The Litigators

THE LITIGATORS

Lindsay G. Arthur, Jr.

SCARLETTA PRESS

MINNEAPOLIS

Library of Congress PCN
2005926330

ISBN 13: 978-0-9765201-0-8
ISBN 10: 0-9765201-0-9

Further information about *The
Litigators*, including Lindsay G. Arthur
Jr.'s blog and schedule of appearances
is available at the Scarletta Press
website at www.scarlettapress.com.

Book design by Chris Long
Mighty Media Inc., Minneapolis, MN

First edition | First printing

10 9 8 7 6 5 4 3 2 1

Manufactured in the
United States of America

To My Father
Whose Dreams I Have Shared

CHAPTER One

Arne Bergstrom and his young wife Ruth lived in the house Arne's father built in 1946 when Minneapolis was enjoying the beginning of the post-war boom. It was a charming white stucco home with dark green trim and shutters, set on a deep tree-shaded lot with a creek running through the back yard. Next to it was an abandoned gas station which occupied the corner. Previously owned by Arne Bergstrom's long departed neighbors, the Gustafsons, the gas station had become an eyesore with tall weeds growing out of deep cracks in the pavement around the pumps. Kitty-corner from the gas station was the building that had been Bergstrom's Hardware, one of those small stores with old wood floors, narrow aisles, and jam-packed shelving that ran from floor to ceiling. Customers could climb a ladder to reach merchandise on the top shelves, where they were often met with a sprinkling of dust and dead bugs as they retrieved their selections. Arne, like his father before him, had done nothing else but manage the family business in that building.

Most people in the area used to purchase their tools and household supplies at Bergstrom's Hardware; they also brought in their lawnmowers and snow blowers for tune-ups and repairs. If you were a regular customer, the Bergstroms, senior and junior, gave credit easily and kept a running tab in their heads. After his father died, Arne, always more cautious than his dad, took to keeping track of these debts in pocket notebooks, which gradually became dog-eared and grimy. When customers came in to settle their accounts at the end of the month, they would marvel at how Arne fumbled through his notebook, scribbled a few numbers on a scrap of paper and handed the bill over the counter, accurate to the penny. However informal the system, Arne could recall only a handful of complaints, which was why Bergstrom's Hardware had remained in business on the same corner for over fifty years.

This local loyalty to the Bergstroms and the other small business owners in the area began to evaporate shortly after new malls were opened around the outskirts of the metropolitan area. From then on most of the neighborhood people got into their cars and drove miles to do business with people they did not know who provided none of the personal touches offered by Arne Bergstrom and his fellow neighborhood shop owners. People seemed oblivious to the fact that these small businesses could not survive without their patronage; one by one the local businesses closed, and with their demise, often to the consternation of the very residents who preferred the sterile aisles of Wal-Mart, K-Mart, or Target, the neighborhood was forever changed.

A FOR SALE sign hung in the dusty window of the once busy Bergstrom's Hardware, and across the quiet street at the Bergstrom residence, a sign stuck in the lawn revealed Arne's new occupation:

ARNE BERGSTROM

HANDYMAN

CAN FIX ANYTHING

612-827-2782

His years in the hardware business, especially the many hours spent making house calls, provided him with a steady stream of customers after he closed the store. Over the years he built his new venture into a modest success through his well-earned reputation for prompt service at a fair price. With virtually no overhead, he earned enough to support Ruth and their two young children, and, with the newly flexible schedule in his life, he counted himself a happy man.

One mid-January morning in 2000, Ruth Bergstrom, unable to sleep, arose earlier than usual. She slipped on Arne's huge, hooded sweatshirt which smelled of pine sap and putty, and quietly opened the bedroom door so as not to disturb him. He had been up until the wee hours working on a project for someone. She turned up the heat, and with the sweatshirt enveloping most of her petite frame, stood by the radiator and rubbed at the strange tingling in her fingers that had ruined her sleep. After a few minutes, she shook her fingers a couple of times and walked into the kitchen to plan the meals for the day. She immediately saw a large box wrapped in brown paper with a big red bow. She let out a tiny shriek, and gently opened an envelope marked "My Wife for Life." She opened the card to find a brief message written in Arne's funny, boyish handwriting: "Ruthie, a lovely old name for my lovely young wife. It's still a month to Valentine's Day, but a wonderful girl like you deserves an early gift. Love, Arne."

Ruth ripped off the wrapping paper, opened the top of the cardboard box, and saw a large wooden object inside. She was unable to lift the object out of the container, so she grabbed a kitchen knife and carefully sliced along the cardboard seams. As the sides fell to the floor, a hand-crafted cabinet made of fine-grained wood stood in front of her. She loved the smell of its rubbed oil finish. The top of the cabinet was bordered with maple veneer and had a Pembroke-style inlay in the center; brass handles glistened on the doors. She opened the doors, whispering, "You're a mad lunatic, Arne Bergstrom," and smelled the freshly sanded pine shelves on which Arne had neatly arranged twelve new Mason jars; their beautiful empty shininess made Ruth think of bountiful summers gone by, and she was warmed by the prospect of summers to come. On the inside of one of the doors she saw an inscription burned into the wood: "For Ruthie, January 2000."

She leaned back and slid gently downward against the refrigerator door until she found herself cross-legged next to the cabinet. She remained there quietly for a few minutes, dabbing her eyes with the big sleeves of her husband's smelly sweatshirt. She could scarcely imagine the work Arne must have put into making this gift, not to mention the extraordinary effort he must have taken to avoid discovery. A mad lunatic! She loved him so much her heart nearly burst.

"All right, you silly little woman," muttered Ruth, "time to get practical and feed the five thousand." She got up and, feeling a bit dizzy, steadied herself by opening the refrigerator. "Please don't let's be pregnant. Please only be a sinus infection." She took out a carton of eggs, sausage links, and a package of English muffins, and laid them on the counter beside the stove. She went back for milk, orange juice, and a big can of ground coffee. Her hands felt so numb that she nearly dropped it all. The stove clock said six o'clock. She had not realized it was that early, so she decided to put off making breakfast and retrieve the morning paper from the front porch steps. She would enjoy a few minutes scanning the headlines before Arne and the kids started bumping about upstairs. Her feet felt numb, too, so she found her fluffy slippers in the hallway, and pulling up the hood of the sweatshirt against the cold of the porch, said to herself, "Lucky, lucky little woman."

The alarm clock woke Arne from an exhausted sleep. He immediately sensed Ruth's absence. He got up and walked quickly into the dark second-floor hall, wondering if she liked her cabinet. The stairs down to the front entryway were faintly illuminated by a stream of light through the kitchen doorway. The room itself was quiet, so he descended the stairs and glanced into the kitchen. He noticed the breakfast fixings on the counter and the cherry wood cabinet standing in the middle of the room amidst its torn off wrappings. What caught his attention, however, was the wide-open front door leading to the cold porch.

"Ruthie, where are you?" He called out. No answer came, so he walked, shivering, to the open doorway and shouted, "Ruthie!"

He hurried through the door to the porch and attempted to push open the screen door. It would not budge. Perhaps last night's snow had blown against the door and frozen it shut. He turned on the outside light and looked at the railing leading down the steps to the sidewalk. Only about four inches of new snow had accumulated, not nearly enough to block the door. With rising concern, he yelled, "Ruthie! Ruthie! For God's sake, Ruthie, where are you?"

He ran through the house to the back door, knocking over the telephone stand and sending everything on it scattering across the floor. In his haste he fumbled with the lock on the back door before he could get it open. Barefoot and clad only in boxers, he ran into the cold, leaving the back door wide open behind him. Stars shone through the branches of the giant elm next door and the inside of his nostrils froze as he ran around to the front of the house. The light on the steps illuminated the motionless body of his wife lying in the snow against the screen door.

"Ruthie, dear Christ, what's happened?"

He lifted Ruth under her armpits, hoisted her away from the door, and lifted her upwards so he could carry her with his right arm under her knees and his left under her shoulder blades. He opened the screen door with his toes and edged his way into the house, careful not to bump her head on anything. He laid her on a couch in the living room and wrapped the old crocheted afghan around her.

"Ruthie!" He patted her cheeks and rubbed her hands. "Wake up, Ruthie. Open your eyes. What the hell's going on?" Her eyes were half open, only the whites showing, and her mouth sagged. He had to steady her neck as if she were a newborn child. He leaned his face next to her mouth, and when he felt warm breath against his cold cheek, he shouted, "Thank God," and rushed to the telephone. Its shattered remains dug painfully into his feet in the hallway, so he rushed upstairs to use the telephone beside the bed to call an ambulance.

When he came back down Ruth lay just as he had left her on the couch. Her eyes were more open, and her fully dilated pupils stared unseeing at the ceiling. Her lips and fingers were cyanotic blue and her arms and legs twitched in light, irregular spasms. Arne tucked his mother's old afghan more tightly around his wife and wiped drool from the side of her mouth.

"Ruthie, my darling Ruthie," he pleaded. Water dropped onto her cheeks and he realized he was crying. Then he noticed his daughter, Molly, standing in the doorway in her nightgown.

"Daddy, what's happening? What's wrong with Mommy?"

"Get me a pillow," Arne snapped.

Molly broke into tears.

Calming himself, he said, "I'm sorry, honey. Your mother's sick. I've called an ambulance. If you'd go get a pillow, it might make her more comfortable."

Molly ran to obey, and Arne turned back to Ruth.

"Ruthie, it's okay now. I'm right here. The medics are on the way." Arne put his arms around her, placed his warm cheek against hers and whispered into her ear, "I love you more than anything. You're going to be all right now."

Arne knelt on the floor beside the couch, reached under the blanket and clasped Ruth's cold hands tightly in his.

"I love you, Ruthie," he said again.

Against his ear he heard Ruth's fragile voice, "The cabinet is beautiful."

Arne smiled with relief and kissed her fingers. He could barely see her through the sheet of tears in his eyes. A siren sounded in the distance, but it seemed like an eternity before the ambulance finally pulled up in front of the house and the piercing shriek stopped. He rushed to open the door and bring the team of paramedics into the living room.

Molly returned, dragging a pillow behind her, tiny beside the tall paramedics.

"Molly, you must be a brave girl," said Arne. "Go upstairs, wake up your brother, and tell him to get dressed for school. You're a big girl now, so you must find your own clothes and put them on all by yourself. Go quickly. We'll all be leaving soon."

Molly dropped the pillow and ran from the room. Arne heard her bare feet pounding up the stairs and along the hallway to Brett's room. He heard her yell in her bossy little voice at her sleeping brother, "Brett, wake up! We gotta get dressed."

Arne heard Brett fussing while the medics made Ruth comfortable on the gurney. He longed to go comfort his son, but he had to stay with Ruth.

The ambulance took Ruth away at 6:45 and Arne quickly went upstairs to Brett's room, sat on the edge of his bed, and cuddled him. He explained to Brett that his mother had fallen and was being taken to the hospital but that everything would be fine. Though upset, Brett still got up and pulled on the clothes his mother had laid out for him the night before.

Frightening images and suspicions tortured Arne's mind as he drove with the children to the hospital. What could this be, cancer? A stroke? No, she was as healthy as a horse. He kept shaking his head as he drove. The children hugged each other in the back of the car, sobbing quietly.

In the ER, Arne anxiously gave Ruth's vital statistics to a maddeningly calm duty nurse. He refused to take a seat but stood at the nurse's station with the kids clinging to his legs. Finally, the phone rang and the nurse smiled, and he was escorted back to where several nurses and a doctor surrounded Ruth.

"How is she?" Arne asked the medical team collectively, still ten feet from the examining table. To his surprise, Ruth's voice answered, "Arne, I'm fine."

As he got to the examining table, the team surrounding Ruth parted and he saw that color had returned to her face.

"Boy, you really threw a scare into us," Arne said. "What on earth happened?"

"What a little sneak you've become, love," Ruth replied. "I adore the beautiful cabinet you made me."

"Ruthie, don't be silly. I thought we'd lost you."

"I wouldn't leave you and the kids. You'd never make it on your own."

The children stood on either side of Arne, looking up at their mother with big eyes. He couldn't believe how light with relief his legs felt.

"Nothing happened, Arne, really," said Ruth. "I fell and hit my head, but I'm fine now. I'm ready to go home as soon as these nice people let me."

"Mrs. Bergstrom," interrupted the attending doctor. "We all want to know what happened. Did you slip on some ice? Did you faint? Did you become dizzy? We really must know why you fell."

"I don't really know," Ruth said. "I went out to get the newspaper. As I bent over to pick it up, my legs gave out from under me. I don't remember anything else."

"Well, what were you doing up so early?" Arne asked. "Were you having those tingling sensations again?"

"Tingling sensations?" asked the doctor. "Have you had any previous episodes like this?"

"I've never fallen, doctor," Ruth said. "I've had a little numbness in my hands and legs recently. It's nothing."

"She's already seen our family doctor about this," Arne said.

"Dr. McCosh did run a few blood tests," Ruth added. "But he didn't find anything."

"After I put a suture in the back of your head, I'll call Dr. McCosh and find out what tests he ran," the doctor said. "Then I'm going to talk with the attending neurologist on staff here. We may also need to do some additional blood work and an MRI. This can all be done in the next few hours, and, if everything looks normal at the end of the day, I'll let you go home for dinner."

"You kids are going to be late for school," Ruth said. "Molly, those are the same pants you wore yesterday. They're filthy."

"What are all those green lines on the television set, Mom?" Brett asked, climbing onto a chair at the side of her bed.

"They're checking my heart to make sure it's working right."

"Is there something wrong with your heart, Mom?" asked Molly.

"My heart's fine," Ruth reassured her. "The doctors here just have to check out everything. It's time for school now. If you're lucky, maybe your dad will take you to McDonald's for breakfast on the way. I'll be home for dinner. Run along now."

Arne kissed Ruth and started to leave the room. As the kids walked out ahead of him, he turned and said, "I'll be back. I'm going to cancel my appointments for today. Someone's got to be here with you to make sure you tell the doctors the truth."

"Don't talk silly, sweetie," she laughed.

The ER doctor came to Ruth's cubicle to suture the laceration on the back of her head. He touched her so gently she barely felt anything. Like many young men he was a little breathless around her and questioned her guardedly about her relationship with her much older husband. The neurologist came as promised and ran a battery of tests. He flirted with her, too, soon disconnected the EKG, and told her she would be out dancing by the weekend. He ordered her a private room on the next floor. The ER staff all came to say goodbye and wish her luck, especially her young doctor, for whom she felt a little sorry. His attention flattered her, but she longed for Arne to come back and sit with her.

Ruth gradually regained her strength and, by late morning, felt more like a prisoner than a patient. Arne came back and did not help matters; he would not let her get up and bullied her into eating an institutionally nourishing lunch. At four o'clock, their private physician, Dr. McCosh, came to her room to meet with her and Arne.

"I see you're doing better this afternoon," McCosh said, walking briskly to the side of Ruth's bed. "You certainly had the docs in the ER all excited this morning."

Ruth laughed and said, "How nice of you to stop by."

"I'd hardly miss the chance to practice my bedside manner on my favorite patient."

"Well, don't be counting on me to give you any more opportunities," Ruth replied.

"I should hope not," McCosh said, picking up her chart and intently studying the results of the many tests that had been run during the day. As he read them, he absently said, "By the way, did you ever call the city about that gasoline odor you told me about?"

Ruth frowned and looked at Arne, who answered for her. "A city inspector was out to the house last week, but he didn't find anything."

"Well," McCosh said, "I see you have reduced sensation in your toes, and the reflexes in your feet are somewhat slow, just about the same as the last time I saw you. Only thing is," McCosh continued, "now you've also got this numbness in your fingers. This has been going on now for over a month, and I..."

Interrupting McCosh, Arne said, "Almost two months. She refused to see you right away. Stubborn as a mule."

Ruth laughed, slapped Arne's hand, and said, "Can I go home now, please?"

"Ruthie," Arne sighed, "let the man finish."

"I don't know what's causing your paresthesia, this tingling and numbness," McCosh said. "The blood tests were normal. The MRI was normal. All your tests were normal. As a precaution, I'm going to give you some antibiotics, but I believe it would be wise to have you go down to the Mayo Clinic for a full-scale physical."

"The Mayo Clinic? What for?" Ruth asked, abruptly raising herself onto her elbows. "I'm not going all the way down there. I have the kids to look after."

"The neurologists there regularly see many unusual disorders that I may see only once or twice in my career. We've got to find out what's causing these symptoms so we can prevent another collapse." From the end of the bed he wiggled her toe and said, "Any more bumps on the head could make you even more stubborn."

Arne laughed and said, "There, Ruthie, a second opinion!"

Ruth glared at both of them.

Dr. McCosh said, "I'll let you go home tonight, but I'm going to schedule an appointment for you at the Mayo. My office will call you with the details."

Ruth sat upright, peeved, and said, "Next week's not good for me, doctor. I've got work to do, and I have a PTA meeting, and..."

Dr. McCosh interrupted her and spoke firmly. As he did, he

momentarily made direct eye contact with Arne. "Ruth, I don't want to alarm you. This will probably turn out to be nothing serious, but I can't be sure. This isn't something we can afford to take too lightly. It's imperative that we arrive quickly at the correct diagnosis so that any permanent neurological damage can be prevented."

"He's right, Ruthie," Arne said, adjusting Ruth's hospital gown. "You've signed on for lots of years of cooking my dinner, and I've no intention of letting you off the hook because of some piddling disability." He turned to McCosh and said, "We'll be there, doctor."

"Say," Dr. McCosh asked as he started towards the door, "did you find out anything about the company taking soil samples out at the gas station last summer?"

"They're still there," Arne said. "They've been pumping something into the ground around the old gas tanks. The city inspector gave me the name of the company that's doing the work. Ruth wrote them a letter a few days ago asking for information, just like you suggested."

"Well, let me know when you hear something," Dr. McCosh said. "It's a bit curious, if nothing else."

CHAPTER TWO

Boyd Campbell untangled himself from his wife's arms and slipped from under the eiderdown comforter. A glass of water with a crust of ice on its surface sat next to the alarm clock on his bedside table. He tucked the comforter around Kathleen's neck and closed the window. Shivering, he pulled on his polypropylenes and Patagonia shell, and, within minutes, was outside in the minus-ten-degree morning.

One of his jogging routes took him alongside a city lake not far from his house. Four inches of overnight snow weighed down the weaker tree branches, forcing him to duck as he passed under them on the unshoveled sidewalks. The snow had moved on through, and the Arctic air had come in behind it, leaving the sky clear and star-lit. He loved running on mornings like this when few people ventured out; he could enjoy the last minutes before dawn and shuffle through virgin snow. He felt a surge of joy in his chest and ran hard until his heart rate peaked. He had been running thirty minutes when he encountered the first car of the morning, its engine muffled by the snow and its headlights revealing the tire marks of an earlier vehicle, perhaps a bus. Beautiful. Boyd Campbell felt lucky to be on exactly this small patch of earth at this precise instant in time.

A siren suddenly wailed in the distance as he turned away from the lake and ran toward home. It was an unusual time of day, he thought, for the sounds of sirens. The sirens made him think of his wife, Kathleen, a physician, who would just now be stepping from the shower and thinking about her morning rounds at the hospital. Boyd, the earlier riser of the two, took it on himself most mornings to make sure she ate breakfast before she left the house. He picked up his pace to try and get home and start the coffee before she beat him into the kitchen.

Boyd kicked off his running shoes in the mudroom and came into the kitchen dripping sweat. Kathleen sat at the kitchen table drinking juice. The coffee pot gurgled on the counter. "Wow, lover, you're up early," Boyd said, taking English muffins out of the refrigerator. Kathleen looked up from the open folder she was studying, and said, "Today's battle is already joined, I'm afraid."

"Another day annihilating strep bacteria and flu viruses?"

Kathleen came over to the kitchen counter, grabbed him by the chin and pulled him toward her. With her other hand she tweaked him gently on the nose. "You're only jealous I'm out in the world saving lives," she said, "while you're in your boring old lab growing bugs for a living."

"You mean you're killing God's little creatures while I'm inventing new ones."

"You always say that," Kathleen replied. "After fifteen years you should be able to come up with something more original."

"After fifteen years living as your financial inferior, oh my queen, you should expect at least a modicum of verbal rebellion."

"After fifteen years," she laughed, "I figure you'd know better than to challenge me."

"Well," Boyd said, dropping the pre-split muffins into the toaster, "I've often thought the bugs you're destroying may have some greater purpose for mankind. I may be married to a murderess."

"Their greater purpose is to earn a living for us," Kathleen said, poking him between the shoulder blades. "And thank God the reward for killing microbes is more lucrative than for creating them."

"It's encouraging to have such spousal enthusiasm and support," Boyd said. "Perhaps you'd care to increase your investment in my company?"

"*Your* company? Are you forgetting who your number one shareholder is?"

"With that attitude I can tell you're about to have a fine day. All my friends envy me being married to such a rich and humble woman." With that he grinned and kissed her on the mouth.

"Bastard," she said, "don't say something shitty and then kiss me." She folded her arms and turned away while he laughed and poured her a cup of coffee.

"Okay," Boyd said, "What time do you have to stop killing bugs today? I'll be famished by seven."

Eyes triumphant as she sipped her coffee, Kathleen said, "Today's the fourteenth, sweetheart, an even number. You cook or you buy."

He shrugged and sighed, "No harm in trying."

"See, you're a trickster."

"A veritable old coyote. How about a candlelit dinner in front of the fireplace?" Boyd said, making big eyes. "With a little Brahms in the background."

"With the Afghan rug spread in front of the sofa, no doubt. You're a dirty old letch."

"I thought we might celebrate tonight."

"Celebrate?" said Kathleen.

"Yes," Boyd replied. "This is the day we start to become millionaires. Henry Holten has set up a meeting with investment bankers so we can get started on the IPO."

Kathleen frowned. "I don't know why you work with Holten. He strikes me as very arrogant."

Boyd smiled. "Well, apart from his being a fellow Princeton alum, they say he's very nice to his wife."

"I don't suppose he ever cooks dinner for her, though," Kathleen said with a wry smile.

Boyd Campbell had spent his entire professional life in academia. A biochemist by training at Princeton, he worked his way up through the professorial ranks teaching molecular biology at the University of Minnesota. His principal research program developed entirely by accident: an early October snowfall had covered their yard except for a compost pile near Kathleen's vegetable garden. This would have been no surprise to any reasonably experienced gardener, since for centuries it has been known that organic matter produces heat as it decays. But to a biochemist the heat was produced by microbial organisms consuming and metabolizing the organic matter, initiating a natural process of degrading and recycling the organic wastes. Because nature had created its own garbage haulers, a specialized corps of bacteria and other organisms, an endless garbage pile of animal corpses and vegetable wastes was avoided.

Campbell's laboratory research had focused for several years on processes to eliminate or reduce hazardous wastes. If microbes are so efficient in recycling natural organic matter, he theorized, these same organisms could also be used to degrade the mountains of manufactured toxic wastes created by humans. Campbell understood that most hazardous substances are also organic compounds that are molecularly similar to the organic deposits in his wife's compost pile. Just change the positions of a few atoms here and there, and the molecular structure would be identical. Perhaps with a little genetic manipulation, they could persuade the bacteria in the compost pile to degrade hazardous wastes. All Campbell needed to do was develop the organisms. His eventual success was a major scientific achievement.

That was 1988. In July of 1994 Campbell began his first field trials at the site of a nearby abandoned gas station that had been leaking gasoline through its deteriorating underground storage tank. There was no telling how far the contamination had spread, but many homes in the area had been affected, and there was danger of the spill reaching the aquifer. Cleaning the site with conventional technology would require digging up and hauling away all the contaminated soil to a landfill, which was enormously expensive, especially where the digging would have to be done underneath buildings or other structures.

Campbell had found a strain of bacteria, a pseudomonas he named P-27, that seemed to survive in gasoline contaminated soils. Following several years of laboratory work, he was able to improve the organism genetically so that, at least in laboratory experiments, it readily degraded gasoline into water, carbon dioxide, and other harmless components. If they could pump Campbell's new organisms into the soil along with some appropriate nutrients to encourage their growth, perhaps they could degrade the gasoline and destroy its hazardous additives with no excavation at all. Presumably, the waterborne bacteria would follow the same path as the gasoline and degrade most of the toxic hydrocarbons.

Successful field trials and the publication of an article detailing his research generated considerable interest in the scientific community. Recognizing the business potential of this research, patents were obtained, a business plan was prepared, and the Campbell home was refinanced. On July 15, 1995, Boyd Campbell took a leave of absence from the university and became president of EnviroClean, Inc. Five years later, the company was poised for success.

January 14 was a special day in the life of EnviroClean. Campbell had an appointment with his lawyer, Henry Holten, and some investment bankers Holten wanted him to meet. Feeling invigorated by his early morning run, Boyd swept through the company's reception room and down the hallway to his office. Amy, his secretary, already occupied her desk.

"Mr. President," she asked, as Campbell glided past, "who are you trying to impress this morning?"

Amy Wilcox had been the first official employee of EnviroClean, arranging for office space, desks, supplies and other necessities, even before Campbell himself formally left the university. She had been in the steno pool in his department for a decade, had taken a liking to Campbell from the very beginning, and assumed an "in loco parentis" relationship. Scientists, in her opinion, were helpless once they took even a single step away from the lab. They definitely needed someone to help them through life's little challenges. Amy was quite pleased to have served as Boyd Campbell's surrogate parent all these years, and she was proud her charge had done so well under her tutelage.

"I knew you'd wear that tie," Amy continued. "Whoever coined the phrase 'dress for success' undoubtedly didn't know any scientists. How can your wife let you out of the house dressed like that?"

"She left before me, and besides, Kathleen's my wife, not my mother, and she knows I have two mothers already."

"Do all you science types actually plan these pathetic color combinations?"

"Excuse me?"

"There's gotta be a manual that tells you all how to look like scientists. You can't possibly come up with these costumes on your own."

Campbell's one reluctant exception to his traditional dress code was a mid-weight permanent press from Brooks Brothers, recommended by his banker. This suit could be worn in acceptable comfort in either the cold of winter or the heat of summer. Campbell had sent it to the cleaners every year since he bought it in 1990.

Amy handed her boss a thin box which obviously contained a necktie. "Here, I picked this up on the way home last night. It's more suited to your role as a corporate mogul. You've got to look the part if you want these financial wheeler-dealers to give you any money."

Knowing there would be little benefit in arguing the point, he accepted the gift graciously and changed ties on the spot.

"Why don't you let me have this polka-dot number for safe keeping," Amy suggested. "Next time you're asked to speak at an American Legion bowling night, I'll give it back to you."

Campbell, although he would never say it aloud, felt there was little out of sorts about his tall, athletic physique, which he managed to maintain through regular workouts as he crept into midlife. Unlike most men his age, the entire circumference of his belt remained parallel to the floor. But it was true that he was not one to think too much about clothes; in fact, he thoroughly disliked the idiom to which his secretary obviously adhered: 'The clothes make the man.' On the contrary, he believed the man made the man, and that dressing people or things up too much in superficialities was one of the aspects of human nature that humanity could seriously do without. But arguing with Amy was not an option. Once the tie was knotted, he said, "Why do I surround myself with women who are bullies?"

Amy laughed and said, "Because we love you, boss."

"Thanks," Boyd replied. "You can inscribe that on my headstone, 'His women loved to bully him.' Is Dick Blair in yet?"

The levity left Amy's face, and with some concern, she said, "You know what, boss, I'm not sure he even went home last night. I'll ask him to step into your office."

Richard Blair was the company's number-cruncher. A pudgy, somber man, he had succeeded in avoiding all forms of physical exercise. Were it not for a failed attempt to be exempted from a general sports program required of all students in his ninth grade class, he would never have seen the inside of a gymnasium, at least not while he was wearing athletic shoes.

The two men met in Campbell's office for several hours going through all the plans and numbers item by item. They needed $2 million to acquire additional fermenting equipment so they could grow all their own organisms internally. They needed $2.5 million to upgrade their production facilities to be able to service the anticipated growth of customers. Another $1.5 million was needed to cover salaries of newly hired employees. They also wanted to pay off their existing debt to the bank to eliminate the heavy interest payments and to remove the second mortgage from the Campbell home. Finally, he hoped to raise an additional $4 million to undertake the necessary field trials and obtain government approvals for a second product line. $10.5 million. Was there any real possibility they could raise this amount through a public offering? Campbell could hardly imagine anyone would want to invest so heavily in his little company.

"The truth of the matter is that you don't have any real choice about going forward with this public offering," Richard Blair said after noting the vacant stare of his boss. Richard leaned back in his chair, forcing it onto its two back legs. "If you don't expand this company now," he said, "someone else will do it for you. You've published an article that's been widely circulated throughout the industry. Now there are a host of other companies trying to establish themselves in this market. They'll develop their own products and they'll beat you to the punch if you don't do it first."

"Maybe that'd be just fine," Boyd responded. "I could just stay here with my small, easily managed company, and they'd have all the headaches of trying to run a big operation."

"It doesn't work that way," Blair replied. "Once someone else becomes firmly established in other markets, they'll come here also, and when they do, they'll take over this market, and you'll have nothing left. There's a small window of opportunity now. You've got to take it or ultimately you'll lose everything."

"No one else has the patents I have," Boyd countered. "They can't just start some company when they don't even have a product, and they can't get a product without violating my patents."

Blair sat forward in his chair, returning it to all four legs. He took off his glasses and flipped them casually onto Boyd's desk. "You have patents on a particular organism to clean up gasoline contaminated soils. Do you really think this is the only organism that can do this job? You were able to engineer P-27 in only a few years. Someone else could undoubtedly engineer another bug that would do the same thing, perhaps even better. These patents only give you a head start on the competition. They don't insulate you from it."

"I'm a professor," Boyd said, "not a ..." He struggled to find a term, coming up at last with Amy's phrase, "not a corporate mogul. What do I know about running a big company? I don't know if I'd even be happy heading up a big operation."

Blair gathered his papers and rose from his chair. "If you're really serious about making some meaningful contribution to the environment, then you owe it to yourself, to the world, to give it your best shot."

"Well," Campbell responded, "we'll see what the lawyers and investment bankers have in mind."

Boyd had half an hour to read the mail before he had to leave for his luncheon. At the top of the pile, where it was certain to gain his immediate attention, Amy had placed a handwritten letter. It was on plain white typewriter paper, with neat, clearly legible handwriting. Amy had affixed a Post-it note asking Boyd to read it ASAP. Curious, he sat at his desk and read the letter:

Dear Sirs,

My husband and I live at 3605 Nassau St., next to the abandoned gas station your company was working on last summer. I'm not sure exactly what you were doing there, but the city engineer's office told me you were using some new procedure to clean up all the gas that leaked out around the station. We are very grateful to you for your work because my husband and I are worried about possible contamination of the ground water.

However, for the last few months I have not been well. I have started to lose strength in my legs, and from time to time it gets rather painful. Unfortunately, the condition only seems to be getting worse with time. I spoke to my doctor about these symptoms, and he thinks I may have been exposed to some toxic substance. I asked him about the gasoline contamination, because there is a small creek running behind our property that sometimes smells of gas. Dr. McCosh did not think my symptoms were consistent with gasoline exposure, but he suggested I write and ask you whether whatever you were doing out there might be causing me some allergic reaction.

I'm really sorry to trouble you about this because I know you must be very busy with other more important matters. However, if you have any information about this, it would be helpful to us in attempting to find out what is causing my symptoms so Dr. McCosh might know how to treat them.

Thank you very much for your attention.
Sincerely,
Ruth Bergstrom

Campbell immediately dialed the phone extension of Mary Frick, his vice president of research and development.

"We got a letter from a woman asking about the potential of our P-27 to cause an allergic reaction. What do we know about that possibility?"

"Amy said you'd be calling me," Mary Frick replied, "and she's already given me a copy of the letter. I've never heard of anything like this with any genus of pseudomonas, but, as a precaution, I'm running a Web search for any possible published articles that may be relevant."

"I'm meeting with Henry Holten today to discuss our public offering," Campbell said. "As long as I'm seeing him anyway, I'll give him a copy of the letter and see what he thinks we should do."

"In the meantime," Mary Frick said, "I'll review any abstracts the computer may turn up. I wouldn't worry about it, though, boss."

CHAPTER Three

Boyd Campbell wove his way through the mob of loud-talking people in gray and blue suits. He liked the ornate lobby of the Bengal Club, but disliked crowds, particularly when alone, so he found a comfortable place to stand near the revolving doors where his lawyer, Henry Holten, now considerably late, would easily notice him. Boyd's secretary, Amy, had been dead-on about the tie; the polka dots of his confiscated one were so out of place in this den of attorneys that he was reminded of high school and the merciless bullying that unusual apparel could bring down on a person of quiet disposition. His gray Brooks Brothers suit felt the worse for wear, and even the new navy tie, decorated with stylish amoebas, felt strangely alien. Despite the presence of several other gentlemen who also wore little amoebas, Boyd imagined everyone's attention drawn to him, and they would be wondering who could possibly have invited this aging geek to the Bengal Club?

Boyd's shoes, well-worn reddish-brown loafers which did not match his suit, embarrassed him. Discretely he wrapped first one foot, then the other, behind the opposite leg and brushed off the tops of his shoes on the back of his pants. He saw no improvement. He was just planning a retreat to the restroom to try again with water and hand towels, when a man in a tuxedo, holding a slip of paper, touched his arm and said, "Dr. Campbell?"

Still on one foot, Boyd lost his balance, prompting the man to catch him in a firm grip and steady him. The man of about sixty, looking completely comfortable in a black tuxedo with the small, but nevertheless grand, coat-of-arms of the Bengal Club sewn over the breast pocket, was a head taller than Boyd.

With a slight arch of the eyebrow, the man repeated, "Dr. Campbell, I presume."

Feeling like an idiot child, Boyd answered, "Yes, I'm Boyd Campbell."

"Mr. Holten has reserved the Senators Room for your luncheon meeting. Let me show you the way."

Situated on the third floor toward the back of the building, and dominated by a large, round table over which hung a crystal chandelier, the Senators Room made Boyd Campbell feel like a schoolboy. It was the combination of oak paneling and the glaring, thick-framed portraits which hung around the room that did it. The table, set for six, with crystal goblets filled with white linen napkins, sported at each place setting the coat-of-arms of the Bengal Club.

"May I have your waiter bring you anything, Dr. Campbell?" asked the tall man.

"Thank you," Boyd replied, "I'll manage. Is there a men's room nearby?"

"The second door on your right, sir. Will you be needing anything else?"

"No, thank you. I'll be fine."

Boyd strode down the hall to the men's room. He took a hand towel from the counter next to the sink and found an empty stall where he could clean his shoes without detection. The towel was real white cotton, and he felt decadent soiling it on his shoes.

When he returned to the Senators Room, four of the other guests had already arrived, everyone except Henry Holten. Boyd stood in the doorway quietly facing the group.

An attractive young blonde woman stepped forward, holding out her hand. "I'm Allison Forbes," she said. "I can't tell you how pleased I am to meet you. I've heard so much about your bio-remediation research. You're really quite a celebrity, you know."

With a tight smile, Boyd replied, "Pleased to meet you," as Allison took his arm and eased him into the room.

"I'm Henry Holten's partner in the litigation department," she said. Laughing, she added, "Let me introduce you to the people with all the money." Two men and a woman rose from their seats at the table and shook hands with Boyd while Allison introduced them. "Geoffrey Firestone is the chief executive officer of the best investment firm in town, Firestone and Pyne. Christopher Walker is the group vice president for F & P's biotechnology division, and Deborah Dodge heads up their IPOs."

Boyd sat next to Allison, and with a slight frown, asked, "Litigation?"

Allison smiled broadly and said, "One can't be too careful these days. Our most important mission is to assist our clients in avoiding litigation. It takes a good litigator to know how to do that and Henry is one of the best in the state."

"I didn't realize he specialized," said Boyd. "I heard him speak once at a Princeton Alumni meeting, and we got to talking and discovered that we'd lived in the same dorm a few years apart. So when I needed a lawyer, I called him."

"It never occurred to me I'd need a trial lawyer," Boyd went on. "My greatest ambition is to survive a full and satisfying professional career without ever once seeing the inside of a courtroom."

"A worthy ambition, to be sure," Allison said. "But, as with any IPO, there are a few landmines along the way. That's why I'm here, to guide you safely through them." She smiled sweetly as she added, "There's really nothing to worry about. The investors are very interested in your new process, and Henry and I think this should be a very beneficial meeting."

"I've heard a lot about EnviroClean," Christopher Walker said, unfastening the button on his pinstripe suit and revealing a gold watch fob in his vest. "In fact, I've read your article describing the success you've had using microbes to clean up leaking underground storage tanks. The hazardous waste industry is ripe for exploitation with a process such as yours. We've been looking for the right opportunity for several years."

Boyd explained his research program to the group. Both laboratory studies and field work had gone very well using genetically mutated organisms to degrade the contaminants. They had even recently completed a contract to clean up some toxic soil underneath a local gas station. It was just a pilot project, but it ran according to plan and within budget. Of course, Boyd told the group, before large-scale commercialization could occur, they would need more field trials, more small pilot projects with inevitable product modifications and redesign.

"That's always the case, Dr. Campbell," interrupted Firestone. "Every business has its risks. These must be balanced against the potential profits. In your case, the potential is enormous. Did you bring any data to show us?"

Boyd opened his briefcase and handed Firestone and the others each a sheaf of papers containing summaries of his field results in a series of graphs, charts, and other data. As Allison thumbed through the materials, her attention was drawn to a sheet of paper that appeared out of place.

"What's this?" she asked Boyd, holding up the letter Ruth Bergstrom had written him. "Is this a testimonial from one of your customers?"

"Well, not exactly," Campbell replied. "This is a letter from ..."

"I see you've all met one another," Henry Holten interrupted, striding into the room and grasping the hands of his assembled guests. Holten was a tall man, impeccably dressed in a dark blue suit and gleaming white shirt. At his collar was his signature red bow tie, hand-tied, his symbol of individuality in a world of four-in-hands.

"Geoffrey, where have you been keeping yourself? You're too young to retire and too smart to use another law firm." Holten walked over to Allison and placed his arm around her shoulders. "This is one hell of a fine lawyer we have here. You could never imagine all the maneuvering I had to go through to get her in my department. And God help any bastard who tries to steal her away from me."

Allison smiled without looking at Holten.

"Well, let's get to the menus," continued Holten. "Boyd, you sit here with Geoffrey and Christopher so you can get to know each other better. After lunch Allison and I will retreat to the sidelines and watch meekly as the entrepreneurial spirit erupts."

"Meekness," Firestone replied, taking a sip of water from his crystal glass, "is the least of your virtues."

Holten picked up a small bell that had been placed at the head of the table to alert the wait staff they were ready for service. "In the legal profession, it's not a virtue at all," he said, ringing the bell several times.

"Though, of course," Allison interjected, "Henry's certainly capable of a touch of strategic humility when the need arises." The Firestone and Pyne contingent chuckled.

"So, Henry, I understand you've just returned from Bermuda," Deborah Dodge said.

"Ah, yes, Bermuda. Charming little island," Holten said. "Can I offer anyone suggestions from the menu? Everything's excellent, but the salmon is especially good."

The waiter arrived to take their orders. Everyone but Allison requested the salmon; she ordered a Maurice salad.

"That's what I like about my young partner here," said Holten. "Just to prove she's a freethinker, she's perfectly willing to suffer through a plate of rabbit food while we all enjoy the best item on the menu. She's just as spirited on behalf of our clients, I might add. Well, enough of the chit-chat. We didn't invite the best of Firestone and Pyne to engage in idle gossip. We're here to get our hands on your billfolds. What can we tell you all about EnviroClean?"

Over the next forty-five minutes each of the investment bankers asked a series of questions about the nature of the business, the status of the technology, the direction Boyd wanted to take the company, and the proposed use of the money that might be raised in an IPO. Campbell had provided them each with a copy of his business plan as well as the cash flow projections that he and Dick Blair had gone over that morning. Nothing in the financials appeared to diminish the enthusiasm of the three venture capitalists.

"There haven't been any legal claims, have there?" asked Walker. "That can be a big problem for companies in the hazardous waste business."

"Of course not," interjected Henry Holten. "We'd certainly not allow EnviroClean to get into any legal problems."

"Nothing so far," Boyd added. "But, Henry, I'd like you to take a look at a letter I got this morning."

"Letter?" Holten asked.

"Yeah, some lady wrote asking us whether our P-27 might have caused her to have an allergic reaction. That's quite impossible of course. Nevertheless, I thought you might have some suggestions on how best to reply."

"Well," Firestone replied, looking directly at Henry Holten, "you'd better put a quick end to that little deal. We're sure as hell not going to buy into any law suits."

"I wouldn't worry about it," Henry said stiffly. I'll personally see that it's dealt with appropriately and immediately."

"Debbie," Walker said, "when can you get started on this? An early summer offering would hit the market at the best possible time, so we need to get on this right away."

"I can be at your office first thing in the morning, Boyd," Deborah Dodge said. "How does eight o'clock suit your schedule?"

"There's nothing on my calendar that can't be moved. I can make Dick Blair available also, if you like," he said.

"Okay," Dodge replied, smiling brightly. "Good deal," and then tucked into her dessert.

Everyone departed cheerfully from the street entrance of the Bengal Club. After the investors hands had been thoroughly shaken, Henry Holten caught Boyd by the arm and said, "You better come up to the office and discuss this damned letter." Boyd, Holten, and Allison crossed the street under the skyway, ignoring the blistering wind gusts which characterize winter in the man-made canyons of downtown Minneapolis.

Although Boyd had been to the offices of Darby and Witherspoon a few times during the last eight years, he never lost his sense of awe as he walked from the elevator into the grand reception room on the thirty-second floor of the First Northern Tower. The architectural decor was Minnesota marble. Intricate patterns in the rock had been meticulously selected, cut and preserved, and carefully positioned to create a series of Picasso-like forms and figures on the walls. This natural artwork was complemented by several sculptures strategically placed about the room. Indirect floodlights recessed behind marble panels in the ceiling created their own patterns on the walls, highlighting the magnificent geology displayed in the room.

Three receptionists sat at a long, curved mahogany desk. Behind them was a solid glass wall, extending the entire width of the reception area and revealing a large conference room with a panoramic view of the Mississippi River, St. Anthony Falls, and the skyline of St. Paul in the far distance.

"I don't understand why you thought it necessary to mention this letter in front of the Firestone and Pyne people," Holten said as they entered his office and seated themselves in the wing chairs surrounding a large glass coffee table.

"I was concerned about it," Boyd replied. "I was concerned that someone might actually believe our process could induce human allergies. And I thought I needed to answer Mr. Walker's question honestly."

"Honesty is not the question here," Holten said. "All they asked you was whether there were any pending legal matters. By that they meant lawsuits. This is not a legal matter. This is a letter, a handwritten letter. Letters like this are written thousands of times daily and don't turn into lawsuits. There's absolutely no reason to get Firestone and Pyne all worked up by some letter that has no legal significance."

"I hope I didn't make things difficult for us," Boyd said.

"We'll take care of this for you," Holten responded quickly. "We must nip this thing in the bud. Mrs. Bergstrom must know that she has no valid claim and that it would be futile for her to consider the matter further. Believe me, I'll make that quite clear to her."

Campbell looked relieved. "Fine," he said, "you write the letter. Mary Frick and I will go out to the creek behind her house and take a couple of samples so we can definitely rule out our microorganisms."

"That's not a good idea," Holten said. "Initiating any investigation at all will only cause undue concern by the investment bankers. If they think we're concerned, they'll be concerned. They must believe, as we do, that this is an inconsequential letter from a misinformed woman."

"Sampling won't take any time at all," Boyd countered, "I don't feel comfortable just letting this thing dangle out there unresolved."

"Science moves about as fast as a herd of bureaucrats on Monday morning," Holten said. "We can't afford the potential of any delays. It's better not to get started at all, at least not at this time."

"May I make a suggestion?" Allison interjected after having read the letter. "Mrs. Bergstrom's letter is very polite. She doesn't write in the tone of someone who is claim-conscious. She's not even making any allegations. I agree that we must respond with a letter that convinces her there's nothing to worry about, but I think the letter should come from Dr. Campbell, rather than from this office. I think it should be courteous and nonlegalistic, and I think we should send her something that demonstrates our microbes can't cause these symptoms anymore than gasoline could."

"I kind of like ..." Campbell began.

Holten interrupted him. "The problem with a letter from Boyd is that it then becomes legal evidence in the event of any subsequent proceedings. I don't want to take any chances of that happening. A letter from this office will immediately let her know she's up against the best law firm in the state and that any legal action would be hopeless. Certainly we should be courteous, but firmness will carry the day."

"Henry," Boyd stated finally, "I've got to tell you I feel more comfortable with Allison's approach here, but I'll leave the decision up to the two of you to work out. In the meantime, we'll continue our Internet search for articles, and we'll make arrangements to get a few samples from Mrs. Bergstrom's creek."

Holten stood up and pushed his vacant chair into its proper place at the table. "I have no objection to your reviewing whatever publications you think appropriate," he said, leaning on the back of the chair, "but do yourself a big favor, hold off on the sampling. Allison and I will work on a response to Mrs. Bergstrom. I'll call you in a few days. For the time being, just sit tight and stay away from that creek."

CHAPTER Four

At 7:00 A.M. on Monday, January 17, 2000, Henry Holten strode into the glass-walled conference room on the thirty-second floor of Darby and Witherspoon's Minneapolis office. The lawyers were already sitting at the elliptical marble table awaiting his arrival.

Holten was wearing a well-cut pinstriped suit. He always wore suits. He also wore his usual red bow tie, his one departure from an otherwise staid, stuffed-shirt appearance. It was a statement of his distinction from the rest of the blue bloods in whose circles he normally traveled.

Nancy Sellers had made arrangements for coffee, rolls, and fresh orange juice. The juice had been poured into a large glass decanter set on a sterling tray surrounded by tumblers. The sweet rolls were divided equally between two ceramic platters on either side of the tray. She had also set up the overhead projector at one end of the conference table and had lowered the screen from behind a valance at one end of the room. Each attorney had been provided with a legal pad as well as a product data sheet describing EnviroClean's Leaking Underground Storage Tank business.

"Good morning, gentle people," Holten greeted the group. "I welcome everyone's willingness to accommodate the scheduling of this meeting on such short notice. But then, I suppose L.U.S.T. is a strong motivating factor for some of you."

Holten looked at Allison Forbes for her anticipated chuckle. "Never before noon," she said gaily, giving him the desired reaction.

"Of course," Holten continued, "our associates are well acquainted with sunrises from the thirty second floor, but I suspect each of you have had to expedite your normal routines somewhat. By the way, happy Martin Luther King Day, Mr. Edwards."

Morrison Edwards was Darby and Witherspoon's first person of color to be promoted to full partnership. He was a member of the firm's government regulations department. Edwards was a behemoth of a man who had played tight end for the Vikings in the 1970s while attending law school part time. Graduating at precisely the time when most of the established firms began actively seeking black attorneys, his celebrity and his minority status together insured he would be heavily recruited.

"Thank you, Henry," he replied, "but is there some reason why you would not also wish our colleagues a happy Martin Luther King Day? Perhaps you assume this is only a day for people of color as Mother's Day is only a day for mothers. Actually, today is a national holiday to honor a hero of monumental importance to all Americans."

Henry Holten was rarely put on the defensive, and the others in the room took silent pleasure in his discomfiture. "No one could ever confuse today with Mother's Day," he said. "Now *that* is a serious holiday, and if you ever forget to send flowers to your mother, you will quickly be reminded of the day's importance. King is gone, but mothers are here forever." Holten paused briefly. "Happy King Day, everyone."

The yellow edge of an oversized sun broke the surface of the horizon, creating a long, thin sundog in the icy blue eastern sky. Inside, the assembled team of lawyers began their work week, oblivious to everything outside the confines of their immediate world.

The attorneys in the room had been painstakingly recruited from some of the most prestigious law schools in the country. All had held distinguished clerkships for noted jurists in the circuit courts of appeals or state supreme courts. The firm published a grand four-color brochure describing its history and practice groups to lure gifted lawyers into the fold. It was stylishly laid out with a combination of photographs of the firm's art collections and line drawings of the offices and historically significant members of the firm. Each of the seven practice groups also published its own brochure describing its practice and clients. These materials were widely distributed in law schools and court houses across the country.

To the right of Henry Holten was Allison Forbes. After graduating at the top of her class she had been randomly assigned to Holten as her initial mentor. When she finished her training rotations through the firm's seven practice groups, Holten requested she be assigned to his department, and she had been practicing under his tutelage ever since.

Wendi Palmer represented the corporate department. A graduate of Harvard Law School, she had clerked for a year in the eighth circuit before garnering an invitation to clerk at the United States Supreme Court. She had been with the firm for fifteen years, specializing in high-technology start-up companies.

Stephen Patton from the securities department and Thomas Dodd from the environmental law department rounded out the group. Dodd had earned an undergraduate degree in molecular biology and a master's degree in ecology before attending law school.

"I assume you've all read the materials Nancy provided you late Friday afternoon," Holten began. "We're about to take EnviroClean public to raise the necessary capital to permit its entry into additional markets and to fund further product development research and field trials. I spoke briefly with Stephen about this a few weeks ago, and I want him to direct the IPO team. As soon as we're finished here this morning, I'd like him to call Deborah Dodge at Firestone and Pyne to coordinate efforts with their office. Wendi will be reviewing all the legal documentation because, as you all know, she's responsible for the firm's technology group. I think it best that she serves as principal liaison between this office and Boyd Campbell. His controller, Richard Blair, will provide you all the numbers you'll need."

"I've got to tell you this is an outstanding company," Palmer said. "Another year or two of coddling it through its infancy and we'll have a nice new client for the firm."

"We have one minor issue that needs our immediate attention," Holten continued. "Some of the biological processes Dr. Campbell has developed use genetically engineered microorganisms to degrade hazardous compounds. These organisms, which the company calls P-27, are dissolved in water with nutrients and injected into the ground around filling stations that have had leaking underground tanks.

"As some of you may be aware, there are several groups of pseudo-scientists who are opposed to the use of any genetically engineered organisms, despite well-documented scientific proof that no possible harm could result. It's particularly ironic that these so-called environmentalists might object to something that will actually make the environment cleaner. But we've got to keep this in mind when drafting the Securities and Exchange Commission filings so there's nothing that could conceivably arouse these sleeping tigers. We must be keenly sensitive to this issue in all contacts with anyone outside this firm. The best tactic will be to say nothing at all about genetic engineering, and to notify Wendi in the event anyone hears anything so we can respond through her to any questions deemed significant."

"I need to hear about it immediately," Palmer interrupted. "We've got a PR firm ready to assist us in quashing any potential threats, but we've got to react quickly."

"In that regard," Holten said, "there's a matter of a letter Dr. Campbell received the other day. It's of no legal significance, other than that it came to him at precisely the wrong time, and Campbell inadvertently mentioned the letter in front of the people at F & P. I've already considered our response, but I told Campbell I'd pass it by each of you for your thoughts before acting on it. Allison, could you put the letter on the overhead projector?"

The projector was turned on, the recessed overhead lighting dimmed, and the louver blinds electronically rotated to block out the rising sun. However insignificant Ruth Bergstrom's letter may have been, it now filled the entire southern wall of the Darby and Witherspoon conference room, and six of the brightest attorneys in the state of Minnesota focused their attention on her letter, each pondering the appropriate response.

Thomas Dodd was the first to speak.

"What do we know about P-27?" he asked. "I assume the standard battery of toxicity testing has been run on this organism. Are there any data to suggest the possibility of some allergic reaction?"

"I've spoken with both Dr. Campbell and his R and D director, Dr. Mary Frick," said Palmer. "Both have indicated all tests are negative for any reaction of this type. In addition, they have no knowledge of any similar strains of pseudomonas causing symptoms like Mrs. Bergstrom's. I might add that the organism cannot survive outside the carefully controlled environment EnviroClean provides to stimulate its growth. Even if it were to migrate from its underground plume, it'd quickly perish."

"There's no way for the organism to come into contact with humans," Holten said, "since it's injected into the soil and penetrates deep into the subsurface where it remains until the gasoline is degraded. With the toxins gone, the P-27 organisms promptly die from lack of nutrients, causing no possible harm."

"I doubt that anyone can say precisely where the organism might wander once it's injected into the ground," added Dodd. "We don't even know where the gasoline itself goes once it leaks from the storage tanks. The easiest way to prove our point is to take some samples from the creek bed."

"It's not that simple," said Holten. "The sampling and testing is expensive. This could take a year or more. The public offering cannot be delayed. The company needs the infusion of capital now. It's not worthwhile to do all this because of a single letter from one woman who has no scientific training whatever."

"There's another reason not to undertake any testing at this time," interjected Stephen Snyder. "We'd be required to disclose the issue in all our SEC filings. It would reduce the value of the offering, and, given the volatility of biotechnology stocks in the current market, it could even result in an outright failure of the entire offering."

"From our perspective in Government Regulations," added Edwards, "we most definitely don't want to create any suspicions about the safety of P-27. If any of the EPA people take an interest in this question, they'll indefinitely delay the issuance of further permits. P-27 could be temporarily removed from the market. Worse yet, if the do-gooder pseudo-scientists get wind of this issue, we'll become firmly enmeshed in a regulatory quagmire."

"My thoughts exactly," said Holten. "There can be no doubt about our need to keep this matter under wraps. I've already prepared a draft response to the letter. Nancy's typing it as we speak. I'll have her bring it in for your review."

"Perhaps," Allison Forbes said, "I might play the devil's advocate for a moment. I think there's an ethical consideration here. What if the P-27 actually *is* causing Mrs. Bergstrom some problems? We have some responsibility to her, as well as to thousands of others who could become infected as well. I think it's dangerous for us to bury our heads in the sand and pretend there's no problem when we don't really have any definitive answers. Have we not..."

"Ms. Forbes," Holten said rising from his chair, "I doubt there's a law firm in the state that is as concerned as we are with promoting the highest standards of professional responsibility. But ethics is not some vague philosophical ideal, it's such an important part of the fabric of this profession that it's published in the Code of Professional Responsibility, as you well know. If there's anyone in this room who thinks the action we're proposing compromises even a single word of that code, then I'd like to hear about it now."

Holten paused for a few seconds to create the impression that he actually wanted to hear such a citation, even though he knew full well there would be none.

Allison sat quietly, her hands on the table, a slight frown on her face.

"On the other hand," he continued, "if the code does not specifically prohibit our advice, then we're mandated by our duty of loyalty to our client to take whatever steps are most prudent in furthering his business objectives. We're not social judges of the niceties of corporate responsibility. We're sworn to be advocates for our clients' interests."

Nancy Sellers entered the room with an overhead transparency of Holten's proposed letter to Mrs. Bergstrom. She removed Mrs. Bergstrom's letter and placed Holten's on the projector.

Dear Mrs. Bergstrom,

Your letter of January 11 to EnviroClean, Inc., has been forwarded to my attention for response.

EnviroClean manufactures a product called P-27. This is a biological product that is used extensively in treating soil and ground water that have been contaminated by gasoline leaking from underground storage tanks throughout the United States. The product has undergone extensive testing and evaluation. It has been approved for use by the Environmental Protection Agency, and it has been reviewed and issued permits by the Minnesota Pollution Control Agency. P-27 has been found to be both entirely safe as well as extremely effective in cleaning up toxic materials. Our team of scientific advisors has concluded there is no possibility the product could cause any allergic reactions or other medical symptoms in humans or other animals.

As counsel for EnviroClean, we take very seriously any allegations that it could be responsible for a health hazard caused by its product.

Please understand that we would vigorously defend EnviroClean and its products against any such frivolous charges to the fullest extent of the resources of this firm. I trust, however, that such pointless litigation and expense will not be necessary.

We are very sympathetic to your recent medical problems, and we wish you the speediest of recoveries.

Sincerely,

Henry Holten

Morrison Edwards was the first to break the silence. "I think this is an outstanding letter, Henry. It's quite to the point and very convincing that P-27 has been thoroughly tested and is safe. I don't know about the paragraph referring to litigation possibilities, but I certainly defer to your judgment. My only suggestion would be to delete the reference to both the EPA and the MPCA. I'd substitute 'federal and state regulators' in their stead. If this woman should want to pursue this matter further, giving her the names of the appropriate agencies to contact merely invites that possibility."

"Good point. I can live with that change." Holten glanced around the room, conspicuously avoiding eye contact with Allison Forbes. "Are there any other suggestions?"

"I agree with Morrison," said Thomas Dodd. "But I'd go a step further. I see no reason to mention the product by name. If she should call someone to make further inquiries and not know the name of the product, it'll be that much more difficult for her to gain any additional information. Furthermore, we should delete the reference to P-27 being a biological product since this is a red flag for some groups and individuals. She may even become disconcerted to know a biological organism has been used next door to her residence."

"I appreciate these suggestions," said Holten, "and they can readily be incorporated into the letter." He finally looked at Allison, his facial expression clearly intimating he felt no need to hear further from his junior partner. "Allison, do you have anything that might cast additional light on this discussion?"

"Not at the present," she said slowly, recognizing her cue.

"Good," said Holten. "Since we're all in agreement, Allison, let me suggest you put together a second draft of our letter and circulate it to all of us for further comment. Dr. Campbell will be here at 1:30, so I hope you can get right on it. Does anyone have anything further?"

No one did. The group broke from the meeting, and Allison returned to her office to write a second draft of the reply letter.

"I apologize for speaking brusquely with you," Holten said, appearing suddenly in the doorway to Allison's office. "I shouldn't have rebuked you publicly."

"It doesn't pay to have thin skin in this business," she replied.

"Will it be difficult for you to take on this assignment, under the circumstances, that is?"

Forbes turned from her computer and calmly smiled at her mentor. "I can write a script for Arnold Schwarzenegger as readily as for Mother Teresa."

Holten moved from the doorway and sat on the edge of Allison's desk. He looked directly at her, and she met his gaze straight on.

"I suppose every gifted lawyer has a touch of schizophrenia," he said after a few seconds. "Just how many personalities do you have in your repertoire?"

"How many do you want me to have?"

"Well, there's not much need for the Mother Teresa routine at the moment," he said, "but you might work on a character with a bit more tact than Schwarzenegger."

Holten walked across Allison's office and paused a few moments, staring out her window. "Look at the magnificent clock tower of the old courthouse. When it was originally constructed, long before either of us was born, this majestic building could be seen from anywhere in the city. It was an architectural monument to an era when government was still capable of erecting buildings of substance and style, before government budgets were devoted primarily to interest obligations and entitlement programs. Look at the grand promenade of granite steps fanning out from the arched entryway to the sidewalk below."

Holten paused for a few moments, but he had obviously not completed his thought, so Allison remained silent in her chair facing the window.

"Today the law is little more than a confusing morass of regulations imposing absurd restrictions on our freedoms and destroying our creativity. God, I feel sorry for entrepreneurs like Boyd Campbell."

"It all seems so unnecessary, doesn't it?" said Allison. "Especially all the senseless lawsuits. People certainly should be able to work out their differences without hauling each other off to court all the time."

"Yeah, but it's sure damn good for the law business," Holten said, turning from the window.

Holten leaned against the window ledge as Allison sat in her chair facing the window a few feet away. She pulled her skirt down to the knees of her crossed legs, but several inches of thigh still drew Holten's attention.

Allison smiled and rotated her chair back toward her desk. "I suppose I'd best get on with the job at hand if you want me to have the project done by noon."

"No doubt there'll be another opportunity for us to wax philosophical," Holten said, patting her on the arm and walking out of her office.

Allison contemplated softening the tone of the letter somewhat. She had no doubt that the safest approach for her to take was to stay close to Holton's draft. But there was also no doubt that Mrs. Bergstrom was a woman of some sensitivity. She did not deserve harsh or threatening language. She decided to write as one woman to another, with a gentle but firm denial of the possibility of any involvement from Campbell's process.

She rang Mr. Holten's secretary. "Nancy, does Henry have a squash game at noon today?"

Hearing the expected affirmative response, she told Nancy she would have the revised draft on Holten's desk by the time he returned.

Boyd Campbell stood in the reception area waiting for Holten to arrive. He looked anxiously at his watch and then glanced out the window of the thirty-second floor and saw Holten crossing the street from the Bengal Club. It was 1:30.

"You're certainly punctual, Boyd," Holten said as he entered the room and walked directly in front of his client to the corridor leading to his office.

"Are you ready for me?" Boyd asked.

"Well of course. Come on back. Allison's been working with me on our response to Mrs. Bergstrom's letter."

Holten arrived at the door of Allison's office several paces ahead of his client. "Have you completed the re-draft?" he asked her.

She looked at him with an exaggerated frown. "Have I ever missed a deadline?"

"Good. Bring that ready wit of yours into my office," Holten said, turning and walking away.

A decanter and glasses were on a coffee table in Holten's office. "Would either of you care for some iced tea?" Holten asked, pouring two glasses without waiting for a response.

"No thanks," Allison said.

He picked up three copies of the re-draft, which had been placed at the center of his otherwise empty desk. He handed them to Allison and Boyd, and they each took a few moments to read the letter.

Dear Mrs. Bergstrom,

Thank you very much for your letter of January 11. The president of EnviroClean has asked me to respond to the questions you raised in your letter.

EnviroClean manufactures a product which is used to clean up gasoline that has leaked from underground storage tanks threatening contamination of the ground water. We are pleased that EnviroClean has been able to treat the soil in your neighborhood and rid it of this hazardous substance. We are sure you and your husband will notice a reduction in the noxious odors around your creek next spring after the snow melts.

Our product has been used extensively in cleaning up similar contaminated sites throughout the United States. Naturally, we have subjected it to extensive testing and evaluation. It has been approved for use by federal and state regulators, and it has been reviewed and issued permits by the State of Minnesota. All testing has proven it to be both entirely safe and extremely effective in cleaning up toxic materials. We have discussed your questions with our team of scientific advisors, and you will be pleased to know there is no possibility the product could cause any allergic reactions or other medical symptoms.

EnviroClean takes very seriously any concerns people like you may have about the safety of its product. After all, the very foundation of the company is to prevent possible health hazards. Because of EnviroClean's unblemished record of product safety, we are very comfortable represent-

ing the company and its outstanding products. I trust, however, that our explanation will satisfy your curiosity so you and your doctors can focus your attention on whatever may actually be causing your symptoms.

Thank you for writing EnviroClean. We are very sympathetic to your recent medical problems, and we wish you the speediest of recoveries.

Yours truly,

Allison Forbes

"Well, I see you've made a few changes, Allison." Holten's voice and tone were mild, but the steely glare of his eyes betrayed his disapproval.

"Henry, this is very good," Campbell commented, still looking at the letter. "I really appreciate your sensitive approach. I also like the idea that Allison will be signing the letter. I think it's better to have the response come from a woman."

"Allison's a very talented young lawyer," Holten replied. "Of course, there are a few minor changes I'd like to make to insure Mrs. Bergstrom is persuaded to give no further thought to this matter. We can have that taken care of as soon as you leave, and get the letter in the mail this afternoon."

"Good," Campbell said.

"And I do think the letter should come from me," Holten added. "In case the response finds its way into the office of some unscrupulous lawyer, he'll quickly know who he's really up against."

"Whatever you think best," Boyd said. "You haven't steered me wrong yet."

"I expect you're going to be meeting with Wendi Palmer this afternoon to get the public offering started," said Holten. "Allison, why don't you take Boyd down to Wendi's office while I put a few finishing touches on the letter."

As Holten rose from his chair to close the meeting, Allison recalled their earlier dialogue about further testing of the P-27. "This morning we discussed setting up a continued testing protocol for..."

"Thank you for reminding me, Allison," Holten interjected. "Boyd, we all agree you should continue with your research and development program for P-27. No doubt part of that program will include renewed toxicity testing of this and other strains you may develop. However, and I believe we are all unanimous on this, it would undoubtedly be more productive to proceed as usual with your standard testing protocol rather than to attempt any sampling at the Bergstrom's creek. I suspect that would only dilute your testing program for no real scientific gain, and, from a legal perspective, field testing at Bergstrom's is clearly inadvisable at this time."

Campbell rose from his chair and took a final sip of iced tea. "Sounds good to me. I'll discuss this with Mary Frick when I get back to the office. Thanks for your help, Henry."

"That's what I'm here for, Boyd." Henry walked his client the few steps down the hall to Allison's office. "I'm sure this is the last you'll hear from Mrs. Bergstrom," he said, shaking Boyd's hand and heading off to his next meeting.

CHAPTER Five

Dillon Love liked to dress comfortably: washed-out blue jeans, soft old shirts, and worn and scuffed cowboy boots. Growing up in a small, blue collar northern suburb he had early-on acquired a strong pride in his working-class origins and it colored his approach to life. That pride stretched to include the way he dressed and his choice of the legal profession as a way to make good money.

He had the broad shoulders, muscular arms and large hands of a man who had gone to work young and worked hard through law school. His big neck was defined by bulging arteries, permanently distended from excessive testosterone. He had a thick untrimmed beard, and, probably as a result of stress and all the excess testosterone, he was balding prematurely. He didn't mind the thinning-hair look; in fact, he felt it encouraged trust in his clients. His wife Laurie liked it; her dad was bald.

There was little in Dillon Love's life that diminished his confidence, because after his father abandoned him and his mother to run off with another woman, Dillon had become the man of the house at fifteen. Early responsibility had toughened him and made him self-reliant. He was not in the least bit interested in dressing for what others considered success, and his appearance more closely resembled a north woods outfitter fresh off the trail than a downtown lawyer. Well, he was not exactly downtown; he was on the edge of downtown. In other words, he could park for free behind the rundown office he rented cheaply from an Iranian.

In his last year of law school Dillon Love did not interview for positions with the big firms that promoted themselves with four-color brochures and recruitment kits. He had not been recruited by any firms despite standing fairly high in his class. The lack of enthusiasm potential employers demonstrated might have been summed up in a T-shirt given him by some of his classmates the semester before graduation: "Does not play well with others." Dillon was not a team player and he hated discipline.

He did not seek a judicial clerkship when he could not find a law firm to hire him. Insulted and angry, he stopped seeking any other position; he did not want to accept help from anyone. Instead he did the unthinkable, which seemed to him to be the right thing, the only thing. The week he passed the bar examination, he stenciled his name on the window of a long-vacant storefront a dozen blocks from the courthouse, had business cards printed at Kinko's, and started practicing law. The independence learned from long hours of low-paying jobs wasn't going to be sacrificed.

In place of a legal secretary, he traded the basic Apple that had gotten him through college for a souped-up used Macintosh from Computer Renaissance. The county law library was only a few blocks away, so there was no need for expensive books. He bought a huge battered steel desk, a few chairs and two big rusty file cabinets from Goodwill. The day Dillon Love carried those items into his shabby office and switched on his Mac, his feet barely touched the ground. He was practicing law, wearing blue jeans, and he was his own man. It was Dillon Love heaven.

Gradually, the tenacious stubbornness and intensity he brought to his work garnered him a reputation which began to produce a decent practice. He could afford to get married. Instead of a honeymoon, he and Laurie spent a long weekend redecorating the office. He hired a legal secretary, a retired friend of his mother's who delighted in bossing him around as she had been doing since he was a child. The Mac was replaced with a pair of pre-networked iMacs, also from Computer Renaissance. A few reference books accumulated in a rickety bookcase next to his desk and more comfortable seating in the guise of three mismatched sofas (from Goodwill, of course) were added near the front door to accommodate waiting clients. His secretary, Cindy, contributed a better coffee maker from home and actually kept it clean. A fabric-covered room divider was installed to separate his desk from the rest of the office and provide a modicum of privacy for his clients to meet with him and discuss their problems with the appearance of confidentiality.

On Friday, January 21, Love parked his old black Jeep Cherokee in the alley at the rear of his office. He kicked through the few inches of snow that had blown against the back entrance, bounded inside, and threw his coat on one of the sofas in the waiting area.

"Muffins and coffee, boss," Love said to Cindy as he sat on the edge of her desk and plunked a large paper sack in front of her. "Skinny lattes and a couple of blueberry muffs. Hot damn, you must love working here, girl. Look at all the perks."

Unimpressed, Cindy shrugged her shoulders and said, "Oh, dear me, yes, and the presentation is so elegant. Christ, Dillon, this stuff's leaking all over my work," and swept the sack to the side of her desk.

"Shall I retrieve the silver service from the china cabinet, milady?" Love said, lifting his coffee from the sack.

"What's with this designer coffee anyway? Your mother just bought you and Laurie a new coffee maker for Christmas. You could've made me a cup at home and it would've been hotter and better than this. Two bucks for some lukewarm crap in a paper cup, what a deal. You kids are so wasteful."

Sixty-two year-old Cindy Stanhope had never found a man willing to submit himself to her dominating disposition. She had retired recently after forty years of civil service and had found her way into Dillon Love's law practice through her long-standing friendship with his mother. Dillon had no filing system, no established procedures for sending or paying bills, and no reliable calendar for keeping track of deadlines on his pending cases, so the two women conspired to convince him that he needed a strong woman to bring some order into his law practice. Cindy graciously accepted Audrey Love's invitation to perform that role, and Dillon was in no position to demur. That was how she got hired, despite being a bit of a thorn in his side. Glancing at Dillon Love's red flannel shirt and rumpled blue Dockers, she said, "I see by your attire that you're in wood-splitting mode today."

"Let me guess, Cindy. You didn't get laid last night."

"Idiot. Could you maybe consider attending to the Gonzales hearing before Judge Brown at 9:30?"

"Judge Brown? Damn, he hates me."

Cindy shook her head as she sipped her coffee and squinted at him. "You've had a good up-bringing," she said. "Hard-working mother who made a concerted effort to provide you with a proper education and good manners. And yet..."

"Here we go again," he said, turning his back to her and walking over to his desk.

"I just don't understand it. Where did she go wrong?"

"It's the same old boring song," Love said, playing air-violin behind his desk. "What's wrong with this shirt anyway?"

"If you want to be successful, you first have to look successful."

"Oh what crap! Synaptic activity is equally profound regardless of one's outward appearance," countered Love. "I see no advantage to wearing duds that are more expensive and less comfortable than my woodcutter's wardrobe."

Cindy could not help laughing, but said, "I'm sure Judge Brown will be impressed."

The only true vestige of gentility in Love's profession, the Rules of Judicial Decorum, mandated coats and ties for male lawyers in all courtroom proceedings. Someday, perhaps, he would challenge the rule's hypocrisy, but for now he tolerated the requirement in order to concentrate his energies on his clients' affairs.

"Get me the Gonzalez file, will you," Love said. "I'll throw on the old corduroy."

Love walked around the corner to a small area where they kept the coffee maker and a desktop copying machine. A beige corduroy jacket hung in the broom closet which lacked sufficient space to accommodate a hanger. The coat hung from a hook that after eight years in the same spot had produced a vertical nipple just below the collar at the back of the coat. Like an old pair of boots that finally become thoroughly comfortable only when they are ready to be replaced, the corduroy was now perfectly molded to the contours of Love's torso. What it lacked in style, it made up for in comfort and sentimental attachment. On the same hook he kept a solid navy polyester clip-on tie which, together with the jacket, would at least not clash with almost any combination of clothing he might happen to wear on a given day.

He slipped on the coat and threw the tie over his shoulder, deferring the eventual choking of his neck until the last possible moment.

"Impressive!" observed Cindy. "That red flannel really makes the outfit. If the court should somehow miss the logic of your arguments, you'll at least distract your poor adversary."

"Jesus, Cindy," said Love as he caught sight of the Gonzales file. "Where do you come up with this crap, anyway?"

"I'm just telling you the truth," she replied.

Love grabbed the file and hustled toward the front door. "Thanks, Mom. I love you."

"The Burroughs Neighborhood Association will be here at 10:30, so don't dally at the courthouse all morning. I don't have time to sit around drinking coffee with all your freeloading clients."

"That's the main reason you work here. That and your insatiable maternal instincts." Love let the door slam behind him and took off jaywalking across the street toward the courthouse.

Minneapolis has both a courthouse and a government center. The courthouse is a majestic granite building with a tall clock tower. The interior has wide marble hallways with twelve-foot ceilings. A classic staircase leads visitors in 360-degree revolutions as they move from floor to floor. Love liked to cut through the old courthouse and walk some of its empty corridors on his way to the Government Center.

He wondered what it must have been like to practice law in that building. The abandoned courtrooms were located on just two floors. Next to each courtroom were the judge's chambers, and these were easily accessible to both the lawyers and the public through broad corridors circling the perimeter of the building. Hand-carved wooden benches were strategically placed along the walls and served as meeting places. Love could imagine lawyers standing with one foot on the bench talking with their clients and with each other, as they prepared to assemble in the various courtrooms. Practicing law in that building must have been a friendly and civil occupation. The architects who designed it had not only built a physical structure that was proud and stately, but they also made an important contribution to the quality of justice.

All that ended in 1975. The magnificent courthouse is now a largely unused municipal office building, and court proceedings are now held across the street in the brand-new, thoroughly modern Government Center. The new building is also granite, but it is tall and drab. The rough texture of the granite, so much a part of the spirit of the Old Courthouse, was smoothed out on the new building and monotonously stacked to create a huge brown fortress. Love had heard that the architects claimed the new building was linked to the history of the Old Courthouse because the building is divided in half and separated by glass so that if one stands in precisely the right spot on the sidewalk a block away, it is possible to see the clock tower of the Old Courthouse through the glass walls of the Government Center. Distraught people sometimes take advantage of the open design and hurl themselves to a mangled death among the bushes and fountain in the courtyard below.

Love descended one floor to the underground tunnel that connected the Old Courthouse with the Government Center across the street. The staircase was lined with Minnesota marble and led to a walkway constructed of imported Swiss tiles. Once through the tunnel, he took an escalator up two flights to the service area, which provided access to the elevators in the rest of the building.

There are twenty floors of courtrooms in the Government Center, served by elevators that are invariably crammed with teaming masses of humanity, and stop painstakingly at virtually every floor on their way to and from the eighty courtrooms in the building. In search of security, the judges now lock themselves in chambers behind their courtrooms, out of touch with the lawyers and the people they serve. In doing so they also distance themselves from most of their judicial colleagues. No one really knows many of the judges anymore, and the judges themselves do not know each other very well.

There is no charm or dignity to the new building. There is no warmth or character. Where the Old Courthouse brought people together in a collegial and venerable atmosphere, the Government Center stands as a stark and impersonal set of barriers that effectively isolates everyone involved in the judicial process. Beginning in 1975, the quality of justice in Minneapolis underwent a dramatic change.

Love waited for several minutes with about twenty-five other people for the next elevator. From past experience he knew to position himself so that he had the best chance of making it onto the first elevator. Those infrequent visitors who made the miscalculation of arriving during the morning rush hour might stand in the hall for several cycles of elevators as the experienced people repeatedly passed them by. Or they might inadvertently step too soon toward the opening doors of an arriving elevator, only to be forced to retreat by a stampede coming out.

Getting off the elevator was no easy feat either. With a constant change of riders at each floor, one almost inevitably found himself at the rear of the elevator by the time the desired stop was reached. So determined are most of the regulars to enter and depart at the same moment that any poor soul burdened with meekness of character might end up riding an elevator for hours.

Ricardo Gonzales was waiting nervously by the eighteenth-floor elevators when Love stepped from the car at 9:25. Love asked him a few questions as he fiddled with his clip-on tie, and the two men walked toward Judge Brown's courtroom. Gonzales had brought a few photographs of his apartment as well as a building inspector's citation which had been posted on the front door of the building. Love reassured his client that everything would be all right as they sat down in adjacent chairs at the back of the room.

The judge's clerk walked in and one by one called all of the cases that were on the calendar that morning. Dozens of people who had business before the court were waiting for the opportunity to be heard. Fortunately, Gonzales's case was to be called first, so they would not have to wait through everyone else's.

"Everyone please rise," said the clerk. She finished the first reading of the calendar and then immediately pounded a gavel against a wooden block on her desk, thereby giving the judge his cue that she was ready for him to enter the room. "Hear ye, hear ye. This court is now convened, the Honorable Byron Brown presiding."

"You may be seated," said the judge after sitting down himself. "Good morning, everyone. Call the first case."

"George Linden versus Ricardo Gonzales," the clerk said loudly. "Please come forward and be sworn."

The parties stepped through the gate separating the courtroom from the audience, and both Linden and Gonzales took the necessary oath. Linden was represented by an obese attorney who was dressed in a dark suit with a white dress shirt and tie. The suit was soiled with food stains that had apparently not seen recent dry cleaning. He had thinning silver-gray hair that had been blown about in the wind and not combed back into an orderly appearance. He spoke first.

"Your Honor, this is a simple, straightforward case. Mr. Gonzales has not paid his rent for almost three months, and we're asking the court to evict him from the premises immediately. Mr. Linden is here with all the records showing the arrearage in this man's lease payments, should Your Honor wish to hear this testimony. I doubt that will be necessary, however, since it's obvious he has not paid his rent. We have a new tenant ready to move in tomorrow, and we want to have Mr. Gonzales out of there today."

That was just the speech Love needed to hear to get his juices flowing.

"Your Honor," he began, "this is one of the most callous and despicable landlords in this city. We've had too many cases involving this man and his slum properties. The court would be well advised to check the index with the clerk's office, and you'll find scores of cases that have been filed against this man by his tenants and by the city inspectors. This apartment building is a rat-infested pigsty that violates virtually every building code in the city. The radiators are so clogged with iron deposits that practically no heat gets through to the apartment units. Many windows are broken and haven't been repaired despite repeated requests by Mr. Gonzales. The plaster is falling in over his bed because of faulty plumbing on the floor above him. Look at these pictures my client took yesterday, and you'll see why he's withholding his rent. Look at this report of violations by the building inspector. This apartment is a disgrace, and this landlord is an embarrassment to the community."

"Your Honor," responded the silver-haired attorney, "if this is such a lousy place to live, why doesn't Mr. Gonzales just move out and let us rent the unit to someone who really wants it? Obviously he doesn't actually believe what his attorney is saying, or he'd be long gone. The truth is, the man's a deadbeat. He has no money to pay the rent, and this is all a bunch of malarkey so he can live there for free at my client's expense."

"I can't believe my ears," Love said, jumping to his feet. "Where would they have my client go? He's struggling to support his wife and child on a minimum-wage job. There's nowhere else for him to go, unless of course Mr. Linden wants to rent him a cardboard box so he can sleep under a railroad bridge with a bunch of derelicts. Mr. Gonzales has a right to stay in his apartment, and he has a right to force his landlord to fix the place up properly. It's time the court put a stop to this man's profiteering at the expense of the poor and helpless people of this community. It's time to shut him down right now. The slum lords of this community must get the message loud and clear, the plight of these poor people can and will be improved so they can once more live in dignity with their families as they so well deserve."

Judge Byron Brown looked at Linden and then at Love over the top of his reading glasses. His eyes rested on Love's red shirt for a second, then locked onto Love's face. Dillon grinned and nodded, which prompted an almost imperceptible shaking of the judge's head. "I'll take the case under advisement," the judge said. "Call the next case."

The four men walked from the courtroom, each attorney whispering to his client.

"I'll call you as soon as I hear from the court," Love advised Gonzales. "In the meantime, you're free to stay in the apartment as long as you want. I really hope the court gives us this one. It'll be a big help to you and to hundreds of others just like you. Call me anytime if you have questions."

Love would have just enough time to make it back to his office to meet with the Boroughs Neighborhood group. They were concerned about a fourplex on their block that was becoming rundown and shabby. They were worried it might attract drug dealers or other misfits who would drastically alter their neighborhood for the worse. He was going to help them organize an effort to force the building's owner to make some improvements.

He would be meeting later with clients who had claims involving possible wrongful termination from their employment, a divorce client, a man charged with shoplifting, a man who had been beaten in an encounter with the police, and a woman who had been injured when she slipped on some ice in front of a grocery store. Such was the typical day of Dillon Love.

The corduroy and tie could now come off.

CHAPTER Six

Laurie Love was an outdoorsy type just like her husband Dillon. She worked as a buyer for the city's biggest outfitter. The two met a few years earlier at a Nordic skiing lodge off the Gunflint Trail, just outside the Boundary Waters wilderness area. They were married six months later on a granite outcropping at East Bearskin Lake. They were both busy with their careers and kept promising each other a real honeymoon in London or Paris. Since then their marriage had revolved around their work schedules, with cross-country skiing trips in the winter or canoe trips in the summer punctuating their busy lives. They used mountain bikes all year round to try and keep fit, but it was never enough, and neither quite felt comfortable trying to fit into the clothes they got married in.

On Saturday, January 22, after a horrible week during which they had barely seen each other, they absolutely had to get out for some exercise. There was fresh snow on the ground so they went to Theodore Wirth Park and hit the groomed ski trails that wound through the woods. The air was frigid with a dangerous wind chill even in the relative shelter of the trees. To escape the wind for a minute they stopped at a small lean-to. Dillon pulled a packet of gorp from his fanny pack and offered a handful to Laurie. Ice had formed on the whiskers around his mouth and in his eyebrows. She wanted to kiss him, and pulled him down to her. She loved his clean breath.

"What's that for?" he asked.

"Well, Dillie, I guess I'm about ready to make babies."

"It's a little chilly at the moment," Dillon said, laughing.

"I'm serious. My job has a great maternity leave package and your practice is going great, and, well, I'd like to have kids. Wouldn't that be wonderful!"

"We'd have to give up all our trips, you know."

"No way. There are those baby carriers I just ordered for the store, we just strap the little tyke on your back, and off we go."

"I'm not taking a baby on a canoe trip."

"Oh, come on, Dillie. Our trips can wait a few years. I want a family. You and me, Dillie, perfect parents, perfect."

"It's almost 4:30 and the wind chill's dropping. Let's get out of here. Maybe later tonight you can try and seduce me, Laurie, if I'm feeling generous."

"Stingy old bastard. If I get back to the Subaru before you, I'm leaving you behind."

Laughing, they raced to the parking lot.

At six o'clock Dillon and Laurie walked into the basement of St. Mary's Catholic Church. Their plan was to volunteer for an hour and then escape to catch a movie and some dinner. The room was going to be used to hold a rummage sale to raise money to improve handicapped access to the parish school. Everyone involved in the project was gathering to sort and organize the clothing that had been delivered to the church over the previous four weeks and to prepare the tables for the crowds anticipated the next day.

Laurie had to suppress a gasp when she saw her friend Ruth Bergstrom sitting in a wheelchair in front of a large wooden table, attaching price stickers to items of clothing that her husband, Arne, set in front of her. Their kids contributed too, Molly carrying the marked items and stacking them neatly at the assigned location while under the table Brett was covering his arms with blank stickers.

"Do you know the Bergstroms?" Laurie asked Dillon, pulling him in their direction. "Ruthie, what are you doing in that wheelchair?" Laurie asked. "This is my husband, Dillon. What on earth happened to you?"

"It's nice to meet you, Dillon. Laurie talks about you a lot. This is my husband, Arne, and these are our two children, Molly and Brett."

"What's going on, Ruthie?" Laurie insisted, frowning.

"Brett, come on out of there now!" Ruth said, reaching under the table. "Just look at you!"

"Ruthie..." Arne was about to scold Ruth for avoiding Laurie's question, but she interrupted him before he could finish his sentence.

"I wish I knew what was wrong," she said. "A few months ago I started getting pain in my legs, and it's gradually gotten worse. A week ago I slipped on some ice, and I haven't been able to walk since."

"You didn't slip on any ice, Ruthie," said Arne. He looked at Laurie and said, "There might be something wrong with her legs or it might be neurological. We don't know yet."

Laurie knelt beside the wheelchair and took Ruth's hand. "Oh, Ruthie, I'm so sorry," she said.

"I guess you can imagine how many times someone has poked and prodded me all week long, running endless tests. I do know it's not MS, and we're all really grateful for that. I should hear something more next week."

"They think she might have been exposed to some chemical," Arne said, "and that she's having an allergic reaction to it."

"Now, Arne, don't go telling them stuff like that. Rest assured I haven't been fooling around with any chemicals."

"You'd think she was a doctor the way she talks," Arne laughed, ruffling her hair. "Dr. McCosh thinks that's possible, and he certainly knows more about it than you. I'm taking her to Mayo on Monday."

"The Mayo Clinic," Laurie said. "That's great. I'm sure they'll figure it all out."

"I do hope so," Ruth answered, "but I'm sure they won't find any chemicals in my blood."

"Dr. McCosh thinks it's from the gas station next door," Arne said.

"Gas station?" Dillon broke in. "Hasn't that place been shut down for several years?"

Ruth ignored Dillon. "Arne," she said, " that's not what Dr. McCosh said."

"I was there too, you know," said Arne.

"And now we've gotten that letter from the lawyer saying there was nothing wrong at the gas station," said Ruth.

"Lawyer?" Dillon asked. "What's this about a lawyer?"

Arne told Dillon about Ruth's letter to EnviroClean and the response from Darby and Witherspoon. The reply indicated there was nothing at the gas station that could have caused her symptoms. In fact, the lawyer had seemed quite sure on that point.

"Did you write your letter to the company directly?" Dillon asked.

"Yes," Arne replied. "Ruthie wrote to EnviroClean. The city inspector gave her the name and address."

Dillon appeared puzzled and Laurie had the first twinge of suspicion that if she really wanted some time alone with her husband she should not have introduced him to Ruth Bergstrom. Dillon scratched his beard and said, "It's strange that you'd write the company and get a response from its lawyer."

"I thought that's what lawyers did," Ruth said. "Write letters and that sort of thing so everything is clear and legal."

"Did you save the letter? I'd like to take a look at it."

"It's at home," Arne said. "If you want, you could stop over after we're finished here and I'll show you it."

"Now, Arne, these guys have a lot more to do on a Saturday night than come home with us and read some silly letter."

"Actually, we don't," Dillon said. Laurie looked up at him and found him looking down at her. "Do we, Laurie?" he said.

"I guess not," she said, disappointment in her voice. She realized it was pointless to argue with Dillon when he scented a potential client.

After a few pleasantries at the Bergstrom's, which included cracking open some cans of beer, Dillon's curiosity got the best of him. "Let me see both letters," he said, "the one you wrote and the one you received."

He read Henry Holten's letter through twice.

"They're hiding something. EnviroClean wouldn't hire the senior partner of the largest law firm in Minnesota to write a letter to Ruth if there wasn't something very funny going on. The guy probably bills his time at four hundred dollars an hour. By the time he met with the EnviroClean people and ran through a couple of drafts, he had over a thousand dollars put into this letter."

"You can't be serious," Ruth said. "A thousand dollars for a single letter? That's criminal."

"That it is," Dillon said. "But that's the mentality of these humongous law firms. And they wouldn't do it if their client weren't scared of something."

Dillon's mind focused intently on Holten's letter as he read it a third time, looking for further clues as to its real purpose. "This is bullshit," Dillon said finally. He clenched his fists together and sat uneasily on the edge of his chair. He could feel the heat coming into his face. Laurie, who sat opposite him in a chair next to Ruth, looked at him curiously.

He then began talking rapidly and intensely, almost stumbling over the words. "There's no doubt in my mind something funny's going on here. Why would they have a lawyer write a response to your simple letter? Why would they have it written by the senior partner in the largest law firm in the state? Why would this legal superstar, presumably a man of culture and propriety, write such a harsh, strongly worded letter? 'Frivolous charges,' 'pointless litigation.' Bullshit, there haven't even been any charges filed for chrissake. It's all very suspicious. If there's something from the gas station harming you, it may be affecting the children, too. You have to let me ..."

Ruth suddenly slumped forward in her wheelchair. Her face was taut, and tiny beads of sweat formed on her brow.

"Ruthie!" Arne shouted.

Ruth did not respond. Her entire body began shaking, and her legs rattled against the foot supports of the wheelchair. The muscles in her neck flexed tensely and she appeared oblivious to the world around her. All stood paralyzed for a moment as the room became agonizingly quiet except for the eerie clatter of Ruth convulsing against the aluminum chair.

Breaking the tension, Arne ran for the phone and dialed 911. Laurie got a wet towel from the kitchen to cool Ruth's forehead. Horrified, Dillon stayed by Ruth's side to keep her from falling out of the chair. Gradually the muscle spasms and quivering of her torso subsided, and by the time the paramedics arrived, she had regained her senses.

All the confusion and excitement had attracted the attention of the Bergstrom's children. They stood in the doorway staring at their mother as the paramedics walked through the front door. Too scared to move any closer, they remained silent in the doorway, side by side, intently focused on the pained expression on their mother's face.

After conducting a preliminary examination, one of the paramedics asked, "How long have your legs been swollen like this?"

Wincing in pain, Ruth said, "Ever since they put me in this dumb wheelchair."

"I'll call Dr. McCosh and ask him to meet us at the emergency room," Arne said.

"I'm already going to the Mayo Clinic on Monday. Can't we wait?"

"Ruthie, we're going to the emergency room now," Arne said. "I can't stand you suffering like this."

"I don't want to go, I'm..."

"If not for your own sake, then at least have mercy on my middle-aged heart. It's not meant to take all this stress."

"Dillon and I will stay here with the children," Laurie said. "Don't worry about a thing."

Dillon stood watching the medics remove Ruth to the ambulance, his heart pounding with fury. 'They cannot be allowed to do this,' he thought, 'They have to be fought, they have to be crushed. I will not let this go.'

Dillon slept badly that night. He could not get his mind off what was being hidden from the Bergstroms. By six-thirty he was fully awake, distractedly reading the morning paper and sipping coffee. Every few minutes he looked over at the clock to verify it was still too early to call Jackie Lockhart, their city council member. Jackie was a good friend, and she would know about EnviroClean and the work being done at the gas station.

By eight he could wait no longer.

"Dillon Love here. Did I get the Right Honorable council member from the fifth ward out of bed?"

"You've got to be kidding. I don't have the luxury of lawyer's hours. I've been up since six thinking up new and ingenious ways of spending your tax dollars on everyone but you."

"Well, I'm glad you're feeling bushy-tailed this morning," Dillon said. "I need some information. Are you ready to do some work for your favorite constituent?"

"Who might you be referring to, counselor?" Jackie Lockhart said.

"Wasn't it my favorite constituent who missed my last campaign fund-raiser with some feeble excuse about being in a jury trial?"

"So," Dillon said, "that's what it takes to win your favors, cold hard cash. Do you always shake the pockets of everyone who calls you, or do you just treat friends like me with special regard?"

"You're such a special friend," Lockhart said, "I'll save you a dozen tickets for my next fish fry."

"Listen, Jackie," Dillon said, "do you recall Arne and Ruth Bergstrom? They live over on Thirty-sixth and Nassau next to the abandoned gas station."

"Isn't he the Bergstrom's Hardware guy who had to shut up shop?"

"I guess so, yes."

"That sucked."

"It gets worse. His wife, Ruth, has suddenly come down with a strange medical condition. One of her doctors thought it might have something to do with that gas station. Apparently there's a company called EnviroClean working over there to clean up the site from a leaking underground gas tank. I thought I might look into this for her as a friend."

"Gee, that's a shame. All I can tell you is that EnviroClean is a promising new biotech company that uses microorganisms to degrade toxic substances in the soil," Lockhart explained. "I've heard very good things about it. Its founder was a highly regarded scientist at the university when he came up with this new idea."

"What kind of permits did he have to get before he could work on this project?" asked Dillon. "Is there some kind of proposal with supporting scientific data that would be on file with the city?"

"Permits would have been issued by the Pollution Control Agency," Lockhart replied. "The city engineer's office would have on file whatever company literature EnviroClean might publish. I assume there's some type of technical data sheet. Frankly, Dillon, I think you're spinning your wheels on this one. This looks like a solid company with good local people behind it."

"Do you know a lawyer named Henry Holten?" Dillon asked. "He's with the Darby and Witherspoon firm."

"Sure," Lockhart answered. "Doesn't everyone? How's he involved?"

Dillon explained to Lockhart about the correspondence between

Ruth Bergstrom and EnviroClean. He told her his suspicions about Holten's letter and that this was the reason he wanted to look into the matter further.

"I think you're reading more into this than is really there, Dillon," she said. "But if you want to come on down to my office on Monday, I'll give you everything the city has on this company and on this particular clean-up site."

"I'll be there."

"Dillon, there's one thing you ought to know. Holten has made substantial contributions to virtually every current member of the council, including me. You and I have been friends a long time. I suggest you be a bit more delicate than normal in making your inquiries."

"All I want is the truth," Dillon replied.

"Just the same," she suggested, "a modicum of discretion would serve you well in this instance."

Dillon's next call was to an old college friend, Ken Butler, an environmental engineer who worked for a firm of consulting engineers and owed Dillon a favor for getting him out of a bad lease. He told Ken, who had a social conscience similar to his own, all about what had happened to Ruth Bergstrom. Dillon learned that Ken's firm had long-standing ties with Darby and Witherspoon and that this would prevent Ken from looking into the case on a formal basis. So Ken agreed to look around the Bergstroms' neighborhood informally, but he warned Dillon that although the temperature had risen to twenty-five degrees, the conditions were not ideal for searching the ground for unknown toxic substances. What water remained in the creek would have frozen solid a month before. Snow would be covering the ground and the soil would be frozen, making samples difficult to gather.

"Never mind all that," said Dillon, "Let's meet at Thirty-sixth and Nassau at noon."

"Make it one o'clock," Ken Campbell said. "I'll need to stop by the office to pick up my bag of tricks and some topographical maps of the area."

Ken and Dillon arrived at the old gas station at the same time. They shuffled a hundred feet through the snow to the creek bed behind the station, then jumped down a two foot bank, and walked along

56

the creek toward the Bergstrom's house about seventy-five feet south of the station.

The creek cut through the Bergstroms' property at a slight angle so that it approached within fifty feet of the house by the time it traversed their land to its southern boundary. The land sloped gently away from the house toward the creek. On the western side of the creek was a park with woods that gave way to several large athletic fields. It was a serene, almost pastoral setting.

They walked along the creek bed, Ken pausing from time to time to consult one of the several topographic maps he had brought with him. Periodically he stopped to brush snow away from the edge of the bank and poke around with a small hand pick. As they walked back toward gas station, something caught Ken's attention. Under the branches of a large silver maple that overhung the banks of the creek, he dropped to his knees in the snow.

"Look at this," he said, pointing to a small area where the snow had risen to form a small mound about a foot above the surrounding area. "Interesting."

Ken carefully slid his hands under the base of the mound and lifted it away from the surrounding snow. Underneath was a hole about ten inches deep and six inches in diameter, revealing frozen black humus at the bottom. He pulled out his pick and a small plastic bag and began digging away at the frozen soil. He placed about a cup of dirt into the plastic bag, sealed it, and rose to his feet.

"I don't know what to make of this," Ken said, as he stood up and started to walk back towards his car. "I think that's about all we can accomplish today," he said a few moments later as the two men got into Dillon's Jeep to escape the cold. "One thing I do know is that there's a lot of bacterial activity in this stream. I don't know what it is, what caused it, or whether it's in any way abnormal, and I surely don't know whether it could be related to Mrs. Bergstrom's illness."

"Damn suspicious though, right?" Dillon asked.

"The soil I removed is very black and rich. Look at it. Do you see these maple leaves that have almost fully decayed? Those leaves fell from the trees only a few weeks before the ground froze. Rapid degradation like that only occurs in the presence of very active microbes."

"Microbes?" Dillon said, "you mean like bacteria?"

"Exactly. The soil where I took this sample obviously froze well after the ground around it, because the heat from the decaying leaves melted the snow as it fell. It was not until the most recent snowfalls that this soil froze and the winds blew a cap of snow over the area."

"So you reckon the bacteria must be the cause of Ruth Bergstrom's illness?" Dillon asked.

"You lawyers always jump to the most convenient conclusions," Ken said. "I'm a scientist. I need data and we have no data. We don't know what bacterial organisms may be present and whether they're harmful to humans. We don't know whether they're capable of producing the symptoms Mrs. Bergstrom has experienced. We don't know how the microbes in the creek could infect her, and we don't know why, if they could, they've only infected her, and not the rest of the family or anyone else in the neighborhood. In short, we don't know anything."

"But you did find bacteria," Dillon said. "Everyone knows bacteria cause disease."

Ken laughed. "There are billions of different microbes, the vast majority of which are not in any way harmful to humans. Your own body is at this moment teeming with millions of bacteria that are busy helping you digest your lunch. Bacteria perform many evolutionary functions, most of which are essential to the preservation of human life. There's no way I can tell you that what I found could cause anyone to become ill."

"That's the trouble with science," Dillon said. "You scientific types are so blinded by empiricism that you lose sight of what's patently obvious to anyone with open eyes and reasonable intuition."

"The trouble with the law is its lack of concern for the truth," Ken replied. "All you guys care about is what suits your interests."

"What else do you have to do to prove I'm right?" Dillon asked.

"Listen, Dillon," Ken said, "I explained to you that I can't be involved in this officially because of my firm's relationship with Darby and Witherspoon. This has got to be on the QT, agreed?"

"I just want the truth," Dillon repeated with a smile.

"I can run a few tests at the lab to determine the identity of the organism and then see what the medical literature says about it. That's the next step."

"Fantastic. Call me as soon as you learn something."

As Dillon drove home, he thought to himself that at some time in every lawyer's career there comes an opportunity to handle one stand-out case, a case above and beyond all other cases. Most lawyers fail to recognize the opportunity when it arrives. Others recognize it but are too fainthearted to accept the challenge. "This is my case," Dillon said loudly inside his Cherokee. "I'll never see another one like it the rest of my life. I'll never again have a client who will allow me to use all my talents to serve the cause of justice in such a profound way. I am ready. Goddamn, am I ever ready for this."

Laurie was not home. She was probably visiting Ruth in the hospital, so Dillon settled into the comfort of an old stuffed chair in his study. Tired from not having slept much the night before, he threw off his boots, flipped on his CD player, and slid his feet onto the coffee table. The restful violins of Brahms soon took his mind to a place well beyond the events of the last twenty-four hours. His whole body became enveloped by the soothing strings, and he fell asleep, dreaming of triumph.

CHAPTER Seven

"**A**llie, sweetheart, Dillon Love here. How the hell've you been?"

"Dillon?" Allison Forbes replied. "It's nice to hear your voice. How're you doing?"

"Better than most of the other hapless saps you've hung out with over the years."

"Get serious," she laughed. "My heart looks more like the Liberty Bell than an instrument of love. But I'd jump at the opportunity to tease you again, that's for sure, Mr. Love."

"Then you're in luck, how about lunch today?"

"You have time for lunch? Hell, the shit just really hit the fan here this morning. I'm chained to my desk."

"Come on, beautiful, you still have to eat. I remember how cranky you get when your blood sugar gets low. One of my many distinguished clients just canceled lunch, so I'm buying."

"I'm surprised you have any clients at all, and it's unbelievable that you actually have a distinguished one."

"Well, babe, I've got no sterling-silver pimp trotting a parade of big spenders through my office like you do. But I'm one helluva hustler, and I've got a case going right now that'll make anything Henry Holten throws your way look like dog meat."

"Wowie! Do I sense a male ego on the rise this morning? Perhaps it'd be too stressful for you to have lunch with me and hear about a truly stimulating law practice. Though I suppose I could let you allude briefly to your new case, however little time that may take."

"You'd better keep your afternoon clear," Love laughed.

"Are you still working out like a maniac, Dillon?"

"No, just working like one. How's that lovely mouth of yours?"

"I know what you're thinking and you can forget it."

Love laughed and said, "Just as well. I'm a married man, you know."

"So I heard. No invite for poor little me to the wedding."

"I wonder why."

Allison laughed and said, "Ah, me. It's a strange life, isn't it?"

"It sure is. Okay now, let's get serious. How about Paul's Place at 11:45?"

"All right, I'll be there," Allison said. "You should've been a car salesman. It'll be fun to reconnect the old partnership of Forbes & Love."

"Wasn't that Love & Forbes?"

"Actually, as I think about it," Allison said, "I recall it as Forbes & Associates."

"In your dreams, Hot Lips," Love said. "See you in two."

Dillon sat back with his hands behind his head and blew out air. Boy, Allison would be furious when she found out it was his shit that just hit her fan. He had banished her from his mind until he found out she was part of Darby and Witherspoon's litigation team protecting EnviroClean. Just talking to her created the usual discomfort in his nether regions and he had to shake away images of his past with her in order to get his mind back on the case. He was not entirely clear why he wanted to take her to lunch. Was it to show her what a stud he was? Maybe piss her off? Or was his wife, Laurie, just way too sweet for him and he needed to be around a dangerous goddess with a multiple personality disorder. He realized she would have changed some by now, she was no longer a kid. For a man who had grown fatter and balder since taking on the Ruth Bergstrom case, he nevertheless harbored secret longings to weasel his way back into Allison's favor. Great way to do it, buddy, hauling off and filing suit against EnviroClean.

Dillon's mind wandered back to the second year of law school when he and Allison hooked up. They were an odd couple, Allison an outwardly proper Edina girl, Dillon a rebel from the sticks. Their affair had been brief, finally broken up by Allison's impatience with Dillon's casual attitude toward school and toward her. Dillon had not understood her not very subtle demands for more of his time. When she broke up with him it hit him hard, reminding him of his father's defection. He bitterly resented her good grades and popularity and the ease with which she had started dating some of their classmates.

The last two months had been overwhelming for Love as he became thoroughly engrossed in Ruth's case, a case whose complexity would challenge even a well-seasoned trial attorney in one of the larger firms. For a sole practitioner with only fleeting experience in the personal injury arena, it was a monumental undertaking. He had spent days at the public library reading everything he could about biodegradation technology, the scientific process behind EnviroClean's product. He studied textbooks on genetics and genetic engineering. He consulted several books on hydrology to understand how pollutants could migrate from the surface and contaminate water supplies. He contacted several governmental agencies for assistance, the Department of Natural Resources, the Pollution Control Agency, and the Environmental Protection Agency. He also met with the city engineers who had been involved in the gas station project. He went so far as to enroll in a legal seminar on environmental law so he could become familiar with this fast-developing field.

Lawyers in big firms would have hired out most of this work to consultants, experts in specific fields who would conduct the research and then meet with the attorneys to counsel them on the technical details of their case. Such an approach was expensive, and Love had no budget for this kind of program since he had taken the case on contingency. He would have to do the work himself, however time-consuming it might prove to be.

Cindy Stanhope approached Dillon's desk with an armload of the books he had dumped on her chair. "Where would you like me to deposit all this garbage you keep hauling in here?" she asked.

"The distinguished scientist from Stanford who wrote the book on top of that pile would not regard his life's work as 'garbage,' I expect," said Love. "And I know you'll find a good home for his scholarship, because that's why I'm paying you such an exorbitant salary."

She dumped the pile of books on the floor beside his desk, dusted off her hands, and then said, "Sam Wadkins came in yesterday to pick up the final decree in his divorce. The only problem is you haven't even drafted the order for the judge to sign. The man's not a happy camper, nor, I might add, is his fiancée. You'd better give him a call this morning." Cindy waited a few moments for a response, but Love was so absorbed in his reading he did not bother to answer. "You know," she continued, "this isn't the only client you've neglected lately. I'm worried about you. You're going to lose all the clients you've worked so hard to develop over the last eight years."

"Cindy," Love replied, "Ruth Bergstrom *is* the client I've worked eight years to represent. This is the most important case for the most deserving client any lawyer could ever want. She's a splendid human being who desperately needs me to help her through some terribly difficult legal obstacles. I can't let her down."

"Are you doing this for her, or for yourself?"

"Christ, Cindy, this is same shit I get from Laurie at home. What the hell's wrong with you two anyway?"

"What do you plan to do about Sam Wadkins? And the others like him?"

"Look, everything'll be fine. The Ruth Bergstrom case is no big deal in the long run. I've finished all the initial work-up. There'll be a couple of sets of interrogatories and a few depositions, then it'll probably be settled. Besides, we can always hire some law clerk if the need arises."

"Last I heard," Cindy said, "law clerks expect paychecks. As your bookkeeper, let me assure you there's no room for anyone else on the payroll."

"Things have a way of working out," Love said. He turned his back to Cindy and pulled a file out of the cabinet behind his desk. "And there's always my friendly neighborhood banker."

"Bankers are friendly until you need them, not one minute longer." After a short pause she added, "By the way, I hear you canceled your cross-country ski trip with Laurie."

"You've got your nose in all my business, haven't you?"

"Lucky for you I do. Laurie's pretty disappointed."

"She never said anything to me."

"That doesn't change the way she feels."

"People need to say what they mean, not gossip behind a guy's back."

"She's trying not to add to the pressure you're under. What's the matter with you, can't you see that? For a lawyer you know very little about people."

"Cindy, look, I'm busy right now."

"Okay, but it's March already, and there won't be enough snow up north for a ski trip if you put it off. I think you ought to reconsider."

"There's nothing to reconsider. You said yourself I'm behind in all my work. Hell," Love said, affecting a smile and pounding his fist on the desk, "what's a guy supposed to do with such an array of evil-mongers and scum bags out there and so few good lawyers willing to take them on?"

Cindy started to withdraw but stopped, turned, and said, "You aren't Robin Hood. You are not God's gift to the poor. You're getting fat because you don't exercise like you used to and you eat junk food on the fly in your pigsty of a Jeep. If you weren't so damned stubborn, you'd trade a bucket of testosterone for a snippet of common sense. At least the women in your life would be better off for the trade."

"Wow, you should be a trial lawyer, Cindy, you're a real bitch."

"And you should be a real husband, instead of an obsessed jerk."

Love looked up from his file, shook his head, and returned to his reading.

At 11:35 Dillon left his office for the short walk to Paul's Place. Paul's was a small casual French café located in an old print shop. Some of the original presses and other equipment, left behind by the pre-vious owner, remained as the only noticeable decorations in the room. The duct work for the heating system had been left exposed and painted in bright colors. Love remembered how it had been described in *City Pages*, the local weekly, "The intentionally understated ambiance is pleasantly complemented by simple, well-presented selections." The pomposity of the statement made him laugh, but it was true.

As Love approached the restaurant, he saw Allison's elegant blond profile through the window. Typically, she had arrived early and had been seated at a table for two. Their eyes met as Love neared the front door. A stab of longing shot through him. She flipped her long blonde ponytail in front of her lips and winked at Love through the glass. He paused and pressed himself against the windowpane like a splattered frog and kissed the glass, which made her laugh.

Inside, she stood to hug him, and her breasts pressing against his chest, combined with her lovely scent, made his throat dry. He had forgotten how much he liked her height. What came out of his mouth was way goofier than he intended, "Allie, goddamn, it's great to see you. How about a little kiss for your old boyfriend?"

Allison did not back away from the embrace but remained a few seconds looking into Love's eyes. "That was a long time ago, and I don't kiss married men."

"Pardon me," Love said. "Has that big law firm in the sky forced some antiquated morals on little Miss Hot Lips?"

She smiled and gently squeezed his biceps. "Besides, you're getting fat and bald."

"Hey, come on," Love said, puffing out his chest, "I'm a rock-hard stud like Samson."

"You'll never make it in a Rogaine commercial. What happened to all your mighty curls?"

"Sweet, ain't it?" he said, running a hand across his pate. "Brings in business."

Allison laughed and tugged at his thick beard. "With your shaggy pelt and bald dome," she said, "you look like you've got your head on upside down." She was smiling into his face, so close he could smell a hint of tea on her breath.

"The testosterone does it, you know."

"You always had an excess of that. Jeez," she laughed, shaking her head slightly. "I kind of like it though. You look like Attila the Hun."

"I was hoping for the Robin Hood look."

"Forget it," she said, finally stepping back. "He was a gentleman."

They sat down and Dillon asked, "So, sweet Allison, do you like working at Darby and Witherspoon?"

"Of course. Are you kidding?"

"Is there any satisfaction in what you do there, other than the big salary, I mean?"

"Darby's a great place to be. It's very stimulating with all the bright people there. The training program's outstanding for young associates. And to work with Henry Holten, hell, I'm on my way to becoming one of the best trial lawyers in Minnesota."

"That's fine, but are you working on any cases that are meaningful to people who truly need your help?"

"At $250 per hour, you better believe they need my help. They sure think so anyway."

Love found it amusing to watch Allison's personality change from sex kitten to earnest advocate for a money grubbing mega-firm in the blink an eye. She had not changed much since law school. Theatrically, he said, "$250 an hour! Holy shit." He leaned forward, took her hand and added, "You're not that friggin' smart, woman."

"Our clients have complex problems that require creative solutions. They want the best legal advice available, and we provide it for them. I love my job. I love getting up every morning to come to such an exciting and challenging place to work. What about you?"

"You know," Dillon said, "in law school, none of us saw ourselves representing clients who were justly accused of some travesty. We all wore ten-gallon hats and rode white stallions. Our imaginary clients were always innocent, and their oppressors were always villains who, but for our singular talents, would continue undaunted in their subjugation of the weak and downtrodden. Then, one by one, we costumed our slovenly bodies in the unnatural garb of the legal establishment. We suddenly realized that the few clients who had the money to pay us were those very people who, for three years, we had seen as the objects of our scorn and our principal targets. So most of the smart lawyers ended up in firms like Darby and Witherspoon, firms whose principal objective is to help make rich people richer. Where's the social validation for dedicating your entire life to such a purpose?"

"Take a bath!" Allison said, pulling her hand out of his, "You're rolling around in your own bullshit. Tell me you're not serious."

"I am serious, Allie. Look, you know there isn't a lawyer I respect more than you. I'm just curious as to your perspective on this issue."

"Darby's a very community-spirited firm. We're all expected to spend 10 percent of our time on pro bono work. The firm's a leading contributor to every legal aid program in town. Most of our partners are members of charitable boards and have committed many long hours to community service. There's no way any small firm can possibly make the contributions to this community that we do."

Dillon sat back, crossed himself, and placed his hands in an attitude of prayerful supplication and said, "All praise the newly sainted Allison Forbes."

Allison rolled her eyes, said, "So where's the transcendent social purpose in representing a bunch of deadbeats who care so little about their own futures they drop out of high school, take no tangible steps toward productive careers, and can't even manage their personal lives without public assistance?"

"Don't tell me their plight isn't the grand design of Corporate America."

"Do you still believe all that conspiracy crap they taught us in law school?" Allison said. "You and I are doing the same thing. What difference does it make who our clients are?"

"I guess the main difference is that I'm able to justify my existence through my legal work for the disadvantaged, whereas you gain your sense of worth through outside activities, sponsored by your over-advantaged clients."

"Are you appointing yourself the judge and jury of who's 'over-advantaged,' as you call it? Is someone who has dedicated a lifetime of hard work and long hours carefully growing a good business at considerable personal sacrifice 'over-advantaged'? Frankly, Dillon, I'm proud to be dedicating my life to these wonderful people. They deserve a good lawyer like me as much as any of your clients deserve you."

"Sounds like I hit a nerve," Dillon said with a wry smile. "Goddamn, Forbes, you're cute when you get all riled up."

"And you're a goddamn chauvinist, Dillon Love. That's why I loathe you," Allison said.

He laughed. She sat back, looked out of the window for a second, and then said, "So tell me about your practice."

"You know the program, a little bit of everything. If it walks in the front door, I take the case. It's not that easy getting a practice going from scratch."

"I bet."

"A lot of David and Goliath stuff. I'm the David, in case you don't recognize me."

"You look more like Goliath."

"Nah, Darby and Witherspoon's the Goliath. It's just me and my slingshot against the rich and powerful."

"Oh jeez, gag me with a maggot, Dillon!" Allison said. "I know you better than that. What's this slingshot crap? You're no David, you're more like that idiot Samson who brought the temple down on himself. You'd be a stubborn opponent and you're probably a rotten husband."

"Ah, the exacting analogies of a biblical upbringing. You should reread that good book."

"No, you should. Then maybe you'd figure out you're not Jesus Christ Himself."

The conversation paused as the waiter arrived and took their lunch orders.

"Why the hell do you women always order rabbit food?" Dillon asked as the waiter left. "You can eat that shit at home any time. Here we sit in one of the best restaurants in Minneapolis, and all you can think of is lettuce."

Allison smiled, and sat up straight and sucked in her abdomen so the hollowness enhanced the rich protuberance of her breasts. She cocked her head slightly to one side and said, "So I won't wind up a fat slob like you."

"Oh, I'll get back to my former self," Dillon said. "Once I get everything stabilized. Just you wait, I'll be Hercules Unchained."

"More like the Kraken released."

Dillon did not get the Kraken analogy, so he just laughed.

"Listen, Dillon, we haven't got all day, and I've got to tell you about my new case. This is the first major lawsuit where I'm going to have primary responsibility for the file. Talk about deserving clients, this guy's at the top of anyone's list. He's a former professor at the university who invented this new biotech product and spent ten years developing it through lab studies, field trials, and test markets. He's building up his own company from scratch with nothing but his own talents and boundless energy. Not only that, but he's about the nicest person I know, and honest as they come."

"So what's the big case, Allie?"

"It's a new product liability case involving a very innovative new product used in the bio-remediation of hazardous wastes. It's been proven effective and safe in countless rigorous studies. The lawsuit's completely frivolous."

"You don't know who the other attorney is yet, do you?"

"No, I haven't seen the summons and complaint yet. The client was just sued this morning."

"Oh really, just sued this morning?"

"Yeah, the guy's totally distraught about the whole thing. He was almost crying on the phone to me, but I assured him that with Darby and Witherspoon behind him he's in good hands."

"So I suppose Henry Holten's been doing his Mr. Tough Guy routine for the poor soul?"

"Damn right. There's no way we're not going to bring him home a winner. *I'm* going to bring him home a winner."

"You may have some interest in hearing about *my* new case," Love said. "Mine's also a product liability case. I represent a remarkable woman who's suffered catastrophic neurological injuries as a result of poisoning from mutant bacteria. She's practically paralyzed and is constantly plagued by horribly painful muscle spasms throughout her body. The whole family's devastated." He paused a moment, then added, "I just sued the case out, Allie. This morning in fact."

"You son of a bitch! You goddamn son of a bitch."

"Bingo," Love said, laughing. "You and I are now enemies."

"You bastard, Love. You're damned right we're enemies, you mangy fuck."

"I figured Henry Holten might get you to do his dirty work for him. And when I realized you didn't even know I had the case, hell, you were fair game."

Allison recovered herself, relaxed back into her chair. She took a sip of her water, set her glass deliberately back on the white table-cloth, cocked her head and smiled. "You're a slimy worthless shit, and I promise you you're going to pay dearly for this."

"This is going to be really fun," Dillon said. "We're going to have a goddamn blast working together again. It'll be just like law school, only for real."

Allison reached across the table and pulled Love's hand into hers. For several seconds he allowed the smooth, white skin of her long, slender fingers to cover his large, doughy palm.

"What happened to all that feigned anger of yours?" Dillon asked.

"It was just a mood swing. I wouldn't rest easy if I were you."

"When are you going to get a stone to complement this gorgeous hand, Forbes?" Love asked, gently taking hold of her ring finger.

"The pain's not worth the pleasure," Allison replied. "You know," she said, pulling her hand away, "I have no doubt your client actually believes EnviroClean is responsible for her illness. I mean, I certainly don't mean to impugn her motives. But I want you to know it's just not possible. P-27 has been thoroughly tested, and it can't cause neurological problems."

"Listen, Allie," Love said, "I don't know what propaganda they've been feeding you, but we've conducted some tests also, and we think P-27 did cause Ruth Bergstrom's debilitating injuries. We've taken soil samples and found rich deposits of bacteria, genetically engineered bacteria."

"Where the hell do you think the bacteria came from?" she interrupted.

"Who cares?"

"You better care, because P-27 can't harm humans."

"That may be the party line, but releasing mutant organisms into the environment is a damn stupid thing to do. EnviroClean is playing God for greed, gambling with the lives of innocent people simply to return a dividend to its shareholders. It's got to stop and this case will make it stop."

"The biggest threat to Ruth Bergstrom's health is from the carcinogenic additives in the gasoline that has saturated the soil around the gas station and her own house. It's companies like EnviroClean that are doing something about these hazards. Genetic engineering is a danger only in the paranoid minds of small-thinking people. The real danger is that these blindered half-wits could slow down progress. That'd be the true tragedy of the Bergstrom case, that she might win, and endanger the lives of countless others who are facing greater risks from mountains of hazardous, highly toxic wastes."

"Allie, for crying out loud, you can't actually believe all that crap your public relations department feeds you?"

"It's not PR, it's science."

"Science, my butt. It's unadulterated bullshit."

"By the way," Allison said, "I'm surprised you never responded to Henry's letter before blithely filing suit. I personally wrote back after Dr. Campbell got Mrs. Bergstrom's letter."

"Holten's letter was pretty nasty and way over-the-top."

"I wrote that letter myself," Allison said, "and it was reassuring and conciliatory."

"Holten's letter was just plain rude. I can't imagine you wrote it—unless you have ice in your veins."

"Henry must have changed the letter without telling me. After all, he's the boss."

"I guess."

"But it doesn't change the fact that we're right. Dr. Campbell deserves a vigorous defense, and I'll supply him that. And, besides, you sure as hell could have contacted the company to discuss the matter before taking it so far as to actually file. Ridiculous!"

"Well then, let's discuss it. I'll give you an extension of time to answer the complaint. All I need is a copy of the toxicity testing and pre-market field trials for the P-27. I'll also need to have the engineering notes for the project next door to the Bergstrom's."

"Those documents are all highly confidential," Allison replied. "You're really not entitled to them. I'll have to clear it with Henry."

"I'm sure you don't expect me to settle the case without having all the data to evaluate," Dillon said.

"Settle the case? You have to drop the case, Dillon. There's no merit to it. It should be dropped before either of us invests any more time or money into it."

"Bullshit. Don't even think about it. This case is a winner. But you can be damn sure I won't even consider settling it until I've been provided with the complete company records."

"You've taken the case on contingency, haven't you?"

"Indeed I have."

"I don't want you to get hurt by thinking there's some chance of a settlement," Allison said. "We go too far back for me to let that happen. But this case will not be settled, not now, not ever. We'll get it dismissed, and if it goes to trial we intend to win. I'll still be your friend, but I'm going to win this case, that's simply all there is to it."

"Maybe you will, maybe you won't. In the meantime, I want those records. When I have them, I'll send you a proposal for a settlement. If you want to pay up, fine. If not, that's fine too."

The waiter came and they sat back as he laid out their food. When he had left, Allison leaned over her salad, pointed her fork, and said, "You don't fully appreciate the importance of this case to EnviroClean. It's just a start up company for chrissake."

With a mouthful of crab cake, Dillon pointed his knife and said, "Allie, love of my life, heart of my heart, this case will be settled, or it will be won by me."

CHAPTER Eight

Allison Forbes arrived early next day at Darby & Witherspoon, eager to begin her defense of EnviroClean. Expecting to be the first lawyer at work, she was mildly disappointed as she passed Henry Holten's office to see him through his open door, standing like a colossus at the window.

"Henry," she called, "do you have a minute to discuss the Enviro-Clean lawsuit?"

"Of course," Holten replied, turning. Allison experienced the nagging feeling in her gut that Holten may have expected her even earlier. Appearing pensive, perhaps even a little world-weary, something she had never seen in him before, he motioned her in, and, without any sort of greeting, said, "Nancy faxed me the legal papers in Bermuda yesterday so I could study them on the plane. Frankly, I'm shocked at the gall of this Dillon Love character, taking on a spurious case like this. Is he some sort of maverick? He must not realize what he's getting himself into."

"I know Dillon quite well, Henry. We were law school classmates. And you're right, he doesn't have a clue. He's bright, personable, and energetic, but he's got zero experience with this type of case. He's a sole practitioner, landlord-tenant squabbles, divorces, misdemeanors, that's his bread and butter."

"We're being sued by a bottom-feeder. Unbelievable. How the hell does he think he'll manage a case like this?"

"Dillon's full of bravado. He's taken this case on contingency and is banking on a quick settlement."

"We'll draw some quick blood from the son of a bitch. He'll get the message damn fast."

"I agree," Allison replied. "I really feel sorry for Boyd Campbell."

"Yeah, he's coming in this afternoon to discuss the case, so I suggest you spend the morning developing an outline for our defense strategy. The first thing that needs to be done is look over Enviro-Clean's insurance policies; they must have coverage for this kind of situation."

"I'm a step ahead of you," Allison replied. "I've already done that. Boyd's secretary faxed a copy of their comprehensive liability coverage policy, and I've read it cover to cover. There's no coverage for this."

"You're kidding me! How can that be?"

"They're fully covered for automobile and worker's comp, but there's nothing for completed operations, for product liability. I'll put a copy on your desk and you can check it out yourself."

"How did this happen?" Henry asked. "How did that slip through the cracks?"

"It didn't slip through the cracks at all," Allison said. "I called and talked to Richard Blair and he told me they tried to get coverage, but the insurer turned them down when he found out they were developing mutant genetic strains of bacteria to be injected into the environment. Blair even went to Lloyd's of London; they agreed to cover it, but the premiums were so high EnviroClean decided they couldn't afford it."

Henry thought about this for a moment. "Then we need to get rid of this lawsuit as quickly as possible. I need you to get me a plan of action by 1:30."

"I wrote a draft last night," Allison said. "By the way, what took you down to Bermuda?"

"Oh, nothing much," Holten replied, turning back to the window. "We've got a client down there, a small genetics company. I stop to see them once in a while, just an excuse to get back to Bermuda really. Wonderful place. It's a British territory, you know. They still do things right there."

"Is that so?"

"We stay at this colony of cottages at one end of the main island where you still see men wearing blazers with Bermuda shorts and knee socks and riding around on mopeds and scooters. About what you'd would expect of the Brits, like something out of 'The Prisoner.' You remember that show, Allison?"

"A bit before my time, Henry."

"Anyway, Louise loves this little resort, so she's always ready to pop on down there at a moment's notice."

"So why would a genetics company end up in Bermuda? There's no scientific community there to support the technology."

"I don't know much about it myself," Holten replied. "Our corporate group sees some opportunities in Bermuda for our high-tech clients. Wendi Palmer went along with me this time, an impressive young lady."

"I don't want to hear about it."

Henry laughed, turned to face her. "Well she's no Allison Forbes, of course, but she sure knows government regulations. That's the point of Bermuda, really, not much government interference and good access to venture capital through the British investment banking community. Actually, I don't have that much to do with it. It's Wendi's project. I just open a few doors and spend most of my time relaxing."

"Any relationship to EnviroClean? I imagine Dr. Campbell must know these people."

"You know, I've never even asked Boyd that. Not that I know of anyway."

"Well, it's good to have you back," Allison said. "I assume you've set up the meeting for half past squash time."

"You know me all too well, Allie, and you must also know I want to see a very aggressive litigation plan by 1:30."

"May I make a suggestion, Henry?"

"I'd expect nothing less."

"Well, I've already given this some thought. Clearly the client's interests will be best served by getting this case resolved at the earliest possible opportunity so EnviroClean can get on with its IPO. This case could drag on for years in the courts. Even under the best of circumstances, we'd expect a delay of at least six months just to get a hearing on a motion for dismissal. In my opinion, the best chance for an early resolution is to try an alternative approach. Mediation would be my preference."

"Mediation! Good god, what would that accomplish?"

"It'd bring everyone together to discuss the case before both sides invest a huge amount of time and money in a lawsuit. As soon as Dillon's put a lot of money into the case, he won't be able to afford to resolve the case short of trial. With luck we can reach some understanding. At worst, we'll have wasted a day or two."

"Are you planning a retreat before the battle's even begun?"

"Look, Henry, if we schedule mediation now, we can blow Dillon Love out of the water. He's bound to agree to participate in the mediation because he'll think it means we're willing to pay his client some settlement money. He'll think our offer is a sign of weakness. Psychologically, he'll get all geared up for settling the case rather than litigating it. In reality, we'll put together a team of lawyers, legal assistants, and experts and prepare the hell out of the case. We'll catch him totally off guard. We'll have all the scientific data to support our position. The mediator will immediately recognize the strength of our case and Love's complete inability to respond to any of our points. His clients will be there to witness the debacle, and he'll be humiliated in front of them. The process will dilute his blind bravado, and his clients will see first hand, instead of through Love's prejudiced interpretation, the overwhelming evidence that supports EnviroClean. The mediator will push hard to force them to accept a nominal settlement, and the case will be over."

"Settlement?" Holten said. "There'll be no settlement. Mediation is nothing but an infantile concession of principle to expediency. This firm is not built on a foundation of compromise but on a foundation of fortitude and perseverance. We're not going to sacrifice our client's objectives. We're not going to cave in, we're going to win."

"You seem rather firm in your views."

"Unshakably firm, my dear."

"Well then, I guess I know what I've got to do."

Allison wasted no time fretting over the summary rejection of her recommendation. She returned to her office and became immediately engrossed in her work until, several hours later, her concentration was suddenly broken by the voice of Henry Holten at her door.

"Boyd Campbell's here," Holten said. "Are you ready?"

"I'm just finishing up," she replied. "Let me print copies and I'll join you in a minute."

Allison polished a couple of sentences in her litigation plan, sent the file to the printer, took the pages and walked briskly into Holten's office where she encountered a haggard looking Boyd Campbell. "Good afternoon, Dr. Campbell. I hope you're not unnecessarily concerned about this lawsuit. I'm sure you'll find it to be nothing more than a minor nuisance that we'll get dismissed in short order. Henry and I have been working on a plan to get this done as quickly as possible."

"Boyd," Holten began, "we're going to take a very aggressive approach to this lawsuit. The young lawyer who brought this case has no experience as a litigator. He's incapable of handling a case like this. We intend to bombard him with paper, use the whole arsenal of legal procedures to stop this nuisance law suit. He'll never know what hit him. He'll be begging us to let him dismiss the case before we're through with him."

"I don't know, Henry," Boyd replied. "That letter you wrote last January didn't exactly scare this guy away. Maybe it would be worthwhile sitting down with him to see if the case might get resolved. Wouldn't that be a lot cheaper in the long run?"

"How many sites like the gas station next to the Bergstrom's have you treated?" Holten asked.

"I believe we're on our fifty-first project as we speak," Boyd replied. "Our business plan projects ten new sites per month during the next twelve months, increasing to twenty-five per month after our public offering."

"Do you want to sit down with fifty-one lawyers tomorrow and settle fifty-one different cases?" Holten asked rhetorically. "Because that's exactly what'll happen if you pay this guy even five cents. Every two-bit lawyer in the country will hear about the settlement, and you'll be paying extortion money until you're broke and EnviroClean's ancient history."

"You're kidding," Boyd said. "How would anyone even find out about a nominal settlement in this one, isolated case?"

Holten got up from his chair, his tall frame looming over his client. Leaning down, he said, "Boyd, these plaintiffs' lawyers are a contagious plague. They have a national network, which they pretentiously call the American Trial Lawyers Association. Each state has local chapters. They use newsletters to brag about all their grand victories. They have a computer system that keeps track of similar cases, and this is available to every personal injury lawyer in the country. Pay any one of these piranhas, and you'll have hundreds more nipping at your billfold until hell freezes over." Holten's face was getting red as his voice rose.

Campbell lost what color remained in his face. He looked at Allison and sagged in his chair. Seeing this, Holten exploded, "And don't forget about your public offering, Boyd! We'll have to disclose any sort of settlement in our SEC filings. Nothing will scare off investors faster than the threat of serial law suits. Boyd, you have no choice, take my word on that, my friend. We must go forward. We must do it aggressively, and we must win at all costs. It's either that, or you can give up all your dreams and go back to the university and teach biology to zit-faced morons. Your entrepreneurial days will be over."

"I just can't believe that, Henry," Campbell said.

"You understand science, Boyd, I understand law. Trust me. We'll do right by you and your company."

Campbell squirmed uneasily in his chair. "This is not my style, Henry," he said. "It just doesn't sit well with me. How much is all this going to cost me anyway?"

"Far less than if you don't fight the battle at all and have to respond to dozens of other lawsuits around the country."

"What are we talking about anyway?" Campbell asked. "Ten thousand dollars? A hundred thousand? What's it going to cost me to get this case thrown out?"

"Well," Holten replied, "there's no way it'll approach a hundred thousand. By moving aggressively to get the case dismissed quickly, we should be able to minimize costs and avoid protracted litigation."

Campbell stood up and went to the window, where he stood with his hands behind his back, breathing hard. After some tense minutes of silence, he said, "Allison, what do you think? What do you think is best for my little company?"

Allison uncrossed her legs and folded her hands in her lap. She sympathized with the confusion on Campbell's face and reflected on the advice she had given her senior partner a few hours ago. In her peripheral vision she also caught the stern intensity of that very powerful senior partner. Being put on the spot like this annoyed her, but she smiled and said, "I don't believe we can expect Dillon Love to cave in to an aggressive strategy. But I agree with Henry that this approach offers us the best opportunity for an early dismissal of the case."

"I hope you're right, Henry," Boyd said. "This whole thing's mighty scary for me. I never had to make this kind of decision at the university." Campbell paused for a few seconds, took a deep breath, and exhaled the air slowly from his lungs. "Let's get on with it, then," he said, sitting back down at the table. "What do we have to do?"

"First," Allison began, "we'll prepare a response to the suit, denying all liability and raising every affirmative defense available to us. I recommend we counterclaim against Ruth Bergstrom on the grounds that it is a suit brought in bad faith and seek all our expenses and attorneys' fees. That may scare her and her husband into thinking that this suit, which Love has taken on contingency, is not without its risks, and that they could end up actually paying money to *us*."

Campbell put his face in his hands, rubbed vigorously, and said, "Counterclaim against Ruth Bergstrom? She's in a wheelchair."

"It's just a ploy, Boyd, so they'll withdraw the suit," said Holten, patting Campbell's shoulder forcefully. Allison continued, "Second, we're going to file a Rule 11 motion for dismissal. I'm sure Love has no scientific proof for his allegations and is only on a fishing expedition to see if he can develop something through us. Rule 11 requires an attorney to have a sound factual basis for the claim before signing his name to the complaint. We'll draft a comprehensive set of discovery demands. We're going to have interrogatories, document productions, demands for statements and other investigative materials, demands for the names and phone numbers of all his witnesses, requests for authorizations to get all the medical records for his client and her family. We're going to note a series of depositions to take testimony under oath from his clients, all the witnesses Love lists in his answers to our interrogatories, any expert witness he may have had look at the site and take samples or run tests. If, when this is all done, he still hasn't withdrawn the suit, we'll file a motion for summary judgment to make sure this case never gets in front of a jury. The law is on our side, and Love has an enormous burden of proof he will never be able to sustain."

Campbell looked dazed.

"Now, Boyd," Holten said, giving Campbell's shoulders another pat, "aren't you glad I've brought Allison into this case?" He walked over and sat behind his desk, obviously the man in charge.

"This is just the beginning," Allison continued. "We'll put three or four lawyers on this case, and Love will be so overburdened by its complexities he'll have no choice but to abandon ship."

"These cases are expensive to prosecute successfully," Holten said. "Love will need several scientists and hydrological engineers, all with complete laboratory facilities. He'll need a computer system and a team of data entry people to keep track of all the documents that we will generate. I expect there'll be over a hundred thousand pages of records from government files, scientific publications, medical journals, doctors' charts, and legal pleadings. There'll be tens of thousands of deposition pages. He can't do this on his own, and I doubt he has the money to hire all the staff he'll need to do it for him. He'll be completely out-gunned, and he'll either quickly recognize this obvious fact and give up, or he'll be thrown out of court for failure to prove his claims. The ultimate result is completely predictable."

"You know, Dr. Campbell," added Allison, "you have an outstanding company and an outstanding product. It's exactly the kind of product the people of this state need. I know I'm doing more than representing an honest client and a just cause, I'm also representing the best interests of the public."

"You're kind to say so," said Campbell with the glimmer of a smile.

"By the way," continued Allison, "I'll need to stop by your office in the next few days to review some of your internal records. I want to look at your pre-market field tests and other technical materials documenting the effectiveness of P-27. I'd also like to see whatever you have that shows the origin and distribution of all P-27 manufactured to date. I assume you keep that sort of record, don't you?"

"We keep batch records for each of our fermenters, documenting that each lot produced meets all specifications."

"Good," Allison said. "When can you have them ready for me?"

Before Campbell could answer, Holten cut in. "Why don't you let me send over one of our legal assistants to check those records for you," he said. "I know how busy you are, and you can better spend your time running the business."

"That'd be fine," replied Campbell.

Holten closed the notebook lying before him on the desk, and without further comment rose from his chair. "Thanks for coming,

Boyd," Holten said. "We appreciate your business. I really appreciate your business. I intend to win this one for you, and very soon."

Holten turned to Allison as he and Campbell walked from his office. "Ask Nancy to have the rest of the team meet us in the Witherspoon room. I'll be there after I see Boyd to the elevator."

The Witherspoon room was a large conference room named after one of the founding partners, Horace Witherspoon. The esteemed Mr. Witherspoon had departed the corridors of Darby & Witherspoon so long ago that only a few current partners had even met the gentleman. Most of them agreed that it was appropriate that the largest conference room in their suite of offices be named to honor his memory. The rest agreed the name was more dignified than some combination of numbers and letters.

The group had already assembled when Holten entered the room. "Give us all an overview of our litigation plan," he said to Allison, who was now standing at the head of the table.

Nancy Sellers arrived propitiously with a few overhead transparencies hot off the photocopier. One after another Allison focused them on the large screen at the end of the room and using her laser pointer, explained the aggressive plan of attack she had developed.

"There you have it," she said, turning off the projector as Nancy electronically opened the drapes to allow the warm afternoon sun to fill the room. There was general movement in the group, and, since she was younger than most of them, Allison wondered if there was any resentment of her being put in charge. Boldly, she continued, "We need volunteers. The team will be composed of five main groups. First, I want someone responsible for expert witnesses. We'll want to recruit the finest scientists in the country. We'll need a hydrologist, a geneticist, a molecular biologist, a chemical engineer, and an environmental engineering firm with a first-rate laboratory. We also need to get any information we can on whatever experts our opponent comes up with: testimony from previous cases, copies of all published articles. And dirt, whatever we can turn up out there on these guys." The assembled lawyers laughed and looked at each other. Her heart fluttered a little, she had made them laugh, and she could feel the atmosphere of the room getting more relaxed.

"Second," Allison continued with more confidence, "we need someone to coordinate all legal research and writing. I want a database search of every significant environmental case decided in the last ten years. Whoever's going to take on this responsibility can get started on our Rule 11 and Rule 12 motions right away.

"Third, I want someone else to be responsible for all discovery initiatives, depositions, document demands, medical records, interrogatories, and the like. We're not going to leave a stone unturned in our efforts to uncover every single detail of the plaintiff's claim so we can systematically undermine whatever theory Dillon Love may develop."

Allison felt her voice failing and drank some of the water Nancy had thoughtfully provided.

"Fourth, I need a group leader who will be responsible for the organization and management of all documentary evidence. We want to obtain all pertinent government records, including EPA, MPCA, and local records. We'll have to obtain all EnviroClean's testing and R and D records. In addition, they have sales materials, product and technical data sheets, and relevant invoices and purchase orders. There are many published articles in the academic literature that must be located. I expect in excess of one hundred thousand records in all. Janet Laughlin will be responsible for digitally scanning all of these documents. We can use litigation management software to abstract and organize the information. We might as well integrate this with our graphics department so they can take the information and generate charts, diagrams, and other colorful displays for courtroom use. I assume Janet will coordinate this with Carla Osborne in Graphics.

"And finally, we'll need a corporate liaison. Wendi Palmer will play that role because of her experience with high-tech start-up companies and her familiarity with this client. As some of you may know, EnviroClean is in the midst of launching an IPO to raise capital for expansion and new product development. We must coordinate all our efforts with Wendi to make sure we do not run afoul of some objective our corporate and securities people may be working on."

Allison looked around the table, sipped more water. She had them; they were furiously scribbling notes. 'I love this fucking job,' she thought. Putting down her glass firmly, she said, "I'll coordinate the work of the whole team, no doubt under the watchful eye of Mr. Holten. For the time being at least, I want every piece of paper we generate to come through my office before it's finalized. I don't intend to interfere, but I do need to know all the details so the defense can go forward in a coordinated fashion."

Forbes turned to Holten. "Henry, have I left anything out?"

"Hardly," he replied. "Frankly, I'm impressed with how quickly you've got all this organized. Unless anyone has some strong feelings to the contrary, I'm prepared to accept Allison's organizational scheme." He paused briefly, as if awaiting suggestions from the assembled group, and then continued. "I'm also prepared to accept the following volunteers as group leaders. Morrison Edwards will be responsible for all documents, since most of these will be governmental records and technical articles, and he chairs our governmental regulations department. Tom Dodd will be group leader for expert witnesses, as he has degrees in molecular biology and ecology. Charles Jadwin, of our appellate department, will head our legal research and writing group, and Tim McCarter from Litigation will be group leader for discovery. Allison will be lead trial counsel."

Holten looked around the table, obviously not expecting comments. No one spoke.

"Allison," he continued, "can you have an EnviroClean primer prepared for each of the group leaders so everyone will have sufficient background on this client, its products and technology, as well as the factual circumstances surrounding the law suit?"

"Will do," said Allison. Her face felt hot. She was Henry Holten's deputy in this. She imagined Dillon Love, gagged and hog-tied, squirming under her feet.

"I'd like you to keep this primer updated as the case progresses," continued Holten. "Janet Laughlin can create a special directory for this file, along with appropriate sub directories. As documents are imaged and CD-ROMs become available, they'll be distributed with all imaged documents and legal research." Holten paused again to look around the table at his team. "I'm proud of this outstanding group we've put together. You're the best attorneys in this state. Together we're one of the most formidable litigation teams ever assembled. I expect nothing less than the highest conceivable caliber of work. Cost is not a factor. There'll be no settlement. There'll be no compromise. The client deserves to win this case. The people of this state deserve to win this case. For them, for the environment, for our client, we must succeed. I simply must insist on a total victory."

CHAPTER Nine

On the morning of April 2, Ruth Bergstrom woke to find that her collection bag had leaked. Her urine-soaked nightgown, cold against her buttocks, sent chills throughout her body, and the smell made her gag. Unable to move her legs, she shifted her torso from one side to the other, tugging at the hem of her nightgown to pull the saturated fabric upwards under the small of her back. Quietly, with as little movement as possible, she wiggled it over her head and dropped it to the floor.

Shivering, she re-fastened her collection bag, reached across Arne's chest, and pulled herself against his hairy back. She reached down and tugged her legs together to tuck under his buttocks. Without waking, Arne instinctively rolled in unison with her, allowing her to fold her nakedness against the matching contours of his large frame. Her left hand slid under his pillow and her right drew the comforter over them both. In the moments that followed, she began to get warm and with the warmth came a faint spark of desire. She thrust against him gently with her hips. It was their old signal, Hey, wake up, I want you. She pressed her torso against his back, kissed his shoulder blade.

The buzzing of the alarm clock made them both jump. Arne, startled into consciousness, lifted his head and looked around the room. She knew he understood what her nakedness against his back meant and she held him as hard as she could, but she was too weak, and he sat up, escaping her.

"Dammit, Ruthie, you've got to wake me up when your bag comes loose. It's stupid to lie there freezing all night."

Ruth pulled him down so that he faced her, and whispered, "You can smell it, then?"

"Yes," he said.

She knew the moment had been lost and let go her grip. "I guess it's not very sexy," she said.

"That's not the point. I won't let you lie here humiliated in your own pee."

"I can't expect you to attend to me all day and then again at night. You need your sleep more than me."

"Nonsense," he said, looking into Ruth's eyes, inches away from her face. "You need all your energy to fight off whatever's screwing up your system. And I won't have you uncomfortable."

Reaching for him again, she said, "Lying next to you is all the comfort I need."

Arne pulled away and sat on the edge of the bed. "What's wrong with that goddamn bag anyway? You'd think all these hotshot drug companies and these know-it-all doctors could come up with a system that doesn't leak in the middle of the night. What the hell's wrong with them anyway!"

Ruth caught an edge to Arne's voice, something unfamiliar. "The doctors are doing everything they can," she said, "they aren't to blame. We just have to be patient."

"I'm fresh out of patience," Arne said. "Those hotshots at Mayo have been working on this for two months now, and they've gotten nowhere. I want some answers, goddamn it!" He shot up from the bed, his face crimson. "I'm calling McCosh."

"It's so early, Arne."

"I'm calling him at home, Ruthie. I can't take any more of this."

"Wait awhile and call his office."

"No, we're going to his office this morning to get this figured out."

Arne strode naked to the door, ripping his bathrobe off the hook and slipping into it. A few minutes later, Ruth heard him speaking on the phone in the hallway. She smiled. For all his passion he was a mild-mannered man and spoke reasonably with poor Dr. McCosh. She heard him replace the receiver and fill the kettle for her morning herbal tea. He made coffee for himself. Then he returned to their bedroom, which was the old back study, now converted into an invalid's boudoir, and said, "He didn't want to give us an appointment, wanted to wait until our scheduled one. But I insisted."

"Good for you."

"He'll squeeze it in later this morning."

Although Arne's bathrobe was now tightly tied around the middle, Ruth said, "I wish you'd squeeze it in."

She hated the way he tried to disguise his recoil, and she felt the smile fade from her face.

"I have to get the kids up, and you know, Ruthie, Dillon Love's coming by this morning to discuss the court case."

"Oh, good grief, do we have to go through all that again?"

"Let's get you up and bathed," Arne said, frowning. "We'll worry about Dillon later."

She suddenly did not feel well; the giddiness was back. She said, "No, Arne, I'm not ready. Get the kids up. I think I'll lie here for a while."

He pulled the comforter up to her chin and left the room. Once, not long ago, she had been so lithe and lusty, and he could never get enough of her. The mornings were their time, before the children woke. She remembered how it felt to climb on top of him, how generous he was, how he let her take all the pleasure she wanted. She pushed her face into the pillow and cried hard, soundlessly, until her temples throbbed from the pressure.

The morning routine for the Bergstroms had become both tedious and strenuous. Arne usually ran Ruth's bath water while he got her into her wheelchair and brought her to the bathroom to brush her teeth and take her morning medicine. While Ruth bathed, he got the children moving and made their breakfast. As the children ate, he scrubbed Ruth's back, got her out of the tub and helped her with her personal hygiene. When all went according to plan, Ruth was ready in time to say goodbye to Brett and Molly as they trudged off to catch their school bus.

This morning went well, but Arne felt awful. After the children left, he poured a glass of orange juice for Ruth, brought her the newspaper, and made himself breakfast, bacon and eggs because it was fast and he liked it. He rescheduled a wiring job he had undertaken a week ago, and called Love's cell phone to make sure the lawyer would not dilly-dally as he had learned Love was wont to do.

Arne brought his breakfast to the table and sat with Ruth. Suddenly he could not face the food and pushed the plate away.

"What's the trouble, Arne?" Ruth asked. "You've gone very pale."

He felt perspiration on his forehead. He took a deep breath and massaged his breast bone.

"Heartburn. I guess the old stomach's not very happy with the recent decline in cooking around here."

"Arne, you're covered with sweat. Are you okay?"

"I've had a lot of indigestion lately. I'll take a couple of Tums."

"Please don't come down with this thing I've got."

"No, Ruthie. It's the stress. I don't know where to put it all. And remember I'm an old fart compared to you."

"Oh Arne, you're only ten years older. I worry so about you and the kids. Supposing I'm contagious?"

"Remember what McCosh said? You can't pass this on and we're not in any danger."

"I'd rather die than have you or the kids get this."

"Ruthie, don't talk like that," Arne said. "You're going to get better." He took up his knife and fork and ate the bacon and eggs to show her he was all right.

Arne was loading the dishwasher when Love knocked at the front door. They had not seen each other for a month and from the lawyer's expression Arne could tell he was shocked by the deterioration in Ruth's appearance. Love's own appearance had changed too; he looked fuller in the face and wore jeans which were worn through at the knees and had white threads hanging out.

Love had no words for a situation like this and nervously blurted out, "I've got great news about your case. The results of our initial testing came back yesterday. We've identified an unusual organism in the soil behind the gas station. My engineer friend thinks it's been genetically altered. DNA testing shows some clear but unexplained differences from previously identified species. He also did a careful literature search. A similar organism has been linked to isolated neurological disorders in a group of factory workers in Japan; same thing, just like you."

"How could there be any genetically engineered bacteria in our creek?" Arne asked. "How'd they get there anyway?"

"EnviroClean," Love replied. "They use mutated organisms to clean up gasoline spills, and they used them next door. That's where those bugs came from."

"But I thought their bugs have been tested and cause no problems," Arne replied.

"EnviroClean won't give me any test results," Love replied quickly. "I've requested copies of all their tests and have spoken with their attorney several times about this. If their tests are so damn convincing, why won't they give them to me? Wouldn't that be the easiest way to get rid of us? They're hiding something from me, something critical. I can feel it in my bones."

"You've been saying that all along, but what's there to hide?" Arne said. "Whatever they put in the soil is just sitting there. Can't we just dig it up and look at it?"

"Sure, and what we'll find is a bunch of genetically engineered bacteria that no one knows anything about."

"So what're you going to do?" Arne asked.

"I'll tell you what I think the problem is," Love said. "This Frankenstein professor was playing God in his lab one day and fabricated some new organism that he hoped would degrade gas and oil coming from leaking underground tanks. Knowing how much contaminated soil there is, he saw his chance to get rich. But rather than commit the money necessary to conduct careful testing of the potential dangers of releasing this new organism into the environment, he just started using the stuff. And the organism turned out to be damned dangerous. Now that we've come along and have threatened to ruin his risky little business, he's hired the best law firm in the state to keep the whole thing quiet. If he'd done adequate testing of these organisms before pumping them into your creek bed, his lawyers would give us those test results. There are either no tests, or the tests prove I'm right. They're in big trouble if the truth comes out, so they're doing everything they can to make sure the truth is buried."

"How'd Ruth get exposed to the bacteria?" Arne asked. "You don't go swimming back there, do you, Ruthie?"

"I bet that's exactly what she does," grinned Love.

Laughing, Ruthie shook her head. "Oh, you guys."

Love spoke confidently. "Look, just to recap, I don't know the answer to that yet, but I'm sure as hell gonna find out. The first step is to prove scientifically what our common sense has already told us, that the bacteria are causing Ruth's problems. If they are, and I'm sure of it, finding out how she was exposed is just a question of putting in the time."

Love explained to them more of the details of Ken Butler's laboratory testing and outlined what still needed to be done to tie all the loose ends together. They would have to run some tests to demonstrate the toxicity of the organisms. They would need a medical opinion that these organisms were the cause of Ruth's illness. They would have to compare known samples of P-27 with the organisms found in the creek to establish EnviroClean as their source. They would need an explanation for how Ruth became exposed to the organisms. And they would need an explanation for why only Ruth became ill, and not anyone else in the family or anyone else in the neighborhood.

"These are just details required by the court to prove our case legally," Love explained. "It's only a matter of time before we prove the bacteria are the culprits. After that, everything else is bound to fall into place." Love ran both his hands across the top of his head, reorganizing his few remaining hairs. He paused for a few seconds with both hands clasped behind the base of his neck, exposing identical rips in each armpit of his shirt. "Unfortunately," he continued, "these tests all cost money. They must be done, and we can't afford any shortcuts. I'm going to need an advance of ten thousand dollars to get them started. I know that's a lot, but it's worth it. You've got a great case."

Arne was stunned. He looked at Ruth and saw that her jaw had dropped open. Her big blues eyes stared astounded at Love. "I thought you said you'd take this on contingency, Dillon," Ruth said. Seconds passed in awkward silence until Arne said, "We don't have any money. Things have been tough, what with all the medical bills and my not working as much."

Love, red with embarrassment, looked from one to the other, then shrugged. "You know," he said, "I think I can come up with the money. You can pay me back out of the settlement later on."

"I hope that's not too much of a problem for you."

"I'll figure it out. Now let's talk more about the case."

Ruth slouched despondently against the side of her wheelchair, her eyes staring vacantly into space. She said nothing as Love launched again into the encouraging results of his investigation and all that yet needed to be done. She interrupted him suddenly and said, "I don't really understand anything about this case. Why can't we just talk with this Dr. Campbell and work it all out with him without all this blessed fuss? Let's just call him up and ask him over for coffee."

Love looked pained by Ruth's naïve suggestion. Arne agreed with her but remained quiet. "These things just aren't that simple," Love said, trying not to sound condescending. "Old Campbell's a brilliant scientist. As smart as you are, you're a mother and homemaker, Ruthie, and I'm just beginning my investigation. We'd never come out on the winning side of that discussion."

"I don't know," Ruth said. "We've never even spoken with this man, but now we've sued him, hoping to prove he's done something wrong. It just seems like we ought to talk with him to hear what he has to say before all this gets out of hand."

"He's spoken to us through his lawyers," Love replied curtly. "They won't give us any information. They don't want to talk, they want to fight. They've made that choice, not us."

"It's all so confusing to me," she said faintly.

"Trust me, Ruth," Love said. "This is my job. This is what I've been trained to do. We can't talk to a brick wall. We're going to have to push this case along for a while so they'll know we're serious. I don't want to go to court any more than you do, but unless Dr. Campbell and his lawyers know we're fully prepared to do so, they'll have no incentive to discuss the case. Don't worry about all this, I'll do the worrying for all of us. By the way, Arne tells me you're seeing Dr. McCosh this morning. Do you mind if I tag along? I'd like to talk with him about the case for a few minutes."

They drove in separate cars to Harold McCosh's office because Love would have to go on to work afterwards. Ruthie's weight loss and shrunken legs, not to mention the saucer-like quality of her eyes, had bitterly shocked Love. A ghastly smell, which permeated the Bergstrom home, now lingered in his clothes, making him nauseous. The vivacious and energetic woman had been reduced to a listless invalid. Arne Bergstrom looked like shit, too; his hair had new gray streaks in it, and the creases that ran from his nostrils to the corners of his mouth had deepened, giving him an uncharacteristic sneer.

Love helped the Bergstroms into the clinic, then waited in the reception area, jotting down a few questions he wanted to ask Dr. McCosh. After about half an hour, Arne emerged from the examining area and without speaking motioned Love to follow him. The two men entered a small office at the end of the hall. Ruth sat in her wheelchair, and Dr. McCosh stood at her side.

"Mr. Love, I presume," said the doctor. "I'm Harold McCosh. It's nice to meet you. The Bergstroms speak very highly of you." Dr. McCosh paused for a moment, looked at Ruth, and added, "I'm afraid we're sending Ruth back to Mayo this afternoon. There's been continued deterioration in the muscle groups in her lower extremities, and today I noticed that her reflexes are abnormal in her left arm. She needs to be hospitalized."

"I'm sorry to hear that," Love said.

"Arne said you had a couple of questions for me about Ruth's court case," McCosh said. "How can I help?"

"We've found some organisms in the soil around the creek in the Bergstrom's backyard. They're pseudomonas. We believe they were genetically engineered by a company called EnviroClean to break down the gasoline that's leaked into the ground around the adjoining gas station. I suspect Ruth has been exposed to these organisms and that they're the cause of her illness. Arne tells me you're of the same opinion."

"Well, actually, I don't think I can be much help to you," the doctor said matter-of-factly. "My days in the field of genetics are long past. Frankly, I don't have the foggiest idea what's causing her symptoms. It may very well be some bacterial infection, but the lab hasn't been able to isolate any likely culprits. I wish I could help you, because if I knew what was causing Ruth's symptoms, I could find some way to treat her."

"Doctor," Love continued, making himself sound surprised by McCosh's answer, "I thought it was you who initially suspected the gas station as the probable source of Ruth's problems. Have you changed your mind about that?"

"Not at all," Dr. McCosh replied. "That's the likely cause. But there's no way I can ever prove it, because I just don't know. It's entirely possible we'll never find the answer."

Only mildly discouraged by the lack of assistance from McCosh, Love left the clinic and returned to his office. He trusted that help would be forthcoming from other, more specialized doctors. He would have to schedule an appointment with Ruth's Mayo specialist. Cindy could get right on that after lunch.

"How about I buy you lunch at Paul's Place?" Love asked Cindy as he walked into the office. "I've got some things to go over with you, and we might as well get ourselves properly fed in the process."

"God only knows what this free lunch will cost me," Cindy replied. "Last time I ended up working all weekend on your tax returns."

"Your unfounded insinuations won't dampen my generosity," Love said.

"And the lunch won't repay your indebtedness to me."

They left the office together and walked to Paul's Place. It was a beautiful spring day, the kind that makes Minnesota winters seem almost worth the trouble.

"I want your advice, Cindy," Love began, once they were seated at a table in a corner of the restaurant. "Pretend you're on the jury in the Bergstrom case. You spend two weeks listening to a lot of technical testimony about genetic engineering and bacteria and gasoline contaminated soil. You understand only a small portion of what you hear. Doctors describe an unusual medical condition that's afflicted Ruth Bergstrom. They discuss their efforts to learn what caused this disease. It was probably some bacterial infection, but they've not been able to learn the precise modality. They agree whatever the cause, it's unprecedented in medical annals.

"No one disputes the fact that it was probably some unusual organism, something genetically engineered, but no one can say that with certainty. You also hear testimony about an unusual, previously unknown organism found in the Bergstroms' backyard, an organism that is related to a strain of bacteria that have previously caused similar adverse reactions in Japan.

"Then you listen to the most heart-wrenching story of immeasurable suffering on the part of one of the most wonderful people you've ever met, the kindest, most selflessly loving woman, and her long-suffering family. Tears roll down your cheeks as this gentle person stoically tells you how her life has changed since the day EnviroClean put something into the soil next door to her house.

"Finally, the defendant presents his case. He has all the top scientists in the country, who swear all over the courtroom that nothing EnviroClean did could possibly have caused this problem. These scientists are outstanding in their fields, and they're persuasive, but they cannot themselves totally rule out the possibility of some strange reaction by the plaintiff to an unknown, mutant organism.

"What do you do when you go into the jury room with this case? How do you resolve these uncertainties, in favor of the sympathetic plaintiff or the corporate defendant?"

"Do I assume from your question, Dillon, that you can't prove your case against EnviroClean? Is that what you're telling me? Am I supposed to ignore your lack of proof because of the tears I've shed for this unfortunate Ruth Bergstrom and her family?"

"The circumstantial evidence all points to EnviroClean," Love answered. "Every piece of evidence you hear suggests this is what happened. But there's no scientific certainty, and the jurors have to make a leap of faith. Is Ruth Bergstrom worthy of this leap of faith?"

"Faith is for the devout," Cindy replied bluntly. "Proof is for courtrooms. You better give up the case if this is all you've got."

Love replied abruptly. "The advice I want from you is not whether to keep the case or withdraw, because I'll never withdraw. The question is only how much more I need in order to win. And you've answered it. I still have a lot of work left."

"Dillon," Cindy responded somberly, "I'm worried about you. Your mother's worried about you. Your wife's worried about you. You're not the same person you were three months ago when you got started on this marathon. Your practice is falling apart. Your money is running out. Your common sense has been tossed to the winds. You're not looking after yourself either, you look like you're sleeping in a gutter or something. Give it up now, when you can still salvage the good practice you've worked so hard to build for yourself."

"This is the case I've been building my practice for. This is my chance to do something really important. It's my chance to shut down a company that has placed these mutant bacteria on the market, that's preying on the public for the sake of big profits. This is my big case, my chance to make my mark, and I intend to see it through."

"I know you mean well," Cindy replied. "I know how desperately you want to help Ruth and Arne Bergstrom. No one can say they don't deserve everything you're doing for them. But you're all by yourself against the biggest law firm in the state. You have none of the resources that are available to them, the specialized lawyers, the legal assistants, law clerks, fancy computers, mountains of money. You can't compete with these people. This is a battle you can't win on your own."

"I *can* win this battle, and I'm going to win it, and win it big. Justice has a way of finding itself in a courtroom, where the power and influence of the litigants are equalized. The rich and poor both play under the same rules. They'll be allowed only a single lawyer to speak for their side. They'll have only one opening statement and one final argument. They'll be bound by the rules of evidence and the rules of procedure. The jurors will be everyday people like Ruth Bergstrom. They'll see themselves in her, and they'll know her and love her. The truth will come out. It always does."

"You sound like some naïve first-year law student," Cindy sighed. "The truth will come out only if you present evidence that convinces the jury that the Bergstroms are right. That evidence will come out only if you find it. And you haven't found it. You may never find it. You certainly won't find it by yourself. You need doctors, engineers, hydrologists, laboratory facilities, and God knows what else. You need to have these people do a lot of work that has not yet been done."

"No problem."

"Yeah? And you need a whole lot of money that you don't have. Without money, there'll be no evidence. Without evidence you have no case."

"I discussed this with Laurie last night," Love responded. "We had a long talk about the Bergstroms, about their case. She's been a friend of Ruth's for fifteen years. Ruth has done more for our church than any other single parishioner. She's spent countless hours helping homeless and disadvantaged people. We can't abandon this woman now that she needs us. Laurie and I are committed to doing whatever it takes to help the Bergstroms through these difficult times. We're prepared to raise the necessary money by taking out a second mortgage on our house."

"Laurie said that?"

"Yeah."

"I doubt it."

"Ask her yourself, then."

"Don't do that to Laurie," Cindy pleaded. "Don't risk everything you and Laurie have made together for this one case. It's been stressful enough on your marriage already. It's just not worth it."

"My marriage is fine. And it's none of your damned business anyway," Love said.

"It may be none of my business," said Cindy, "but I know it's strained. Your mother and I…"

"I have to do this, Cindy," Love interrupted. "I have to do this. I'm committed to Ruth and Arne Bergstrom. Laurie understands that. She knows what it's like being married to a trial lawyer. Once the case is over, our lives will return to normal. In the meantime, I intend to go after these corporate profiteers. These are bad people, Cindy, and they have to be stopped."

It was nearly two in the morning, and Love arrived home to a dark house. He took off his shoes in the back hall, used the downstairs toilet, and quietly ascended the stairs to the master bedroom.

"I suppose you've been at Pete's Piano Bar all night," Laurie said, fully awake in the dark room. "Do you find Joe Clapp a more stimulating conversationalist than your wife?"

"Joe Clapp?"

Laurie snapped on the bedside light as Love took off his clothes, which smelled of liquor and smoke, and tossed them into the closet.

"Yes, Joe Clapp. Joe Clapp Investigations. Former FBI agent. Divorced. Private investigator extraordinaire."

"You've talked to Cindy, I see."

"Don't you think it's a little sad that I should have to find out from your secretary what you're up to?"

"I'm sorry, Laurie. I needed some help, and this was the only time I had available to talk to Joe. I thought of calling you, but I figured you'd know I was just working on the case anyway. I'm sorry. I should've called."

"No, you should not have called, you should've been here. Do you still love me, Dillon?"

"What kind of stupid question is that? Of course I love you. You know I do."

"Then it's high time you started proving it to me. You're certainly proving the opposite when you leave me alone every night. When do I start getting some of your time?"

"Laurie, we have our whole life together. This case will be over in a few months. Try to understand that. You, of all people, should understand what I'm going through now. Isn't that what a marriage is all about, understanding and tolerance?"

"Well, if it is, I'll have none of it. I'm a jealous lover, Dillon. For me a marriage is about companionship. It's about wanting desperately to spend every conceivable moment of time together. When do you suppose we last had sex? Is Ruth so important to you that you don't even want to make love to your wife?"

"I'm sorry if I've hurt you. You're everything to me. I want you to understand that. I want you to understand that I'm here for the long haul. I do love you, Laurie, however poorly I've shown it to you lately."

"You haven't shown it at all."

"How about if we went up to the Boundary Waters in a couple of months. I should be able to take some time off in June. A week of renewal just for the two of us? What do you say?"

"I say I want more than that. You're going to have to figure out what's important in your life. And if I'm not important to you every day, then I just might not be around when you're ready to take this little canoe trip of yours."

CHAPTER Ten

Kathleen Campbell was in the study reading a medical journal and sipping from a glass of white wine when Boyd arrived home from work much later than usual. He called hello from the kitchen and she heard him go to the bedroom to change and then turn on a tap in the bathroom. When he left the bathroom to join her in the study, Kathleen detected a lack of enthusiasm in Boyd. Her suspicions were confirmed as he entered the room, his eyes glazed and his forehead furrowed in a frown, and slumped onto the couch at her side. She offered him a sip of her wine, but he shook his head. Kathleen reached around his shoulder and gently pulled his head down into her lap. She massaged his temples and the back of his neck until the signs of tension began to ease. He closed his eyes, and she could feel him holding back his emotions.

"I'm worried about you, lover," she whispered as Boyd opened his eyes minutes later. "You'll end up in one of my coronary units if you keep pushing yourself like this. And you don't have enough life insurance for that to be particularly attractive."

Boyd did not respond. He rolled onto his side, wrapped his arm around Kathleen's waist, and hugged her like a sick cat, snuggling next to her womb for comfort. It broke her heart to see him so beaten down. She ran her fingernails across the top of his head in long, soothing strokes, stimulating his scalp and soothing his tight muscles. She reached for a small blanket that had been draped over the arm of the couch and covered his shoulders. Almost immediately he fell asleep, and his light snoring could almost be mistaken for the purring of the poor battered old cat she imagined him to be.

Keeping as still as possible, Kathleen drained her wine and returned to the article she had been reading while Boyd sank deeper into a heavy slumber in her lap. She quickly became uncomfortable and after finishing the article, laid the journal aside, then lifted her husband's head. She whispered, "Sweetie, just stay here while I make us some dinner," and carefully eased herself free, slipping a pillow from the corner of the couch under his head. This was new; he had never come home and fallen asleep like this before and it alarmed her.

She went to the kitchen and pulled down a large stainless steel pasta pot from the hanger above the butcher-block island, filled it with water, and put it on a back burner of the stove to boil. Then she took down a twelve-inch copper-bottomed sauté pan from the hanger and put it over a medium flame. Next she pulled some fresh portabella mushrooms and basil from the refrigerator and set them on the island. After rinsing them and drying them on a paper towel, she sliced the mushroom caps into thick strips and halved them. She poured herself some more wine. Next she chopped the basil leaves into one-inch pieces and minced a couple of cloves of garlic; she and Boyd loved garlic.

As the water began to boil, Kathleen took the package of fresh fettuccine from the refrigerator. Then she poured a generous amount of extra virgin olive oil into the pan, put a teaspoon of salt into the now boiling water, and dropped about half the package of pasta into the pot. She took a few sips of wine and then put the mushrooms in the pan to sauté. Kathleen was always careful not to add the garlic and basil too soon. Salt and pepper and a few splashes of white wine came next. When the wine had reduced a bit, she added the final ingredients. As she did, a rather disheveled husband materialized in the kitchen doorway.

"My God," Kathleen said, "he's risen from the dead."

Boyd, heavy-eyed, faked a smile, but said nothing.

Sympathetically, Kathleen said, "I hope you feel better than you look."

"Oh man. Long, awful day," Boyd replied, scratching his scalp.

Kathleen walked over, kissed him on the lips, and ran her fingers through his hair to straighten it. "Why don't you get a couple of candles from the cupboard, and we'll have a relaxing dinner. The pasta's almost ready. I'll pour you a glass of wine."

Boyd found a box of matches on the counter by the stove. "That smells magnificent, Katie! How lucky I am to have such a gourmand for a wife," he said with a smirk.

"That's *gourmet*, you ass," said Kathleen, whacking her husband on the behind. "Light the candles already."

Boyd lit the candles and Kathleen followed him to the dining room table with two steaming plates of pasta. "This looks wonderful," said Boyd as she set one of them before him. "I'm glad you chose medicine, but you sure would have made a damn good chef."

"Sure you're glad. You get the best of both worlds, a sizable income *and* great food." Kathleen was having trouble making him laugh tonight, but she smiled brightly as Boyd refilled her wine glass, the candlelight reflecting in the wine-filled glass, the bottle, and his bleary eyes. "So what's been going on at the shop today that made you so miserable?" she asked, raising the glass to her lips.

"I hardly know where to begin," Boyd said. "It's as though my desk were sitting at the bottom end of a giant funnel with a dozen demons poised at the top, pouring in a perpetual cascade of crises from every nook and cranny of the universe."

"Oh dear," she tried, reaching for humor, "quite an extended metaphor."

He ignored her and said, "The public offering has been delayed because of the lawsuit. Without a new infusion of capital, we can't upgrade our production capacity or expand our marketing group. Without improved production and additional sales force, we can't generate the revenue to sustain our cash flow requirements. Our reserves are dangerously low. Morale's poor. Everyone's worried about the future. We may have to lay off some people and close down our R and D efforts. If that happens, there'll be a stigma attached to the company. Our best people won't be able to risk remaining with EnviroClean. With a stream of departing employees, the company won't look appealing to the investment community, so raising capital will be difficult. Without the capital, more people will leave. Eventually there'll be nothing left but me and an empty laboratory."

Kathleen got up from the table, put her arms around her husband's shoulders, and kissed the side of his cheek. "I love you, Boyd."

"You know, I hardly have time to deal with any of these problems. Every day there are meetings with someone from Darby and Witherspoon—trial lawyers, legal assistants, environmental and government lawyers. This lawsuit's taken on a life of its own. They've even got computer technicians over there imaging all our papers and scientific records. I have to meet with all the consulting experts they've hired to present our case in court. There's no end to the information they demand from me. You realize we've already spent fifty thousand in legal fees on this case? And there's no end in sight."

Kathleen thought Boyd was about to break, but he took a deep breath and said, "This is no fun anymore, Katie. God, it'd be nice to go back to the university to teach and do research."

Bemused, Kathleen asked, "How can this one lawsuit delay the public offering?"

"Henry says that the investors are worried that the lawsuit might be indicative of some basic flaw with P-27, and they won't invest in a company with dozens of potential lawsuits to defend."

"I'm an investor," Kathleen replied. "Don't forget that, a major investor. But, like everyone else, I know you've done ten years of laboratory research and field tests on this product to prove it's safe. Just show them all your data and test results."

"You're an investor, but you're also my wife."

"That doesn't diminish the pain of losing money."

"Look, corporate investors don't care about scientific data, they care about lawsuits. They don't know whether the court will accept our data. Maybe the jurors will be overcome by some sense of sympathy and ignore the science. And, really, I can't blame them for feeling that way. Who'd want to be embroiled in a string of lawsuits? I only wish there were something I could do to get myself out of this case."

"What does Henry Holten say?" Kathleen asked, sitting back down in her chair. "Can't he meet with the other lawyer and work this out?"

"Holten says that's impossible," Boyd replied. "As far as the investment community is concerned, a settlement is an admission of responsibility. Holten says the case can't be compromised. We have to fight it to the bitter end."

"Well, what do you think? Is there any merit to the case?"

"None whatever," Boyd replied. "That's the sad part. We've got a great product. P-27 makes the environment safer. If we lose, the environment loses with us."

"Well, if there's no basis for the lawsuit," Kathleen said, "how can it be brought in the first place?"

"I wish I knew. Henry's working as hard as he can to get the case dismissed, but he says judges are reluctant to deny injured people their day in court. We have to prove our innocence, and that takes time and money."

"And you've got neither."

"You're right about that. But neither do the Bergstroms. I can only guess this must be as hard on them as it is on us. Wherever can they get the money to prepare this case properly?"

"Who knows," Kathleen replied. "What are they claiming anyway?"

"All I know is Ruth Bergstrom wrote us a letter asking if our bacteria could be responsible for some allergic reaction she was having. Henry Holten wrote her back and told her it was safe, and the next thing I knew, the sheriff showed up to serve the legal papers."

"My God, Boyd," Kathleen said, "a single letter is written, then, with barely the blink of an eye, a lawsuit is filed, EnviroClean is crippled, and your life's work is placed in jeopardy. What a waste!"

"I don't know what more we can do," Boyd said.

"Settle the case."

"And compromise our position with the investment bankers?"

"Sounds like it's already compromised."

"I know. That's the problem. There's no way out of it."

"That's ridiculous," said Kathleen. After pausing a few moments to regain her composure, she continued. "I think you should pick up the phone and call Mr. Bergstrom to see how his wife's getting along. I think they'd really appreciate your concern. Maybe it'd even be the start of some dialog that would resolve this ridiculous mess." Kathleen reached over, took Boyd's hand, and squeezed it tightly. "I can't stand to see you so unhappy, Boyd. The anguish this lawsuit is causing you has affected you more than you realize. You've got to take control of this situation. Whatever may happen to EnviroClean, your health and your peace of mind are far more important than the success of P-27."

"I'll call Henry in the morning and see what he says."

"Forget about Henry Holten," Kathleen said. "He's not paid to settle cases, he's paid to litigate them. This is your case, not his. Something's got to give. If Holten's right, you can't afford to settle. If you're right, you can't afford to fight. Either way you lose. Go ahead. Make the call, maybe it'll do some good."

"I don't know," Boyd said. "What you're saying sounds so simple, so easy. But I have no experience in these matters and I've put my trust in Henry."

Kathleen held Boyd's hand firmly in hers for a minute and watched Boyd's moist, candle-lit eyes staring into his wine glass. She smiled, picked up his fork, and loaded it with pasta and mushroom. "Come on, lover," she said, "eat." That got him to smile a little and he let her feed him a mouthful.

CHAPTER Eleven

Just as Love crossed the street, a UPS truck pulled up in front of his office. A burly man with tattoos and absurdly tight shorts stepped from the truck, lumbered around to the rear, and raised the back door. He disappeared inside for a few moments, activated a hydraulic platform, and then reappeared on the tailgate with a four-wheeler stacked high with cardboard boxes. Love stopped in the office doorway and watched the load descending on the platform.

"Dillon Love?" the man called over the hum of the hydraulics. "This has gotta be signed for."

"What is all this stuff?" Love called back.

As the man rolled the boxes through the door, he said, "I just deliver the stuff, I don't inspect it. Where do you want it?"

Cindy was already at the office door, holding it open. "Stack it all there please, young man," she ordered, pointing to a free wall. Before he unloaded it, the driver held up a clipboard for someone to sign. Cindy scribbled her signature, then plunged into the first box the driver took off the stack. Love sat down on his desk, stunned.

"Your Easter basket just arrived from Darby & Witherspoon," Cindy called out. "Either that or a late April Fool's joke." She paused for a few seconds while she rummaged through some of the papers. "I'm no legal scholar," she continued, "but I don't think this is a very thoughtful gift from the distinguished Mr. Holten."

"Quite the contrary," Love said, as he walked over to look. "I suspect he's given it considerable thought. What Holten and his fellow conspirators lack in sensitivity, they make up for in thoughtfulness."

Cindy removed the tops from each of the six banker's boxes. They were all filled with legal papers.

"Assholes," Love said loudly. It was going to be a monumental task just to read the documents, let alone respond to them. Love turned to walk back toward his desk. As he did, he kicked one of the boxes, spewing its contents across the floor. "Jesus Christ, that guy's a flaming asshole."

He grabbed the brim of his baseball hat, yanked it off his head, and flung it across the room. It hit yesterday's half-full cup of coffee, spilling its contents over the papers littering his desk. Cindy remained by the boxes, silent and aloof, as he wiped the spilled coffee onto the floor with his bare hands. He rubbed his hands on the seat of his jeans and fanned a few of the saturated papers. Tossing them aside and putting his wet cap back on his head, he looked back toward the reception area at the stack of boxes from Darby & Witherspoon.

"We might as well have at it," he said. "This shit ain't gonna sort itself out."

The two worked silently together through the morning and into the early afternoon. Cindy completed an initial inventory of the documents and handed Dillon a typed index.

"There are several sets of motions," said Cindy, "including one for summary judgment, another for dismissal under Rule 11, and a couple of others I don't even understand. There are hundreds of interrogatories they want us to answer, a large set of requests for admissions, whatever those are, and a whole series of deposition notices all over the country—Washington, Chicago, Boston, New York, St. Louis—not to mention another fifteen or twenty scheduled in Minneapolis. The Bergstroms are first. They're set for three days next week. Every day after that for two solid months D & W have scheduled other depositions, except for the day the motions are to be heard. Those are all scheduled for April 24. Dillon, what in God's name are you going to do about all this?"

Dillon took the list from Cindy and pondered its implications. Holten had obviously assigned half a dozen lawyers to work full-time on the case. They had prepared several motions, the effect of which would be to dismiss the case outright or severely restrict the evidence Love could present. The motions were well-researched and eloquently argued, just as he expected. Even though few judges would grant such drastic relief this early in the case, the motions had to be taken seriously because of their dire consequences. Under the rules, three weeks' notice for such motions was required, and Holten had given him only the bare minimum time to respond.

"Those bastards," Love muttered to himself as he realized the strategy Holten had devised. The motions would be heard in three weeks, but the depositions would begin immediately, so Love would have little time to prepare a proper response. He fumed silently for a few minutes, the pulse in his temples beating visibly. A surge of adrenaline filled his arteries and roused his resolve to fight, but it did little to foster any confidence that he could come up with a considered reply to the crucial motions he would face in only three weeks.

Dillon stared vacantly across the room, his feet resting on the messy stack of coffee-stained papers covering his desk. Cindy worked quietly across the room without glancing in his direction. "Stop your goddamn gloating," Love yelled at her across the room before returning to the papers on his desk.

Cindy ignored the remark, even suppressing an almost involuntary snort, and continued with her work.

"Listen up," Love said several minutes later, swinging his large legs off his desk and sitting erect in his wooden swivel chair. "Call Ruth Bergstrom. If she doesn't have a doctor's appointment next week, I want you to make her one. They can't force us to go to a deposition if she's under medical care at the time."

"Just what kind of appointment am I supposed to schedule?"

"Who the hell cares? She's a sick woman. She must need something. You figure it out."

Love rose from his desk, pulled down the brim of his hat, and started for the door. "I'm going over to the law school to find a couple of students looking for part-time work. While I'm gone, call a temp agency and have them send over a paralegal with some environmental experience. I can get them started answering some of these discovery requests."

"While you're at it, knock over a couple of banks on your way back so we'll have some cash to pay all these people," Cindy said.

"I can get a bank loan any time I want it," Love said. "Oh, and call Allison Forbes. I want a meeting with her as soon as possible. See you in a couple of hours."

Love was successful at the law school, and two students agreed to meet with him the next afternoon to begin responses to the various motions. Cindy lined up a paralegal temp to help gather the detailed information needed to answer the interrogatories and requests for admissions. She would also start the next day.

The meeting with Allison Forbes was arranged for seven o'clock. They met at Pete's Piano Bar for a beer. They had both visited separate happy hours before meeting and were already primed for their usual heated interchanges. As they seated themselves in a booth with their beers, Dillon jumped right in, "I know you appreciate frankness, Allie. It was damned inappropriate to have Kathleen Campbell call Ruth Bergstrom and try to talk her out of this lawsuit. That's an unethical intrusion into my attorney-client relationship. I just can't believe Darby & Witherspoon would stoop so low."

"Campbell's wife called Ruth Bergstrom?" Allison said. "That's news to me. I certainly didn't put her up to it, and I seriously doubt anyone else at D&W did."

"Well, she'd never make the call on her own initiative, that's for sure. Hell, she's not even involved in the case, and her husband never had the courtesy to respond to Ruth Bergstrom's letter last winter."

"We told him not to. Henry wrote the letter, don't you remember?"

"Only too well."

"So, what's your point?"

"Someone must have told her to make the call to Ruth in order to break her resolve to take this case to court. Boyd Campbell doesn't even take a piss without calling Holten."

"It's a little dangerous to jump to conclusions about our motivations without any evidence to back them up."

"Holten's an easy read, victory at all costs."

"So what was Ruth Bergstrom's response?"

"She was whining about why can't we all just get along and sort things out without lawyers. When I reminded her of Holten's bellicose letter and that he'd do whatever it takes to destroy this case, including having Kathleen Campbell do his bidding, she calmed down and saw my side of things."

Allison shook her head, pulled her hair back, and said, "Your whole problem is that you're ready to leap to absurd conclusions whenever it suits your fancy. Henry will have a shit-fit when I tell him Kathleen Campbell tried to intercede. Dillon, this whole thing is stupid. You've got no proof of anything. You've got no qualified scientists to support your claims. You've done no testing of the soils, no analysis of the active microorganism. You rely totally on the temporal relationship between the remediation EnviroClean was undertaking and the onset of Ruth Bergstrom's illness. That's it, that's all you've got."

"How would you know what I've got?" Love asked. "You just served me with the interrogatories, and I haven't revealed any of my case to you yet."

"Dillon," Allison said condescendingly, "it's our business to know these things. We simply called all of the qualified laboratories around town to see if any of them had conflicts of interest that would prevent them from consulting with us. Funny thing, none of them had a conflict, so they certainly aren't working for you. It's obvious that you either have nothing at all, or you have some totally unqualified pseudo-scientist from God-knows-where helping you. I suppose with your budget, that's about what's to be expected."

"I guess you'll have to wait thirty days to see what I have, won't you?"

"Actually," Forbes replied, "I suspect we'll find out a little sooner. By April 24 you'll have to provide the court with any evidence you've got if you want to avoid an order of dismissal. And we'll find out more when your client's depositions are taken next Monday."

"You won't be taking Ruth's deposition," Love said, "because she'll be at the Mayo Clinic."

"We'll just do it the following day then."

"Actually, she's having a whole series of tests done. It'll take most of the week."

"You were given proper notice, and I must insist on going forward with her deposition before April 24."

"If you're so goddamn sure this case is going to be dismissed on April 24, why have you noted so many depositions and sent out so many discovery demands? It wouldn't by any chance be an attempt to distract me from the motions? You know the Code of Professional Responsibility prohibits that kind of harassment."

"Don't lecture me about ethics, Dillon. Henry Holten is the chair of the Professional Responsibility Committee of the State Bar Association, so I can assure you we know what's required, as well as what's not permitted."

"So that's his strategy for avoiding censure," Dillon sneered. "Chair the committee that's responsible for disciplining his behavior."

"That's really cute."

"Look," Love said, "I'd like an extension on the discovery schedule you've set up. There's no way I can prepare answers to your discovery requests and respond to your motions, all while I'm attending your friggin' depositions."

"I understand your position, Dillon," Allison said, "and I truly sympathize with it. I've known you a long time. Unfortunately, your lawsuit, your unfounded lawsuit, is causing irreparable damage to EnviroClean, and I've got to consider the best interests of my client before I can extend special favors to anyone. It's nothing personal. I hope you understand that."

"What I understand, Allie, is that Darby & Witherspoon is attempting to take unfair advantage of me in order to deny Ruth and Arne Bergstrom a full hearing of their case in court. What I understand is that you're a part of this conspiracy against truth and justice." Dillon Love slid abruptly from the booth without finishing his beer. "What I understand is that I'm going to kick your friggin' butt."

"I'm sorry, Dillon. I really am. I may be lead trial counsel, but this is still Henry's case. And between having my butt kicked by you or Henry, I'll take you anytime."

Dillon jumped onto the bench across from Allison and slammed his large foot on the middle of the table, bouncing a basket of popcorn onto Allison's lap. "Before you choose your poison," he said, "take a good look at this little shit-kicker."

"I was speaking metaphorically." She smiled, calmly brushing popcorn off her sweater. "I'll talk to Henry when he returns from Bermuda. I can't promise anything, but I'll talk to him."

"Bermuda?" Dillon said, breathing hard and stepping down from the table.

"Yeah, his wife loves the place, and he has some little client down there to pay for the trips."

"A client in Bermuda ... that's interesting."

"And convenient."

"God, Allie, why are you so damn cute? I want to kill you."

"Listen Mr. Extrovert, after you kick my butt," Allison said, "why don't we all hop on a plane to Henry's hideaway and set our bruised little fannies on that warm, pink sand."

Dillon paused briefly to reflect on Allison's spontaneous metamorphosis from articulate advocate to disarming seductress. He was glad he knew her as well as he did. The familiarity neutralized the feminine advantage she might have over other males.

"You're a fucking dangerous woman, and that grin of yours reminds me of a crocodile," Dillon said.

"There you go," she said, drumming her fingers on his hand, "jumping to conclusions again."

The next morning, Love drove the ninety miles from Minneapolis to Rochester to meet with Ruth Bergstrom's consulting neurologist.

He entered the large, congested lobby and asked at the central information desk for directions to the office of Dr. Richard Gauss. He found his way to the elevator bank, and within a few moments was standing at the nurse's station in the neurology unit. Dr. Gauss was expecting Love, so the nurse gave him directions to the doctor's office.

As he walked down the corridor, he had the feeling he was in a medical factory, a streamlined, well-oiled assembly line where human beings are shuttled from station to station for each practitioner to perform his own specialized medicine on the particular body part associated with that unit. The beauty of this place, Love thought, is its organizational resourcefulness, unfortunately achieved at the expense of enduring, nurturing relationships between patient and physician. But if I'm ever seriously sick, he thought, this is where I'm coming.

"You must be Dillon Love," said an enthusiastic young man in navy slacks and a pink cotton sweater, offering his hand to shake. "I'm Rick Gauss. I've been looking forward to meeting you. Ruth and Arne Bergstrom speak so warmly of you. Please come in and sit down. Can I get you some coffee?"

So much for the dehumanization of this place, Love thought as Dr. Gauss guided him into his small, cluttered office. "No thanks, doctor."

"Please, let's forget this 'doctor' stuff, my name's Rick. I don't want to feel any older than I already am."

"This is an amazing facility you have here," Love said.

"Yeah," Dr. Gauss responded, "when I first started here, I had to carry a cell phone with me so I could call my office for directions whenever I got lost. Now the clinic seems to have shrunk. It's really a wonderful place to work. Everyone's busy, frightfully so, I'm afraid, but people here always seem to have time for a smile and a short chat in the hallway. I do like it here." He paused a moment, his face taking on a more somber tone. "I've been doing a lot of thinking about Ruth Bergstrom's situation," Dr. Gauss said. "Her condition is medically quite rare. It's called eosinophilia-myalgia syndrome, or EMS. I suspect she's had long-term exposure to some triggering chemical. I don't know yet what it is, but I hope to isolate it soon, and then we can begin looking for a treatment protocol. The challenge is to succeed before it destroys her central nervous system."

"I think I know the source of the contaminant," Love said. "I found an article in the *New England Journal of Medicine* which linked similar neurological disorders to a species of pseudomonas. I brought along an extra copy for you."

"I'm quite familiar with this article," Gauss replied politely. "Unfortunately there's a minor flaw with your theory. We've not been able to culture any pseudomonas from her blood. I plan to..."

"Well, I've found genetically engineered organisms in the creek bed behind her house," Love interrupted. "Given the study in the *New England Journal*, there's got to be a connection."

"That's not an assumption I'd be comfortable making, there are too many other possible explanations. But I'd be interested in seeing that lab report. Possibly..."

"I'm *certain* there's a link between the microbes and the EMS," Love interrupted again.

"Look, we may never be able to establish that scientifically," Dr. Gauss said. "Whatever microbes she may have had in her system were killed by the antibiotics she's been taking."

"What are you saying, doctor?" Love asked hotly. "When are you going to figure this thing out?"

"I'm saying we'll never find any bacteria in her blood. However, I also doubt her EMS was directly caused by bacteria. It's more likely a chemical of some kind. What we need to do is find that chemical. Once we've identified it, it's likely we can trace it back to its source. I've ordered some chromatographic studies for tomorrow morning. Hopefully, we'll observe an unusual spike and identify the contaminant."

"Chemical?" Love asked, "where'd this chemical come from? I thought we were talking about P-27."

"I don't know, but it's entirely possible that the metabolic processes of the bacteria produce some toxin and that it is the toxin, rather than the P-27, that does the damage."

"You mean the bacteria could be responsible for making the toxic chemical?" Love asked.

"It's conceivable."

"I need you to help me figure this out. And eventually someone's going to have to explain it to the jury so they understand what happened."

"I'd be a bit cautious about jumping to conclusions too quickly," Dr. Gauss said. "We've got no proof yet."

"Of course," Love replied. "I need proof also. But scientists like you are always searching for absolute proof. The law does not require that. All I have to do is prove it's more likely true than not. And I already know that."

"Oh?" Dr. Gauss asked.

"Yeah, there are genetically engineered organisms in Ruth's backyard. Studies with similar organisms have shown that people exposed to them develop similar symptoms. There's no other known source of infection. There's no other logical explanation."

"Perhaps that's how it will all work out," Gauss responded with a smile. "For the moment, however, there's simply no evidence that links Ruth Bergstrom's EMS with any bacteria, genetically engineered or otherwise. Nevertheless, I do intend to look for the cause. And when I find it, I'm sure one side or the other will want me in that courtroom."

CHAPTER Twelve

The judge Darby & Witherspoon had expected to preside over the *Bergstrom v. EnviroClean* case had been taken ill suddenly, and Allison Forbes watched fascinated as Henry Holten's face and neck turned crimson on hearing that Pamela Cleveland had been assigned to adjudicate. Holten rubbed his eyes harder than a middle-aged man should while, in considerable distress, he chose his words. "She's the worst judge we could get, Allison," he said finally. "She's just a kid, not much older than you, and between you and me they gave her a judgeship because she's black. Get me the lowdown on her immediately."

Not wanting to argue with Holten in his present mood, Allison merely said, "I'll get right on it," and left Holten's office, but she did not like his attitude at all. She knew a good deal about Judge Cleveland and was looking forward to working with her.

Pamela Cleveland was a success story from the slums of the Near North Side. Minneapolis does not really have slums, at least not like St. Louis or Chicago, but there are several sections of the city which accommodate various social miscreants whose aspirations are focused elsewhere than on neighborhood beautification. The childhood home of Pamela Cleveland was in such an area.

She was born to a teenaged mother and never learned who her father was. By his absence, however, her father played a significant role in her education; she learned that life in a dilapidated fourplex surrounded by crack dealers and prostitutes was hell on earth. She considered herself made of different stuff; there would be no teen pregnancy or AFDC for her, no sweet-talk from flashy street boys would distract her from completing high school and college. And she would find a man driven by his mind rather than his insecurities.

This inadvertent paternal legacy of self-determination gradually matured into a full-scale obsession to succeed. She graduated college with honors in African-American and Women's Studies, and immediately took a job in a shelter for battered women. Two years into this career she succumbed to the futility of the endless parade of helpless women who dragged themselves into the shelter, bleeding and bruised, only to return to their assailants after a few days to repeat the cycle ad infinitum. Pamela Cleveland came to believe that poverty and an unfair social system caused the battering of women and the humiliation of men. Determined to do something about it, she enrolled in law school to become a lawyer and take more substantial action against social inequities.

Law school challenged her, but she labored into the wee hours so she could both complete her studies and retain her job at the women's shelter. It was during this time that she met her activist husband, Lonny Palahniuk, a man now on the fast-track to DFL stardom. She graduated in four years in the top third of her class and turned down several lucrative offers from major firms needing to pad minority hiring statistics. Following her heart, she took a position with the Legal Aid Society.

After only five years as a legal aid attorney, Pamela Cleveland found herself sitting in the governor's office being interviewed for an opening as a district court judge. Hiring a black female was a rare political opportunity, and her lack of experience would be less obvious to the public than her color and her gender. Three months after donning her black robe for the first time, Judge Cleveland would assume responsibility for the case of *Bergstrom v. EnviroClean*.

Before heading together through the skyway to the Government Center, Allison briefed Henry Holten and the courtroom team on their judge. They huddled together around the table in the Witherspoon Room while rain slashed against the windows. In front of the others, and to Allison's puzzlement, Holten seemed to have a touch of censure in his voice when Allison finished speaking. He said stiffly, "One judge should be just as acceptable as another, Allison."

Without looking at Morrison Edwards, who had been drafted onto the courtroom team much to his unvoiced displeasure, she replied, "I couldn't agree more, Henry."

Allison's pulse accelerated as she entered the courtroom leading the Darby & Witherspoon entourage. Two parallel tables for opposing counsel were situated a few feet in front of the bench. She took her place as lead counsel and leaned forward as Henry Holten, Morrison Edwards, and Wendi Palmer slipped behind her to their assigned seats. With a lovely phrase stolen from the classical orchestra, Holten had ordered Morrison to sit at second fiddle and Wendi at third, with his humble self in the conductor's position at the far end. Behind Allison and her colleagues sat several legal assistants and law clerks with large briefcases filled with documents. The Darby & Witherspoon table was covered with legal papers and note pads carefully arranged in neat stacks covering most of its surface.

Allison remained standing while the others sat. She looked around the courtroom. At the other table sat Dillon Love in his corduroy sports jacket. He had nothing but a bulging file folder on the table in front of him and was gazing intently at notes scratched on a legal pad. She felt a little disappointed that he did not acknowledge her, but she was relieved that he had chosen not to bring Ruth Bergstrom to court. She had not wanted Boyd Campbell in court either since he would look far too tanned and healthy in comparison to Ruth Bergstrom if Love had chosen to put her on exhibit. She loved the smell and atmosphere of the courtroom, even if this was only an initial hearing with few people in attendance. She had dressed the part, too; they had all dressed in the Darby & Witherspoon "uniform," navy blue suits and brilliant white shirts or blouses with blue ties or scarves. Of course Henry Holten was the exception: he wore his signature red bow tie. Straightening her jacket and smoothing her skirt in a state of hyper-awareness, Allison glanced once more at Dillon Love, then sat and forced herself to relax.

The assembled lawyers rose from their seats as Judge Cleveland walked into the courtroom without a formal announcement by the bailiff. She was shorter and heavier than Allison expected. At her bench the judge stood for a few moments and surveyed the faces of the suppliants before her. The lawyers in turn focused intently on her as she assumed her chair and opened a large journal to record the proceedings before her. As those standing in front of her waited for her to speak, she adjusted the sleeves of her black robe as if reflecting momentarily on the power the robe gave her over the lives of the people in that courtroom.

Judge Cleveland took a deep breath, looked over at Henry Holten and said, "Before you all take your seats, I wonder if you'd have a few of your folks move to the other side of the courtroom. There's a risk of it toppling sideways and catapulting Mr. Love through the wall before he gets to speak."

Dillon chuckled, looked at Allison and winked. She knew what he was thinking, that the judge had seen through the facade of strength the defense had mounted and that in spite of their superior resources they sat in this courtroom as equals. What he did not understand, because he did not understand people, especially women, was that Cleveland was incredibly nervous and had cracked a joke to try and ease the tension she felt. Allison had confidence that Judge Cleveland would not fail to see the frailty of the suit.

Still smiling, the judge said, "Who's going to present the argument on behalf of EnviroClean?"

"I have that privilege this morning, your Honor," said Allison, rising from her seat. "May it please the court, I'm Allison Forbes, with the firm of Darby & Witherspoon, attorneys for EnviroClean."

"You may proceed, Ms. Forbes," the judge said. "I've reviewed all the briefs that each side has filed, so you needn't repeat anything from those materials in your oral arguments."

"Your Honor," began Forbes, "there are actually three separate motions before you this morning. The first is a motion to dismiss based on Rule 11. The second is a motion for summary judgment based on Rule 56, and the third, if the court even needs to consider it, is a motion to compel discovery based on the inadequate responses to our discovery requests by opposing counsel. I'll deal with each of these motions separately."

The many hours of preparation by Allison and her law clerks had created an aura of professionalism that she felt advanced the sense that she spoke not just as an advocate for one of the parties, but as an advocate for the truth as a whole. This was why she went to law school, this was why she trained under Holten; she had arrived. She stood tall and proud and said, "The court is well aware of the requirements of Rule 11. An attorney is prohibited from signing any pleading, including the complaint filed against my client in this case, without having first developed a sound evidentiary basis to support his allegations. This rule has not been followed in the case before the court. As my affidavits clearly indicate, Mr. Love has failed to develop any scientific basis for his bald assertions that EnviroClean's product, P-27, caused harm to Mrs. Bergstrom.

"His whole case is based on the fact that he apparently found some bacteria in the creek behind the Bergstrom home and that these bacteria were similar to some organisms EnviroClean uses to decontaminate toxic gasoline spills. The problem is that there are literally thousands of similar organisms, many of which are commonly found wherever there are decaying organic materials, exactly as there are in Ruth Bergstrom's creek. Counsel has no proof that the organisms he found were put there by EnviroClean. We know this because he has not conducted the appropriate testing procedures to prove this. He admits this, your Honor. The matter is not even in dispute.

"Secondly, he has no evidence to prove how these organisms, if they were EnviroClean's, somehow found their way from the creek into Ruth Bergstrom's body. He has not presented any evidence that she came into contact with water from the creek at any time. Even if she had, it would be practically impossible for the bacteria to get into her bloodstream, and counsel has suggested no theory as to how this could have happened.

"Third, he has no evidence that these organisms can cause the type of problems Ruth Bergstrom is experiencing. Indeed, her symptoms can be caused by any number of medical conditions. Without recognized medical opinions documenting the organisms' capacity to cause such neurological symptoms in humans, he has no case at all. Your Honor, Rule 11 requires counsel to establish this evidence before he commences a lawsuit and forces good companies like EnviroClean to underwrite huge expenses to establish their innocence. He has not done this, and his case must be dismissed."

Allison closed the notebook containing her notes and materials concerning this first motion. Simultaneously she was handed a second notebook by one of the legal assistants who had been sitting behind her. The book was already open to the page she needed to continue her arguments on the second motion.

"My Rule 56 motion is based on these same facts, your Honor, but this rule requires counsel to go a step further than Rule 11. Rule 56 requires counsel to come forward with sworn affidavits supporting his position, and these affidavits must contain sufficient evidence to establish a prima facie case of liability against EnviroClean."

Allison removed from the notebook in front of her one of the several affidavits she had filed in support of her Rule 56 motion and read a short excerpt from it to the court.

"As the court's file will reflect," she continued, "Mr. Love has not filed a single affidavit supporting his position. The rule clearly requires this. This rule does not exist to create a burden on litigants or unjustly punish lawyers who neglect its requirements. The rule exists because it is a fair rule, because it seeks to protect the public from capricious lawsuits that cannot be supported with credible evidence. Rule 56 clearly requires a dismissal."

Again there was an exchange of notebooks between Allison and one of her legal assistants. With only a brief pause to find her place, she began her third argument:

"My third motion to compel discovery is based on the fact that Mr. Love has yet to respond to any of our interrogatories or requests for production of documents on a timely basis. His responses are now three days overdue. Ordinarily we would be entitled to sanctions for this non-responsiveness. We are willing to waive the sanctions if the case is dismissed. The main point here, your Honor, is that it's obvious the discovery has not been answered because Mr. Love has no information to furnish us. He has nothing to answer because he has nothing to support his case. His lack of responses only further supports our position that he has no evidence and that this case must be dismissed.

"Your Honor, EnviroClean is a company whose very purpose is to advance the cause of the environment. EnviroClean does not poison the environment. It spends hundreds of thousands of dollars in research developing products that clean it up. Indeed, that's precisely what it was doing at the gas station next to the Bergstrom's, cleaning up the contaminated soil and ground water. EnviroClean is making the Bergstrom's property far less toxic, not more toxic.

"What we're asking of the court is not only what the law requires, but also what principles of fairness and decency require. It's unjust to summon anyone before this court to incur huge expenses defending themselves without even a scintilla of evidence that they've acted improperly. Such harassing tactics to extort undeserved settlements are not only improper under the rules, they are also unethical. I cannot begin to explain to the court how severe an impact the mere existence of this suit has on EnviroClean. It could literally be forced out of business before being fully exonerated by a jury. I request that the court put an end to this frivolous litigation today."

Allison sat down emphatically and crossed her arms, looking across at Dillon.

"Mr. Love," Judge Cleveland said, "would you care to respond to Ms. Forbes's arguments at this time?"

Love rose to his feet and strode confidently to the center of the room, positioning himself directly between Allison and Judge Cleveland. Allison could see only the back of his wrinkled corduroy jacket. She understood that he would not want her to see his face, because it was going to be full of bullshit. To hell with him, Judge Cleveland would get the real picture.

Love's neck reddened, and he stood quietly a few seconds, apparently looking at the legal pad filled with notes. He shuffled briefly through the pages, then dramatically turned and tossed them onto the counsel table behind him. Planted firmly on both feet he raised his arms toward the judge and said, "I'm overwhelmed by the responsibility I strongly feel at this minute for Ruth Bergstrom. And I'm humbled by the stature and prestige of those who would have you summarily abrogate her constitutional right to have her day in court before a jury of her peers. Counsel's eloquence is a formidable tool for shielding us all from the indisputable truths of this case. I wish I had her poise, and I wish I had the seemingly limitless resources of Darby & Witherspoon for my client.

"Ruth Bergstrom was a healthy, vibrant young mother and wife." Love paused and turned to face Allison. He glared at her, and his voice suddenly rose, "Until she was poisoned in her own home by the company Ms. Forbes represents here today. She was poisoned by a genetically mutated organism her client cavalierly discharged into Ruth Bergstrom's backyard. Ruth Bergstrom was in the prime of life until this defendant decided to play God and create a new, dangerous life form, one never before known to mankind, never before tested by scientists or medical professionals.

"I wish I could stand before the court and represent that we have every detail of our case all ironed out and that we're ready for trial. Your Honor, this case has just begun. Our work has just begun. We don't understand precisely what caused Ruth Bergstrom to get sick, but we do know the basic parameters. We know that the defendant uses genetically altered bacteria known as pseudomonas in a product it calls P-27. We know that organisms such as these were found by our consulting expert in the creek bed behind Ruth and Arne Bergstrom's home. We know there has been a great deal of research on similar organisms and that at least one published study has documented the bacteria's toxicity. We know from the scientific literature and from Dr. Richard Gauss at the Mayo Clinic that organisms such as these produce various chemicals as a part of their normal metabolic processes. Some of these chemicals are toxic and capable of destroying the central nervous system. We know that, except for the P-27 released into the environment by the defendant, no other medical explanation has been found to account for this catastrophic illness, which is ravaging the lives of Ruth and Arne Bergstrom. All the talent and experience of the finest doctors at the Mayo Clinic have found no other explanation for her life-threatening and totally debilitating illness.

"Can I represent to this court that P-27 clearly and unequivocally is the cause? I only wish I could. But we do have a great deal of circumstantial evidence supporting this conclusion, and, very soon, there will also be direct evidence. I'll prove this to the court's satisfaction, but I need time in order to do so. I need time for the doctors at Mayo to complete their research to solve this medical puzzle. I need time to obtain necessary testing to demonstrate the toxicity of P-27 and compare it with the toxins in Ruth Bergstrom's blood.

"Your Honor, EnviroClean apparently has not done these tests itself. Or if it has, its lawyers are keeping that a secret from me and from this court. If EnviroClean's lawyers are so convinced its product didn't cause Ruth Bergstrom's injuries, they could have run the same tests I plan to run. They could have brought those results in here today to support their motions. We can only assume they are afraid to run the tests because of what they will surely show.

"Counsel has scheduled depositions virtually every day for the next two months. As the court will readily observe from the entourage before it, Darby & Witherspoon has numerous lawyers to attend these depositions and still bombard me with an avalanche of paperwork. My office is me. Yet they expect me to have my case put together flawlessly at the same time they require most of my time to attend all the depositions they schedule and respond to all the demands for discovery which they continuously deliver to my office.

"The Bergstroms and I cannot be expected to have answers for every question the defendant might raise at this moment. This is a complicated product liability case that is taking time to investigate and develop. All we ask from the court is the chance to do so, the only chance Ruth Bergstrom will ever be given, her one opportunity to have a jury look at the evidence, her one opportunity that is guaranteed her by the constitution and laws of this state.

"Ms. Forbes says she comes to this room seeking fairness and decency. I have no idea how the well-heeled lawyers from Darby & Witherspoon can possibly know what is fair and decent for Ruth Bergstrom. They have never met her, never met her family, never been to her home. They have not seen the agonies and indignities she has been forced to endure through the unconscionable behavior of her client. If there is any fairness left in the world, it will pour forth generously on behalf of this gracious, suffering woman."

Allison shot up from her chair before Dillon Love had even regained his place at the counsel table. "May I respond briefly, your Honor?" she said.

"I do not believe that will be necessary, counsel," Judge Cleveland said perfunctorily. "Your points are very well taken, Ms. Forbes, and the law supports your conclusions. But I also have a responsibility to Ruth Bergstrom. My job is about fairness and justice, not untempered adherence to procedural rules. I'm going to give Mr. Love six months to gather evidence to support his case. In the meantime, I'll take your motion under advisement, subject to further affidavits and briefs at that time. Is six months adequate for you, Mr. Love?"

"I think that will be sufficient," Love replied.

"I'm also giving Mr. Love a thirty-day extension to respond to the interrogatories," the judge announced. "The depositions you have scheduled will have to be postponed until after July 4 to give Mr. Love a chance to prepare his answers. I don't see how he can be asked to attend depositions every day and respond to your discovery requests at the same time."

No one from Darby & Witherspoon spoke as they began to rise from their seats and put their papers back into the multitude of briefcases and boxes.

"Before I let you all go," Judge Cleveland said loudly, "I must say I'm concerned about the direction of this case. I can only guess that this one hearing today cost EnviroClean at least ten thousand dollars, and the case has hardly begun. Where will all the money come from to fight this case as it is being fought now? From what I have read, EnviroClean is just a start-up biotech company and must have enormous need for cash to build its business. The cost of winning may be more than the company can afford. And, my God, how in the world will the plaintiffs finance their case? Neither party can afford to lose, but I wonder whether either party can afford to win. So I'm going to order both parties to appear before a mediator to attempt a settlement. I want this to be completed within ninety days. You can either agree on a mutually acceptable mediator, or I will appoint one myself."

Allison, shocked, looked at Henry Holten who was rising abruptly to assume command. "With all due respect, your Honor," Holten said, "we are not interested in a settlement. We will not compromise the integrity of our client by paying extortion money to every Tom, Dick, and Harry who sues the company. Mediation would be a waste of time and money for everyone. This case is simply too important to our client to compromise."

"That, Mr. Holten, is precisely why you will be mediating this case," Judge Cleveland snapped.

"Again with all due respect, your Honor," Holten replied, "I do not see where in the rules the court has the authority to order mediation. I respectfully request the court reconsider its position."

"My order will follow shortly." Judge Cleveland rose from her chair and walked briskly from the courtroom.

"I want a notice of appeal ready by the end of the day," Holten demanded in a voice intentionally loud enough for Love to overhear. "And I want to get this judge off the case. Fairness and justice, my ass. She ignores the rules, she ignores logic, she ignores justice. I want her off this case."

Allison saw the disdain in Holten's eyes as he looked over at Love. "This is not some little game we're playing here," he said, turning to face him. "The fun's over, sonny. Our guns are drawn and the battle's only begun."

"At the moment," Love replied, standing, bushy-bearded and disheveled, "it appears your gun's pointed at your foot. As far as I'm concerned, you can fire at will."

CHAPTER Thirteen

Arne Bergstrom jolted awake. He must have been dreaming because he was full of sadness, but could not remember the dream. The orange glow of a late September sunrise was refracted into a serene spectrum of colors on the white living room ceiling by the chrome framework of Ruth's new bed. He sat up, feeling slightly dizzy and sick at the thought of having to get the kids up and make breakfast. He wondered if the settlement money would be enough to allow him to hire a housekeeper.

He swung his legs off the couch, rubbed his face, and said, "Ruthie, time to wake up." Outside, a rich blend of reds and yellows from the changing fall leaves along Nassau Street filtered the sun and filled the room with a warm and placid hue. Her new adjustable bed, provided by their church, was placed under the big picture window so she could see the neighbors walking on the sidewalk a few yards away.

"Ruthie, come on."

He shook off the dizziness, went over to her, and found her tangled up in the sheets in a dead faint. He could always tell a faint because her eyes rolled back and her mouth went slack, usually producing drool. He no longer panicked as he had eight months earlier when he discovered Ruth passed out on their frozen front stoop. Repeated episodes had provided an odd reassurance that life would soon return to her limp body.

Arne pulled a hypodermic needle and a small vial from a black leather satchel on an end table at the side of the couch. He prepared the adrenaline injection, carefully inserted the needle into Ruth's vein, then patiently combed his fingernails across her scalp, waiting for her to return to consciousness. However mechanical this routine had become, his heart still raced and his chest tightened. Today, he also felt a great heaviness beneath his breast bone, and an ache that radiated across his entire chest to his shoulders.

Ignoring his own discomfort, Arne waited. He gazed through the window at the serene fall morning outside. The solitude of the setting was broken by a man jogging from the south end of Nassau Street. As he watched the jogger approach Arne wondered what made them do it, these runners, wasting their energy. Tall, lean, and middle-aged, the jogger paused briefly in front of the house and looked in Arne's direction. Arne could not recall seeing him previously in the neighborhood. As their eyes met for the first time, Arne smiled. The man returned the smile and took a hesitant step toward the front door.

Ruth made a snorting sound and shuddered. A pillow fell off the bed. Arne reached for the pillow, but it was a few inches beyond his grasp. He nodded to the jogger then dipped down to pick up the pillow. When he bobbed back up with it the jogger had started moving off down the street again. Arne watched him as he continued on toward the corner, where he stopped at the filling station. The man looked back again at the Bergstrom residence, kicked his foot against one of the abandoned gas pumps a few times, and them ambled out of sight.

Ruth opened her eyes and smiled. "How're you doing?" she asked softly.

Arne laughed and said, "Me? I'm fine, you turkey. It was you who was just in a faint."

"How'm I doing, then?"

"Pretty damned sassy as usual," he said.

Arne ran his fingers through Ruth's hair and massaged her temples.

"I'm hungry," she said.

"Liar," he said.

Arne helped Ruth into the small bathroom next to the kitchen. Holding tight to the sink with her left hand, she grabbed her toothbrush in her fist and let Arne apply toothpaste to it. Then she looked up at him and said, "Arne, you needn't stand there watching me brush my teeth. Why don't you make your coffee and get the newspaper."

"Bossy as well as sassy this morning, I see. I'm not going to leave you here to smash your head on the toilet."

"Nonsense. I don't need a nursemaid."

"Shall I get your wheelchair, or would you prefer to slither to the kitchen on your belly when you're done here?"

"I don't need a doting husband, either. Don't I get any privacy or dignity around here?"

"God knows, there's no chance Ruth Bergstrom will ever lose her dignity."

Ruth gave him an insincere, toothpaste-smile.

"Dillon is coming by later this morning," Arne said. "He's got news about some laboratory testing he's done. I told him to stop by around nine. Will that give you enough time to get ready and have breakfast?"

"Not unless you leave me alone, bozo."

Arne brought the wheelchair and found Ruth emptying her collection bag into the toilet. She gave him a dirty look, but sagged thankfully into her chair. "You've been using your legs for nearly ten minutes," Arne said. "I'm impressed."

"They hurt terribly. My God, how they ache."

"It's a start though, isn't it?"

"I guess, but who knows what other damage all this medication's doing."

"Come on, Ruthie, this isn't like you to be so negative."

"I'm sorry. Maybe I'm just hungry."

Arne cooked up a great pile of fluffy scrambled eggs, made with cream cheese the way the children liked them. Ruth ate more than usual, even finishing the whole-wheat toast left when the kids rushed off to catch their bus, but Arne dared not make anything out of that just yet; he'd seen the cycle of improvement and relapse several times before.

He was turning on the dishwasher when Dillon rang the doorbell.

"Cup of coffee?" Arne asked, closing the door behind Love.

"Absolutely," he replied, "your coffee puts hair on my chest."

Laughing, Arne said, "Come on into the kitchen, Dillon. Ruthie and I just finished cleaning up."

"I haven't done a thing, Dillon," Ruth said, as the two men passed through the doorway. "I've just been sitting around all morning looking pretty."

"Pretty indeed," Dillon observed. "I haven't seen you in weeks. I hope you feel as good as you look."

"You're a shameless liar, Dillon Love."

"And you're exceptionally modest."

"I think I'm finally over the hump," Ruth said. "I haven't felt this good in a long time."

"Are you forgetting you were in a faint at six this morning?" Arne said.

"Are you forgetting that I used my legs for ten minutes right after that?" Ruth said.

Dillon raised his eyebrows and said, "I know it's a strange thing to say, but..." Then he closed his mouth. They looked at him while the dishwasher hummed. "Never mind," he said.

"Anyway, she's not well," Arne said. "She'll never admit it, but she's just not doing real good with these fainting fits."

"Hogwash," Ruth said.

"I hope you're not getting dementia along with everything else."

"Arne, I'm sure Dillon doesn't want to waste his day listening to us argue."

"Who's arguing?" Arne barked. "I'm just telling it like it is."

"The way you carry on, you'll just work yourself into an ulcer, and I'll have to look after you," Ruth replied. Turning to Dillon, she added, "Please sit down and tell us what you've been up to."

"I've got great news," Dillon began, as he took a seat at the table. "Ken Butler's been able to prove unequivocally that the bacteria samples from the creek bed have been genetically engineered. The lab pathologist told me he's never seen an organism quite like this one. It looks like a pseudomonas, but it doesn't behave like one. It's more active and can reproduce itself every fifteen minutes. He thinks it's an entirely new species that's been created by EnviroClean."

"What's Dr. Gauss have to say about this?" Ruth asked.

"I spoke with him yesterday. He reviewed the laboratory results with me over the phone and reminded me that last spring he had run a chromatographic analysis of your blood and found some chemical toxin that he believes caused your EMS. We're a step closer to proving our case against EnviroClean. It's only a matter of time before we trace this contaminant to the P-27."

"I don't understand," Arne said. "What's this chemical got to do with EnviroClean? I thought they use bacteria."

"They do," Dillon answered, "but the antibiotics Ruth took killed all the bacteria before Dr. Gauss could get a culture."

"Then how do you know the bacteria have anything to do with Ruthie's condition?" Arne asked.

"We're not completely sure," Dillon said. "Either EnviroClean adds some chemicals to its P-27 to improve its effectiveness, or the bacteria themselves produce the chemical as part of their metabolic process."

"How do we prove this?" Arne asked.

"That'll be easy," Dillon replied. "Finding the chemical was the hard part, figuring out where it came from will be a piece of cake."

"Does this mean we can get this case settled now, Dillon?" Ruth asked.

"This means we're going to win the case," he said. "Why would we want to settle now that everything is falling into place? We're going to make them pay for what they've done to you. They're going to pay dearly so they'll never do this to anyone else."

Ruth fidgeted with a paper napkin as Love spoke, squeezing it into a tight ball.

"Why would we want to hurt them?" she asked.

"Things are a little tough around here financially," Arne added. "With Ruthie so sick I've had to turn down jobs so I could take care of her. What little savings we had are gone. We'd really like to see the case settled. Ruthie and I just want to get on with our lives."

"We don't care to make an example of anyone," Ruth said. "We don't care to punish anyone. We all make mistakes once in a while."

"Listen..." Dillon started, but Arne interrupted: "If we can just get our medical bills paid, and a little money to cover our living expenses until Ruth's better, that's all we'd ever want."

"Anyone who'd create some new organism," Dillon continued, "and throw it into the creek without any testing, without any effort to prove it won't harm humans, is a callous, uncaring person. This case is about the greed of a company that gambles with the health of other people for the personal profit of its executives. They cut corners just to save money. How can you feel sorry for anyone like that? Besides, they must have insurance. All that will happen is that the insurance company will pay our verdict. It won't be any big deal for Boyd Campbell."

"We can't afford to wait for all this to happen," Arne said. "We can't last through a long court battle. I may have to sell the house to pay our bills if you can't get a settlement soon."

"I hate to tell you this, Arne," Dillon said, "but you won't be able to sell the house. With the polluted creek back there, no one would ever buy the place."

Arne looked nervously at Ruth to see how she would react to that news, but she was holding up just fine. "I hadn't thought of that," he said.

"Don't worry, I'll be building that issue into the damages, too. We should be able to get a trial date by next spring, so everything will be resolved by then. Just hang tough a little longer."

"Why can't we just sit down with Boyd Campbell and work it all out?" Arne asked. "I'd think he'd want to settle the case too, especially if you tell him about the genetic testing you've done."

"I'm sure as hell not going to tell him about that," Love said. "It'd just give them a chance to conjure up some phony response. This is the sort of thing I want to keep under wraps and surprise them with in court when they'll have no chance to explain it away."

"But if we tell him about it, maybe we won't have to go to court," Arne said.

"There's no chance of that. They've told me more than once they have no interest in a settlement. Besides, if you talk with Boyd Campbell, anything you say can be used against you in court. His lawyers would just trick you into saying something that would harm your case."

"I don't know, Dillon. I ...," Arne began.

"Look," Dillon interrupted, "the guy never even responded to your letter last January. He just shipped it off to the most obstructionist law firm in town to do his dirty work for him. Why do you suppose he'd want to meet with you now if he wouldn't even answer your letter eight months ago?"

"His wife seemed like such a sincere person when she called

me on the phone last April," Ruth said. "You've got to admit it was thoughtful of her to make the effort for us."

"She was only put up to that by the lawyers," Dillon said, throwing his hands in the air. "I told you that before. They figured you'd fall for the old woman-to-woman routine. It was nothing but a sham. I told Allison Forbes to make damn sure it never happens again."

"I don't know," Arne said, "what do we really have to lose?"

"Listen," said Love, "I can't allow you to meet with them. You're not experienced in these matters. You must trust me to do the best I can for you. That's my job. I know the delays are frustrating, but it'll all work out in the end. The legal system protects people like you."

CHAPTER Fourteen

When Dillon left the Bergstrom's he drove directly to the bank. Aside from needing to touch base with them, he had gone to their house partly with some notion of asking for more money, but once he saw the state they were in he skipped it. It worried him slightly that, aside from her fainting fits, Ruth was getting stronger, which could reduce the amount of the verdict. He would need to keep moving this thing along; therefore, he would bite the bullet today, then go kick the lovely ass of Allison Forbes.

His loan officer, Jay Marx, was one of the more gregarious people Dillon knew in Minneapolis. It was only by virtue of some quirk of fate that Marx found himself in the banking business without acquiring the slightly aloof personality generally required for success in consumer lending.

As he met Love in the bank's lobby, Marx said, "Dillon, good to see you. How the hell you doing these days?" He had a warm, hard handshake. "Come back to my office and tell me what you've been up to."

"Whatever," Dillon joked, "but I thought you'd already have your coffers open and ready for me."

They entered a cloth-paneled cubicle and sat at a small round table with a stack of files covering most of its surface. "No such thing as a check and a handshake anymore," Marx laughed, transferring the papers to his desk, which was also littered with paperwork. "If we don't generate at least five pounds of paper on every loan, the bigwigs think we haven't worked hard enough. What the hell, if that's how they want to spend their money, I can shuffle papers with the best of them."

"Jay, I need some help financing a case."

"Yeah, I hear you've got a real barn-burner going. That's great."

"It's as close to a slam dunk as anything I've ever seen," Dillon said. "I can't wait to get these people in front of a jury."

"How can we help?"

"I'm going to need fifty thousand to hire an investigator, finish some genetic testing, and cover the salaries of a couple of law clerks. You remember that you guys previously loaned me ten thousand for some initial testing. Now that the results are so encouraging, I need to get the final trial preparations done and put the last nails in their coffin."

"I heard Henry Holten over at Darby & Witherspoon is on the other side," Marx said.

"Last I heard, Holten still puts his pants on one leg at a time," Dillon said, sneering.

"Yeah, but he brings a few other pairs of pants with him, and some skirts as well. The resources of Darby & Witherspoon are enormous."

"I know what I'm doing, Jay, I..."

"Have you given any thought to associating yourself with a larger firm that has more resources to engage in this sort of litigation?"

"This is my case to win. I know it backwards and forwards. I don't need another law firm. What I need is a little money. I'm good for it. You know that."

"Hell, Dillon," Marx replied, "if you say so, that's good enough for me. Your word is gold in my book. Unfortunately, I don't make the rules around here. Banks are not loaning money on people's good word any more. I need collateral. If you want a home equity loan, I can give you fifty grand tomorrow. That's about the best option you have."

"Fine, Jay. Can we get that done right now?"

"We'll need your wife in here to cosign."

"I owned the house before we married and never added her name to the title."

"Just the same, Dillon..."

"You don't understand, Jay. It was a precaution against exactly this sort of thing. My house is all mine to lose."

Jay Marx sighed and said, "Well, I can make the loan against your office equipment and receipts."

"That'll work," Dillon said, and pulled open his briefcase.

An hour later Love walked from the bank with a load off his

shoulders. A second mortgage would be no big deal. He would surely not need the entire fifty thousand, but this gave him a good safety margin to make sure he would not have to cut any corners in preparing the case properly.

Love called the office and told Cindy he would be taking the afternoon off. Laurie would be home, and it would be a nice afternoon for a bike ride around the city lakes. A little time with his wife would be a welcome reprieve from his harried schedule. Cindy merely harrumphed and hung up the phone.

He stopped off at a fancy supermarket and bought a dozen yellow roses.

Summer had been largely lost to the pressure of the case. There had been a dozen or so depositions of research scientists, engineers, and government regulators. These had taken Dillon across the country, almost without a break. When he was not traveling, he was immersed in his own continuing investigation and research and in the undone work for the few other clients who had remained loyal to him despite the distractions caused by the Bergstrom case. So Dillon had not kept his promise of taking Laurie on a Boundary Waters canoe trip.

He would make amends for his inattentiveness. What the hell, he thought. We'll go up North tomorrow. Why not? A short break in the deposition schedule would allow him a few days away from the office, and the tranquillity of the north country would be the perfect catalyst for renewing his relationship with Laurie. They could spend the afternoon picking up supplies, and head out early next morning.

Dillon pulled up in front of the house and grabbed the roses from the back seat. He hustled toward the front door with an extra bounce to his gait. In his enthusiasm he did not see the Sheriff's Department squad car parked across the street.

"Hey there, hold up a second," a voice shouted out from the sidewalk just as Love reached the top step to his house. "Are you Dillon Love?"

"I'm your man, Deputy," Dillon said playfully. "I suppose you've got some new epistle from Darby & Witherspoon."

"Wrong law firm," the deputy said as he approached Dillon and handed him a large envelope. "Consider yourself served. Have a nice afternoon."

Love stuffed the roses under his left arm and opened the envelope. He saw immediately that it was a court summons. The caption read, "Laurie Love, Petitioner, versus Dillon Love, Respondent."

"Holy shit. Holy fucking shit."

Dillon slumped down on the top step; the yellow roses fell from his hand and cascaded to the concrete, landing a few feet in front of him. He stared at the papers but could not force himself to read them. His eyes welled with tears, and he crumpled the summons against his face and buried his head in the document. It took him several minutes to regain his composure sufficiently to walk inside.

In the kitchen, he noticed an envelope lying in the middle of the table, with the words "Dillon Love" neatly printed on the front. He tossed the legal papers onto the table and picked up the envelope, ran his forefinger underneath the seal, and jerked out the letter inside.

Laurie's penmanship was impeccable, the lines running flawlessly across the page without smudges or corrections. The margins were equal, side to side and top to bottom. He stared at the letter for several minutes, having difficulty comprehending the words written on the two pages before him:

Dearest Dillon,

In all likelihood you'll have received the divorce papers by the time you read this letter. I'm truly sorry it's all come to this, as I've loved you deeply. I probably still do. I wish it could continue, God only knows how I wish it could continue. You must know I would do anything to rebuild our love together as it once was. I only wish I could believe it was still possible.

I need to be loved, Dillon. I need to be the only love in your life. I need your strength and your support. I need the warmth of your body beside me on the couch at night. I need you to listen with interest to the trivial things I've done every day and share them with me and make me feel important. I need you to sit on the counter and talk with me as I fix our dinner, to go shopping together, to do all the simple things that used to be such an important part of our lives. I need you to play with me and tease me and touch me, to reach under my clothes and caress me.

Maybe it's my fault that I've not adapted as modern women are supposed to adapt. Maybe there would be some hope for us if I'd developed my own career and had fallen in love with it as you've fallen in love with yours. That's not me. I have no career as such, no big case to make

*me feel important and useful. I am Laurie Love, mother-in-waiting. And
I am lonely.*

*I'm lonely for the man who used to bounce through the front door with
enthusiasm radiating from every fiber of his vibrant masculine physique.
I'm lonely for the man who used to chase me around the house and rav-
ish my body with love and warmth. I'm lonely for the children he and I
dreamed of having once his career was established. I'm lonely for all our
friends who no longer fit into your schedule.*

*My clock is ticking, and I need to find a new Dillon Love before it's too
late. I'm sorry, I'm so terribly sorry. Please forgive me for what I must
do.*

I wish you all the best.
Laurie

Dillon folded the pages and dropped heavily into a kitchen chair.
He slumped at the table, numb and slack-jawed, and stared at the letter for several moments before suddenly sweeping the legal papers
onto the floor. Only Laurie's letter remained on the table, and, seeing it still there in front of him, he pounded his fists repeatedly
against it. The vibrations knocked over a salt shaker which rolled
into his lap.

"Fuck!" he yelled at the top of his voice. "Bitch!" He pitched the
shaker as hard as he could against the window above the sink where
it shattered the glass, hit the screen, bounced back inside, and broke
in the sink. He reached for the acrylic pepper mill, clubbed the letter with it, and threw it against the wall. It bounced back and hit
him in the shin.

"Fuck, fuck, motherfucking fucker."

He grabbed a large piece of broken glass from the sink and shattered it against the kitchen floor, then leaned against the sink, breathing hard, his eyes streaming. "Okay," he muttered, "Okay, get a grip,
Dillie." He turned the faucet full on and drenched his face in cold
water. Still dripping wet, he walked across the room to the refrigerator, popped a can of Budweiser, and chugged its contents. Tossing
the empty can onto the floor, he pulled his shirt tail from his pants
and wiped his wet face, then opened a second can and sat again at
the kitchen table. In a few minutes he had finished the second beer
and tossed it onto the floor near the first. He reached for the folded
letter and flicked a shard of glass from it.

With his shirt cuff he wiped a trickle of beer from his chin and read the letter again, slowly. He scrutinized every word dispassionately as though the letter was a legal document, trying to understand the true mood of the author, looking for hidden meanings, for loopholes he might grasp to influence the direction of events. In the back of his mind he had a sudden vision of Allison leaving him in law school. She had left a note, too, afraid to face his anger. When his father left there had been no note.

Apparently Laurie still loved him and only needed to be convinced he loved her too. He did, so he figured he'd easily be able to persuade her to come back. That was his gift, his profession, persuading skeptical people to adopt his views. He would call upon those skills, and he would get his wife back. She would be at her best friend Mattie's house, that nosy trouble-making bitch with the fat ass. He would call her there and say what needed to be said.

Dillon saw Mattie's name and number, hastily scribbled in Laurie's lovely handwriting on an outfitter's calendar beside the wall phone. Laurie was everywhere around him, she had bought the beer, hung the calendar, filled the salt shaker and pepper mill. He started to dial, then stopped. He pressed the disconnect button and held it firmly with his thumb, and muttered to himself, "This is one of the most important moments of your life. Your future depends on the next few words out of your mouth." Resting his head against his fists, with the phone still clutched in his hand, he searched for the right words. But the arsenal of verbal skills he had spent his professional life perfecting now eluded him.

He dialed the number anyway.

"Mattie, this is Dillon. Laurie's not there by any chance, is she?"

"She's a bit upset at the moment, Dillon. It might not be a good idea to talk with her right now."

"Mattie, I've got to talk with her. Her timing's terrible. I planned a canoe trip for us this weekend, brought flowers home and everything. I've been sitting here bawling my eyes out. I can't give her up, Mattie, I love her. I've got to make her understand that. Please! Ask her to come to the phone."

"She just got back from her lawyer's. He told her not to discuss the divorce with you. She doesn't feel she can talk with you right now."

"Look, I'm not going to discuss any divorce with her. I don't want a divorce. I want to apologize. I want to do whatever I have to do to get her to come back. I'll do anything she wants. I mean that. Anything."

"She says her lawyer was adamant about not having any contact with you. She doesn't feel she should ignore his advice. You of all people should understand that."

"You've got to be kidding. I'm her husband. I love her. No lawyer can tell me not to talk with my own wife. He's got no right. Laurie's my wife, for chrissake, she's my wife."

"We've been friends a long time, Dillon," Mattie said. "Please do me a big favor. Do yourself a big favor. Let it go for now. There'll be another opportunity. There'll be another time when you're both less emotional. This is not the time. I hope you can appreciate that."

"Mattie, you're being condescending."

"Dillon, you're being unreasonable."

"You put her up to this, didn't you, with all your feminist shit?"

"Have you been drinking?"

"Put my wife on the line, you fat bubble-butt bitch!"

"Bye, Dillon," Mattie said as she hung up.

Dillon slammed down the phone. He grabbed Laurie's letter and spat on it. He crumpled it forcefully into a ball and threw it across the room.

"Then fuck the bitch. If she won't even fuckin' talk to me, fuck her."

He strode angrily around the kitchen, kicking the chairs and the table legs.

The afternoon drifted into nightfall; more and more crumpled beer cans littered the kitchen floor. Dillon rose stiffly and walked the few steps to the refrigerator, grabbed the rest of the twelve-pack, staggered into the living room and threw himself on the couch. As the room darkened he continued to drink, lobbing the empty cans at a picture of Laurie.

"Her marriage vows mean nothing to her. A solemn oath in a goddamn church. *I need to be loved, Dillon.* Need to be loved! She must have a goddamn lover. *I need to be the only love in your life, Dillon.* Maybe she's fuckin' pregnant! Yeah, I'll bet the bitch screwed some asshole when I was out of town and she's got herself knocked up. Whoever the bastard is he's welcome to her whining dingbat bullshit. *I need your strength, Dillon.* You need my wallet, that's all you fuckin' need. Fuck off! *I need you to listen with interest to all the trivial shit I whine about all day.* Gimme a break. Oh, yes, ha, and I have to make her feel important. Important. Well you can kiss my spotty pink ass!"

He threw a half-filled can at her picture and missed. Then he thought about her pretty face looking up at him that winter day when she said she was ready to make babies and he started to cry, seeing in his mind's eye the two of them cross-country skiing with a little Dillon strapped to Laurie's back. *I want a family. You and me, Dillie, perfect parents, perfect.*

After a series of deep, chest-wrenching sobs, Dillon pulled himself together. Grabbing the phone from an end table, he dialed the number of the only person he knew would understand what he was going through. When she answered, he said, "My fucking wife's left me."

"Dillon?" said Allison Forbes.

"Who else would be loser enough to have his wife leave him?"

"Happens every day in our trade, hon."

"One minute she wants to make babies, the next she serves divorce papers."

"You've been drinking."

"Goddamn right. Nothing else to do 'round this shit hole, looking at pictures of her, smelling her on everything."

"I guess that's how Laurie must've felt."

"What the hell do you mean by that?"

"You tell me. Why'd she leave you?"

"Because she's a mindless cunt who wants to monopolize my entire life."

"Shhhhh, don't call her that. That's over the top, Dillon."

"Well for crying out loud, I'm supposed to make her feel *important*."

"I had the same thing. I got left because I cared more about my work than I did about my fiancé. Eric couldn't understand that I didn't want to travel with him or join the Peace Corps or feed the hungry children in some third world country. For all I know he's teaching lacrosse to some kids in darkest Africa."

"So that's why your heart looks more like the Liberty Bell than an instrument of love."

"You got a memory like a trap, counselor."

"Right now my memory's an instrument of torture. Laurie's letter reminded me of the letter you wrote me. God this hurts!"

"Dillon, we're not responsible for making other people happy. They need to make themselves happy and learn to live with us that way. A partnership is a hundred percent each, not fifty percent each. Laurie needs to take responsibility to make herself feel important."

"I knew you were the right person to call."

"I learned it all in very expensive therapy. You owe me a hundred bucks."

"I've never felt so down, Allie. I feel like I'm sinking through the floor."

"It takes about a month and two bottles of wine a night to get over it."

"Man!"

"So what are you going to do?"

"How should I know? She won't talk to me because her asshole lawyer told her not to."

Allison laughed.

"It's not funny."

"Not funny, no, but it is ironic."

"What the hell are you talking about?"

"Skip it. Look, you're hurt and angry. Maybe you're the one who wants a divorce."

"That's up to her."

"If it's up to her, she's already had her say. So that makes it up to you. Are you going to let her walk out of your life without a fight?"

"I'm not sure I'm interested in dealing with it now," Dillon said. "She's pissed me off royally."

"You've got your priorities screwed up. Laurie's more important to you than Ruth Bergstrom."

"Don't start, Forbes. Maybe in the long run, but Ruth Bergstrom's case is like a war. It's going on right now. Sometimes a man has to leave his family to go and fight. That's what Laurie can't seem to understand."

"Sounds to me like she understands perfectly, just like my handsome Minnetonka hunk did."

"Yeah? So what do you think I should do?"

"Back to the gym, buddy, get yourself in shape. Remember how good you used to feel when you worked out? You're a big man, Dillon. You have to work that body of yours. Right now your attitude's as flabby as your gut. It's always your attitude that gets you in trouble. You shut people out."

"I mean about Laurie."

"I do, too," Allison said. "You'll think more clearly if you spend more time working out and less time drinking beer. Lawsuits come and go, wives are forever, or should be, and it's about time you figured that out."

"Tell that to Laurie."

"Tell her yourself."

"The bitch won't talk to me."

"You'll have the chance, Dillon. Sooner or later there'll be an opportunity for you to make your peace with her. Just don't blow it when it happens."

"Thanks, Allie. It means a lot to me to talk to you this way."

"I've been there, Dillon. I know how hard it is, but no matter what happens, you'll survive."

Dillon hung up the phone, stumbled across the dark room, and turned on a porcelain lamp next to the television. The bulb blew, making him jump. Furious, he ripped the cord from the socket and smashed the lamp against a wall.

The beer was all gone and his bladder ached. He found a bottle of vodka in the kitchen cupboard and took it with him to the bathroom. He did not lift the seat as he urinated, and the stream kept missing and splashing his trousers. He took a mouthful of the vodka and looked at his swollen face in the bathroom mirror. "To hell with the bitch!" He said to the mirror. "She won't even talk with her own goddamn husband." He took another big swig and saw himself swaying. He felt a little sick. "I'll have that goddamn lawyer's ass. Fuckin' A, I'll have his ass for goddamn sure. Motherfucker."

Dillon stumbled back to the living room and collapsed on the couch, where he downed the rest of the vodka. He drifted like a man on a raft, muttering increasingly inarticulate curses against his faithless wife, until sleep took pity on him.

CHAPTER Fifteen

Boyd Campbell let himself into the EnviroClean offices at 6 A.M. and kicked the snow off his shoes. It was January, a year had passed without a resolution to the Bergstrom situation, and he could barely sleep unless he was completely exhausted; at least insomnia got him into work early. He made his way through the dark hallway and found Mary Frick waiting for him alone in the laboratory.

"Mary," he said, surprised, "what are you doing here so early?"

"I haven't been home yet. We've had a problem with our fermenters. I can't get enough bugs to meet our production needs."

"Why don't we have the lab techs jump-start the system with a shot of glucose?"

She stared at him, her eyes watering a little. "The lab staff up and quit last night, Boyd," she said. "It's just you and me."

"Oh," Boyd said, stunned. He set his brief case on the lab bench and rubbed his face.

"They were scared for their futures. I tried to talk them out of it, but I couldn't."

Boyd stared vacantly at Mary Frick, his mouth dry, and when she was about to continue he held up his hand and said, "I don't blame them. I understand. We look like a sinking ship. Not that I think of them as rats."

There was a long silence, then Mary said, "I've been trying to keep things going on my own, but it just won't work. We had a slight rise in the pH of the tanks, and some of the organisms were killed."

"You should've called me. I was awake anyway."

"No, Boyd. You're already here too much."

"How will we get the organisms grown, Mary?"

"We can either hire more people, or contract with that outside vendor we used before. That's about it. Otherwise, we'll have to shut down some of our job sites."

After a few moments of silence, Mary said, "There's one other thing, Boyd. Most of our vendors have put us on a C.O.D. basis now. I know it's none of my business, but, well, my heart and soul are here with our little company. I want to do anything I can to help out."

"You're a real trouper, Mary," Boyd said. "I appreciate your loyalty. Things are tight, you know, with the delays in our public offering. But we'll get through it all right. Henry Holten thinks the court's going to dismiss the lawsuit in a few weeks."

"Look," Frick said, "I know I speak for everyone in the company. We're all behind you 100 percent. Would it help if we all took reduced paychecks to tide you over for a while?"

"No way. Forget it."

"You can always make it up to us after the public offering's completed. I want to help out, boss, and I know the others feel the same way."

"You're truly generous, Mary," Boyd said. "And I'm touched by your offer. I'm meeting tomorrow with Henry Holten and Geoffrey Firestone to work out some bridge financing, so we should be able to get through the winter."

"Well that's something."

"It's a start. Now you go on home and get some sleep."

"And the fermenters?"

"I'll call BioTech this morning and get them to grow some bugs for us like they did once before. When the bridge financing's in place in a few weeks we can replace the staff and resume normal production."

Boyd left Mary Frick in the lab and headed for his office. Once he was alone he collapsed into his chair and let his façade of strength dissolve; he gazed vacantly at the ceiling. The tranquil security of his lab at the university was only a distant memory, separated by five and a half years of enthusiastic anticipation and fulfillment and a seemingly endless year of fear and frustration as the Bergstrom case inched slowly through the courts. The dreams that had excited him as a research scientist now left him dispirited and depressed as an entrepreneur.

He could not focus his thoughts. He revolved his chair and stared through the window behind his desk. He was immediately mesmerized by a light snowfall backlit by a street light. Gusty winds whirled the frozen crystals about and flung them against the window at his feet. The tempest outside, he thought, was far more hospitable than the chaos of his inside world.

Amy Wilcox arrived at eight o'clock and stuck her head through his door. "Deep in thought?" she asked. Boyd, swiveling his chair to face his secretary, forced an uneasy smile and replied, "I've got the beginnings of one whale of a headache."

"Can I get you something?" she asked.

"Nah. I'll be all right. Thanks."

"Sorry to hear about the lab techs. Pretty unfair of them just to leave you in the lurch like that."

"You know, Amy," Boyd said, "I was actually thinking about the Bergstroms. It's a bit strange, I know. These people are suing me. They've stalled the IPO that we desperately need to breathe some life back into the company. And if they happen to win, they'll destroy my entire life's work, everything I've tried to build during the last ten years. I should despise these people. But I don't. I don't even dislike them."

"What's brought all this on?" Amy asked.

"Oh, God, you'd never guess. I did something weird back in the fall. I wanted to meet those people ever since I got their letter, just to talk with them, to extend my sympathy for what they must be going through. And, you know, I've always felt that if only I could talk things over with them, they'd realize our bugs were not the problem. But that sort of thing never happens in a legal proceeding. I'm only supposed to talk with my lawyers, and the Bergstroms talk only with theirs. Then the lawyers supposedly talk with one another. In reality they don't talk at all. They argue. Kathleen even tried calling the Bergstroms one day last spring just to connect, you know. Ruth Bergstrom seemed pleasant and receptive, but when Henry found out, he had a fit and told me never to call them again. We'd just say something that'd compromise our position in the case. That's what he said anyway."

"He may be right."

"I don't know," Boyd said. "But when Henry told me not to talk with them, I figured at least I could see where they lived. I thought maybe I could learn something about the people who were suing me, seeing their house and all. That's pretty naïve, I guess. Anyway, I looked up their address, figuring I might as well go for a run in their neighborhood as anywhere else. In my mind I pictured this house sitting next door to a gas station, run down and poorly maintained, with old cars and junk lying around the yard cluttering up the place. I figured it would look like the house of some deceitful freeloaders who spent their days scheming for a free meal ticket at somebody else's expense, whatever the house of a freeloader is supposed to look like. That's what I thought anyway. So I got in my car and drove over there. I felt like a naughty boy doing something I knew my mother wouldn't approve of, so I ran around the neighborhood for a while to build up my courage. As I said, this was last fall, late September I think, and despite the beautiful morning I was scared just to see their house, for pity's sake. Finally, there I was, self-conscious and sweating outside their neat, well-kept house."

Boyd stood up and faced the blowing snow outside.

"What I saw was the face of a man, presumably Arne Bergstrom, staring forlornly from a big front window. I'll never forget it. The face was barely visible above the sill. I don't think of myself as someone who understands people at all well. I'm not sure I can read anything in a face, but the emptiness of this man's gaze struck me as so sad. I haven't been able to shake it. It was like all his zest for life was gone. What had brought that look to his face, staring from a window at six o'clock in the morning? I can only imagine it was Ruth Bergstrom's illness. It's been four months since I ran past their house, and I still can't forget that look on his face."

"That's incredible," Amy said.

"Our eyes met briefly and we nodded to one another, and then he ducked away for some reason. I thought of going up and talking to him, but instead I turned away and pretended to inspect our job site next door."

"Why didn't you just go on up and say hello?" Amy said. "You were standing right there looking at each other."

"In retrospect I wish I had," Boyd replied. "When he nodded back at me, I thought for an instant maybe he might even know who I was and want to talk with me. But he just sat there by the window. Then I realized he couldn't possibly know me, so I figured it'd be unfair to take him by surprise like that."

"It would've been a nice gesture," Amy said.

"That's what Kathleen said. But I just couldn't bring myself to walk up those steps."

"Well, I suppose that's what the lawyers are paid for anyway, to do the talking for you."

Boyd paused for a moment, as though he were focusing on Amy's last remark. "I know I'm not responsible for the condition in which I found Arne Bergstrom. Our bugs cannot cause the neurological injuries Ruth Bergstrom has apparently suffered. There's no doubt in my mind. Yet somehow I find myself attracted to this family because of the tragedy of their lives. I want to do something to improve their situation. Actually, it's not just something I want to do, it's something I need to do. I need to do it for myself. This has been bothering me for months now. Does any of that make sense to you, Amy?"

"You're a fine person, Boyd," Amy replied. "What do you have in mind?"

"I wish I knew," Boyd said.

The weather outside turned into a blizzard. Boyd sat back in his chair and swung around once again to face the storm. The wind howled, and tree branches brushed noisily against the side of the building. The drumming of ice crystals against the window and the pandemonium produced by the howling wind created a mesmerizing cacophony that partially drowned out the turmoil of the day.

"My morning run's the one thing that's kept me sane," he said with his back to Amy. "Look at it out there. I can't even do that now."

Amy walked around Boyd's desk and stood next to him, watching the storm. "It won't last forever," she said.

Eventually Boyd said, "Let's keep this conversation between ourselves. I'm not sure it would be productive if this discussion found its way back to Henry Holten."

CHAPTER Sixteen

Dillon awoke to the stench of his own vomit. His head clanged with a hangover. He could not at first recall what had happened the night before. Then the sports bar came back to him, and then the Super Bowl playing on a huge screen. The waitresses all had big breasts, and the drunker he got, the more obnoxious his behavior became. He remembered some snippets of dialogue, lustful gropings, things which made him cringe now. He could barely remember his companions. He could not remember who won the game. He could not remember driving home but had obviously thrown himself on the bed fully clothed. The bed reeked of vomit, beer, and stale cigarette smoke. He staggered into the bathroom and retched into the toilet, producing nothing but dry heaves, before turning on the shower and stepping fully clothed into the spray.

As the hot water beat on his head, he began to remember more. There were two women who spent a lot of time at the bar with him. He bought drinks for them and finally propositioned one of them. She turned him down flat. It seems she objected to his attitude, to his being rude and insisting on talking about himself all night, about what a big shot lawyer he was and how this case he had was going to make his name. She was not thrilled to discover he was married even when he swore up and down he was separated from his wife. That only seemed to make it worse.

With the emotional clarity that often accompanies a hangover he could recall all the feelings of rejection starting with his father. Add to that Allison and Laurie and all the law firms that did not even want to recruit him, and last night's unsuccessful try at seduction was just more proof that he was a loser who could not even get laid on Super Bowl Sunday by a woman in a bar. She had obviously been looking to hook up with somebody.

Months of sexual frustration and self pity welled up in him and he wanted to cry. He had not been with a woman since before Laurie walked out, his neglect was one of the reasons she left. Even in his debilitated state he could feel the anger start up again. 'Bitch,' he thought. Then he remembered how close he had come to scoring the night before. 'All women are bitches,' he thought. 'They lead you on and then walk away, everybody walks away.'

Viciously he kicked off his filthy clothes, rubbed a great handful of all-purpose body wash into his beard, and massaged his scalp vigorously in a futile effort to dull the pain that throbbed in his temples. He guzzled the hot water as it fell on his face, then lathered his whole body until it tingled. His butt felt crusty and he could smell his own armpits. Realizing dimly that he had not actually bathed like this in several days, he trampled the now sudsy clothing under his feet, so as to save money on laundry. Laurie would not have let him get away with this lifestyle.

He made his way naked to the kitchen, kicking aside piles of empty beer cans, opened the refrigerator, and forced down a twelve-ounce can of V-8 juice. He tossed a couple of Pop-Tarts into the toaster. Leaning against the counter, he rubbed the throbbing sides of his head and waited impatiently for the Pop-Tarts to brown.

Next to the toaster was the crumpled letter that had precipitated his misery. The wad of paper caught his attention, and a sharp pain shot across his chest. Laurie's letter and the divorce papers had been lying next to the toaster for nearly four months. He saw them every day, and every day he meant to do something about them. "Fucking bitch," he muttered to himself as the Pop-Tarts sprang up in the toaster.

He sat on a stool next to the counter and stuffed the pastries into his mouth. But his attention was riveted on Laurie's wadded letter. He reached for it, pried open the crumpled pages and pressed out the wrinkles over the edge of the counter top. After staring at the letter for a moment he tossed it aside and went upstairs to dress for work.

He pulled on a pair of khakis and an old sweatshirt. He sucked in his stomach to fasten the button above the fly, but it popped off and shot across the room and rolled under the dresser, leaving frayed threads. Without the button he could not zip his fly to the top, so he threaded a belt through the loops of his pants to hold both sides together while he worked at the zipper once more.

He grabbed the beige corduroy jacket that had been hanging from the top of the closet door for several days and went downstairs, ignoring the wet clothing soaking in the shower and the vomit-stained sheets on his bed. He also ignored the beer cans strewn across the living room and kitchen floors, but for some reason he picked up Laurie's letter, folded it carefully and stuffed it into the inside pocket of his jacket.

When Dillon walked into the office around midmorning, Cindy was on the war-path.

"You got a new shipment from Holten's crew this morning," Cindy said through gritted teeth. "You're not going to like what you see, especially if you feel as bad as you look. I've moved the chairs out of the reception area, and the boxes are stacked up over there. God only knows what you're going to do with all that stuff."

Dillon tossed his jacket on the chair next to his desk and poured himself a cup of coffee.

"Have you got enough sense yet to give up this craziness?" Cindy asked.

"For chrissake, Cindy, not this morning," Dillon replied. "I've got one helluva a headache."

"This case has destroyed your practice, ruined your finances and wrecked your marriage. How much more is it going to take for you to come to your senses and give up?"

"The more I get backed into a corner, the more I fight. I'm never going to give it up."

"What you are you going to fight with, Dillon? You're out of money."

"I'm selling the house," he said, "so we'll get some money to pay Howard and Jim. And I was wondering about your niece Barbara, didn't you say she was looking for a part-time job? Is she still available?"

"If she needs the money badly enough, maybe she'll come in despite what I plan to tell her about you," Cindy replied.

"Loyalty to your employer," Love said. "That's your greatest virtue, Cindy."

"Loyalty's a virtue about which you obviously know precious little, Dillon."

"I spoke with Ken Butler yesterday about our final testing protocol," Love said. "And our investigator, Joe Clapp, is ready to lay out his findings."

"Was it them you were drinking with last night?"

"Yes."

"Fool. You should see yourself."

"All right. It was supposed to be a working session, but the Super Bowl was on and we didn't get much done. Can you call them? I'd like to get everyone together here tonight to develop a game plan."

"Game plan? Do you think this is a game?"

Dillon glared at her and said, "You know what I mean. Stop being so stupid."

"This is my last day," Cindy said. "I can't stand it here anymore."

"Order in a couple of pizzas before you go," Love said.

"You're such a bastard. Order in your own goddamn pizza."

Dillon spent the rest of the day reading the new discovery demands and deposition notices that had arrived from Darby & Witherspoon. He would get Howard Canon and Jim Fine going on preparing responses and drafting his own discovery requests and interrogatories.

The mail also contained copies of the decision of the court of appeals reversing Judge Cleveland's order of mediation on the basis that she had exceeded her authority by ordering mediation against the wishes of both parties to the case. However, the appellate court refused to disqualify Judge Cleveland, as Henry Holten had so vehemently argued.

Dillon smiled at this, one of his small victories. "That sure as hell isn't going to make Judge Cleveland any great friend of Henry Holten. I bet the son of a bitch is still fuming."

He went to the file cabinet and tossed out his own crumpled and coffee-stained copies of the decision and replaced them with the snowy white ones from Darby & Witherspoon. "Keep it coming, you assholes," he said, laughing harshly.

Joe Clapp and Ken Butler arrived around six thirty. Barbara Hansen, Cindy's niece, was still available, in spite of Cindy's warnings to her, and was able to attend the strategy session, along with Howard Canon and Jim Fine.

"Thanks for coming on such short notice, folks," Love said after everyone was seated. "I've ordered a couple of pizzas. Should be here in a minute. Ken, what's left to do to complete your engineering work?"

"A lot. We've not had much luck with our recent genetic testing and can't tie EnviroClean to any bacteria that may have infected Mrs. Bergstrom. As we expected, no suspicious bacteria have been found by the Mayo Clinic. All we've got is the report from the pathologist there. He identified a chemical toxin believed to have caused Mrs. Bergstrom's symptoms. Unfortunately, they haven't been able to learn where the chemical came from. It could be from the P-27, but it could just as well have come from a host of other sources. I've even examined several samples of P-27 furnished by Darby & Witherspoon, but none of them contained the chemical identified at the Mayo Clinic."

"No pizza for you tonight," Love joked.

"But my theory still holds up," Butler replied. "As Dr. Gauss reported, some bacteria are capable of producing toxic compounds as part of their own process of metabolism. Assume for the moment that the P-27 is capable of doing this, even though we haven't been able to replicate it in the laboratory. Mrs. Bergstrom would probably have been exposed to P-27 over a long period of time, so the bacteria could easily have established a foothold in her system. Once it entered her body, it could very well have continued to produce the toxin until eventually she became severely ill. We know Dr. McCosh gave her antibiotics when he first saw her, which would have killed the bacteria but not the chemical they had produced. This explains why the Mayo doctors didn't find P-27 but did find the toxin. All we have to do is prove that P-27 can produce this toxin in the first place."

"When will that be done?" Love asked.

"I'm already on it," Butler said. "I've isolated small amounts of this same chemical from the soil samples we obtained at the creek. I ran them through chromatographic analysis, and they match the Mayo samples perfectly. That proves that the creek bed is the source of her exposure. And that definitely points the finger at the gas station, and at the P-27. Unfortunately, I've not been able to replicate this with the P-27 itself. I just can't get it to produce the toxin. But here's the rub. The P-27 Darby & Witherspoon finally handed over to us rendered no genetic match to the bugs we recovered from the creek. That's the problem. The samples don't match. It smells a little fishy to me. Why don't the samples match?"

"Holten's playing games with us, that's why," Love snapped. "What do you think?"

"Well, I'm only guessing, but I suspect a little detective work would not be a bad idea."

"Maybe the stuff we got from EnviroClean was not the same bug they used at the job site," Clapp said. "Maybe they changed bugs along the way. Maybe they had some quality control problems and got a different batch for that job. Maybe they ran out of bugs and had to order some from another source."

"Or maybe there's some chemical in the soil at that site that caused a mutation of the EnviroClean organisms," Butler added. "Hell, we don't know, we're just speculating. This could be a wild fishing expedition in a fished-out lake."

"Anyone else got a better idea?" Clapp asked. "If not, we can't take a chance. We've got to check it out."

"I sure as hell don't trust Darby & Witherspoon," Love said. "They've got precious little incentive to help us find the right bugs, and they have every reason to lead us astray. If EnviroClean uses different organisms, Holten may simply have given us a clean batch."

"I'll do a little midnight snooping," Clapp said. "I'll look in the dumpsters behind the company's plant and at their job sites. I've found a shit load of evidence in the enemy's garbage in other cases. How much you want to spend on this?"

"Whatever it takes," Love said. "You find the evidence. I'll find the money."

"I don't want to tell you how to do your business," Clapp continued, "but it might be wise to sift through all these boxes. I have a hunch there's something interesting in there."

"Well then, sweetheart," Love said to Barbara Hansen, "I guess we're about to find out how good you are."

"You mind telling me what I'm looking for?" Hansen asked.

"Anything that might explain why the two organisms don't match," Love said. "Could be some internal memorandum, some lab records, correspondence, invoices, purchase orders. Could be just about anything. In the meantime, Jim, I want you to put together a draft of interrogatories to EnviroClean asking for information about their P-27. I want to know if they grow all their own organisms in their own fermenters, or whether they purchase some from outside vendors. I want to know if they've ever made any changes in the formulation of P-27. Howard, you get going on our discovery responses and put some witness kits together for each of the depositions that are coming up. I'm going to be pretty much out of commission for the next thirty days attending all the depositions Allison Forbes has noted."

The pizza boy arrived at the front door, which was mostly blocked by the stacks of newly arrived banker's boxes from Darby & Witherspoon. Love made his way through the reception area and pried open the door just enough to reach through for a couple of pizza boxes and two six-packs of beer. He cleared a mound of papers from his desk and tossed them into a corner. Barbara Hansen sniffed and said, "I hope you're not expecting me to pick those up."

Love laughed and said, "I can tell you're your aunt's niece, Barb. You'll do just fine."

The group pulled chairs around the desk and cracked open cans of beer.

"These David and Goliath legal battles aren't everything that the romantics make them out to be," Love quipped. "The modern day David needs a hell of a lot more than a rock and a slingshot. This is one hell of a lot of work."

"Let's hope we're playing from the right script," Butler said. "At the moment, I feel more like Don Quixote."

"Let's make no mistake about who we are," Love said. "Our enemy's no illusion, and this P-27's no windmill. It's a monster, a real monster, threatening real people, people like Ruth Bergstrom. And the excruciating pain she suffers every day of her life is real. We've got one helluva battle to fight, and we damn well better win it. Let's also not forget that there are thousands of Ruth Bergstroms out there, good people who are invariably taken advantage of by corporate tyrants whose lifeblood is profit and greed. Boyd Campbell doesn't care about people. He doesn't care about their lives and families. He cares about money. Well, we're going to take his money away from him and give it to Ruth Bergstrom."

"I don't know," Butler said. "You can worry about all that stuff if you like. For me, either we match the bacteria or we don't."

Later, encouraged for no particular reason, Love climbed into his Jeep and headed home. The house, dark as a grave, stank. He thought about cleaning up a bit, washing his bed sheets and throwing yesterday's soaked clothes into the dryer, but his headache was back, so he threw himself on the living room couch and was soon fast asleep.

CHAPTER Seventeen

Allison Forbes looked up from her papers and caught the sad and dejected gaze of Arne Bergstrom across the courtroom. After a moment he looked at his wife and pulled some unruly hair away from her face. He had the eyes of a gentle man whose energy and enthusiasm had been sapped through months of struggling with the health of the woman he loved. This impression disturbed Allison, and in spite of herself she looked at the frail figure of Ruth Bergstrom slumped in a wheelchair next to her husband. She saw the body of a woman who was crippled and pathetic, barely able to sit upright despite the belt around her waist that held her firmly in the chair. Allison also saw a remarkable, kindly warmth radiating from the emaciated woman's face. The face smiled, unnerving Allison so that she coughed, looked nervously down at her papers and shuffled them aimlessly.

Behind Henry Holten and the Darby & Witherspoon litigation team sat Boyd Campbell and his wife. Boyd looked tired and forlorn, much like the Bergstroms. Allison was struck by how, despite his long-standing discomfort, his personality still projected warmth and sincerity; he was similar in this way to the Bergstroms, and Allison suddenly wanted to be like them, and not like herself, sitting next to the dour Henry Holten who glared at everyone like an Old Testament patriarch. Suddenly she hated his pretentious red bow tie. A lump rose in her throat and she looked across at Dillon who sat at the other table with two male assistants. She wondered if he was feeling the same sorrow at having to pursue this case. She hoped so. Dillon looked much thinner in the face and he had finally bought a suit, which made his large frame look slimmer. He had even visited a barber and was looking neater than usual, although not as obsessively neat as her colleagues. He caught her looking at him and flared his nostrils at her. That was just what she needed; stinking bastard, she would kick his arrogant ass.

As Judge Cleveland entered everyone stood. Allison looked again at Arne Bergstrom and saw a peculiar look of fear in his face. He looked ill. She hardened her heart and prepared to cause another setback in his life. Henry Holten fiddled with papers through the preliminaries, shooting dirty looks at Pamela Cleveland who shot them back, so that Allison felt a sense of relief when she finally stood to address the court.

"Your Honor," she began, "today is March 21, and, as the court well knows, this case has now been scheduled for trial on May 29, less than three months away. It has been pending for over a year, during which time there has been extensive discovery, including over twenty-five lengthy depositions, and production of more than one hundred thousand documents. A score of experts have conducted virtually every imaginable test to determine the cause of Mrs. Bergstrom's illness. I think it safe to say that no stone has been left unturned.

"And where have all the time and colossal expense we've invested into this case gotten us? Nowhere. It's all been wasted. Your Honor, the plaintiffs are no closer today to proving the microorganisms from EnviroClean's P-27 caused Ruth Bergstrom's illness than they were the day their lawyer filed this frivolous law suit. We've been forced to spend hundreds of thousands of dollars defending ourselves in this spurious litigation. My client has suffered enormous financial hardships. The company has been unable to proceed with its planned public stock offering because of the shadow hanging over its future by virtue of this lawsuit. Its cash position is desperate and its future is hanging by a thread. The jobs and economic well-being of the many fine EnviroClean employees are in jeopardy. And perhaps worst of all, the public is effectively being denied the use of a product that has been proven effective time and time again in eliminating highly toxic chemicals that have been leaking for decades from the underground storage tanks of tens of thousands of gas stations throughout the United States.

"It's time to put a stop to all this. It's time to force Dillon Love to come forward and tell this court exactly what evidence he has that the P-27 caused Ruth Bergstrom's illness. With less than three months until trial, we must now begin our extensive and costly final preparations. We should not be required to incur this further hardship and expense when there's no direct evidence against EnviroClean.

"Let me review the evidence as it now stands and the holes in that evidence. We know from the Mayo Clinic that Mrs. Bergstrom is suffering from eosinophilia-myalgia syndrome, or EMS. This disease often produces severe neurological dysfunction, including quadriparesis and paralysis of the respiratory system. Fortunately, Mrs. Bergstrom's illness has not progressed this far, and she still has limited use of her arms and does not require ventilator support. Her mental function is normal, except for some impairment of her short-term memory. She's able to live at home with her husband and two children.

"There are a variety of causes of this condition, including allergic reactions, parasitic infections, and long-term ingestion of certain triggering substances. In this case, the Mayo Clinic suspects there was a triggering agent, and it has identified an unknown contaminant by chromatographic analysis. The theory Mr. Love is advocating against my client is that the P-27 produced this triggering chemical. Unfortunately for him, neither the Mayo Clinic nor any other laboratory has made the same leap of faith.

"There are several significant gaps in his chain of proof, gaps which are absolutely fatal to his case. First, the Mayo Clinic has not found any P-27 in Mrs. Bergstrom's blood or tissue. P-27 is actually a species of bacteria known as pseudomonas, a very common organism, generally harmless to human beings. The Mayo Clinic has taken numerous blood and tissue samples in an attempt to culture some organism that might be the cause of her illness. Pseudomonas was never found.

"Second, not a single doctor or other scientist is prepared to say that pseudomonas can cause EMS. Indeed, Mrs. Bergstrom's own physicians at the Mayo Clinic don't believe it caused her EMS. On the contrary, they found a toxic chemical in her blood which they believe was the source of her illness. That chemical is not contained in P-27, and that fact is verified by opposing counsel's own witnesses. So Ruth Bergstrom had to have been exposed to it from some other source.

"Third, none of the scientists involved in this case has been able to match the pseudomonas found in the creek bed with those contained in P-27. They are different. They had to have come from some source other than EnviroClean.

"Fourth, plaintiffs have no explanation for how Mrs. Bergstrom could have been exposed to the P-27. How did it find its way into her bloodstream from the soil beneath the gas station, more than fifty feet from her house? Despite all the depositions and investigations that we have undertaken in this case, there's no explanation for this critical supposition advanced by the plaintiffs. P-27 does not have wings to fly, Your Honor, and Mrs. Bergstrom was not drinking water from that creek.

"Fifth, there's no evidence that P-27 has caused EMS or any other illness to anyone other than Mrs. Bergstrom. If this is such a dangerous product, why would there be no evidence of other people becoming infected at one of the many other sites where P-27 has been used to clean up leaking underground storage tanks? Why would no one else in her family have gotten sick? Not Arne Bergstrom, and neither of their two young children? Why not the people at EnviroClean who work with the organism in the plant? Why not the people at the job sites who inject it into the soil? Why is she the only person in the world who has gotten sick?

"Your Honor, we've had at least a dozen medical doctors, molecular biologists, geneticists, and environmental engineers study every last detail of this case. These people are distinguished scientists with impeccable credentials. In fact, even Mr. Love has had some yet unidentified engineer and physician review the facts of this case. Not a single scientist, including Mr. Love's own, has offered an opinion that the P-27 is the cause of Mr. Bergstrom's EMS. Not one! Indeed, not a single medical doctor has advanced the opinion that P-27 can cause any injuries to human beings. They have no study to show it's harmful, because it's not harmful, a fact long ago proven by EnviroClean's own pre-market studies and tests of P-27.

"At the beginning of this case I called some of these problems to the attention of the court and opposing counsel. I asked for a dismissal of the case at that time to avoid all the expenses we have subsequently incurred. It was understandable that the court would at least want to give counsel an opportunity to develop his case, to give Ruth and Arne Bergstrom a chance to have their day in court. They have now had that chance. Their attorney has had that chance. Their scientific consultants have had that chance. It's time now, finally, to put an end to this litigation so my client can get on with the rest of his life."

Allison sat down. Henry Holten's eyes bored into her, but she could not fathom their meaning.

"Mr. Love?" Judge Cleveland said simply.

Dillon walked around to the front of the counsel table, looked around the court, and began, "Thank you, Your Honor. We have not come here as scientists defending a dissertation in molecular biology before a group of academicians. We make no pretense that our investigations satisfy the rigors of scientific certainty that may be demanded by such institutions. Nor are we held to that standard. As the court well knows, our burden of proof is very limited. We need not prove with scientific certainty that Ruth Bergstrom's EMS was caused by P-27, we don't have to prove unequivocally that it's true. We need only establish that this is more likely true than not true.

"The law permits us to satisfy this burden of proof by direct evidence, or we can do it by circumstantial evidence. It makes no difference under the rules of the court. While science may not permit circumstantial evidence, the law does. Do I wish I had solid, scientifically undisputed proof? Most certainly. Do I have any obligation to produce such proof? Most certainly not.

"Your Honor, we've satisfied our legal obligations, because we have amassed considerable circumstantial evidence that the P-27 caused my client's illness. Let me summarize some of the salient points for you. We know that Ruth Bergstrom lived in her house without incident for fifteen years. Her husband and his family had lived in the house without incident for twenty-five or thirty years before that. Nothing in the neighborhood changed during all that time, and the residents of that quiet neighborhood lived without incident year after year.

"Then one day EnviroClean decided to create a new form of life. Its genetic engineers took apart the DNA of some pseudomonas bacteria and rearranged the genes to create an entirely new organism. Your Honor, this is all undisputed. EnviroClean does not deny it has created this invisible monster. They created it, and they knew nothing about their new life form, except that it was apparently able to thrive deep underground and degrade gasoline and the toxic chemicals added to gasoline. They never considered that a microorganism powerful enough to prosper under such conditions and degrade something as toxic as gasoline might also be powerful enough to cause serious neurological injuries to human beings. These people came into the Bergstrom's neighborhood and injected millions of their genetically engineered organisms into the ground and forever changed the lives of Ruth and Arne Bergstrom.

"Your Honor, it's undisputed that these dangerous organisms leached through the soil and found their way into the creek bed behind the gas station. From there, they moved with the hydrological flow to the bank directly behind the Bergstroms' home. This is undisputed because both defense counsel and I have had this soil tested, and both of us have found these mutant bacteria in the Bergstroms' backyard.

"We also know, because it has been published in the *New England Journal of Medicine*, perhaps the most prestigious of all medical journals, that similar species of pseudomonas have produced similar neurological dysfunction in other people. Counsel complains that we have no proof that the precise species of pseudomonas involved in this case have been shown to cause such symptoms in any scientific study. Counsel would have us undertake some experiment to inject a group of people with these mutant organisms to see if they get sick.

"As far as I know, Your Honor, no one from Darby & Witherspoon has volunteered to take part in such a study. They have 250 lawyers in the firm, and not one of them has offered to help their client by submitting to such a procedure. They have it within their own power to prove me wrong, but they do not dare to try the experiment. Apparently they are not all as interested in scientific proof as Ms. Forbes would have this court believe.

"We also know that the Mayo Clinic has studied this matter quite thoroughly. Dr. Richard Gauss heads a team of physicians and technical support people who have conducted this investigation and who have treated Mrs. Bergstrom's devastating injuries. These renowned physicians have concluded that Mrs. Bergstrom had some exposure to a toxic substance and that this contaminant was the cause of her injuries. They've run gas chromatographic analysis of some blood and tissue samples and identified a suspected contaminant, which they've labeled as 'Peak E' on the graph. Your Honor, I've included in the appendix to my brief copies of two graphs produced by gas chromatography. Please take a look at these, because they are most interesting and extremely important to this case. Notice that the first graph is of a normal tissue sample and the second graph is a tissue sample from Mrs. Bergstrom. Notice also the one large peak on the second graph, Peak E, that's not present in the normal sample. This is what caused her injuries.

"The Mayo Clinic has yet to identify precisely what this Peak E actually is, but they do know it's toxic and that it could have been produced as a part of the process of metabolism by some microorganism. They cannot conclusively say the organism was P-27, but they can say that related pseudomonas have produced similar human responses.

"Dr. Gauss can also say that Ruth Bergstrom was most likely exposed to the contaminant for several months. Your Honor, I have an environmental engineer who has calculated the amount of time necessary for the P-27 to move through the soil and leach into the creek behind the gas station. Using that information we have been able to calculate that Mrs. Bergstrom would first have been exposed to the bacteria about three months before she started having noticeable symptoms. That's entirely consistent with the etiology projected by Dr. Gauss.

"EnviroClean has come forward with no proof of its own. Ms. Forbes says EnviroClean and its lawyers have spent hundreds of thousands of dollars studying this problem. Presumably much of that money has been spent trying to establish some other cause of Ruth Bergstrom's illness. Obviously they have found no other explanation, or we'd be hearing all about it today. Given the tremendous circumstantial evidence pointing to P-27, and given the lack of any other reasonable explanation, this court has no choice but to allow this case to proceed to trial and let a jury decide which side is right. That's all we ask, our one and only chance to present our evidence to a jury. This is Mrs. Bergstrom's constitutional right. This is what fairness and justice demand."

Dillon retreated behind his table and sat down. The courtroom became quiet.

Judge Pamela Cleveland sat back in her chair and looked at her sleeves, shaking her head slightly.

"I have before me four nice people and several clever, persuasive attorneys," she said finally. "Whatever decision I make will be the wrong decision, because no judgment I make can possibly do justice to the people whose lives have been entrusted to me. My power is frightening, but it is also limited. I can only say yes or no. I can allow or disallow a trial by jury. I have no other options. And because I have no other options, I cannot do what is right for all of the people in this room. It's unfair, but it's one of the limitations of the system.

"I'm going to take this matter under advisement for six hours. If I have to decide how to proceed with this case, I'll do so by 4:30 this afternoon. I know what I'm about to say will annoy Mr. Holten and Mr. Love, but I know in my heart this is the right course. Between now and then, I want all of you to meet to discuss settlement of the case. I'll make the jury room available to the defendants to caucus, and the plaintiffs can use the attorneys' conference room just outside the courtroom. I want you all to discuss your positions carefully and find some way to compromise those positions so this matter can be settled. That way you can all win. If either the jury or I decide the case, at least one of you will lose.

"Make no mistake about the importance I attach to everyone's genuine, good-faith participation in this settlement process. I'll have my clerk summon you at 4:30."

"Your Honor..." Love said rising from his seat.

"Your Honor," interrupted Henry Holten. "I appreciate the court's willingness to assist the parties in resolving this case. As I said before, it is a waste of time. We will make no offers and we will accept no offers. That's our final position. I must confess to being astounded at the court's persistence in pursuing this remedy."

"I agree," Love said. "This is the one thing we both agree on. We do not intend to compromise our position. We've demanded $5 million in settlement, and unless it's paid, we intend to go forward with our case."

Allison heard Kathleen Campbell gasp behind her.

She turned her head and her attention was caught by Ruth Bergstrom who was looking over at Boyd Campbell. As their eyes met for the first time during the year and a half since their lawsuit had been filed, Allison thought to herself that each of them looked bewildered. Having finally heard the opposing views argued so convincingly by their lawyers, they stared silently at each other, apparently uncertain for the first time about the probable outcome of the case. Allison saw only the pathos of a very sick woman, not the body of a battle-hungry seeker of easy riches.

She turned further and looked at Boyd Campbell who was slumped uncomfortably against the back of his seat with his arms stretched out along the bench. His unbuttoned suit coat fell open to the sides, revealing large rings of perspiration edging from under his arms towards the front of his shirt. His face was ashen.

Judge Cleveland was silent for a few moments while her face contorted with controlled anger. "I am the one astounded," she said in a very low voice. "No settlement? A $5 million claim? Let me briefly reiterate my position."

Henry Holten cast his eyes to heaven and flung himself back in his seat.

"Clearly," said Cleveland, "I am the only one who recognizes, and I might add have recognized from the outset of this case, its importance to both parties. I have the distinct impression that Boyd Campbell and Ruth Bergstrom would prefer to settle, but they have failed to do so on the advice of counsel. This makes the law look ridiculous, and I believe, as adherents to the legal codes which all the professionals in this room share, it behooves you, the litigators, to get the law out of trouble here. These people need our help. For me to decide for the plaintiff would require EnviroClean to spend considerable additional money, which it apparently doesn't have, to defend what is at best a weak case. It would further delay its public offering and create a dangerous cash flow shortage for the company. To find for the defendant would deny Ruth Bergstrom her day in court, her only opportunity to have a jury weigh the evidence and make a determination on the merits of the case. To deny her this chance would be a harsh and rare judicial procedure. Between you, you have the power to do the right thing. I'll see you all back here at 4:30." Cleveland rose from the bench, cutting off further discussion. "I hope you use the time wisely."

Allison jumped at the banging of the clerk's gavel. She turned with a look of sympathy to the Campbells, and saw Ruth Bergstrom's eyes meet Boyd's and him nodding in uneasy acknowledgment. This unauthorized contact with one another was quickly interrupted by the commotion of the lawyers packing up their files. Boyd Campbell was left staring at an empty chair as Henry Holten bolted from his seat and left the courtroom rapidly without explanation.

"What's gotten into him?" Campbell asked Allison.

"Beats me," she said. "I'll be right back."

Allison left the courtroom and hurried towards the elevator bank to chase down her mentor. The corridor was empty. Allison stood alone, wondering what to do. But she was not alone for long.

"It doesn't matter," Boyd Campbell said, suddenly next to her. "I'm sure Henry's quite comfortable leaving you in charge, and so am I."

"I just can't imagine what got into him," she said.

"Forget it," Campbell said. "What's our next move?"

"We try the case."

"What do you really want to do, Allison?" Campbell replied quickly. "Forget about Henry. Before we got into this damned mess, you seemed to be advocating a conciliatory approach. What's different now?"

"Henry never agreed with that approach," she said.

"I like that judge. She's right, I'd like to put all this behind me," Campbell said. "I can't take much more of it."

Allison thought for a moment. "I'll see if Dillon's softened up at all," she said. "Maybe he'll be more receptive after Judge Cleveland's appeal. I'll meet you back in the courtroom in a few minutes."

Dillon sat on a bench outside the courtroom with Arne Bergstrom, Ruth beside them in her wheelchair; he was whispering to them with great intensity. Their eyes looked glazed and troubled. Allison approached and said, "Got a minute?" He followed her a few paces down the hall without saying a word.

"Nice suit," she said.

"Thanks," he said, "I'm desperate."

"And you're working out again."

"Just because I can't afford to eat," he said, laughing.

"Look," she said, "Maybe we should see if we can find some common ground. This case is killing both our clients."

"Does your boss know you're talking to me?" Love asked. "Or are you flying solo?"

"Cut the crap, Dillon," she said tartly.

"I'm surprised at you, Allie. I thought you were hell-bent on getting that first notch on your pistol. You a little nervous maybe, with Horrible Henry shooting out of the courtroom like a maniac? What was that all about anyway?"

She shrugged, shook her head, tried to quench the frustration flooding through her. "Don't you think we have an obligation to our clients to work something out? Look at those two," Allison said, briefly turning her head in the direction of the Bergstroms. "They're exhausted. They'll never make it through a trial."

Dillon looked past Allison back toward the bench where he'd been sitting with the Bergstroms. "Goddamn it," he said loudly, pushing Allison aside and taking off down the hall. "What the hell do you think you're doing, Campbell?" he yelled. "Get away from my client."

Allison followed, feeling sick to her stomach. Boyd Campbell rose from his seat next to Ruth Bergstrom's wheelchair. "I'm so sorry," he said to her softly, as Dillon pushed himself between them.

CHAPTER Eighteen

Judge Cleveland resumed the bench at precisely 4:30. "My clerk advises me that you've made no progress toward settlement of this case," she said. "I can't express how disappointed I am. And I'm shocked that Mr. Holten has apparently dissociated himself from the process. I wish I had the power to force you to do more. Unfortunately, I have no such power. I'm going to deny the defendant's motion and allow this case to go to trial on May 29. It's only very reluctantly that I do so. Indeed, I'm not at all sure I'm doing the plaintiffs any favor by permitting the trial. I'm probably only delaying the inevitable. This is a very weak case. But, weak or not, I'm going to let a jury decide it. I want your pretrial submissions by May 15. I'll see you all on May 29."

With a wink at Allison, Dillon walked out of the courtroom with the Bergstroms and explained the significance of Judge Cleveland's decision. They would have their day in court at last. Regardless of the judge's belief that the case was weak, there would be six impartial people bringing a fresh perspective with them into the jury box. The jurors would probably be extremely sympathetic to Ruth and Arne, and this sympathy would give them a great advantage during the trial. In the meantime, there was a lot to be done to get the case ready. He assured the apparently shell-shocked Bergstroms that he would be working non-stop seven days a week.

Barb Hansen, Joe Clapp, and Ken Butler were already at the office waiting for Love when he returned with Howard Canon and Jim Fine. With arms raised, Love announced, "We go to trial May 29, people!"

The group cheered and Joe Clapp shook up a can of Budweiser

and sprayed beer over the celebrants. "Poor man's champagne," he shouted, tossing a can to each person. "Hot damn! That's good news. No jury will ever give the verdict to EnviroClean, it'll never happen."

"Give it the old college chug-a-lug, guys," Love said, already crumpling his can with one hand and throwing it across the room in the general direction of a wastebasket. "We've got work to do."

"Not so damn fast," Clapp said, tossing another Budweiser to Love. "Suck down another one of these puppies, you sure as shit can use a little mellowing out."

"I'll do my celebrating once we've won this goddamn case," Love replied. "But I will go and take off this goddamn monkey suit before you assholes ruin it. I'll need it May twenty-ninth!"

They all cheered again.

When Love returned from the back room in jeans, carrying a fresh twelve-pack, Joe Clapp, already a little more flushed in the face than he was fifteen minutes before, said, "Where the hell's Cindy, anyway? She sick or something?"

"Retired," mumbled Love, cracking open a beer.

"Retired? Right before trial? You must have one hell of a 401K around here."

"If you're sixty-five and quit, that's retiring."

Barb sat biting her cheek, looking quietly at the floor.

"Legal-speak," Clapp said. "So why'd she quit?"

"She couldn't take any more of me, Joe. I'm too much of an asshole."

"Damn, you're one helluva a ladies' man," Clapp said. "You got any women left in your life?"

"Ruth Bergstrom," Love said.

"What am I, chopped liver?" Said Barb.

"You'll never be in his life," said Ken Butler, "you're way too practical."

Everyone laughed and Love glared at Canon and Fine, who were not allowed to laugh as much as everyone else, but they laughed anyway and chugged their beers.

"Ruth Bergstrom's no woman," Joe Clapp laughed. "She's a case. And she'll be gone, too, in a few months."

"Then things'll get back to normal."

"You mean Laurie will come back?"

"Why not?"

"Bullshit. The Bergstrom case goes to a jury, and overnight you think you're just going to go suck up to Laurie and she'll hop back into the sack with you?" Clapp was still laughing. "For a good lawyer, you're one helluva dumb son of a bitch."

"You my investigator or some kind of goddamn therapist?"

"Don't matter to me," Clapp said. "I'll take your money either way."

"Then let's stick with something you're at least marginally qualified to do and get on with Ruth Bergstrom's case." Love turned away from Clapp and addressed Butler. "What's new on your end, Ken?"

"More dead ends, and no mutated organisms," Butler said.

"Stab me in the heart," Love said, feigning a mortal wound and falling back into his desk chair.

Clapp laughed and covered Love's face with the old corduroy jacket.

Butler continued, impervious to the by-play. "As you know, Joe snuck out to a few EnviroClean sites and picked up some empty canisters of P-27 from the dumpsters. He even got a couple from the gas station next to the Bergstroms. I had the lab look at every one. They're all the same, no Peak E toxin. Campbell's got good quality control going for him over at the plant. We also compared the organisms in the canisters with those I dug up earlier in the creek bed. The bugs from the creek are different. I have no idea where they came from, but they sure as hell didn't come from those canisters. Without a matching canister, we've got no way of proving the bad bugs came from EnviroClean. We have absolutely no link between the toxic substance in the creek bed and any P-27 produced by EnviroClean."

"Did you run any cultures on the canisters?" Love asked.

"Hell, I cultured everything, the bugs from every canister and the bugs from the creek bed. I ran gas chromatographs on all the samples. The samples from the creek bed produced a Peak E that matched the Peak E the Mayo Clinic obtained in its own studies of Ruth Bergstrom's blood. None of the samples from the EnviroClean canisters had that peak. What I've succeeded in proving is that EnviroClean's P-27 doesn't produce the Peak E contaminant that causes EMS, whereas the bugs of unknown origin do. EnviroClean will love the evidence I just manufactured for them. It proves they're innocent."

"Well," Love replied, "you got a match between the toxin in her blood and the toxin in the creek bed. That's no goddamn coincidence, you know."

"Except we can't prove where the toxin came from, and we can't prove how it got from the creek into her bloodstream without infecting anyone else."

"Well, you're the smart-ass engineer," Love said, "and you've got exactly ten weeks to figure it all out."

"If you've got something more for me to look at," Butler replied, "I'll be glad to run the tests. Right now, I'm out of leads and out of ideas."

"I've also drawn a blank on my document review," Barb Hansen put in. "I've looked at every last piece of paper we got from EnviroClean as well as everything we have from its suppliers. I've looked at their production records, batch records, batch test reports, purchase orders, and invoices. I found nothing unusual. There's no difference between the various batches of P-27, at least according to the records they've sent us. I've also looked at their lab notebooks. They've recorded every single lab and field test EnviroClean's run. These science dudes who run their laboratory and field studies for them had no reason to falsify their records. Just the opposite, the preservation of their hides depends on accuracy. And the notebooks are all in page-numbered hardbound binders, so sections could not have been destroyed later by someone trying to cover things up. There's not a single notation of any unusual or suspicious situations."

"I agree," Butler added. "I read over the lab records myself. They're all in perfect order."

"I've also looked at their internal corporate memoranda," Barb continued. "Sometimes in these cases we find memos by a disgruntled employee criticizing the operation for one reason or another. Not here. This is one hell of a cohesive group. We struck out with the memos."

"Is that it?" Love asked.

"I still haven't had time to review all the government documents that have been produced," Barb replied. "EPA, DNR, FDA, and Agriculture have all been out to the plant and stuck their noses into the poor guy's operation. There's a mountain of paperwork to go over, but I haven't had time to do that part of it yet. However, as far as I can tell, they've had no complaints with P-27, at least not from any of these agencies. I also checked state court filings. They've had no workers compensation claims from any employee becoming sick from the stuff, no other lawsuits, nothing. There are no letters from customers or neighbors next to other job sites in any of their records. I can't prove a single person has developed symptoms similar to Ruth Bergstrom's. Hell, I even called all the EPA field offices responsible for each of the sites EnviroClean is treating. No one at EPA had heard of this problem, not even a rumor. I don't know, Dillon. They look clean to me."

"Yeah? To me it looks like one friggin' major-league cover up," Love said.

"There's one small thing I did find that might be interesting," Barb added. "EnviroClean doesn't always grow their own bugs. It appears they've ordered shipments of bugs from off-site, since I found a couple of invoices from a company called BioTech Services, Inc. But I found nothing unusual in the records. Sorry I couldn't be of more help."

"Is that all you guys have for bad news?" Love asked. "Hell, I was really worried there for a while. There's nothing here that a little jury sympathy won't overcome. What about you, Joe? You been having bad hair days too?"

"At least I still got some hair," Joe Clapp replied.

"I'm impressed. What else you got?"

"Holten left court early today." Clapp said.

"I know, Clapper. I was there."

"But I know where he is, Dillweed. Holten's in Bermuda. Now isn't that interesting? The most important court hearing of the case, and he runs off to Bermuda. Well, this is no fucking vacation. He's got a client in Bermuda."

"That's ancient history," Love said, "Allison told me about that months ago."

"Yeah? Well it must be an important client for him to walk out in the middle of the hearing today and get the judge even more pissed off at him. I don't know the name of the client. Not yet anyway. But he went there with Wendi Palmer. You know who Wendi Palmer is, don't you? You sure as hell should, because she's one of your opponents. She's a biotech specialist with Darby & Witherspoon, part of the litigation team defending EnviroClean. So what are they doing in Bermuda? Frankly, I smell fish."

"Same odor I've smelled for months," Love said, crushing a beer can.

"By the way, Babs," Joe asked, "do you recall when it was that EnviroClean bought bugs from BioTech Services?"

"Sure. There were two shipments, both in July 1999," Barb Hansen said.

"July 1999! Here we go. That's around the time EnviroClean started on the project next to the Bergstroms," Clapp said. "If they purchased contaminated bugs from BioTech, the gas station could've gotten a few doses and there'd be no batch samples at EnviroClean for us to find. EnviroClean would have no records. It would also explain why there's no match between the bugs Ken dug up in the creek and the bugs in the EnviroClean canisters. The bugs in the creek could've come from BioTech." Clapp stroked his chin in mock contemplation. "I just might have to pay them an unofficial visit."

His face burning, Love looked hard at his team. "I sense a breakthrough, people," he said.

"Way cool," Barb Hansen said as the men all high-fived each other.

CHAPTER Nineteen

Arne Bergstrom wheeled Ruth from the lobby of the Mayo Clinic to their waiting van in the parking ramp next to the building. After completing the tedious task of transferring Ruth from her wheelchair to the front seat of the van, he folded the chair, loaded it in through the sliding door behind her, and walked, yawning, around the van, heaving himself behind the wheel.

Arne tried to conceal his exhaustion from Ruth, but he supposed that the effort was futile, her being so observant. The last several weeks had proved increasingly difficult. Arne thought how helpless he was, just watching his wife deteriorate with no real solution in sight. Her physicians appeared to be bystanders just like everyone else. They did tests, poked and prodded her, sent her back home, and still she got worse. His mother had died young, and this looked like it was turning into a repeat of that nightmare. He tried to keep all the implications out of his mind, and, despite the assurances of the doctors that Ruth was not contagious, the constant worry that the kids might somehow come down with Ruth's illness compounded his anxiety.

Tonight he would forget all of it.

"Ruthie," Arne said as they pulled out of the parking lot, "tonight's your lucky night. I'm taking you out to dinner."

"Oh, wow," she gasped, "I hope you're not kidding."

Perhaps a half dozen times during their marriage, Arne had organized unexpected dinners alone with his Ruthie. The announcement never failed to surprise her. It was a little something he learned from his father, whom Arne remembered as having always treasured his mother. Arne made all the arrangements himself, usually selecting a small, upscale restaurant with a cozy atmosphere. The evenings had always been memorable for their warmth and intimacy, and he felt bad that he had not done this since Ruth became ill.

"You're such an incredible sap," Ruth said, her eyes bright with excitement.

Ruth reached for her purse, which Arne had placed between the two front seats. Her arms had very little strength and she needed all of it to lift the purse onto her lap. Clumsily, she pulled open the zipper and reached inside for a handkerchief, wiping tears from her eyes.

"I love you with all my heart, Arne. God only knows how I wish I could still love you with all my body, too." Her eyes welled up anew and she dabbed them again with her hanky. "Where on earth could you possibly take me looking like this?"

Arne smiled and said, "You'll see when we get there. I have big plans for you tonight."

The drive from the Mayo Clinic back to Minneapolis took about two hours, but the time passed quickly. It was a beautiful afternoon with crisp late-March temperatures and clear blue skies which faded to light orange on the western horizon as they saw the Minneapolis skyline approaching to the north. Arne drove directly downtown, bypassing their normal route home.

"Where're you going, Arne?" Ruth asked. "I can't go anywhere looking like this."

"Ruthie," Arne replied, "you're going to be looking like the Queen of Sheba."

Arne pulled the van into the valet parking at the front entrance to the Hennepin Inn, a quaint, renovated flour mill on the banks of the Mississippi River. "You get a love dinner, I get a love evening," he said.

"Good heavens, Arne, what am I going to wear? What about the kids? What about..."

"I wouldn't get all worked up about a few details, girl," Arne said. "Have you no faith in your old hubby?"

They checked in and made their way to a room on the second floor overlooking the river. Arne opened the door and wheeled Ruth into the room, where she was greeted by a dozen red roses in a vase on a table by the window. He parked her chair next to the table and handed her a card he had placed in front of the vase. He opened it for her and left her to read it alone.

"I didn't know exactly what you might want to wear so I brought several different dresses for you," Arne said, proudly opening the closet door for Ruthie to see her choices. "The kids are keeping Laurie Love company tonight, so now you've got nothing left to worry about but me. And I'm a lot of man for you to worry about."

Ruth remained silently reading the card. As she did, Arne walked over to a small refrigerator and retrieved a little box. Approaching his wife from behind, he reached around her and handed her a large white corsage. "I didn't know which dress you'd pick, so I thought it best to stay with white."

She clutched Arne's hands in hers and held them against her cheeks, kissing the inside of his fingers. A glowing smile was as close as she could come to summoning a response. Gently she lowered her arms and placed her husband's hands on her breasts. "Kiss me, Arne," she whispered.

Without removing his hands from her breasts, Arne leaned over her shoulder and met her lips as she strained her neck backwards to receive him. They kissed tenderly at first, but the hormones of a young woman, crippled or not, were soon stirred. She opened her mouth, and with her tongue pried open her husband's lips.

Arne caressed her breasts through her cotton blouse until the nipples hardened. He moved his mouth across her face, kissing her cheek and her eyes and her ears. He traced his tongue through the loops of her ear, and Ruthie writhed in her wheelchair. "I love you," he whispered into her ear.

"God, Arne," she said, her voice catching in the back of her throat. "I want to feel you all over me." Her face was hot and her cheeks were wet with tears.

He slid his body around the side of the chair and straddled her legs, assessing the situation. He crouched a bit, careful not to put any weight on her legs, and leaned forward. He looked at her lovingly as he slowly undid each of the buttons on her blouse and unfastened her bra, barely able to balance himself. He placed his face between her breasts and rested there in the safe darkness for a moment.

"If you want to make love with a cripple," she whispered, stroking his hair, "you're going to have to get me into bed. We've gone about as far as we can in this darned chair."

Arne lifted his wife from the chair and carried her to the bed. He laid her on the white comforter and stood, momentarily gazing at her. He quickly finished undressing her and then let his own clothes fall to the floor. He saw before him the white skin of a young smiling woman, vibrant and sensual. Her illness had not after all robbed her of grace and beauty. He leaned over with one knee on the bed and was pleased to see his penis erect. Ruthie touched it with the tips of her fingers, smiling, and said, "It's been a while. Go slow."

He opened her legs and entered her, careful not to put too much weight on any one part of her body, savoring how his chest hair brushed against her breasts. They moved together in the old way, and he waited for her to climax before allowing himself release. The effort set off a kaleidoscope behind his eyes and his orgasm caused a stabbing pain in the back of his head.

They lay together on the bed, breathing heavily, touching shoulder to shoulder, with their fingers entwined.

"That's better," Ruthie sighed.

"I'm sadly out of shape," Arne said.

"That'll teach you to neglect me."

Arne laughed, turned on his side to look at her, and touched a forefinger to her lips. "Now you're asking for trouble," he said. She kissed his finger and said, "Bring it on, big man." He pushed his face into her sweet-smelling armpit and nearly started sobbing, but sensing his emotion, Ruthie said, "So when do I get my dinner? This little whore's earned it, hasn't she?"

"The candles are waiting," Arne laughed, his eyes wet. "Let me help you into the shower."

Within the hour Arne wheeled Ruth to a small table by the window downstairs in the restaurant overlooking the river. A winding pathway to the river was lit with kerosene lanterns.

"Who did you call to arrange for that?" Ruth asked, looking across the river to a rising yellow moon.

Arne reached across the table and took his wife's hand and helped her make a fist around the stem of her wine glass. With his other hand he touched their two glasses, and together they took sips from the fine crystal. "The moon?" He said. "Didn't you know I'm the king of the moon? I order it up when ever I'm love-starved."

"Ah, yes, I forgot," she said. "But you hardly needed the moon earlier."

"And the night's still young, lovely girl."

"Yeah, but you're not," Ruth laughed.

"It's true," he said, "I'm thankful that you fished me out of the junk pile and polished me up."

"You know, Arne, whatever happens to me, I surely am blessed to have a man like you to keep my spirits high. I couldn't manage without you. You're my inspiration."

"You're the inspiration, Ruthie. Your spirit never falters. I don't know how you muster the energy or the determination."

"We do it together, Arne. Whatever else may happen, at least we have each other."

"I've been thinking," Arne said. "Do you remember when Kathleen Campbell called you?"

"At the time I thought it was a nice gesture," Ruth said, "but Dillon Love sure didn't."

"Well, we've never reciprocated, never called them, never done a thing. Maybe we ought to call Boyd Campbell. He wanted to talk in court the other day, and would have if Dillon hadn't been so nasty, like a great bear coming down on the poor guy. Jeez."

"It frightened me."

"Hey, I never told you about this, but Campbell ran by our house once. Last fall. I recognized him immediately. He's no monster."

"Is that so?"

"I think he wants to work something out."

"You're right, Arne. He definitely wanted to say something," Ruth said. "Do you remember when the judge told the lawyers to work on a settlement?"

"Yeah, what a waste of time."

"What would you say to him if you gave him a call?" Ruth asked.

"I don't know. Maybe just chat a bit. Maybe just tell him I wish it hadn't all come to this. Whatever. Who knows if he'd even talk to me."

"Well, after that nice judge urged us to settle the case, Dr. Campbell and I happened to glance over at one another," Ruth said. "I thought he wanted to say something. It seemed like we were all going to talk. Then Mr. Holten got up and stormed out and everyone else left the room. Later in the hallway, he told me he was sorry in such a sincere way before Dillon was so horrible. I guess I just don't understand it all."

"Lawyers don't talk with each other," Arne growled. "I'll bet Dillon and Holten haven't spoken one word to each other outside the courtroom. They certainly don't have any meaningful discussions, unless you consider their incessant bickering to be some feeble attempt at conversation. They're just a couple of grown-up boys driven by massive egos. They're all fools. The whole lot of them are fools."

"Calm down, now. We're no different, Arne," Ruth said. "You can't blame the lawyers. We've done nothing more ourselves."

"Tomorrow that'll change," Arne said. He put two Rolaids into his mouth and chewed as he said, "I'm going to call Boyd Campbell in the morning."

The waiter arrived with their hors d'oeuvres. Arne moved his chair next to Ruth to help her. "Now the candle won't obstruct my view of the fine art," Arne whispered, gazing into his wife's eyes.

He forked food alternately into her mouth and his own. He helped her with a sip of wine from time to time. And when the main course came they ate slowly and talked about the children and how well they were doing in school, and how lonely poor Laurie Love seemed, and how they would go on a lovely holiday when the doctors found a cure for Ruthie's illness. It struck Arne that never once did Ruth mention what she would like to do with any settlement money they might win. He determined there and then to get rid of this bane in their lives. He would call Dr. Campbell in the morning and take matters into his own hands. They needed nothing from anyone; they had each other. To hell with the lot of them!

As Arne pushed Ruth's wheelchair from the restaurant into the hotel lobby, he felt reborn, and his heart pounded with happiness. He was filled with his new mission to lead his family out of its legal quagmire. There would be dialogue! And he pondered the irony of having seized his strength from the frailty of the woman in the chair in front of him.

"With my body and your spirit, we're quite a team," he said to Ruth, gently rubbing her shoulder with one hand.

She looked ahead and said, "How strange."

"What's strange?" Arne said.

Ruth nodded her head in the direction of a group of men talking in the lobby. "Isn't that Henry Holten over there?"

"It is," said Arne, "I recognize him from court."

Arne stopped and stared at the men. One of them was a tall, distinguished gentleman, dressed in a navy pinstriped suit. His white dress shirt appeared crisply pressed and fresh despite the late hour. He wore a red bow tie, knotted just enough off kilter to prove it had been hand tied.

Arne's forearm muscles tensed against his wife's shoulder.

"Whatever's the matter?" Ruth asked. "Let's go up to the room."

"I want to talk with him," Arne hissed.

"You can't talk with him, Arne," Ruth scolded. "It's forbidden."

"Nobody's supposed to talk," Arne said. "Heck, we can't even discuss this case with our friends lest we say something that might find its way back to the other side. God only knows what that could be. What kind of craziness is this anyway? I'm going to talk to Henry Holten right now."

Arne left Ruth in her chair at one side of the lobby and walked briskly toward Holten, who did not see him approaching. Arne tapped him on the shoulder. "Mr. Holten," he said, interrupting the men's conversation, "I'd like to talk with you a minute, if you please."

Holten turned away from the group and, with his three associates, stared incredulously at Arne Bergstrom.

"Pardon me," Holten said, "do I know you?"

"You most certainly do. I'm Arne Bergstrom."

"Mr. Bergstrom, good God. I'm quite certain your lawyer wouldn't want you talking with me. And frankly, I'm similarly disposed at the moment, as I'm sure you can appreciate."

"I don't care what Dillon Love thinks," Arne said. "I can talk with whoever I damn well please. I want to talk with you about the case."

"Listen, Mr. Bergstrom, I don't have any intention of speaking with you. I couldn't talk with you even if I wanted to. It's unethical, and I simply will not engage in any conversations with you. Good night."

"That's ridiculous. How can a simple conversation be unethical? Why did you have to go rushing out of court last week? Please, I beg you, I just want to get on with my life."

"You should have thought of that before you filed your lawsuit. The time for talking is long past. I'll see you in court, Mr. Bergstrom."

Henry Holten turned his back and returned his attention to his companions. Infuriated, Arne pounded his open palms against Holten's back, knocking him to the floor. At the top of his voice he yelled, "I just want to talk, that's all, just talk! Why won't you talk with me? Why won't you talk?"

Two of Holten's companions restrained Arne while the other helped Holten up off the carpet.

"What's wrong with you anyway?" Arne screamed. "Why won't you talk? Why won't anyone talk? I don't want to go to court. We just want to get on with our lives. Nobody cares about that. Not you, not Dillon Love, not anyone."

"You'd better get hold of yourself," Holten said, pulling at his lapels to straighten his suit coat, "or we'll have to call security. I've got nothing to say to you. If you don't leave me alone, I'll have you arrested for assault."

Arne turned slowly and started walking back toward his wife. He saw terror in Ruth's face. He had ruined her beautiful evening and made a fool of himself. The group of men behind him began to laugh. He stopped and looked back and caught their eyes on him; they were grinning and studying him in curious amazement.

He felt a heavy wave of nausea flow through him and he turned once more toward his wife. The taste of steak came into his mouth. He took a step in Ruth's direction. As he did, an agonizing pain shot up his neck and down his left arm and through his chest. He stood still for a moment, understanding in an instant what was happening to him. He thought of his father. He took several more steps, almost reaching Ruth's side, before he fell. He reached out to brace himself against her wheelchair. Someone, a woman with a white corsage, was screaming, "Oh my God, help him, please help him!"

CHAPTER **Twenty**

Laurie Love walked down the aisle toward the front of St. Michael's church and took a seat in the second row, hoping a few moments of quiet reflection might help her understand this second tragedy that had befallen her friend, Ruth Bergstrom. She had come to offer support; instead, she found herself sitting alone in a pew, only a few feet from the spot where she had confirmed marriage vows with Dillon. She sat alone, still childless.

She could not make Arne's death sink in; after all, she had been party to the meeting of Ruth and Arne at the Loring Café ten years ago; it seemed like only yesterday. She had introduced Ruth and Arne. With a sudden pang she realized it was before she'd met Dillon. Now Ruth's sudden widowhood made Laurie seriously question the wisdom of leaving Dillon, which also seemed like yesterday but was six months ago. She was sad and confused, and whenever she thought of Arne's smiling face she wanted to cry, but the grief was not all for him; much of it was for herself.

Dillon, after desperately trying to contact her the night she left him, had made no further attempts, much to her chagrin. His adherence to her lawyer's insistence that there be no contact between them left her feeling apprehensive and insecure. Yes, she had rid herself of a one-sided relationship that had been frustrating and lonely, but her indignation had been replaced by guilt, and the guilt produced pain that proved far more incapacitating than the indignation brought on by being the spouse of a workaholic. The vitality that had been there even during the most difficult times with Dillon had vanished, leaving her lethargic and melancholy. She was bound to see him any minute now. What would she say? What would he say? Would Arne's death produce a renewal of their relationship? Guardedly she hoped so; it was spring after all.

Tall granite pillars rose from stone floors, producing a cold ambiance for the arriving family and friends. A large marble altar stood at the front of the chancel, and behind it a modernistic crucifix was suspended, and the back wall was pierced by an immense stained glass rendition of Christ's passion. Heavy chandeliers hung by long steel chains. Spooky, rather lifeless music droned from the organ pipes, and, as if to underscore the prevailing sense of gloom, the mourners spoke not a word as they solemnly filed in and took their seats in the pews. Laurie stood and turned sideways so she could see the entrance, and when Dillon arrived with Joe Clapp a few minutes before the start of the service, Laurie felt a cramp low in her torso at the sight of the big, shining man. He had lost weight, which made him look taller, and shaved off his beard, which made him look younger. What was that visceral spasm in her? Relief, sexual desire, an egg dropping? Whatever it was, church was probably not the right place to think about it.

Dillon guided Clapp to a seat at one side and toward the rear of the church where he would have the best vantage point for locating Laurie without her seeing him. This semi-concealed position would allow him a good opportunity to monitor her movements while avoiding inadvertent contact with her.

As he took his seat he scanned the congregation for a glimpse of her. She would be sitting alone at the very front of the church, staring straight ahead, demure and aloof. Her petite shoulders would be barely visible above the back of the pew. She would want to avoid contact with him also.

Dillon casually surveyed the assembled crowd without locating the blond head of his estranged wife. He shifted his position on the pew and leaned slightly to one side to adjust his line of sight. There was Laurie, and she was looking directly at him. There was no avoiding eye contact. He leaned quickly back to safety behind the man in front of him.

Within seconds, he realized he was being an idiot, and leaned forward once more to seek the distant eyes of his wife. She was crying. Even from where he sat he could see that her eyes were red and swollen. She dabbed at them with a tissue, smiled modestly, and turned her mascara-stained face towards the front of the church.

The organ droned on as the last of Arne Bergstrom's friends found seats. Oblivious to the beginning of the service, Dillon leaned over once more to peer around the shoulders of the man in front of him. As he bent over, he felt the crinkle of folded paper inside his corduroy jacket. Absently, he reached into his jacket pocket and felt the edges of Laurie's goodbye letter.

"She's crying for you," Clapp whispered.

"Get off it. Arne is dead, she's crying for him, or for Ruth. What's the matter with you?"

"Those are tears of remorse, not tears of mourning. I seen 'em do it before."

"Well, she's only got herself to blame for that," Dillon said quietly through clenched teeth.

Clapp nudged him, grinning, said, "What's that you got in your hand?"

Dillon stuffed Laurie's letter back into his breast pocket. "Nothing."

A woman shushed them. Clapp laughed, said, "God, I love church. You are such a pussy, Dillweed."

Dillon's intended retort was interrupted by the sudden blare of music and the simultaneous rising of the congregation. Dillon stood and mouthed the words of a song he did not remember. The priest invited them all to sit, but Dillon did not hear the beginning of the eulogy the priest spoke to the family and friends of Ruth and Arne Bergstrom.

"Arne Bergstrom was a simple man," the priest began. "But he was also a giant, because he had all the qualities common to great men, vision, ambition, and compassion. Arne's vision was modest, to live in an uncomplicated world focused on family and community. It is a vision that is as rare today as it is noble.

"Though his vision was uncomplicated, his ambition to realize it was tenacious and uncompromising. He tolerated no interference. And he succeeded as few men have succeeded simply by being the best husband and father he could be.

"But perhaps his greatest virtue was his vital sense of compassion for others, a compassion that's uncommon in men of strength and courage. Men who are blessed with the vision and ambition required to achieve greatness often do not possess the compassion found in true greatness. Men born with compassion often seem to lack the foresight and vitality to become great leaders. Arne Bergstrom had it all."

Dillon shifted uneasily in his seat and slid along the pew until he pressed against the shoulders of a stranger next to him. He could barely see Laurie from that position. The crying was not to be trusted, he thought, women could pretty much cry on demand when it suited their interests. Dillon caught sight of Ruth Bergstrom, who sat motionlessly in her wheelchair at the front of the church. Her two children sat in chairs on either side of her. She was not crying.

He slid back toward Joe Clapp. "Great speech," Joe whispered. "It'd make one helluva closing argument."

"What," Dillon said, "what's he saying?"

The priest continued, "Arne Bergstrom was a hero, a man of exemplary valor and fortitude. Valor and fortitude are virtues found not only on the battlefield, or in athletic contests, or in courts of law. Men whose adrenaline permits them to achieve heroic victories in any one of these forums are often shallow and fainthearted once removed from their natural element. These men are not true heroes, and they're not cut from the same cloth as men like Arne Bergstrom.

"Arne respected dignity and self-respect in others as he exhibited them in himself; he was unencumbered by a raging ego. In a world of short-sighted insensitivity, he was a man of discernment. He was self-confident but humble, strong yet sensitive. He had the courage of his convictions and the fortitude to live his dreams. Arne Bergstrom was a hero, a true hero to all of us.

"The world is a little worse today for his passing, but it's far better today because he walked among us for forty-five years. We're all going to miss him. I already do."

The congregation sang a final hymn for Arne Bergstrom. Dillon mouthed the words, but the whole time he was thinking about how Arne's death, especially considering the circumstances surrounding it, brought new strength to Ruth's case. Now she was not only a suffering woman in a wheelchair, she was a widow deprived of her support. Amid the sounds of hymnals sliding into racks on the backs of the pews, the organist began playing the postlude, and the priest descended the few steps from the chancel to Ruth's wheelchair. He touched her gently on her shoulders, then rotated her to face the congregation and pushed her up the aisle past the saddened faces of her many friends.

Dillon and Clapp remained in their seats as everyone else began to walk downstairs to a reception in the church basement. Dillon waited for Laurie to leave so he could find an opportunity to discreetly wish her well in the presence of other people. He watched the other guests walk up the aisle past him, and greeted several of them. He glanced from time to time toward his wife, but she remained sitting alone in her pew.

Dillon thought she appeared disoriented, apathetic, almost paralyzed except for the occasional blotting of tears at the corners of her eyes. "Wait here," he said to Clapp. His heart beat rapidly as he stepped into the aisle and walked slowly towards Laurie. A few feet from her, leaning awkwardly against the side of the pew, he said, "Hello, Laurie."

She turned easily toward Dillon, as though she had expected he would appear at her side. She crumpled the remnants of a tissue into her palm and said, "It's good to see you, Dillon. How are you doing?"

"Remarkably well," he said, "The case looks more winnable every day."

She closed her eyes for second and shook her head slightly. "You shaved off your beard."

"Yeah, new look."

"And you've lost a lot of weight."

"I'm living on breakfast cereal."

"I didn't say you looked starved."

"Well, I'm getting some distance in on the bike. You know, to relieve stress."

"But the old jacket remains," she laughed.

"Some things are sacrosanct. I actually bought a suit, and would've worn it today, but my staff sprayed beer on it after the last hearing. It still stinks."

"You have staff now?"

"Yep. This case has gone through the roof."

"Poor Arne."

"You're obviously pretty devastated by his death," Dillon said. "But Ruth's the one left. And the kids. I have to work even harder for her now."

"They were so much in love," she said, tears welling up again. "They had such a perfect marriage, such a perfect family. I try to picture Ruth attempting to take care of her children when she can barely take care of herself, all alone, without anyone to love her."

"She's a strong lady," Dillon said. "It'll be tough, but she'll make it. She'll have a lot of help from all her friends."

"None of them are as strong as she is. Here I sit crying my heart out, incapable of providing any support for one of my best friends. That's the way it always is with her, I'll go downstairs to offer her some encouragement, and she'll end up encouraging me."

"Would you like me to walk you downstairs?" Dillon asked.

"I'd like it if you'd sit down with me for a minute."

Dillon hesitated for a moment, then obligingly took a couple of steps toward Laurie and sat uneasily a few feet away in the same pew.

"Isn't it ironic," she said, "that in a world full of meaningless relationships, a strong one like the Bergstrom's should be destroyed so prematurely? Here I sit bawling my eyes out for Ruthie when I so casually tossed my own marriage to the wind. It makes you stop to consider what love is all about."

"You tell me, Laurie. What *is* love all about? Perhaps that's a question you should have asked yourself last September."

"I wish I knew," she said. "I know it's got something to do with sacrifice. What I can't figure out is who's supposed to make the sacrifice. At the moment of decision it always seems like it's the other person who ought to be adjusting their behavior. Later it's never quite so clear."

"Is that an apology, Laurie?"

"I have many regrets, Dillon. What about you?"

"I don't know how I feel. I haven't had any incentive to think about it, so I haven't."

"Look, maybe it's hopeless to think we might work things out," Laurie said. "Maybe you don't even want to try. I wouldn't blame you if you didn't. But, well, how'd you like to get together for a little dinner tonight at my apartment?"

"Joe Clapp and I are meeting a couple of witnesses. There's no telling how long it might take."

Laurie stood abruptly, pushed past Dillon, and started up the aisle.

"Thanks," Dillon added quickly, "it's a nice offer, and I appreciate it. Come on, I'll walk you downstairs."

"You're a real piece of work," Laurie said heatedly, turning back to face her Dillon. "But if you should manage to find any time for me, I'll be home tonight."

Laurie turned away and hurried down the aisle, disappearing into the church basement.

Dillon walked into Pete's Piano Bar around five. He and Joe Clapp had planned to meet with two DNR field engineers after they finished work. They had been responsible for investigating the circumstances surrounding Ruth Bergstrom's illness, and Dillon wanted to see the data they had generated. Pete's Piano Bar had become Dillon's conference room, since it provided a convenient meeting place, especially during happy hour. Liquor has a way of loosening the tongues of witnesses.

Clapp hit the men's room while Dillon took a booth near the window. He loosened his tie and removed his coat, tossing it over the back of the booth. He stared vacantly ahead as he waited for the waitress to come to the table. He suddenly felt beat. Boy, did he ever need a beer.

A Budweiser materialized in front of him; the waitress, who obviously knew him better than he knew her, was already moving away. He took a swig and noticed that Laurie's letter had fallen from his coat pocket onto the seat beside him. He picked it up, carefully unfolded it, and held it next to the window so he could read the handwriting in the darkened bar:

I need to be loved, Dillon. I need to be the only love in your life. I need your strength and your support. I need the warmth of your body beside me on the couch at night. I need you to listen with interest to the trivial things I've done every day and share them with me and make me feel important. I need you to sit on the counter and talk with me as I fix our dinner, to go shopping together, to do all the simple things that used to be such an important part of our lives. I need you to play with me and tease me and touch me, to reach under my clothes and caress me.

"What you got there?" Clapp asked, standing at the edge of the booth looking curiously at the weathered piece of paper Dillon was reading. He took a swig from his own bottle of beer.

"A note from Laurie."

"On that shriveled-up piece of paper? What the hell, that ain't some old love letter, is it?"

"It's my termination notice," Dillon replied.

"Shit. What the hell you carrying that thing around for?"

"I just put it in there last fall and forgot about it," Dillon said.

"Bullshit. You're a friggin' sentimental asshole. She invited you over didn't she? You're going to Laurie's tonight."

"Nah. I'm not ready to suck up to the woman who walked out on me. I may be dumb, but I'm no goddamn masochist."

"God what a flaming piss-ant you are. The woman's in love with you, and if you weren't still in love with her, you wouldn't be carrying that goddamn letter around with you. Get your ass on over there and make your peace with the broad."

"I'm not so sure I give a rip about her after what she did to me."

"For six months you carry around the goddamn pink slip the broad gave you, and you're not out of your fuckin' mind in love with the bitch? Jesus Christ, give me a fuckin' break."

"It's none of your goddamn business."

"Listen, asshole, you are my business. You owe me so much goddamn money I can't afford to have you fuck up this case because of some stupid broad. Go on over there and get yourself a good lay. Six months. Jesus Christ, you gotta be fuckin' tired of pissing on the ceiling."

"Maybe I'll go over there after we get a little work done."

"You're damn right you'll go over there, and you'll also stop at the liquor store and buy her a nice bottle of wine.

Dillon and Joe spent a couple of hours with the DNR engineers going over the details of their investigation. There was no question in their minds that something had gone wrong with the P-27 to cause Ruth Bergstrom's neurological problems. They had not been able to find exactly what the problem was, but in their own minds they had ruled out every other source. They would gladly testify on behalf of Ruth Bergstrom, and they would summarize their data in several key charts which would make convincing exhibits in the courtroom.

They were on their third round as the conversation strayed to more casual topics.

"I've got to get out of here," Clapp said as he finished his beer. "Nothing against you assholes, but I've got me something a little better to meet up with. You better get going yourself, Dillon, if you've got any brains in that ugly bald head of yours."

"See you later, midget-dick," Dillon said. "I'll be right back," he said to the DNR guys. "I gotta call my wife and let her know I'll be coming around in a little while."

"We gotta get rolling ourselves," one of the men said. "Give me a call in a few days and I'll have some more information for you."

As the men left, Dillon remained alone at the table for a few minutes. He needed some time to gain his composure and plan a strategy to reduce the risk of the evening becoming a disaster. He nodded to the waitress for another Budweiser then called Laurie on his cell phone.

"All right," he said.

She was silent for a few moments, then said, "Are you sure?"

"No, but Joe Clapp says I'm still in love with you."

Laurie let loose her fine old gurgling laugh, which made Dillon smile a little. "What else does he say?" she asked.

"That I must swallow my anger and be forgiving. I must listen to my wife unload the months of frustration that led to her leaving me. I must not be judgmental. I must suffer through the interminable agony of a woman's tears, consciously avoiding the temptation to defend myself, consciously showing her the sympathy and understanding she apparently needs."

"Wow, Joe Clapp has been doing some serious thinking," Laurie laughed. "Don't worry, no recriminations tonight, just a nice salmon dinner with garlic mashed potatoes and a couple of bottles of white wine, which you can bring."

"I don't exactly know where you live, to be honest. Somewhere around Bryant and Forty-fourth?"

Laurie gave him the address and he said he would be there in twenty minutes.

As he closed his cell phone a man hovered beside the table and said, "You Dillon Love?"

"Who wants to know?"

"Nobody wants to know. I already know who you are, you're Dillon Love. And I work for EnviroClean. That is, I used to work for EnviroClean. I just got laid off."

The man was obviously emboldened by having had a few drinks. "Oh," replied Dillon cautiously, not knowing whether the stranger would be bitter toward EnviroClean for having been fired or bitter toward him for having played some role in the event. "You want a beer?"

"Damn right I do." The man slid into the booth opposite Dillon. He was in his mid-thirties. From his white button-down dress shirt and pale complexion, Dillon inferred he had been employed for EnviroClean in a sales capacity; the company was too small to have middle-management executives. Laboratory staff would not wear dress shirts, and field staff would have a more rugged, outdoor complexion.

"Add it to my tab," Dillon instructed the waitress as the stranger ordered an imported beer. "So how do you know me and why are you here?" Dillon said.

"As I thought. You have questions, but if you want answers, it's gonna cost you a lot more than beer."

"Who the hell are you?"

"I'm Richard Blair. Until a few hours ago I was the controller at EnviroClean. Now I'm an unemployed father of four."

"Oh, man, that sucks. I'm sorry." Dillon hesitated for a few seconds, feeling Blair out in order to give himself the best chance of finding the right words to get some information out of him. "Does your coming here have something to do with your employment situation?"

The waitress rushed by and dropped two bottles of beer on the table. Blair lifted his, methodically drained it, then signaled to the waitress by holding up the empty bottle. "You might say my presence here has to do with my employment situation, yes."

"Do you have some information you think I might find interesting?"

"I find it interesting."

"Is this a game, or what?" Dillon asked. "Am I supposed to guess?"

"You're supposed to pay."

"I don't buy information. It's generally unreliable and unethical."

"Unethical. Bullshit, that's the American way. I've got a family. You've cost me my job with your goddamn lawsuit. The way I got it figured, you owe me."

Two more beers arrived at the table, and the two empties were removed.

"Look, I'm not buying any information from you. Henry Holten would undoubtedly learn about it and bring it out in court. Then the jury wouldn't believe it anyway, so I'd be wasting my money and getting myself in trouble for nothing. If you have valuable information, you have an obligation to come forward with it."

"More bullshit. Why should I?"

"If it was your family I was representing, you'd be damn pissed if some key witness wouldn't speak out unless he got paid. I don't owe you anything, but I suspect you owe something to Ruth Bergstrom."

"I'm not a snitch. Boyd Campbell's a good guy. He's worked damned hard to get where he is today. He's worked damned hard to get EnviroClean to the brink of success."

"I sense there's some dirty little secret buried in the depths of EnviroClean that needs to see the light of day."

"What do you mean by that?"

"Well, you apparently like Boyd Campbell, yet here you are talking to the enemy and claiming not to be a snitch. Why else would you be drinking my beer? Let's have at it. What's wrong with the P-27?"

"The P-27's fine. Hell, it's a great product. You're completely missing the boat, man. Have been all along." Blair paused and took another slug of his beer. "Look, maybe I shouldn't be talking to you."

"Why the hell not? You can talk to anyone you choose. But now that I know you've got some information, you're sure as hell gonna be talking. You can do it informally, or the sheriff can bring you a subpoena. If I were in your shoes, I'd just as soon do it informally."

Dillon raised his bottle to his lips, spilling some beer down his chin. "So what makes you think I'm missing the boat?" he asked, wiping his face with the cuff of his shirt.

Blair did not respond to Dillon's question. Instead, he caught the attention of the waitress and motioned her to their booth and ordered more beer.

"I gotta take a pee," Dillon said, leaving the booth. "They oughta just put the goddamn urinal under the table. After a couple more brews I'll just be pissing on the floor anyway. Are you some goddamn camel or what?"

When Dillon returned, Blair had already finished his beer and had ordered more.

"We just gonna sit around here all night or what?" Dillon asked.

"I suppose you know I've met with Henry Holten a couple times to talk about the case," Blair said.

"Yeah, I remember I've seen your signature on a few legal documents," Dillon said, "and I know Holten would never allow them out of the office without talking to you about them. What's your point?"

"Well, there's a couple of things that just don't make much sense to me," Blair said.

Dillon drained his beer and sat up against the hard wooden back of the bench and waited for Blair to continue.

"For one thing," Blair said, "Holten spent almost a week out at our plant last summer going through all the company records. Apparently you had served Darby & Witherspoon with some papers demanding all sorts of records. I had to drop everything I was doing and organize all the files for him to examine. It seemed a little strange to me. Why would Henry Holten spend all that time out at EnviroClean personally going through reams of records if there's nothing of consequence there? I don't know much about law, but isn't that the sort of thing legal assistants usually do?"

Dillon started on his new beer and signaled the waitress to bring another round. "Is that it? Is that what I was supposed to be paying you the big bucks to tell me? Gimme a break. I'm not that fuckin' dumb."

"Holten was mostly interested in our purchase orders. I bet he spent two days just going through the company's purchase orders and invoices. Two full days. Hell, we're no General Motors. All we got are a few file cabinets."

"Were there any missing when you got them back?"

"How the hell would I know? I don't memorize the damn things."

"So you think Holten's been messing with your records, is that what you're telling me?"

"I'm telling you what I saw. You can draw whatever conclusions you want."

"OK."

"There's one other thing," continued Blair. "I got this fax from Holten when he was in Bermuda a few weeks ago. It was on the letterhead of some company down there by the name of Fermagro. The letter identified Holten as Fermagro's general counsel. He asked me for some information about our costs of growing microorganisms. I didn't know exactly what he wanted, so I called him in Bermuda. The Fermagro receptionist told me I could reach him at a resort there, Oxford Beaches I believe it's called. So I called him there. In our conversation I asked him why he needed this information, and he told me it was related to the lawsuit. So I sent it to him by overnight mail."

"What's your point?" Dillon asked.

"I don't know. If it had something to do with the lawsuit, why was he writing me from Bermuda on Fermagro stationery? Wouldn't he just have asked Allison Forbes or someone else at the Minneapolis office to call me about it?"

"Well, it's interesting," Dillon said. "I'll give you that. But I've got no goddamn time to be chasing down wild-ass leads."

"Tell you what I think," Blair said. "I don't think it's so damn wild-assed. That's my opinion, anyway."

"Look," Dillon said, pulling himself out of the booth, "I gotta get out of here." He slipped Blair his card, saying, "We'll talk properly tomorrow. What the hell time is it anyway? Oh shit. I gotta fuckin' get out of here."

Dillon reached for his billfold in the back pocket of his pants, lost his balance, and fell back into the booth. "Goddamn, I was supposed to be at Laurie's an hour ago."

"I don't think you're gonna be seeing any woman tonight," Blair said.

"This ain't no woman. It's my fuckin' wife."

"Your wife? You mean you don't live together?"

"We're fuckin' separated."

"Sorry to hear that. But I don't think you're in any condition to reconcile tonight," Blair said.

Dillon grabbed Blair by the tie and pulled him toward the edge of the booth. "Look, I haven't got laid in six months. I gotta be the horniest bastard in town. I couldn't even get laid at a Super Bowl party."

"Then one more day isn't going to hurt you," Blair replied. "I'll give you a ride home."

Dillon rose again from the booth and steadied himself against the table. He pulled his sagging trousers up on his hips and tucked his shirt into his pants, leaving one of the tails hanging out. He adjusted his belt buckle and took a couple of shaky steps away from the booth.

"I'm not going home. I'm going to Laurie's."

"If you haven't seen your wife for six months, I wouldn't recommend a reunion in your present condition. I'll take you home. You can see her tomorrow."

They left Pete's and headed for Richard Blair's car. "So where do you live anyway?" Blair asked.

"I don't fuckin' know and I don't fuckin' care. If you're so goddamn eager to take me home, you can fuckin' find it yourself. I gotta take a piss."

Dillon stopped between two pickup trucks parked in the lot alongside the bar, braced himself against the side of each truck, and urinated onto the asphalt. "Jesus Christ you must be a goddamn fuckin' camel," Dillon said, peering at his new witness through the cab of one of the pickups. "Don't you ever have to take a goddamned piss?"

"I believe you got a head start on me tonight," Blair replied as Dillon staggered around the back of the truck.

Dillon followed Blair across the parking lot and stopped beside Blair's car. He held his hand up against the light of a nearby street lamp and looked for a moment at the wedding band he still wore on his ring finger.

"I guess you're right," he said, removing the ring and dropping it into his pants pocket. "I'm too fuckin' drunk to worry about the bitch tonight."

CHAPTER Twenty-one

In the company of two elderly ladies also in electric wheelchairs, Ruth Bergstrom threw small pieces of stale bread to the resident ducks and geese of the small lake in Loring Park. May had brought out the luscious green of the park, the cheerful yellow daffodils and, of course, the gray beards of dandelions. The reflected afternoon sun blazed from the skyscrapers massed just to the east of the park, and the bellicose mallards fought over everything, females, scraps of bread, proximity to the cripples. Ruth and the old ladies laughed at them.

The pony-tailed attendant had parked the three invalids on the small decorative bridge that crosses the lake and wandered off to smoke. The three women felt a bit wicked obstructing the able-bodied people trying to cross the bridge, but the young man laughed and said, "Let 'em come and complain to me." The ducks and geese gathered like harpies in the water and on the walkway of the bridge, desperate for a morsel of moldy bread. From the bridge Ruth could see the bar where she met Arne a decade ago. It was called the Loring Cafe then, but was totally different now with some obscure new name.

She held back her emotion so as not to spoil a pleasant afternoon for her companions, but she missed Arne desperately, and now, looking at the building where they had met that night when she was a single girl out for the night with Laurie, and Arne was the mid-thirties bachelor dragged out for a rowdy night with his buddies, she could scarcely believe she had already lost him and that she was helpless in a wheelchair. One of the ladies put a hand on her arm and said, "Are you all right, honey?" Ruth smiled and nodded. The old lady pointed and said, "Make sure that little duck over there gets a bite. She looks scrawny."

Ruth handed the bread to her companion, who threw a chunk out to the little brown duck. The geese and mallards were quick to follow the bread and descended upon it with a great splashing and flapping of wings so that the scrawny duck was dunked by their aggression. "Poor little mite," said the old lady, but she did not throw any more bread. "That's us," she laughed.

"Tell me about it," said Ruth.

"At least you be young, Ruthie," said her friend, "And you gonna get better."

"I hope so."

"You will. And when you do, give 'em hell for me, sugar."

Ruth laughed, and for some reason thought of Dillon Love, whom she would be seeing later that evening. She had lately begun to think of him fondly and had mildly dared to look forward to the time she spent with him.

The attendant finished his cigarette, tossed the butt into the lake, and returned to herd them back to the big white van parked near the fountain. He walked patiently beside them as they hummed along the path, heavily slimed with goose droppings, and Ruth was aware that he had his eyes on her. She found she liked it.

At the end of the afternoon, after driving by the river and around the city lakes, the attendant dropped Ruth off first because her children would be getting home from school. Ruby, her home-care provider, came out and walked behind her up the newly built wooden ramp which led at a mild angle up to her front door. Ruby's assistance with dinner preparation and bedtime activities with her children was usually the order of the day. Tonight she could have some time off because Dillon had invited Ruth and the children to his apartment for dinner.

Ruth had barely gotten in the house when she heard the clamor of young feet, stampeding up the ramp, through the front door, and into the kitchen. They were early. Dillon must have picked them up at school. Her heart pounded, and before she could brace herself, Brett and Molly ran into the room and surrounded her wheelchair.

"Mommy, Mommy," Brett shouted, "Mr. Love's got an iMac, and he's going to let us play games on it tonight."

"Mommy, look at my homework," Molly shouted, stuffing a school workbook into Ruth's face. "I got every question right."

"Read us a story, Mommy," Brett asked, pulling *Winnie the Pooh* from his small backpack.

"No!" yelled Molly, "That's for babies!"

"When am I going to get my hugs and kisses?" Ruth asked calmly, trying to bring the noise level down. Ruby, who was plugging in the wheelchair to recharge it, said, "And what about me? Am I invisible?"

Brett flung himself at Ruby, nearly knocking her over. Then he kissed his mother's hand repeatedly. Molly frowned at him as if he were a freak.

"Now will you read me a story?" Brett said.

Ruth was just opening the book as Dillon caught up with his temporary wards and arrived at the doorway. He walked in and sat down in a small stuffed chair in a corner and listened as Ruth read a chapter of *Winnie the Pooh*.

The living room of the Bergstrom residence had been fully converted into a bedroom for Ruth. Her bed was placed at one end of the room, but there was sufficient space to accommodate a small couch and two armchairs at the other end near the picture window facing Nassau Street. The walls were covered with colorful artwork her children had produced at school, which gave the room a festive and joyful atmosphere. In a glass vase on a table in front of the window was a large arrangement of yellow daffodils, baby's breath and ferns. The fresh flowers made the room warm and welcoming.

"They're from one of her secret admirers," Ruby said to Love as she noticed him looking at the bouquet. Ruth looked up and smiled at them both as she read. Ruby continued, "She get a new arrangement every Sunday. Pretty ain't they?"

"Who are they from?" Dillon asked.

"Well, if we told you, it wouldn't be a secret, now would it?" Ruby replied.

"As an attorney," Dillon persisted, "I'm sworn to confidentiality. With me this secret will go undisclosed."

"Can I push your wheelchair, Mommy?" Brett asked, interrupting the story.

"You got the attention span of a sparrow," laughed Ruby.

"Mommy's got a new electric chair now, Brett," Ruth said. "It goes all by itself, like a little car."

"Can I ride on your lap?" he added quickly.

"You're too big for that," she said. "Come on along now. We can't keep Mr. Love waiting for us, or he won't ask us back."

"My friend Joe Clapp's going to join us all for dinner," Love said as he drove the Jeep onto the freeway. "His girlfriend's out with the girls tonight and he's a lousy cook, so I suggested he come on over. Have you met Joe?"

"Of course," Ruth said, "he was at Arne's funeral. He's your investigator."

"Joe's one of the best PIs in the state," Love replied. "I'm darn lucky he's taken an interest in your case. He's put in an enormous amount of time following various leads. Shoot, look at this pile up! I'll tell you more about Joe's leads later. For now, let's just enjoy this wonderful traffic jam."

"On whole-wheat or white?" asked Molly.

Ruth burst out laughing.

"What's so funny?" said Love.

"Traffic *jam*. Get it?" said Brett.

"You guys are nuts," said Love.

After the sale of his house, Love had rented a first-floor apartment in a fourplex in southeast Minneapolis, not far from the University of Minnesota and only a short drive to his office downtown. The apartment had two bedrooms, one of which he used as an office, as well as a large living room, dining room, and kitchen. It was in an old building built in the 1920s, when it was still affordable to construct buildings with high-grade materials and custom millwork. The builder had made abundant use of woodwork throughout the unit, including hand-milled moldings and ornate archways between the rooms.

"Dillon, I do hope you're not too lonely living here all by yourself," Ruth said after getting situated in Love's living room. "You need a good woman to look after you."

"The life of a trial lawyer's pretty hectic, and I've got no time for loneliness," Dillon said. "Hey," he added quickly, "are you kids ready to check out my computer games? Come on, follow me."

Molly and Brett followed Dillon down the hall to his office and he got them started on a couple of familiar games. He returned just as Joe Clapp walked through the door with a twelve pack of Budweiser.

"Check these out," Joe Clapp said, throwing the twelve pack halfway across the room for Dillon to catch. "When was the last time that old fridge of yours saw twelve beers all at the same time?"

"Hey, Mrs. Bergstrom," Clapp continued, walking over to shake Ruth's hand. "How're you doing anyway? I hear you got yourself all set up with the home health-care people."

"Nice to see you again," Ruth replied. "But please call me Ruth."

"I had an aunt on home health-care for a while, Ruth. Heck of a good deal. Hell, I wouldn't mind having someone come in and look after me once in a while."

"It's nice," Ruth said. "And it's affiliated with the church. But I don't think I'll need her very long. I go to physical therapy every day, you know, and I'm feeling much stronger lately. God willing, I'll be taking care of myself in a few months."

"You should see the garden some of her neighbors have planted for her," Love said. "It's gorgeous."

"That's what I miss the most, the gardening," Ruth added. "I grew up on a farm and we always had a kitchen garden. My mother had a wonderful green thumb. Last summer Arne took me out back to my gardens every day. I couldn't do much, but at least I could boss him around and get everything done the way I wanted. Now all I can do is look at it. They're very thoughtful though, the neighbors, I mean."

"What kind of garden did you have?" Clapp asked.

"In the spring we had bulbs, crocuses, tulips, and daffodils. When they died out, we'd plant some annuals, whatever I felt like. Along the creek we had a huge border of iris and day lilies. Then, of course, I had my vegetable garden, tomatoes, cucumbers, lettuce, the whole works. That was my favorite, fresh vegetables right from the garden. Now I'm not able to do that."

"Well," Dillon said, "if you like fresh vegetables, you'll love dinner. Linguini with a sauce made from mushrooms, onions, and tomatoes."

"Blender sauce," joked Joe Clapp.

"I'm on a health kick," Dillon said.

"Sounds fabulous," Ruth said.

"I hate tomatoes," Brett shouted from the next room.

"Just ignore him," Ruth frowned.

"I can fix him something else if he'd prefer it," Dillon said.

"Don't be silly. This is what you're serving. He can eat it or go hungry. Molly's the same way. They're both just like their father, they won't touch tomatoes, or any fresh vegetables, for that matter, except potatoes of course."

"Well, I love tomatoes," said Clapp. "My ma cans them every fall, and we eat them all year long."

"Really," Ruth said, sitting up straighter. "Me too. Since no one else eats them, they'd all rot on the vine if I didn't can them. Maybe next year I can get back to canning again."

"Yeah," Clapp said, "that'd be great."

"Arne built me a cherry wood cabinet for my canning jars. It's a beautiful piece."

"Clapper would fill it with beer," jeered Dillon.

"Speaking of which," said Clapp, "who's ready for another?"

"Me," Dillon said right on the tail of Clapp's last syllable.

"You guys," laughed Ruth.

"Yep, Arne was one talented dude," Dillon said, as Clapp poured beer.

"He could do just about anything," Ruth said.

They talked about Arne for a while until, from the doorway, Molly said, "Mommy, we're hungry." Brett stood next to her sucking his finger. Love laughed, then left the room to complete dinner preparations, and shortly returned and set a large platter of pasta and a steaming loaf of garlic bread on the dining room table. On the buffet next to the table he put a wooden salad bowl full of dark green lettuce, croutons, and tomato wedges.

"*Mangia, mangia,*" Dillon urged in a stupid Italian accent from the entrance to the dining room. "Help yourselves. Come on, kids. Ruthie, can I serve you? Some of everything?"

The dinner conversation focused on the children and their progress at school. By all appearances they were adjusting remarkably well to the tragic circumstances that had altered their lives.

"You've been so kind to have us all over, Dillon," Ruth said at last. "I can't tell you how much I appreciate it. It's such a nice change."

"Let's do it every week," Dillon said, laughing and raising his beer in a toast.

"Yeah!" yelled the kids.

"I've been wondering about something, Ruth," Joe Clapp said quietly. "Would you mind if I drove over to your house for a few minutes to take another look around?"

"Sure. Whatever for?"

"I've suddenly got a hunch about something I'd like to check out."

"Of course," Ruth said. "But I can't imagine that you'll find anything new."

"Just the same, I'd like to snoop around a bit."

"What're you looking for?" Dillon asked, "What's going on in that pea brain of yours anyway?"

"It's probably nothing, probably nothing at all," Joe replied, absorbed in thought.

"We'll all go back there together when I drop the Bergstroms off and I'll help you snoop. And then we'll hit the piano bar."

"Oh yeah, right, so you can empty my wallet again," said Clapp. "No thanks. Besides, I have a woman to go home to, unlike you."

"Not for long, once she sees those tattered boxers you'll be history."

"At least I wear boxers. I'll go to Ruth's tomorrow on my own. I don't want you crushing evidence under your big yeti feet."

Ruth laughed until tears ran down her face. They were all laughing, red in the face from the beer. She wanted to stay and laugh with these rude, beer-swilling men forever.

CHAPTER Twenty-two

At five in the morning on Memorial Day, Love pulled on his jeans, grabbed his baseball cap and a banana, and climbed into his Jeep for the short ride to his office. He would be working alone today not just because it was a holiday but because Jim Fine and Howard Canon had graduated from law school and were studying full-time for the bar exam. Citing unpredictable paychecks and a foul-mouthed work environment, Barbara Hansen had found more congenial employment with a large firm.

Love stepped from his Jeep and stood for a few moments staring at the back door to his office. Curls of unkempt hair protruded from the sides of his cap, covering his ears and breaking over the back of his T-shirt. He had not had it trimmed since March, and now he would have to try to have it done before court. His suit still hung where he had put it back in March and still smelled of the beer Joe Clapp sprayed on it. He had lost a lot of weight and his jeans sagged in the butt. The trial would begin soon and huge amounts of preparation had yet to be done. For a moment he wondered if he could continue, but he took a deep breath, exhaled slowly, and walked sluggishly toward the door.

His office was like an obstacle course with boxes stacked three tiers high throughout much of the floor space. File folders full of depositions, court pleadings, legal research, technical data, and investigative reports were scattered everywhere in no discernible order. The entire surface of each desk and table was covered with papers and file folders. Half buried in the clutter on Love's desk were several legal pads on which, a few days before, he had begun to write an outline of questions he would ask the various witnesses who would be called to testify in court.

He had spent much of the night sleepless, weighing the most effective order in which to call his witnesses. Some of them were stronger than others, those with critical information and unquestioned credibility; others possessed only peripheral information or were vulnerable to impeachable partiality. Should he start strong to get the jurors on his side quickly, or should he save the strongest testimony for the end to keep the jurors from sensing that the case had been tarnished along the way? In the whole case, he had only one undeniably strong witness, Ruth Bergstrom, and he decided he would leave her for last. He would call his most troublesome witness first.

Love sat at his desk, took a highlighter from his drawer, and began reading deposition testimony. Occasionally he would jot a note or two on one of the legal pads, but mostly he sat with his feet up on the cluttered desk, highlighting in yellow various points in the testimony he considered significant. If there were a strategic plan in the midst of the chaos, it would not have been readily apparent to an uninitiated observer.

The phone rang on Love's desk, making him jump. He swung his feet to the floor and pushed a crumpled sheet of paper off the top of the phone.

"Yeah?" he answered.

"I thought you'd be there," said Allison Forbes. "No rest for the wicked, I guess."

"I've got stuff to do," he said curtly. "Do you know what time it is?"

"Of course I do. I can't sleep either, Dillon," she said. "Look, I feel really bad about everything that's happened. I just want to ..."

"You got that right, Allie," he interrupted. "This was supposed to be a friendly little lawsuit between old friends. Then Holten sent you in with a team of gladiators for his own amusement. Some friend you turned out to be."

"That's crap and you know it. You're the one who's been playing the part of Spartacus. But that's not what I called about."

"I'm broke right now, so servicing sex-starved lawyer ladies is a hundred bucks a minute."

"No thanks, hon, but at least you still have an imagination."

"Shit, I was counting on the extra income."

"Listen, Dillon," Allison said, "I'd like to try to put a deal together.

We owe it to our clients to give it one good shot. Boyd's willing to put some serious money together to get this case behind him. What'll it take, Dillon? Give me something reasonable to take back to him."

"This eleventh-hour bullshit won't wash with me, Allie," Love snarled. "You're wasting my time. Holten's got you trying to distract me from my trial prep. He figures you and I will waste half a day talking numbers, then he'll just put the kibosh on any deal we agree to, and I'll end up unprepared for court."

"Holten doesn't know I'm calling you," Allison said. "This is my own initiative. I'm totally sincere. I'll take any reasonable settlement demand directly to Boyd. Henry won't even be involved. I guarantee Boyd will make a good-faith response."

"It's too late," Love reiterated. "I got work to do. And shouldn't you be coaching Boyd Campbell on how to make a good impression on the jury?"

"You're a cynical bastard, Dillon."

"If you want to make me an offer, put it in writing and e-mail it over here. I'll talk to Ruth about it when I get the chance." Without waiting for a reply, Dillon hung up the phone, put his feet back on top of his desk, and returned to reading depositions.

Joe Clapp had been standing in the doorway listening, and said, "Mister Hardass, even on Memorial Day."

"How the hell did you get in?"

"I specialize in forced entry," Clapp said. "Actually, you left the back door open like some retard." Clapp walked to Love's desk and tossed a bag of donuts on top of the transcript in Love's lap.

Love sat back and rubbed his face hard, pushing his cap to the back of his head.

"I figured you could use a little help getting things organized for your big day tomorrow."

"Thanks, man. I'll put the coffee on."

"More importantly, are you gonna thank me for the goddamn donuts?"

"You're a hell of a friend, Joe. I really mean that," Dillon said.

"Someone has to feed you."

"I guess you're all I've got left."

"Don't go all sentimental on me. Just get the goddamn coffee brewing."

Love felt as if an avalanche of emotion was about to hit him, but without losing control he said, "Every other fucker up and quit on me."

"The hell they did," Joe said. "I just talked to Butler. He's on his way."

"You're kidding," Dillon said. "Good old Kenny."

"I called the son of a bitch and told him to get his wussy ass out of bed and truck on down here."

"You've got a real touch with people, Joe," Dillon replied. "I'm damn glad you're on my team."

"Even better than my warm and sensitive personality is my unmatched talent as a sleuth extraordinaire. I've got me one fuckin' big surprise for you."

Joe pulled a crumpled grocery bag from a backpack he carried at his side. "Plaintiff's Exhibit Numero Uno," he said. "This is your goddamn smoking gun. You don't fuckin' deserve it either. It's been sitting right under your fuckin' nose for eighteen months. Forget all those bullshit depositions you're reading, here's your goddamn case on a silver platter."

Joe reached into the bag and pulled out a Mason jar and placed it on the desk next to Dillon's feet. "Be damn careful with these canned tomatoes, that jar's probably worth five million bucks."

The back door swung open and noisily banged against the wall.

"It's about time you got here, Butler," Joe shouted in the direction of the back hallway. "You're missing all the goddamn fun."

"Do you mind letting me in on your little secret?" Dillon asked as Ken Butler entered the room. "Or is this some riddle I'm supposed to solve before I get one of your friggin' donuts?"

"You're the fuckin' smartass lawyer," Joe said.

"How about you, Dr. Butler?" Joe asked, placing great emphasis on the word *doctor*. "As our resident nerd, certainly you must appreciate the significance of Exhibit One."

"I suppose you're going to tell me those are from Ruth Bergstrom's garden?" Butler replied.

"You suppose right, doctor," Joe stated.

"You think these tomatoes may have some P-27 in them?" Dillon asked.

"There won't be any P-27," Ken replied. "All the bacteria would have been killed when the tomatoes were boiled in the canning process. But there might be some residuals of the chemical toxin the bacteria produced before they died. Perhaps it could be the mysterious Peak E they found at the Mayo Clinic."

"Bingo!" shouted Joe. "One donut for the nerd." He opened the package and threw glazed donuts to Butler and Love.

"Where'd you get these, anyway?" Love asked.

"The donuts?"

"The tomatoes, you fuck!"

"You remember the other night when Ruth told us about the cabinet Arne made for her canning supplies? Well, there was still one jar of tomatoes left in that cabinet."

"Clapper, you're one helluva a sleuth."

"Damn right."

"So how'd they get contaminated?" Dillon asked.

"I suppose you're going to want to see Exhibits Two and Three now also," Joe responded. "Arne Bergstrom was a serious handy man. I guess we all know that. Hell, you should see their house, he's done most of the wiring and plumbing and carpentry over there for the last twenty years. He was also a damn tightwad. Why pay for city water for your garden when there's a creek right alongside of it? With a small pump and a section of hose, you can water your garden for free. Exhibit Two is the pump I found in Arne's workshop; Exhibit Three is 25 feet of hose that was lying next to the pump. Who knows, maybe you'll find some of that Peak E shit in these exhibits as well."

"So why didn't anyone else in the family get sick?" Butler asked.

"Once in a while your clients tell you something that has some bearing on their cases," Joe said, looking straight at Dillon. "You might want to listen to them occasionally."

"What's your fucking point?" Dillon asked.

"The other night at your apartment, Ruth told us about her gardening. She also told us her canned tomatoes lasted all winter because no one else in the family liked tomatoes or fresh vegetables. That's what made me suspicious in the first place. Thank God there was still one jar left when I got over there."

"One jar left," mused Love. "She's been eating a lot of toxic tomatoes, then."

"I guess I know why I was invited to this party," Ken said. "Let's get that stuff over to the lab right away. With luck, I might have some results for you before this trial's over. How long do I have?"

"It'll take me a week to present all my evidence," Love responded. "Holten's case will start after that, probably Tuesday, Wednesday at the latest. Whatever you can get me better be here by next Monday so I have time to arrange how to present it."

"You know, guys," Ken continued, "I don't want to burst your bubble, but I hope you understand that regardless of what I uncover in my testing, we're not home free yet. Let's say we find Peak E in the Mason jar, the pump, and the hose, so what? That only proves that Ruth got sick from the tomatoes and that the tomatoes were infected with water from the creek. It doesn't prove the contamination came from the P-27 or from EnviroClean. For all we know it could've come from anywhere along the creek. It could be entirely coincidental that EnviroClean happened to be working on the project next door."

"Where else would it come from?" Love asked. "You tell me. Name the spot."

"Don't forget that we've tested P-27 and it produced no Peak E. It was clean. If we've proved anything so far, we've proved EnviroClean is not responsible. I'll run the tests for you, but you guys have still got your work cut out for you."

Clapp left with Butler to transfer the pump and hose from his pickup to the back of Butler's van. All three exhibits, the jar, the hose, and the pump, had been carefully tagged and initialed by Clapp to identify where and when they had been found in order to preserve the chain of custody and prove their authenticity in court.

"I didn't have the heart to remind Dillon that I can't testify in court," Butler said. "Our lab does a ton of work for Darby & Witherspoon and several other major law firms, as well as dozens of big companies throughout the five-state area. I told Dillon about this before I got started on this project. I told him I couldn't testify and could only do some behind-the-scenes lab work for him. But he was desperate because he didn't have the money to hire anyone other than a friend."

"Don't tell me you're thinking of leaving him high-and-dry at the last minute," Clapp said.

"I've mentioned the case to our president. He knows I'm doing this work on my own time, but he absolutely won't allow me to testify. I can get you the results, but I cannot come to court. Maybe you ought to say something to him so he can figure out some other way to introduce the results of the testing to the jury."

"Without you," Joe replied, "the evidence will not be heard by the jury. I suggest you have another little chat with your president."

"It won't do any good," Butler responded. "There's too much at stake for the lab to take the risk."

"There's a lot at stake for Ruth Bergstrom as well."

"Joe, I've given my heart and soul to this case, most of it for free."

"Yeah, but if you're looking for a goddamn medal, you've got to get across the finish line, and we ain't there yet."

Clapp returned to the office and was handed a steaming cup of sweet black coffee in a stained mug. "Don't say I never give you anything," said Love.

"Thanks, man," Clapp said, surprised, "I'm genuinely moved."

He pondered whether to remind Love that Butler could not testify. Butler could easily be subpoenaed, but this would be a harsh thing to do to a friend who had worked tirelessly for eighteen months, practically for nothing. He could lose his job. Clapp thought it best to keep the conversation to himself for the time being.

"You remember when Barb Hansen found an invoice from that biotech company, BTS?" Clapp asked as he walked back into the room.

"BioTech Services?" Love said. "Sure, what of it?"

"I figure if there's no contaminant in any of the P-27 from Enviro-Clean, then it's got to come from some other source. It sure as hell had to come from somewhere. Assume Butler finds it in the tomatoes—hell, I know it's in the tomatoes. So how did it get there? It must have come from BTS."

"Except that BTS got a clean bill of health from the EPA, and its batch samples have all been tested and approved. We can't pin anything on BTS either."

"The trouble with you lawyers is that you assholes spend all your fuckin' time finding something wrong with everyone else's ideas. You never get around to coming up with any fuckin' ideas of your own."

"I'm supposed to sit around here wasting my time being insulted by a mosquito-brained investigator for a box of stale donuts? Make your fucking point. I got work to do."

"Look," Clapp continued, "the invoice Babs found was for a shipment of bugs around the time EnviroClean was just beginning its project next to the Bergstroms. I went over to BTS to snoop around a bit, just like I said I was going to do. Well, it turns out that BTS isn't in the fermentation business any more. They haven't grown organisms since June 1999. The guy they had running that division for them left to set up his own business. Guess where, Bermuda. Bermuda, does that ring any bells with you?"

"Isn't that where Holten went when he skipped out of the pretrial hearing last month?" Dillon asked.

"All right!" Clapp exclaimed, raising his hand to give Dillon a high five. "Henry Holten goes to Bermuda. Some biotech guy who ran a fermentation facility for BTS goes to Bermuda and, guess what? He starts a company called Fermagro. Now what do you suppose Fermagro does?"

"Fermagro. Hell, Holten's the general counsel for Fermagro. Rich Blair, Campbell's former bean counter, told me so a few weeks ago."

"And you didn't think it was important enough to tell me? What the fuck's wrong with you anyway?"

"You think Fermagro made some P-27?"

"Damn right I do."

"Well, goddamn, I guess we've been cleared for a landing."

"But maybe at the wrong airport," Clapp said. "If I prove the contaminated bacteria came from Fermagro, that'll just prove EnviroClean didn't do anything wrong."

"Not quite. We're talking strict liability here. It doesn't matter."

"But EnviroClean obviously didn't know there was anything wrong with the bugs. If anyone screwed up it was Fermagro."

"It doesn't matter. If EnviroClean used the bugs, they're stuck with them, whether they knew it or not. That's the law. They're responsible, even if they did nothing wrong."

"EnviroClean has to pay for Fermagro's screw up. What the hell sense does that make?"

"Well, Ruth Bergstrom did nothing wrong either."

"So they're both innocent? We got ourselves a lawsuit between two innocent parties?"

"Not exactly," Love said. "Ruth would be fine today if EnviroClean hadn't put the P-27 in her creek. They did, they profited from it, and now they're going to pay for it."

"But EnviroClean can turn around and sue Fermagro, right?"

"Absolutely, but that's no concern of mine. Let Henry Holten worry about that."

"That son of a bitch probably owns big stakes in Fermagro. This is looking like a dirty business. Ha! He'll have to sue his own ass."

"Looks like there's a lot going on, Joe, but I have to keep my eye on this case. All we have to do is prove the bugs came from Fermagro. And you have a week in Bermuda."

"I've already booked my flight."

CHAPTER Twenty-three

Love walked into Judge Pamela Cleveland's courtroom a few minutes before the start of trial, wearing a charcoal-gray suit and a brand new white shirt both bought that week right off the rack at Burlington Coat Factory. He carried a briefcase and a large file folder of photographs and documents to exhibit. Ruth Bergstrom sat in her wheelchair behind Love's counsel table, flanked by her neatly dressed children. Her home-care provider Ruby sat at the back of the courtroom. Love winked at Ruth and the kids.

The courtroom was rigged with several computers and television monitors. Technicians scurried about, testing equipment, taping electrical wires beneath the counsel tables, along the front of the jury box, and under flat rubber conduits strung conspicuously across the carpeted floor. The technicians wore maroon sweatshirts emblazoned with DARBY & WITHERSPOON in gold lettering across the chest.

There were eight separate TV monitors, one for each attorney, one for Judge Cleveland at her bench, another at the witness box, three more immediately in front of the jury box, and one for the Judge's clerk. A laptop computer for controlling the system was set out on each counsel table for whichever lawyer wanted to make use of it. At one side of the courtroom was a small table with a third, larger computer.

The sight of his opponents transforming the courtroom into the battleground of their choosing caught Love by surprise. He stood, staring, behind his counsel table. In his mind's eye he pictured himself at the end of the case, rising sheepishly from his seat to hear the jury read its verdict. The jury would deliberate only a few minutes and would then parade briskly back into the courtroom before he had even finished packing his briefcase. Several jurors would laugh openly at him as they walked past the counsel table to the jury box and proclaimed him a hands-down loser.

Then he saw himself leaving the courtroom slinking past the wave of self-adulating euphoria of Henry Holten and Allison Forbes. He would walk from that room with nothing, not even the satisfaction of having defended the weak. He could imagine nothing worse than losing to a man he had grown to despise, *and* to his cocky law school classmate. He supposed Laurie (she who refused to return his phone calls) would be one of the first to hear of his defeat. And then his mother, Cindy Stanhope, his law clerks, his former legal assistant Barbara, not to mention his banker. The entire legal establishment would rapidly learn of the debacle. He had projected such a confident front to these people. What would he tell them now? What would he say to Laurie if he was lucky enough to ever see her again? Had he actually lost his marriage for this worthless case and sold his house to finance it?

Love's heart pounded. He had invested a year and a half and everything he owned in this one day, exhaustively perfecting his arguments, thoroughly convincing himself of the merits of his case. The sobering responsibility he felt for his client, seen against the backdrop of an extravagant show of confidence on the part of his opponents, instantly tarnished the facade of bravado that had for the last eighteen months spurred him into battle each day. Love stood alone, the sole defender of the cause of Ruth Bergstrom, and he was completely overwhelmed, a sandlot ballplayer thrust hastily into the major leagues, an impostor in a suit tailored for someone else.

Trembling, he sat down and began to pull himself together. He believed there to be just the right combination of words in the English language that could persuade the judge and jury of the justice of Ruth Bergstrom's case. They were all words that he knew and understood, simple words. The challenge was to put these simple words into the right combinations and speak them convincingly at the right time.

Love turned from the counsel table and looked at Ruth Bergstrom sitting there with her warm smile and large, innocent eyes. Brett and Molly sat quietly in wooden captain's chairs on either side of their mother, their legs dangling several inches above the floor. Seeing the Bergstroms sitting calmly behind him, their lives entrusted to his persuasiveness, sent a chill down his spine and he felt worse than at any other time in his life. There was no chance of winning. These three wonderful people would leave as losers, and what stability remained in their lives would vanish forever.

The sharp thwack of the clerk's gavel reverberated throughout the courtroom.

"Hear ye, hear ye, hear ye. This honorable court is now in session, the Honorable Pamela Cleveland presiding."

"You may be seated," announced Judge Cleveland, ascending the few steps to her bench at the front of the room. "Are counsel ready for trial?"

"EnviroClean is ready, Your Honor," replied Allison Forbes, rising quickly and confidently from the counsel table at one side of the courtroom. With her at the table were Henry Holten and Boyd Campbell. Seated immediately behind them were Kathleen Campbell and two legal assistants.

For a fleeting moment, Love contemplated rising to admit he was not ready. Ken Butler was in some laboratory seeking clues to the source of the toxin that had injured Ruth Bergstrom. Joe Clapp was in Bermuda searching for evidence that would link this still unidentified toxin to EnviroClean. Most assuredly he was not ready. Recognizing, however, that the question was a formality without remedy, Love stood and responded that he likewise was ready for trial.

"Your Honor," Forbes said, again rising from the counsel table to address the court, "undoubtedly the court has observed the television monitors we've installed throughout the courtroom. Our hope is that we may save a lot of time and expense by eliminating the need for bringing a hundred thousand documents into the courtroom. We've imaged all our documents and recorded them on CD-ROMs so that any document anyone may want to look at can quickly be retrieved and brought up on the monitors for everyone to see at the same time. We've given Mr. Love a computer, so this system will not put him at a disadvantage. I very much hope this meets with the court's approval."

"Mr. Love?" Judge Cleveland said, looking in his direction.

"We may wish to bring some documents in here ourselves for the jury to see. Frankly, I have not used such a system before, and

I wouldn't have the foggiest idea how to operate it. As long as I can use my documents, I have no objection to Ms. Forbes using her computer."

"Very well," Judge Cleveland replied. "Will the bailiff please begin jury selection."

To Love's great relief, after a relatively easy jury selection, opening statements took up the rest of the first day, and court was recessed early to begin testimony the next morning.

On the first day of testimony, Judge Cleveland took her seat at the front of the courtroom and, after all the formalities, said, "You may call your first witness, Mr. Love."

"Your Honor, the plaintiff calls Dr. Boyd Campbell."

Boyd Campbell rose uneasily from his seat between Allison Forbes and Henry Holten. He remained at the table for a moment, confused. Holten grasped his forearm and nodded toward the front of the room. Campbell went and stood in front of the clerk of court and was placed under oath. He glanced back toward the first row of benches and looked briefly at Kathleen, then walked across the courtroom and entered the witness box.

Campbell nervously adjusted the microphone in front of him, and it squealed loudly with feedback throughout the courtroom. He quickly released it and clenched his hands into tight fists, which he then lowered into his lap. His eyes were glazed, and despite the sharp navy blue suit he wore, he looked like an insomniac. His voice cracked with phlegm as he recited his name and address.

Holten twitched in his chair.

Love charged the witness box, and, in a very loud voice, said, "Dr. Campbell, you're not a medical doctor, is that right?"

"No, sir, I'm not," Campbell answered. "I have a PhD in biochemistry."

"Please identify for the jury the names of those medical doctors you have on your staff at EnviroClean."

"We have no medical doctors on our staff, Mr. Love. We're not a pharmaceutical company."

"Well then, Dr. Campbell," Love said, "tell the jury the names of those outside medical doctors with whom you and your staff regularly consult."

"Again, I'd have to answer that there are none. We just do not need that type of consultation."

"Well, certainly EnviroClean has an interest in protecting the public from medical hazards associated with the use of its products. Am I right about that, Dr. Campbell?"

"Absolutely. We are most concerned that our products will be safe."

"That being the case, Dr. Campbell," Love continued, "please tell this jury the names of all medical doctors who conducted tests or safety evaluations of your company's P-27 product line before you injected that product into the soil next door to Ruth Bergstrom's home in the summer of 1999."

"Mr. Love," Campbell said courteously but firmly, "there's no more need for us to have medical doctors evaluate P-27 than there is with some product that you might buy at the hardware store and put on your lawn. Frankly, I don't consider medical doctors qualified to pass on the safety of this product, because they have no experience with the organisms and nutrients that are contained in P-27. The product is entirely safe, and our experience with it confirms that fact."

Campbell made no eye contact with the jurors but locked eyes with Love as if he could throttle him at any moment. He then looked briefly past Love at Kathleen.

"Do I take it by your non-responsive answer that you've had no medical doctors reviewing the safety of P-27?" Love asked sarcastically, speaking in the direction of the jury.

"We've not had medical doctors review it because it's neither necessary nor wise," Campbell said with rising irritation. As soon as this tart reply emerged from his mouth, a look was exchanged between Campbell and his counsel. Allison Forbes dropped her face under her hand and Henry Holten shot Campbell a look of scorn.

"Well, then, Dr. Campbell," Love said, looking back and forth between Campbell and the jury, "who's your director of safety at EnviroClean? Who within your company has responsibility for evaluating the safety of P-27 before it's released into the environment? Who's that person, Dr. Campbell?"

Still focusing on his attorney, Campbell saw Holten tip his head and direct his eyes in the direction of the jury box. "At EnviroClean,"

Campbell responded, looking directly at the jurors, "we all have responsibility for product safety. It's too important to us to entrust to the hands of a single person." The smile Campbell attempted following this statement resembled that of a corpse with its jaw wired shut.

"In other words, you have no director of safety. Is that not the truth Dr. Campbell?" Love's face turned red with emotion as his voice rose.

"I think that responsibility is mine," Campbell replied calmly, obviously attempting by his aura of composure to disarm Love's dramatic gesturing.

Love returned to his seat at the table. "I take it that as a biochemist you're familiar with the disease eosinophilia-myalgia syndrome? Would that be a fair statement?"

"I'm familiar with it now," Campbell replied.

"So you were not aware of this devastating illness at the time you injected P-27 into the soil next to Ruth Bergstrom's house?"

"I wasn't familiar with it then," Campbell answered, "that's true. But that syndrome has nothing whatsoever to do with P-27."

"I'm sure we all appreciate your medical opinions on the subject," Love said, looking at the jury, "but I might ask you to restrict your testimony to subjects for which you are qualified and which are responsive to my questions."

"Objection," Allison Forbes said forcefully, rising from her seat. "To the characterization counsel is insinuating."

"Sustained," Judge Cleveland ruled. "Counsel will confine himself to asking questions and leave the testifying to the witness."

"To this very day, Dr. Campbell," Love asked, "have you done a single medical study to prove that P-27 does not cause EMS?"

"No sir, we have not," Campbell said flatly. "Nor have we tested it for hundreds of other illnesses no reasonable scientist would ever suspect could be caused by P-27."

"Your Honor," Love said, "move to strike the last comment as non-responsive."

"Sustained," Judge Cleveland said. "The jury will disregard that last comment."

Campbell gaped at the judge. He was about to protest, but Love's voice cut him off. "In fact," Love stated emphatically, "to this day you've never even conducted simple testing at the Bergstroms' property to determine whether your P-27 organisms have escaped and contaminated their land. You've not done that, have you?"

"No," Campbell said. "I thought it would be a good idea, but my lawyers advised me against it."

"Your attorney gave you this advice?" Love asked, feigning incredulity. "How can that be? Why would your lawyer not want to know the truth about the condition of the soil in the back of the Bergstroms' home?"

"Objection, Your Honor," said Allison Forbes, rising quickly to her feet. "This calls for speculation, and it also invades the attorney-client privilege of confidentiality."

"Sustained," said Judge Cleveland. "Conversations between Dr. Campbell and his attorneys are protected."

"Well, which attorney was it that gave you this advice, Ms. Forbes here?" Love asked.

"Same objection," Forbes said.

"Sustained," Judge Cleveland repeated.

"Well, Dr. Campbell," Love continued, "you are the president and chief executive officer of EnviroClean, are you not?"

"I am," Campbell replied.

"And I assume that, as such, you would be the one making the final decision about whether to do testing? Am I right about that? It would be you not your lawyers who made that call. Is that fair?"

"Yes," Campbell admitted, "the decision was mine."

"All right then, forgetting anything that was said between you and your lawyers, any confidential conversations, why did you decide not to test the soil at the Bergstroms' backyard?"

"I can't answer that without reference to the conversations with Henry Holten," Campbell replied. "That's the reason I didn't do the testing. I wasn't afraid of the truth. I'm not afraid of the truth today, because I firmly believe that our P-27 did not cause Mrs. Bergstrom's tragic illness."

"Move to strike the last part of that answer, Your Honor, as non-responsive," Love droned.

"Sustained," Judge Cleveland said "The jury will disregard Dr. Campbell's opinion about EnviroClean's lack of fault. That's the question you'll have to answer yourselves."

Again, Campbell seemed flabbergasted by Judge Cleveland's agreement that his last statement was "non-responsive." He looked at the jurors, and they looked back at him, frowning.

"One final question, Your Honor," Love said. "Is it you, Dr. Campbell, who's been sending flowers anonymously to Ruth Bergstrom ever since her husband died from a heart attack last March?"

Campbell had no opportunity to answer the question before Allison Forbes rose to object.

"What possible relevance can this question have to the proceedings in this courtroom? Where on earth does counsel intend to take this line of questioning?"

"Withdrawn," Love said quickly to avoid any ruling from the court. Instead, he lifted his briefcase from the floor and placed it on the table in front of him. Opening the clasps, he reached in and produced a brown paper sack. Rising and approaching the witness, he pulled from the bag a dozen wilted roses. "Dr. Campbell, you sent Ruth Bergstrom these flowers because of the terrible guilt you feel for what you've done to her life. Isn't that the truth?"

"Objection," Forbes said again. "This is outrageous. This is ..."

"You're admitting your guilt, aren't you?" Love shouted. "The flowers are your admission of guilt for destroying her life. That's the truth, isn't it, Dr. Campbell?"

Eyes watering and voice shaking with anger and humiliation, Campbell said, "I've sent flowers to Ruth Bergstrom, yes. But I did it out of compassion, not guilt. That's undoubtedly a difficult concept for a lawyer to understand."

"That, Dr. Campbell," Love said, smiling and stomping back to his seat, "will be for the jury to decide. No further questions."

Campbell shot a stunned and wounded look at Ruth Bergstrom who had drawn her hands up to her face. He then looked forlornly at Allison Forbes, who came to his aid by standing and saying kindly, "We'll be asking you some questions later Dr. Campbell. You're all done for today."

The afternoon session brought to court an official from the Environmental Protection Agency. On direct examination she testified about some of the dangers of biotechnology and how genetically altered organisms can create unexpected risks for humans if they are not carefully tested. She indicated that the manufacturer of such products has absolute responsibility for insuring that all necessary tests are conducted to insure the products are entirely safe before they are released into the environment. She did not favor the use of these organisms because of the unknown risks that might be encountered. Rather, she favored conventional methods of cleaning up toxic spills by excavating the site and sending the contaminated soil to a landfill. As for EnviroClean, she had recommended against granting permits to the company to treat the gas station next to the Bergstroms but had been overruled by the regional director of the agency.

Allison Forbes mounted a vigorous cross-examination. Smoothly and efficiently she brought to life on the television monitors dozens of government records and scientific papers that supported the use of biotechnology in controlling hazardous wastes and that also documented the dangers of landfills. She showed the jury the myriad regulations the federal government had adopted that required stringent, exhaustive, and extremely expensive testing of P-27 before it was allowed to be used at the gas station next to the Bergstroms. The EPA official was shown her own signature on documents that specifically accepted the results of tests performed by EnviroClean to get the required permits. This signature was enlarged on the monitors throughout the courtroom for all jurors to see the government's approval of the dozens of tests that EnviroClean had performed.

Over two hours, Allison Forbes meticulously brought scores of documents, scientific charts, graphic displays, and other exhibits onto the television monitors in front of the jury. When the day's testimony concluded, the innuendo and hopeful speculation of Love's witnesses had been methodically undermined by the precision and careful scientific analysis presented by the EnviroClean defense.

Thursday morning brought Dr. Harold McCosh to the witness stand. McCosh described his ten-year relationship with Ruth Bergstrom as her family physician. He told of her remarkable health and vigor prior to January, 2000. Routine physical examinations had been entirely normal for years. There had never been the slightest sign of any neurological problems such as those she began to experience in January, 2000.

Dr. McCosh described in detail both his efforts and those of the

Mayo Clinic in attempting to learn the cause of the symptoms she began experiencing at that time. All the common disorders such as multiple sclerosis and Hodgkin's and Parkinson's diseases were ruled out. Eventually the diagnosis of eosinophilia-myalgia syndrome was made and confirmed by the Mayo Clinic.

"In January, 2000," Dr. McCosh explained, "paresthesia and weakness appeared in Mrs. Bergstrom's lower extremities. An electromyogram at that time confirmed a moderately severe peripheral neuropathy. Mrs. Bergstrom was given antibiotics in increasing amounts, but her symptoms nevertheless worsened and eventually involved the upper extremities as well.

"By March 1, her physical examination revealed a profoundly debilitated woman with severe muscle atrophy and weakness in all four extremities. She had purple macular lesions on her arms and legs. She had an intense burning sensation and skin sensitivity even to light touch. Her paralysis progressed rapidly, and by July 2000, she was borderline quadriplegic, with some paresthesia appearing in her respiratory muscles. Mrs. Bergstrom had random and intense muscle spasms occurring in her extremities. She developed some cognitive dysfunction in the form of short-term memory loss. Really, Mrs. Bergstrom was a very sick woman. We thought we were going to lose her for a while there."

"Dr. McCosh," Love asked, "have you conducted any research to determine the cause of Mrs. Bergstrom's EMS?"

"Yes, sir, I have," McCosh replied. "I conducted a literature search of all published articles on EMS. These all report that the etiology of the syndrome results from the ingestion of tainted food products. One case study in particular documented a widespread outbreak of EMS as a result of the contamination of a nonprescription drug consumed by thousands of women in the United States. After considerable investigation by the Centers for Disease Control in Atlanta and by our own Mayo Clinic, it was determined that the source of the contamination was a change in the fermentation process of a manufacturing facility in Japan."

"Dr. McCosh," Love asked, "do you have any opinion as to the source of the contamination that caused Mrs. Bergstrom's EMS?"

"Yes," McCosh said. "By a process of elimination, we have ruled out every source other than the P-27 that was released by Enviro-

Clean at the gas station next to the Bergstroms' house. I might add that the fermentation process for producing the microorganisms used in P-27 is virtually identical to the process used by the Japanese firm that sold the contaminated tablets in this country several years ago."

"Doctor," Love continued, "do you have an opinion as to what the future holds for Mrs. Bergstrom?"

"Yes, I do," Dr. McCosh replied. "Ruth Bergstrom doesn't have a bright future ahead of her. She'll have continued severe neurological dysfunction, affecting both her legs and to a lesser extent her arms. She'll never get out of her wheelchair. She'll never be able to live alone and take care of herself and her children. She can do limited cooking, provided everything she needs is kept at a level she can reach from her wheelchair. She can take care of her personal hygiene, dressing and undressing by herself at the present, although only with considerable time and effort. Eventually, however, as she gets older, she'll no longer be able to do these things for herself and she'll need twenty-four-hour assistance. Her life will be a constant struggle for her, and her struggle will only become more profound the older she gets."

"Your witness, Ms. Forbes," Love said confidently, feeling perversely delighted by the misery in his client's life.

"Dr. McCosh," Allison Forbes began, "you're a family physician, are you not?"

"Yes ma'am," he replied.

"Have you ever in your life seen another case of EMS besides the case of Ruth Bergstrom?" Forbes asked.

"No, ma'am, I have not."

"So you certainly don't consider yourself an expert on this disease, then, given your total absence of professional experience with the condition."

"Well," he replied, "I'm a medical doctor, and I've read all of the published studies on this illness. In addition, I've consulted with the physicians at the Mayo Clinic who've treated Mrs. Bergstrom, as well as with those who participated in the study of the Japanese pharmaceutical company. This is a rare condition, so no one is really very familiar with it from a clinical perspective. I suppose I have more experience than any other family physician in this state. But yes, you're correct. I've treated only one patient."

"So are you an expert or not?" Forbes asked again.

"With one or two exceptions, I'm about as expert as you'll find in this area," he said.

"So no one's much of an expert on EMS, is that what you're saying, Dr. McCosh?"

"I suppose you could say that," McCosh said.

"Perhaps I could have a minute, Your Honor?" Allison Forbes asked Judge Cleveland. "I'd like to set up a few relevant exhibits."

On that cue several Darby & Witherspoon legal assistants rose from their seats and retrieved from the corridor outside the courtroom a large model of the entire area surrounding the Bergstroms' house, the gas station next door, and the creek that ran behind both properties. The exhibit had been constructed to scale, and it included both precise models of the Bergstrom residence and the gas station, as well as accurate topographic representations of the contour of the land and the creek. Four paralegals carried the exhibit to the front of the courtroom while others brought in a large collapsible stand to hold the exhibit and position it in front of the jury box.

"Dr. McCosh," Forbes began, "you recognize this as a scale model of the Bergstrom residence and surrounding area, do you not?"

"Actually," he answered, "I've never been to their home, so I'll accept your word for the accuracy of your model."

"You mean you have come into this courtroom to tell this jury that Dr. Boyd Campbell is the source of all Mrs. Bergstrom's problems," Allison asked, walking along behind the chairs at the counsels' table and placing her hands on Dr. Campbell's shoulders, "without so much as having set foot on the property to see for yourself what it looked like?"

With some irritation rising in his voice, he replied, "My opinions are based on Mrs. Bergstrom's history, the medical charts, and the published literature in the field."

"Well, then, I'm sorry to catch you by surprise, Doctor, but would you be willing to answer a few questions about the layout of the land? Specifically, I'd like to ask you about what had to have happened for the P-27 to be the culprit here."

"I'll try my best," McCosh said.

"Please assume, doctor, that this is the area where the P-27 was injected into the ground," Allison said, standing at the large model in front of the jury box and focusing a laser pointer on a small dot at the front of the gas station. "For the P-27 to have caused the EMS, it would have to migrate first from 25 feet beneath the ground in front of the gas station, then find its way to the creek bed on the other side of the building, then travel all the way back to the creek about a hundred feet away. Are you with me so far?"

"Yes, I agree," McCosh answered. "That must have been what happened."

"Then," Allison Forbes continued, "the P-27 would have to be carried by the water in the creek, where it would somehow hop out of the water and climb up the twenty-foot incline separating the creek from the Bergstroms' home, finally entering the house mysteriously and carefully selecting only Mrs. Bergstrom to infect."

"Hopping out of the water?" McCosh chuckled.

"Let's not play games, doctor. The bacteria had to migrate from the water into the Bergstroms' house in some manner, did they not?"

"You're right. Somehow Mrs. Bergstrom had to have been directly exposed to the bacteria. We're not sure exactly how, but there would have to have been physical contact with the waterborne bacteria."

"Physical contact with the creek is highly unlikely, isn't that true, doctor?"

"I don't agree with you," McCosh replied. "Mrs. Bergstrom could have come into contact with the creek by rinsing off her hands after working in her garden or by washing some vegetables in the creek before bringing them in to consume them. I'm sure we can think of many other scenarios as well."

"Has Mrs. Bergstrom ever told you that, on even one single occasion, she washed any vegetables in the creek or that she washed her own hands in the creek?" Allison asked.

"No, she hasn't," McCosh replied.

"And, Dr. McCosh," Allison continued, "Mrs. Bergstrom would've had to have done this many times to have had enough exposure to become sick, correct?"

"That's true, if this is the mechanism of infection."

"So she must have forgotten each and every instance where she washed her hands or vegetables in the creek, right?"

"She doesn't remember any such instance, that's correct," McCosh replied. "But you're forgetting she has a memory problem now, because of the EMS."

"In any event, what you're telling this jury is that she became infected in a way that even she herself denies has occurred."

"Well," McCosh said thoughtfully, "I don't think she denied doing it. I believe she said she couldn't remember. Frankly, I wouldn't expect her to remember such a seemingly innocent event."

"She became sick in January, 2000, am I right Dr. McCosh?"

"Yes, that's correct. That's when she first came in to see me," McCosh replied.

"Do you suppose she might remember washing her hands if she first had to chop a hole in the ice covering the creek to immerse her hands in the frigid waters?"

Some restlessness occurred in the jury box, prompting McCosh to look at the jurors as he replied, "Obviously, that's not how it happened."

"How did it happen then, doctor? Please tell these jurors how it happened."

"I can't speculate on the precise mechanism. I can only state that it must indeed have occurred."

"Perhaps you could at least tell the jury why all the P-27 that you say must have entered the creek by the gas station all got out of the creek at the Bergstroms' residence?"

"I'm not saying it did."

"If all the P-27 did not escape from the creek at the Bergstroms'," Allison added, "then why didn't it infect the thousands of other people who live downstream from the Bergstroms?"

"As I said," Dr. McCosh replied, "we don't know the precise mechanism by which she became infected and others did not. All we know is that's what happened. This is not unusual for diseases of this kind, because they are not contagious."

"What tests have you run, doctor, to show that P-27 causes EMS?" Allison asked.

"I've done no tests," McCosh said.

"What test has anyone else done to prove that P-27 causes EMS?"

"The only tests on the P-27 were done at the Mayo Clinic."

"But those tests indicated that P-27 cannot cause EMS. Is that not true, Dr. McCosh?"

"The tests showed that the particular batch of P-27 that was tested did not produce the toxin that injured Mrs. Bergstrom. However, there are variations between batches, so a negative result on one batch doesn't mean a second batch would not be positive. But you're right, the Mayo Clinic didn't find a batch of P-27 that tested positive for the toxin."

"The bottom line, then, doctor," Allison said, aiming her laser pointer at the model before the jury, "is that you believe some organism that has never been proved to cause EMS surfaced from deep under the gas station and somehow found its way into Mrs. Bergstrom's bloodstream, without infecting any other family members, without infecting any other neighbors downstream, and without infecting any of the dozens of EnviroClean employees who worked with the product, nor any of the DNR or EPA officials who inspected the site and tested the product's effectiveness. Is that what you're telling this jury, Dr. McCosh?"

"You're distorting the truth by the way you phrase that question," Dr. McCosh said. "I don't think it much matters how this happened. What matters is that it did indeed happen, and with extremely severe consequences for Ruth Bergstrom."

"Doctor, it may not matter to you, but it matters very much to Boyd Campbell and all the wonderful people who work for him at EnviroClean. I have no more questions."

Thursday was rounded out by testimony from a couple of lab technicians who analyzed several known batches of P-27 and a few samples obtained at the site. They testified the known samples of P-27 matched the samples found in the creek bed behind the Bergstroms' home. They conceded, however, that they had found no P-27 anywhere else on the Bergstroms' property and had no explanation for precisely how the P-27 could have infected Mrs. Bergstrom. They also admitted they had run no tests on properties downstream to determine if the P-27 had migrated beyond the Bergstroms' to present danger to any other residents in the area.

On Friday morning the jury heard testimony from field inspectors from the United States Environmental Protection Agency. Their testimony was uneventful, essentially duplicating what the jury had already heard from the other technical witnesses in the case.

Afternoon brought to the witness stand Dr. Richard Gauss from the Mayo Clinic.

As Dr. Gauss rose from his seat, the female jurors' heads, in marching band precision, followed him from the back of the courtroom, through the swinging gates of the bar, to the clerk's desk where he was sworn to his oath of honesty. Several loose ends remained in Love's case, and Dr. Gauss was expected to be the last technical expert who could tie them all together. He gave the clerk a warm smile as he was administered the oath and swore he would tell nothing but the truth to the jurors eagerly anticipating his testimony. Clean-jawed and softly clothed, Dr. Gauss exuded an aura of scientific excellence and integrity as he took his seat in the witness box.

"Dr. Gauss," Love began, after eliciting a description of the physician's considerable experience in his specialty, "please tell the jury about the work you've done to determine the source of Mrs. Bergstrom's eosinophilia-myalgia syndrome."

"Certainly. Initially when Mrs. Bergstrom was brought to the Mayo Clinic, I was frankly stymied as to the cause of her EMS. Of course, at that time we were principally concerned with controlling its progression rather than determining its cause. As her condition stabilized somewhat, our attention focused on the source so we could make certain that neither she nor other members of her family might be infected. A group of us at the clinic developed a protocol to accomplish this objective.

"It was my preliminary opinion that this was a bacterial infection. Other strains of pseudomonas have been known to produce similar symptoms. We took several blood samples from Mrs. Bergstrom and cultured them for forty-eight hours. Nothing of interest grew. There were no pseudomonas as I had suspected there might be, and we found no evidence of any other bacterial or viral infection."

"What was the next step you took, doctor?" Love asked.

"We took another blood sample and examined it with high-performance gas chromatography. We used a machine that analyzes each of the component parts of the blood and records them on a graph. In essence, what we see is a series of peaks, each representing a different component of the blood. Since we know what the pattern of peaks should look like for normal blood, it's easy to detect an extra peak, representing something that's not supposed to be there, a contaminant. In this case, that was Peak E."

"Doctor, what is the significance of this finding?" Love asked.

"Peak E was isolated and identified as a toxic contaminant. We were able to establish that this was the agent that infected Mrs. Bergstrom."

"Doctor," Love interjected, "would it be helpful to show the jury the graphs you obtained from the chromatography?"

"Certainly," Dr. Gauss replied as Love handed him two exhibits. "Note that I've labeled the peaks on both graphs as A, B, C, and so forth. Note also that the graph with Mrs. Bergstrom's blood has an extra peak that's not present in the control sample. I've labeled that Peak E."

"Doctor," Love continued, "have you tried to determine where the contaminant represented by Peak E came from?"

"Yes, we did," Dr. Gauss replied. "I think we've looked into every conceivable possibility. The Department of Natural Resources conducted a series of tests of the soil around the gas station next door to the Bergstroms' property, as well as in the creek bed behind their home. Those samples were also analyzed by gas chromatography. We found a substance that produced an identical peak as the Peak E in Mrs. Bergstrom's blood sample. There's no doubt in my mind that these are the same compound, the same toxic substance."

"What else did you do, Dr. Gauss?"

"To rule out any other source, the DNR took samples upstream from the gas station. Those samples were also analyzed but no similar peak was detected. Accordingly, it is reasonable to conclude that the source of the compound was at the gas station. Finally, to rule out any petroleum byproduct from the gas station itself, a number of samples were collected from inside the old underground storage tanks at the station. EnviroClean did not treat the insides of these tanks with P-27. No Peak E compound was found, indicating that this isn't something that was originally contained in the gasoline. We did the same for other known petroleum products, such as motor oils, diesel fuel and cleaning solvents, all with the same negative results."

"Doctor," Love continued, "what's the relationship between the Peak E contaminant you have described and P-27? Is this chemical part of the ingredients in P-27?"

"No, Peak E is not actually part of the P-27 formulation, but it was produced by the bacteria as a by-product of their own metabolic processes. In essence, P-27 can degrade the gasoline because the bacteria use the chemicals in the gasoline as a food source, converting them into less hazardous substances in the process. It wasn't the P-27 itself that caused Mrs. Bergstrom's injuries. Rather, it was the chemical by-products that were produced by the P-27 as it degraded the chemicals in the gasoline."

"Dr. Gauss, just one more question," Love said. "Have you been able to determine whether this compound you've identified as Peak E can produce the type of neurological problem suffered by my client, Ruth Bergstrom?"

"Yes," Dr. Gauss replied, "I have. Some of the amino acids isolated from soils collected from the creek bed were sent to the College of Biological Sciences at the University of Minnesota. A colleague of mine then injected small quantities of the compound into the bloodstream of several rabbits. Within ten days, each rabbit developed significant neurological deficiencies, most notably in their motor skills. There's no question that Peak E is a powerful toxin and that it can produce profound neurological disorders."

"Your witness," said Love, looking confidently toward Allison Forbes.

"Dr. Gauss," Allison began, "as a scientist, you must be motivated by a tremendous concern for thoroughness and attention to detail. Am I right about that?"

"Absolutely," he replied.

"And as such, you will always demand solid scientific data to support your conclusions and opinions. Would that also be accurate?"

"Of course."

"On the other hand," Allison continued, "as a practicing physician you must frequently be obliged to make judgments about your patients with something less than absolute scientific proof, correct?"

"We have to take care of our patients as best we can," Dr. Gauss said, "even where uncertainties exist about either the cause of their illnesses or the best course of treatment."

"And, of course, Dr. Gauss, that's exactly what you've done here, is it not?"

"I don't think so," Gauss replied.

"Well, you've come to conclusions about your patient's illness that are not based on absolute scientific certainty. Is that a fair statement?"

"I think your statement is misleading, Ms. Forbes," Gauss countered. "My opinions are based on a reasonable degree of scientific certainty. They are based on a careful review of all evidence, the soil samples, the tank samples, the blood samples, the rabbit toxicity testing, the published medical literature, and my own examinations and history from Mrs. Bergstrom. I feel quite comfortable with these opinions, and I think your characterization of the degree of certainty is deceptive."

"Well, let's just see how solid this proof is, Dr. Gauss. You've testified on direct examination about what you found. Let's look at what you haven't found. You've not found any P-27 in Ruth Bergstrom's blood, correct?"

"That's correct."

"Well then, Dr. Gauss, how could this nonexistent P-27 produce this toxin?"

"It's not surprising to me that we didn't find P-27," Gauss said. "After all, Mrs. Bergstrom had been given antibiotics before coming to the Mayo Clinic. The antibiotics killed the P-27, but not before it produced the toxin that caused the EMS."

"You've not proven that P-27 can cause EMS, correct?"

"That's not quite correct," Gauss said. "We found that Peak E definitely causes EMS, and we believe Peak E can be produced by the organisms contained in P-27."

"Dr. Gauss," Forbes said, "please identify for me even one single, solitary test you or anyone else anywhere in the world has ever performed to show that P-27 produces the Peak E toxin. Which test is it, doctor? Please identify it for the jury."

"The toxin is produced only under certain special conditions, which we've not yet been able to replicate in the laboratory," Gauss answered.

"Is that fancy scientific talk, Dr. Gauss, for having failed to demonstrate that P-27 produces Peak E?"

"Peak E cannot easily be produced in the laboratory. It's only produced when it's actually metabolizing the chemicals in gasoline."

"But neither you nor anyone else in the world has ever taken a sample of P-27, tested it, and found it to produce the amino acid you believe injured Mrs. Bergstrom. Is that a fair and accurate statement, doctor?"

"Yes," Dr. Gauss said.

"Thank you, Dr. Gauss," Allison said. "Do you have some opinion to a reasonable degree of scientific certainty how the P-27 could've gotten from the creek into Mrs. Bergstrom's blood without having infected any other family members or any of her many neighbors?"

"I don't know how to answer that," Gauss replied. "I'm a medical doctor, not an environmentalist. I haven't been out to her property to look into that aspect of her case. What I do know is that it must have found some way into her blood, probably in a rather unusual manner, which would explain why it didn't infect other family members or neighbors. I'm not sure it makes much difference how it got there. It did, and that's something we know without the slightest doubt."

"Dr. Gauss, do you have some opinion why none of the dozens of EnviroClean employees who work with P-27 at the plant and at the job sites around the country have ever developed EMS? If P-27 can introduce this toxin into people's bloodstreams, why has it never happened to a single other person in the world besides Mrs. Bergstrom?"

"As a clinical physician, that question isn't important to me. My patient was ill, deathly ill. My job was to find out why and to take care of her. I think it's your client, Ms. Forbes, who would want to know how it infected Mrs. Bergstrom so he can take appropriate steps to make certain it never happens again."

"Dr. Gauss, strictly from a scientific perspective, there are some unanswered questions in this case. Is that fair to say?"

"I can agree with that," Dr. Gauss stated. "We know what caused Mrs. Bergstrom's EMS, but the exact mechanism is not clear."

"You've said repeatedly you're testifying from the perspective of a medical doctor faced with the need to treat your patient as best you can. Consider for a moment the perspective this jury must have in order to answer questions about whether EnviroClean is responsible for causing Mrs. Bergstrom's EMS. Consider there's no evidence that Mrs. Bergstrom ever had any P-27 in her bloodstream. Consider that after all the tests that have been done by EnviroClean, by various government agencies, and by Mrs. Bergstrom's attorney, there's not one shred of evidence that P-27 is toxic or produces some compound that's toxic. Consider that not one other human being of the hundreds of people who work with P-27 at EnviroClean has come down with this illness. Consider that no one else in her family or in her neighborhood, all exposed to P-27, became ill. Considering all these elements as a scientist, can you say to a reasonable degree of scientific certainty that EnviroClean's P-27 is the proximate cause of Ruth Bergstrom's EMS?"

Dr. Gauss sat silently for a few moments considering the breadth of the question.

"Considering the way in which you have phrased this hypothetical question, Ms. Forbes," Gauss replied finally, "I don't believe it can be answered to a reasonable degree of certainty."

"In other words," Allison summarized, "you cannot conclude with scientific certainty that the P-27 caused Mrs. Bergstrom's EMS?"

"Not with absolute scientific certainty," Dr. Gauss said quietly.

"I believe that's all I have for you, Dr. Gauss," Allison said politely. "Thank you for your candor." Dr. Gauss stepped down from the witness stand. "Your Honor," Allison continued, "may counsel approach the bench?"

"Step forward," Judge Cleveland said.

"Your Honor," Allison said, "I believe that, except for Mrs. Bergstrom, Mr. Love has finished calling all of the people on his witness disclosure list. Certainly there are no more witnesses with any information on the critical liability issues in this case. As such, since it's now late on Friday afternoon, and we've been here for four full days of testimony, I'd like the court to consider my previous motions for a dismissal. Surely Ruth Bergstrom will be unable to shed any light on the complex scientific issues surrounding this case. We'll be wasting our time working all weekend when the court has enough evidence now to grant a judgment in favor of EnviroClean.

"Dillon," Allison Forbes continued, turning her comments directly to her adversary, "you can't seriously contend you've met your burden of proof in this case. You've given it your best shot. You should be commended for that, to be sure. It's time to summon the fortitude to accept defeat honorably so we can all go home and be done with this case once and for all."

"This is the third time Ms. Forbes has made this identical motion, Your Honor," Love responded. "It remains premature, as I have not rested my case. In fact, I plan to call one or two additional liability witnesses to testify on our behalf. Frankly, I think they may have some rather important evidence on the question of fault."

"How can that be? You've called everyone on your witness list except for Ruth Bergstrom," said Allison. "You better not tell me you've got some surprise witness you've been keeping under wraps."

"Your Honor," Love replied, "we're following up on some leads that only recently came to our attention. The additional witnesses I plan to call are not presently on our witness list. However, I can represent to the court that anyone I call will be well known to defense counsel. There'll be no surprise witnesses on Monday morning, Allie, I can tell you that. But I suspect there'll be some very surprising testimony."

Judge Cleveland looked sternly into the eyes of Dillon Love. "For the sake of Ruth Bergstrom," she said, "I do hope you're right, because I've heard nothing yet that would permit me to allow this case to go to the jury. Either you show up Monday morning with some credible evidence, or I'm going to grant Ms. Forbes' motion to dismiss this case. And you better not attempt to do it with anyone defense counsel doesn't already know, because I'll have no surprise witnesses testifying in my courtroom. Have a pleasant weekend."

CHAPTER Twenty-four

At 10:35 P.M. on Friday, June 1, Dillon walked into the echoing arrivals hall of Bermuda International Airport. The grinning white face of Joe Clapp swam out of a crowd of waiting black people and said, "Goddamn, I'll bet I've had a hell of a lot more fun this week than you." Clapp grabbed Love's carry-on bag, then thought better of it and handed it back to him. "What the hell am I doing? You're bigger than me."

Love, his head aching from the free cognac he knocked back on the plane, forced a crooked grin. He felt hot in the suit he had been wearing all day and had not had a chance to change before leaving for the airport.

"Chrissake, you look miserable, Dillon. We gotta get you on the beach tomorrow."

"You're no fucking beauty yourself, you know."

"Must not have gone that well for you in court, huh."

"I have until nine o'clock Monday morning to produce something convincing, or this case will be history," Love said.

"Well, you've definitely got an attitude," Clapp said. "And I've got just the remedy, sun, sand, and pussy. You're comin' with me to meet a couple of 'em for a few brews right now."

"Forget the pussy," Love said, "we've got work to do."

"You're gonna want to meet this one babe, I can tell you that," Clapp said. "Unless you've gotten lucky without me knowing it, you must be one horny sonuvabitch."

"Fuck you."

"She damn well might," Clapp replied. "Either her or her friend. And she's also gonna be your favorite new witness, with a capital *W*. You're gonna be one happy vacationer."

Love followed Clapp out of the small terminal into the soft, humid warmth of a beautiful night. He stopped for a moment to savor the air, filling his lungs and looking up at the bright stars. "Come on, Dillweed, I've got us a cab," yelled Clapp.

The driver sped along a short road from the terminal and onto the causeway that led south off St. David's Island. A small sign indicated the direction to Hamilton. "Take us the quick way, please," Clapp said and grinned at Love. The driver responded, and they drove along at speeds of up to forty miles an hour (which Love later learned was about twice the legal limit). The causeway was relatively straight, so it was pleasant enough, but it was dark, and Love felt uneasy about what might lie ahead.

Once in Hamilton Parish a few minutes later, Love started thinking about the horrible news reports he seemed to always be hearing about buses on tropical islands careening off narrow coastal roads, crashing onto the rocks below, killing everyone aboard. What was this guy doing? North Shore Road was so narrow in spots that it hardly seemed possible for two vehicles to pass. And they were driving on the left side of the road! Love checked his seatbelt several times in between gripping his armrest and bracing himself against Clapp's seat in front of him. After several near misses with trucks, mopeds, other cars, and pedestrians, they reached Hamilton in about twenty minutes. Love's clothing was drenched, and Clapp couldn't stop laughing.

They stopped first at a small cluster of guest cottages, two of which Clapp had rented. The taxi driver waited, walking up and down in the dark, smoking, while Love went into his tiny cottage, threw off his suit, and slipped into big baggy shorts, a Hawaiian shirt, and flip-flops. The shorts were from two years ago when he was still in shape. They fit comfortably again now that he'd shed some pounds.

It was almost midnight when they parked outside the Red Rock Pub, just across the street from the harbor. The Red Rock was a cozy tavern with the island's customary pink stucco facade and dark green shutters. There was a little patio in front, and two ornate gas lanterns lit the entrance to the main room, a dim space with heavy, stained woodwork, a large bar, a few tables, and several high-backed booths with small, colored glass lamps. The place was not packed, but plenty of red-faced people, mostly white men in colorful cricket shirts and Bermuda shorts, watched cricket on a big-screen TV. A pall of smoke hung in the air, which smelled of spilled beer.

Love followed Clapp through the front bar into a billiards room with two tables, at one of which two women were playing a game of three-cushion.

"Hey, girls," Clapp shouted above the raucous noise of the cricket crowd, "I brought you another Yank."

"Do you mind?" said the woman leaning over the table with her long black hair cascading onto the green felt, "you nearly put me off my shot."

The other woman, a tall blond with a ruddy face and a missing tooth, said, "You're a loud-mouthed ponce, Joe Clapp. We got money on this rack."

The dark-haired woman made her shot, stood up, and said, "Get a round in, and then we'll talk to you. Go on, piss off."

The blond woman laughed.

Joe, unfazed, grabbed Love's elbow and turned him back toward the main bar, and over his shoulder said, "We'll get a couple of brew-skies while you ladies finish your game."

"You'll find your arse sanding the doorstep if you order 'brew-skies' from this barman," the blond laughed. "He hates Septics. But you and the big feller can bring us a couple of Red Stripes if you can get him to serve you."

"What the hell's a 'septic'?" asked Love as they continued to the other room.

"It's wordplay," said Clapp. "'Septic tank' leads to 'Yank.' So we're foreign *and* smell like shit."

"How charming," Love said.

"Look," Clapp said once they reached the bar, "if you don't under-stand what the hell they're talking about, just nod and smile."

"What kind of accents are those anyway?"

"Don't even ask. Hey, you gotta try the porter here. It's like drink-ing blood."

Joe ordered two pints of porter and two bottles of Red Stripe from a large bald man with multiple piercings. Love noticed that Clapp neutralized his nasal Midwestern accent when he spoke to the bar-man. They sipped the porter for a while and watched the women play in the adjoining room. The woman with the long black hair was shooting again. Joe identified her as Johanna Huntington. "They call her Johnnie," he said. "Older than she looks. Runs all the time. She's the laboratory director for Fermagro."

"Fermagro," said Love. "Now I see why you're so pleased with yourself."

"Yep. The night's got more potential than throwing down a few beers and pawing a couple of babes."

They went over and gave the women their Red Stripes and then lingered a few feet from the billiard table to observe the game. The buxom blond with the missing tooth took her beer and gave Clapp a wink as she chugged half of it. Johnnie took a sip, smiled at Love, and placed her bottle on the edge of the table before resuming the game.

Love liked the exotic face of Johanna Huntington. Physically she was a wisp of a woman with pretty hollow cheeks and pale olive skin stretched tightly around prominent jaw bones that framed a full and sensuous mouth. There was a hint of Italian or Brazilian about her, but Love was no good at identifying ethnic traits. Neither was he an expert at telling age but he estimated she might be edging fifty, an exceedingly well-preserved fifty, probably helped here and there by a good plastic surgeon. Her tight-fitting midriff halter revealed a well-toned abdomen. Her eyes were intent and serious as she moved effortlessly from shot to shot without hesitation, sending her ball ricocheting in grand geometric patterns around the table. He imagined her sitting in a Minneapolis courtroom revealing mysterious secrets to a spellbound jury.

"I'm a tit man, myself," Clapp whispered, observing Love's scrutiny of Johanna Huntington, "but it ain't half bad to wrap your palms around that sweet little ass of hers."

"I'm more interested in her potential as a witness," Love said.

"You can't have both? A touch of the older woman syndrome?" Clapp asked. "A good witness and a great lay, now that's a powerful combination. And you'll have a whole new attitude come Monday morning."

"Lawyers aren't supposed to screw their witnesses," Love said. "It doesn't do much for their credibility with the jury."

"Only if they find out about it," Clapp said. "I suppose you ask all your opponents' witnesses if they're sleeping with the enemy. Is that how it's done, counselor?"

"Are you trying to get me disbarred?"

"Anyway, since when have you followed the rules?"

The game dragged on, and Love, annoyed at the seeming indifference of the two women and disliking the smoky atmosphere of the unventalated bar, walked outside and sat at a table that looked out across the harbor to an island-studded bay. He sat back in the comfortable Adirondack-style chair and looked up at the bright stars, dreaming of how it would feel to raise his eyebrows in victory across the courtroom at Henry Holten. Clapp joined him and, sensing Love's irritation, was suddenly all business. He summarized his discoveries of the past week. A visit to Fermagro had produced a copy of its annual report and a listing of all the officers of the company. The corporate secretary and general counsel was Henry Holten, with a local address at Oxford Beaches, a small and exclusive colony of cottages on Somerset Island west of Hamilton across the Great Sound.

Clapp had driven to the spot, wandered the grounds, and asked a few questions. Although the staff there revealed no information about Henry Holten or Fermagro, Clapp found a series of plaques in a corridor of the main building. Each plaque carried the names of the most frequent guests and the number of times each had stayed at the resort. Holten's name appeared on a plaque identifying five-time guests in 1999. By 2001 he was on a plaque for guests having visited the resort twenty-five times. "Obviously," Clapp said, "there's more to Bermuda than pink sand and relaxation."

Clapp went on to tell Love about his cold call to Fermagro, when he posed as a vendor of laboratory equipment and supplies. A couple of days later he found himself being escorted through the lab by its director, Johanna Huntington. His cover blown after only a few simple questions, he confided to her his true mission. She listened intently to Clapp's explanation of the Ruth Bergstrom case without offering a clue she had any information that might be helpful.

"I figured she knew something," Clapp said to Love. "I knew she just had to have some information. All she needed was a reason to give it up, so I asked her to join me for a beer. She brought her friend along for protection, and we been 'getting pissed' together, as they say here, ever since. Speak of the devil, here she comes."

Johnnie sat down beside Clapp and looked over at Love. In the tropical starlight she resembled a mature version of the actress Penelope Cruz. He gave her a grin.

"So you're the bloke who's taking on the illustrious Henry Holten?" she said.

Her friend, smelling faintly of the bar, placed a tray of drinks on the table and sat beside Love.

"I am that bloke, yes."

"This is my mate Janis Mathey, by the way."

"Pleased to meet you, Janis."

"How do you do, lawyer bloke," Janis said, and cackled at her own cleverness. Johnnie laughed, then tapped her finger on Love's hand, saying, "Give me one good reason I should help a bloody fool."

"How about truth and justice?" Love suggested hopefully.

"Truth and justice aren't always the same thing," Johnnie observed, pausing to take a swig of beer. "I tell you the truth, and I lose my job. That's truth, but there's no justice in it."

"If you don't open up, then there'll be neither truth nor justice," Love replied. "Besides, truth is good for your soul."

Johnnie laughed and drank more beer. Her friend said, "He's got you there, Johnnie. What soul you got left needs all the bleedin' rehab it can get."

Johnnie stood up from the table and stared steadily at Dillon. She swayed a little and the light breeze blew hair across her face. By the weak light of the lanterns he could see that her eyes were filling with tears. "You can't get any subpoena down here, you know," she said finally. "And you can't get anything without my help."

"I know that," he said. "I need you."

Johnnie dug her hand into the front pocket of her jeans and retrieved a tightly folded wad of paper. Tossing it onto the table in front of Love, she said, "Take a look at these. I have to go and point Polly at the porcelain."

Janis laughed and got up to accompany her.

Dillon carefully unfolded the papers, two letter-sized documents. He smoothed out the creases and held the papers up to catch the lantern light so he could read them. The first page was an invoice for a shipment of pseudomonas from Fermagro to BioTech Services, Inc. It was dated July 1, 1999. The second document was a letter from Henry Holten to the president of Fermagro, with a copy to Johnnie. It was dated February 12, 2001. The letter suggested Fermagro contact Boyd Campbell with a proposal to supply all of EnviroClean's needs for pseudomonas. Holten also informed Fermagro about EnviroClean's financial troubles and plans to scale back its fermentation capacity and suggested this would be a good opportunity to gain a foothold in the huge American Superfund industry.

"I guess this just about tells the whole story," Love said to Clapp as he finished skimming the two papers. "EnviroClean needed more bugs than it could produce in its own fermenters, so it contacted BTS. Unbeknownst to EnviroClean, BTS was unable to fill the order itself because the key scientific team had moved to Fermagro in Bermuda. Rather than lose customers while it rebuilt its business, it merely subcontracted production of the bugs to Fermagro. Fermagro was only getting started and undoubtedly had insufficient time to complete quality control testing of the systems before having to fill the order. Something went wrong, and contaminated organisms were shipped to BTS, who reshipped them to EnviroClean. EnviroClean knew nothing about this transaction with Fermagro, so no records about the sale turned up during the document production. But Henry Holten knew about it. He had to know about it, and he covered it up to protect both of his clients and conceal his own conflict of interest."

"There's only one minor problem," Clapp said when Love finished. "You can't prove it. Without evidence showing Fermagro bugs produce the toxin found in Ruth Bergstrom's blood, you can't prove anything."

"I can help you there too," Johnnie said, quietly reappearing at the edge of the table. "We keep samples of all our batch production so we can certify compliance with our customers' specifications. It shouldn't be too hard to run a gas chromatographic analysis of the pseudomonas we shipped to BTS to see if we get a peak similar to the one the Mayo Clinic found in the blood samples of Ruth Bergstrom."

"I gave her a copy of some of the Mayo records," Clapp said. "She knows what we need."

"We don't have a lot of time," Love said.

"As you might gather," Johnnie said, "my employer may not be too eager to sponsor this testing."

"And your conscience is not sufficient incentive to help a needy widow?" Love smiled.

"I'm a needy widow also," Johnnie said. "Do you want to help *me*?"

"You hardly look the role," Love said. "But I suppose you know that."

"The truth's often deceiving," Johnnie said. "But I don't have to tell you that, you being a barrister and all."

"What kind of help are you looking for?" Love asked.

"What kind of help you got?" she replied cheekily, hands on hips. Janis came back and sat next to Clapp.

"I don't have money," Love shrugged.

"Money's not my thing," Johnnie said. "My husband had life insurance. Do you want to keep guessing what's missing in my life?"

"She wants a big hairy moron to take her over there and fuck in the surf," said Janis, and cackled like some mad island parrot.

"Look, Dillon," Clapp laughed, "why don't you two figure this out on your own. Janis and I might just take a little spin over to Horseshoe Beach a couple of parishes away. Catch you guys later."

"Your friend's pretty persuasive," Johnnie said as Joe and Janis walked to her car, their arms around each other's shoulders. "And he doesn't waste much time." Johnnie looked past Love and raised her arm. "Missy," she yelled at a waitress who had come out of the bar to pick up glasses, "a pint of porter for the Yank and a rum daiquiri for me."

"Clapp's got all the moves, I'll give him that," said Love.

"He's a bit of a prat actually. Janis'll see to him. He won't know what's hit him."

Love laughed and said, "That kinda stuff doesn't even happen to me in my dreams."

"Ah, dear boy, this is Bermuda, a dreamland for lovers."

"I've heard it's all business here these days."

"During the day, yes, but at night even a stiff-shirted barrister can loosen his bollocks."

A roar came from inside the bar and Johnnie looked inside, laughing. "Someone wins at cricket," she said, "and huge men leap around like electrified marsupials. They're more interested in sport than in a merry widow."

The waitress arrived with their drinks.

Turning to Dillon, Johnnie added, "Alcohol, you know, it provokes the desire."

"You mustn't quote your great countryman out of context," Dillon said. "It also takes away the performance."

"A mediocre performance beats no performance at all."

Love suddenly realized his head was spinning and he needed to stop drinking. The tiny woman was dominating him as if she was the bigger of the two. "You people put down booze like nothing I've ever seen," he said.

"We do. It's the ancestors, you know," she said, moving in on him.

"It's late," he said, "and I've got a bit of work yet tonight."

At this she withdrew instantly, and, with a touch of sadness, said, "You got a little lady back home?"

"I'm married," he said.

"Oh," she said, reaching across the table and unfolding his left hand. "This white skin on your ring finger suggests otherwise. Must be a boomerang ring for traveling."

"Laurie and I are separated, temporarily."

"You must still love her, then?"

"Yeah. She's a little possessive and self-centered, that's all."

"Possessive? About what? Doesn't look to me like you've got a ravenous appetite for other women."

"She thinks I work too hard."

Johnnie laughed. "Really? Doesn't she know putting work before sex is the *normal* male response? Whatever could *possess* the woman?"

"Shit," Dillon said.

"Taking life a little seriously, are we?"

"What am I supposed to do?" Dillon asked. "Sell my goddamn client down the river just to keep some woman from getting bored?"

Johnnie sniffed, dropped Love's hand, sat back, and opened the Mayo Clinic report that Joe Clapp had given her. She thumbed through the report for a couple of minutes, not really reading. At last she said, "My husband was the original director of the laboratory at Fermagro. I was his assistant. He was responsible for installing the new fermentation system when Fermagro opened up shop here in March of '99. By November he was dead. No one knew why. The autopsy revealed an unexplained and rapid degeneration of his central nervous system. Tomorrow night we'll find out if the pseudomonas killed him."

"Oh God, I'm sorry," Love said.

"Ironic, isn't it?" she continued, tears streaming down her face, "it may have been my own husband who was responsible for Ruth Bergstrom's suffering, and it'll be left to his widow to prove that awful fact to the world."

"You're a saint," Love said. "Few people would have the courage to do what you're doing. I'm truly grateful."

"Shall I drive you home? It'll only cost you one fuck."

He must have looked alarmed, because she laughed and said, "I'm only pulling your pisser, you dozy Yank."

"I think I'll walk back. Clear my head a bit and enjoy the lovely night."

"That's the ticket. You be here tomorrow night at ten. And if I've not lost interest in you by then, perhaps we'll go to the lab and have a gander at the samples."

"Thank you," Dillon said humbly like a boy to a ten-foot-tall teacher.

She pulled his head down and kissed him with full tongue, giving Love a taste of her daiquiri, then released him, laughing. "Run along now, boyo," she said, "before wicked old Johnnie gets her leg over."

He started to leave, but she said, "Oh, and by the way, Henry Holten arrived earlier this evening on a private jet. I wouldn't do any swimming out at Oxford Beaches if I were you."

Twenty-five

It felt like hell to Dillon Love to have to wait an entire day for the magical hour of 10 P.M. when he would meet the quick-tongued and firm-assed Johnnie Huntington at the Red Rock Pub. He had never spent a longer and less relaxing day at the beach. Awakened early by the animal shrieks of Clapp and Janis in the next cottage, Love pulled on shorts and running shoes and jogged around the harbor and into Paget and Warwick Parishes, where islands obscured his view of the Great Sound. He ran very slowly but even so he ached the rest of the day from what once, not long ago, would have been a routine workout. Still, this was the way back, one step at a time. Thankful that Clapp and the big blonde were gone when he got back, he went across the road to the beach and set himself up under an umbrella with an attached chaise-lounge, and spread out his depositions and legal pads in the sand. The hours droned on as he scribbled notes to himself in his endless search for the exact right words to utter at the exact right moment to the jury.

Smothered in sunblock, he lay in the sun, read, swam, read, lay in the sun, swam. Shit, he came to think, if this is paradise give me a courtroom any day. At lunchtime he had a boy from the café bring him a cheeseburger and beer on the beach. At dusk he went to his cottage and showered. As he dressed he felt a fluttering in his stomach. Tonight's events meant everything. If he failed to find the information he needed, he would lose the case and would be on the brink of bankruptcy. Here he was, all alone in Bermuda, hanging by a thread. He looked at his red face in the mirror and said, "Christ, what the hell are you doing in Bermuda! You must be nuts!"

Just as the cab arrived to take him to the Red Rock Pub, a fax arrived from Ken Butler. Love folded it into his shirt pocket with the intention of reading it during the short drive.

Clapp sat at the bar with sun glasses on, sipping a soda. He said, "Guess what? They know you're here."

"What are you talking about, Casanova?"

"While you sat on your ass frying your bald head, some guy in a maroon T-shirt lounged near you watching your every move."

"I didn't make any moves."

"Don't look now," Clapp said, "but your new best friend is sitting outside on his scooter."

"Is he bigger than me?" Love asked.

"Considerably."

"Then call the cops."

"He hasn't done anything yet."

"Make something up. How about charging him with being a guy wearing a maroon T-shirt?"

"You should take this seriously. We're outside the land of the free, dude. Shit happens here."

"As Johnnie would say, bollocks. Where is she anyway?"

"We have a new plan."

"Christ, here we go."

"I gave the bartender twenty bucks and a note for Johnnie. They have no way of knowing she's coming here to meet us, and we can't let them make that connection. You're going to walk out the door and stroll casually into town. Your friend in the maroon T-shirt will probably follow you. If he does, find yourself a crowd of people and lose him, but don't let him know that was your intention. At exactly ten-thirty you'll find two black taxi cabs parked at the edge of the harbor by the Hamilton Yacht Club. Climb in the first cab. Johnnie will be there. The driver will take you to Fermagro. I'll be in the second cab, following a suitable distance behind. I've got a cell phone for you. Take it. If you're being followed, the phone will ring once. Don't answer it. They can easily monitor cell conversations."

"Clapp, the sun's got to you, man."

"We don't have time to argue. The driver's name is Billy, and he has instructions on what to do. When you finish at the lab, call me, and then hang up after two rings. We'll pick you up at the service door in the back. Be alert. Holten doesn't know we've recruited Johanna Huntington, but he must know we're close enough to pay dirt, otherwise he wouldn't have brought in the goons."

"All this because of a guy in a maroon T-shirt?"

"There's several more of them. And I think they're armed. I've seen this sort of thing before."

"You're shittin' me."

"When Holten's man loses sight of you, they may get suspicious and go directly to Fermagro. I'll be watching and will call you if I see something. Absconding with Fermagro's batch samples isn't exactly legal, you know."

"What is this? Johnnie's their employee."

"And you better do everything to keep her sweet, too, because the shit'll hit the fan for her after this."

"I hope this isn't all some elaborate ruse to drive up your fees."

"Would I do that to a friend?"

"Yes."

At 10:30 Dillon walked up to a black taxi cab near the Hamilton Yacht Club and, without hesitation, climbed in next to Johnnie. She was slumped down in the seat so as not to be seen from outside the cab. As they pulled away from the curb, a red scooter rounded the corner and followed fast behind.

The cell phone rang once.

"We've got company," the taxi driver said. As they turned the next corner the scooter followed a few car lengths behind. Johnnie looked frightened. Love groaned and said, "What the hell's going on here?"

"I'll let you off at the Red Rock," the driver said. "Walk casually into the pub and order a refreshing pint of Boar's Head Stout."

Johnnie let out a sigh, and said, "Oh Billy, for fuck's sake grow up."

"You have to be kidding," Dillon said, laughing. The driver turned and grinned at him, despite the fact that the cab was doing forty in the narrow road. "Watch it!" Love shouted.

"No worries," said Billy. "Ask the bartender if he's seen Janis Mathey and stand next to the waitress station. Janis will join you, and you'll talk with her until precisely eleven. Then she'll take you through the back door, where you'll leave on her motorcycle. Your maroon mate will be delayed following since his scooter'll be parked at the front. We'll meet again a few minutes later. Janis'll know the spot."

"Has Clapp made friends with the whole island?"

"We're a friendly lot, aren't we, Johnnie," said the driver.

Shrugging, Dillon turned to Johnnie and said, "Here's the fax I got tonight from Ken Butler. The first graph is the test from the blood sample taken at the Mayo Clinic, and the second is from a sample of canned tomatoes from the Bergstrom's house. The third is a graph of a test on P-27, obviously different from the first two. I can't wait to see the graph of Fermagro's bugs."

"You won't have to wait long," Johnnie replied as Dillon stepped from the cab and walked into the Red Rock Pub.

Dillon did exactly as Billy instructed him and at the appointed time hopped off the back of Janis Mathey's motorcycle and back into the waiting black taxi. "Fancy meeting you here," said the driver.

"This is like some bizarre farce," said Love.

"Yeah, brilliant, innit?"

"Not if you're the unwilling customer, it's not."

"Oh, give over, mate, we're just trying to protect you."

"At any rate, it looks like I'm in your hands."

"I've already dropped Johnnie at the lab," Billy said. "I'll take you there now."

Johnnie had left the service door ajar. Love entered the small, single-story building and followed a corridor to a dimly lit room at the far end. As he entered the room, Johnnie turned to him and, holding up a tiny vial of yellow liquid, said, "Here's the evidence Henry Holten doesn't want you to have. I removed this from the company's batch samples. I doubt anyone will even notice it's missing."

They walked over to a lab bench in the corner of the room, where a few small test tubes with wire probes inserted through the top were hooked up to a machine. A roll of graph paper slowly revolved as a needle moved about, converting the data to a readable format.

"Look here," Johnnie said, holding up one of Campbell's graphs next to her own. "Both have identical peaks."

"Which two graphs?" Love demanded.

"The tomatoes and Fermagro's," she said simply.

"We've won!" Dillon exclaimed. "Hot damn, we've done it!"

In his excitement, Dillon did not initially note the tears inching down Johnnie's cheeks. She was seated on a stool, her chin almost touching her chest.

"I'm sorry," Dillon said softly, placing his hands on her shoulders. "I guess my triumph is your despair."

He massaged her shoulders gently for a few moments and said, "You know you'll have to come to Minneapolis with me, don't you?"

"I expected that," she said, moving her hands up to touch his fingers.

A single ring of the phone in Dillon's pocket startled them.

"We've got to get out of here," Dillon said, ripping the graph paper from the lab instrument and tucking it inside his shirt. "Where's the light switch?"

Johnnie turned off the lights, and the two started down the corridor toward the rear service door. Suddenly the door flew open. Silhouetted against the light from the doorway, barely twenty feet away, stood a giant. To Dillon's surprise, his maroon T-shit was faded and frayed and did not have Darby & Witherspoon stenciled on it. The man's biceps bulged like coconuts, and his head was shaped like a black bullet.

Johnnie and Dillon backed into the laboratory and locked the door. Dillon ran across the room, opened a window, kicked the screen free, and jumped out. "Hold on," said Johnnie, "I work here. Why am I running away?"

"Because that guy does not look friendly," said Dillon.

"Point taken," said Johnnie and slid out the window. They ran across the manicured crabgrass and crouched behind some bushes just as the lights in the laboratory came on. The man in the maroon shirt stuck his head through the window. Dillon scanned the area for the black taxi, but it was not there. The big man emerged awkwardly through the window, made a call on his cell phone, and began searching the grounds. Within minutes sirens sounded in the distance.

Dillon pulled his own cell phone from his pocket and called Clapp.

"Where are you?" Clapp said.

"Where the hell are *you?*" Dillon hissed. "The cops are on their way."

"Did you get out of the building?"

"We're in some scrub behind the lab. Get us out of here."

"Let me talk to Johnnie."

"Joe?" Johnnie said.

"Where do you want us to meet you?" Joe asked.

"Have Billy Wiz take you to Young's Bicycle Shop. It's not far from here. Drive round the back and turn the lights off. We'll be there in five minutes."

Johnnie turned off the phone and told Dillon to follow her as they abandoned their hiding place and crept farther into the wooded area, their feet crunching on rotted coconut shells and sending unseen critters scurrying in the undergrowth. Headlights from arriving police cars lit up the trees, and several officers fanned out with flashlights. Johnnie picked up the pace as their cover thinned out, and Love followed at her heels. They climbed over a small rock wall and onto a bike path, then sprinted down the path several hundred yards and back into the woods. Johnnie stopped momentarily to take stock of their surroundings. All was quiet. A couple of minutes later they emerged from the trees a few feet from the black taxi. Dillon's chest was heaving from running and he dripped with sweat. Johnnie was breathing normally.

"What took you so long?" Joe asked as they got in.

"Great fucking plan you got," Love gasped. "I almost get my ass shot off, and you fucking sit in a goddamn taxi picking your nose."

"Where to?" said Billy Wiz.

"Shut it, Billy!" said Johnnie.

"Did we get the stuff?" Clapp asked.

"You're damn right we did," Dillon said. "No thanks to you."

"Then what are you bitching about? Let's get out of here and sink a thousand cocktails."

"Take me back to the cottage," Love said.

"What's the matter, big man," said Billy, "things getting a bit hot for you?"

"He better not go back there," Johnnie said to Clapp. "It's the first place they'll go."

"Why would they know where I'm staying? Ridiculous. Take me home, I've got a shitload of preparation to do now that we have this."

"You're so fucking uptight, Dillweed. You should at least stay at Johnnie's place."

Billy Wiz laughed and said, "You're like the Three Stooges. They'll go to Johnnie's too. Let's take him back to his cottage and trust to the stupidity of the Bermudan constabulary."

"Miserable, ungrateful fuck," said Clapp. They drove in silence.

A few hours later, the door to the cottage flew open, and before Love could gather his wits, the glare of a flashlight blinded him.

"Mr. Love, I presume," the voice said in the lilting accent of the island.

The overhead light came on, and Love saw two police officers staring down at him from either side of his bed.

"No need to be alarmed. I'm with the constable's office," said the older one of the two.

Love wiped his eyes and propped himself up on his elbows.

"Would you mind if we asked you a few questions?"

"Now?"

"The Fermagro plant got burgled tonight. You wouldn't happen to know anything about that would you?" the older constable asked.

"Fermagro?" Love said.

"Fermagro indeed," the constable said. He had coffee colored skin and very blue eyes. "Would it be any bother to you if we had a little look around?"

"It's a bit late," Love tried. "Can't it wait 'til morning?"

"Well of course it could wait," the constable said, "but then we'd have to take you along with us. I wouldn't want to put you to any inconvenience if there's no need for it."

When Love offered no further protest, the two constables slowly picked through Love's suitcase and other belongings scattered about the room, and eventually located the vial of bacteria and gas chromatographic printouts.

"Perhaps you can explain how these items came into your possession, Mr. Love?"

"They're part of the case I'm working on, I ..."

"These things have little intrinsic value," the constable said, "so our magistrate won't take this matter very seriously. A petty misdemeanor, nothing more. On the other hand, lack of candor with the constable's office could be a bit of a problem."

"I'd prefer not saying anything at all," Love replied.

"Well, I suppose that is the American way, isn't it? On the other hand, I've got to complete a full report of my investigation for the magistrate. If it would be convenient for you to assist us, we could finish it all up shortly and leave you to enjoy the rest of the night. Otherwise, I'll have to trouble you to come down to the office until I complete my report. No telling how long that might take."

"I'm not going to be arrested?" Dillon asked.

"There'll be no need for it, you see, Mr. Love. I'll write up my report, and you can come on down to the magistrate's chambers tomorrow to work out the details."

The constables seated themselves and listened while Love related the events leading to his trip to Bermuda. He told them about Ruth Bergstrom, about the trial, and about the trail of evidence that led him to Fermagro. He explained how Ruth Bergstrom's devastating disability was most probably related to the death of Dr. Steven Huntington a year and a half ago and that the vial of bacteria the constable had confiscated would clearly establish that fact. He showed them the two matching graphs that proved the same contaminant was present in both the Fermagro vial and Ruth Bergstrom's blood analysis by the Mayo Clinic.

"I wish I had more time to get this stuff without all the cloak and dagger business, but I don't have any more time. Either I show up in court on Monday with this vial and the graph, or Ruth Bergstrom's case will be dismissed. I only hope you understand."

"Yes, sir, of course," the older constable said, "I most certainly do. I'm quite sure you can work something out with Fermagro so you can take these things back to the States with you."

"I doubt it," Love said, "Fermagro's attorney is the same guy who's representing the defendant I'm suing in Minneapolis. He'll never agree to their release. In fact, I'll bet he's the one who set you on to me."

"Oh, I wouldn't know about that."

"It was him," Love said. "Otherwise you'd never have found me."

"Well, it's not up to him anyway," the officer replied. "The magistrate will have the final say about these matters. He's a good sort, you know. Don't worry about it."

"I don't have time for all that," Love said. "I've got to take these with me."

"I'll be taking them back to the station," the officer said. "They'll be kept with my report. I'm sure the magistrate will eventually permit their release."

"Where can I find him? I have to talk to him now."

"Oh, I don't think so. Today's Sunday, you know. He'll be in chambers in Hamilton first thing on Monday. You'll find him there."

"I have to be in court in Minneapolis on Monday morning."

"That may not be possible, Mr. Love. On Monday morning it'll be necessary to appear before the magistrate on the petty misdemeanor charge. Just a formality, but it's quite necessary, you know. Anyway, you can talk to the magistrate about your evidence at the same time. Though I suppose he may want to delay a final decision until Fermagro's solicitors can be heard. It's their property after all."

By the time the constable left, it was already 4:00 A.M. and there was a lot to be done before Love boarded a plane to Minneapolis and became a fugitive. He got dressed, walked next door, and banged on the door of Joe Clapp's cottage. There was no answer. He peeked through the window and could see that the bed had not been slept in. His second choice was Johnnie's place. He found her in the phone book and dialed her number. There was no answer.

He recalled Joe Clapp's reference to Henry Holten's vacation spot, Oxford Beaches on Somerset Island, and found it on a local map. An hour later, with the sun edging above the horizon, he sat on a hired moped on a peninsula surrounded by sea and beaches.

The grounds at Oxford Beaches were immaculate and the streets were neatly lined by a dozen pink stucco cottages with white shutters. He parked the moped at the side of the driveway and walked along a path into the little colony. If he knew anything about guys like Holten, he knew the son of a bitch would be up early for breakfast so he could get control of the day. Love positioned himself where he had the best view of the cottages and hoped he would see Holten before he himself was discovered and asked to leave. He did not have to wait long. Holten, carefully holding the elbow of a gray-haired woman, emerged from a cottage near the end of the point and walked toward the main building of the compound. Without his power suit, his scrawny limbs clad in baggy shorts and T-shirt, Holten resembled a rooster without its feathers.

"Mr. Holten," Love yelled from the other side of the swimming pool as Holten and the woman were about to enter the building. "Hold on a second. May I speak with you a few minutes?"

"Mr. Love? What on earth are you doing here?"

"I need to speak with you a minute."

Holten turned to the woman and said, "Louise, my dear, why don't you get a newspaper, and I'll meet you at our table in a few minutes." She left and Holten turned back to Love. "What can I do for you? I've very little time to talk."

"I'm sure you know what I found at Fermagro last night. I'm not going to beat around the bush with you. I want you to call the magistrate in Hamilton and have the evidence released to me. I'm entitled to it, and you know it."

"You're talking nonsense," Holten said.

"You know exactly what I'm talking about," Love said. "Fermagro sold the contaminated organisms to EnviroClean through Bio-Tech Services. The batch samples prove it. I need that vial with the contaminated organisms. I want you to call the magistrate to get it released from the constable's office."

"Constable?" Holten asked. "What do the constables have to do with it?"

"Look, I'm not going to play games with you," Love said. "I'll make you a deal. I get the vial and gas chromatograph results, and the Board of Professional Responsibility will never find out about your little conflict of interest for representing both EnviroClean and Fermagro at the same time, or about your withholding critical evidence from the court, evidence you've known about all along. I get the evidence, and we both go on with our affairs as if nothing ever happened."

"So," Holten said, "on top of burglary, you now are prepared to add extortion to your strategies? You're pathetic. I've got no time for you, Mr. Love. I'll see you in court tomorrow, for the last time."

"Have you no sense of justice?" Love asked. "No concern that the jury will be denied the single most important piece of evidence in the case? Do you care nothing at all about Ruth Bergstrom?"

"Whatever do you know about justice? Do you think that the

destruction of the life work of Boyd Campbell is just? The disembowelment of EnviroClean and all the jobs of the people whose lives depend on it, is that your idea of justice? The elimination from the marketplace of a sorely needed product to clean polluted land? If that's your justice, Mr. Love, I'll have none of it."

"Somehow I don't think you give a flying fuck about the environment, Holten. But you should care about justice. Justice is fair compensation for an innocent and desperately deserving woman and her children."

"The whole thing was just an accident," Holten said. "What did Boyd Campbell do wrong? What did EnviroClean do wrong? You want to destroy all their years of hard work for an accident. You're an arrogant, narrow-minded man with absolutely no idea of how your self-righteous behavior affects the lives of the people around you. And you don't really want justice either. What you're after is the percentage you'll get from the exorbitant settlement figure you've conjured up. Why, you'd be a millionaire. No, Mr. Love, you have no notion of the meaning of justice. And tomorrow morning that fact will finally become a reality for my clients."

Holten turned and walked away.

Love walked slowly from the grounds toward his moped. He knew that EnviroClean had used a contaminated organism, but he would never be able to prove that fact in court. He had run out of time, and he had run out of firepower.

CHAPTER Twenty-six

"Judge Cleveland will see counsel in chambers," the clerk said after all the jurors had taken their seats in the jury box.

"Mr. Holten's not with us today, Ms. Forbes?" Judge Cleveland asked as Dillon and Allison entered her chambers.

"Under the circumstances, Your Honor, he didn't think it necessary."

"Oh?" Judge Cleveland said.

"Your Honor, Mr. Holten's in Bermuda. I spoke with him last night, and I understand he met with Mr. Love over the weekend. Apparently Mr. Love indicated that he'd been unable to find further evidence to support his claims. So I assume the court will be dismissing the case this morning. It hardly seems necessary for Mr. Holten to return to Minneapolis for that."

"Mr. Love?" the judge asked.

"I'm not sure where Mr. Holten got that idea, Your Honor," said Dillon. "It certainly wasn't anything I said. We're quite prepared to go forward this morning."

"Dillon," Allison said, turning to address him directly, "correct me if I'm wrong, but didn't you have a bit of a setback in your attempt to locate additional evidence? Perhaps you'd care to explain your weekend adventures to Judge Cleveland."

"Your Honor," Dillon said, "I spent the weekend in Bermuda, where I found a company that supplied some contaminated bacteria to EnviroClean. The company's called Fermagro. It's a sort of spin-off of a local company that used to be a supplier to EnviroClean. In any event, we were able to test a batch sample of these organisms, and we're now finally able to prove they're the source of Ruth Bergstrom's neurological injuries."

"Aren't you forgetting one minor problem?" Allison interjected. "The Bermudan police have confiscated your supposed proof. Your Honor, everything Mr. Love is saying is nothing but inadmissible hearsay."

"Police?" Judge Cleveland asked.

"The evidence was given to me by the laboratory director of the company," Dillon replied. "It all came from her laboratory, with her explicit permission. Mr. Holten, however, conspired to deny me this evidence by reporting to the police that it had been stolen. Since he's an officer of that company, the authorities accepted his word. The police now have the vial with the batch sample of contaminated microorganisms that we tested. I asked Holten to release this evidence to me, but he refused. And for obvious reasons. Your Honor, the evidence is not hearsay because Mr. Holten is himself an officer of Fermagro, and the information can be found in Fermagro's business records, well known to him and under his complete control."

"I object to the evidence," Allison said. "It's not here for the jury to see, so its authenticity and reliability is questionable."

"In fact," Dillon continued, "Holten's known about all this for months and has failed to disclose it to me or to the court. His dual role as attorney for both Fermagro and EnviroClean has created a huge conflict of interest for him, and now he wants to profit from this unethical behavior by denying me the evidence I need to go forward with the case. But I'm prepared to proceed, and I have one witness I intend to call this morning to establish unequivocally the authenticity of the evidence, one very impressive witness."

"That's ridiculous, Your Honor," Allison said, "Mr. Holten would never..."

"Ms. Forbes," Judge Cleveland said, "is Mr. Holten an officer or attorney for Fermagro?"

"I have no personal information about that."

"That's why he's not here," Dillon interjected. "He doesn't want to face these embarrassing questions."

"Counsel has no way of knowing that, Your Honor," Allison said.

"Nor do you," Judge Cleveland snapped. "And Mr. Holten's not here to offer any clarification. Your objection to the proposed evidence is overruled. I'll see you both in the courtroom in five minutes."

Dillon walked quickly from Judge Cleveland's chambers to preclude any change in her ruling. Allison kept pace with him, and as they walked said, "Dillon, Boyd Campbell should not suffer because of Henry's improprieties. I still intend to represent him to the best of my abilities. He deserves that."

Dillon waved her off with a hand and kept walking.

"I'm still going to kick your butt," she called out as he disappeared into the courtroom, her words falling flat in the hallway. She stood a moment as the reality of the situation flooded over her. This explained why she was lead counsel on the case, because Henry could not be. This explained why he had been so aggressive. Her entire body shook with indignation. She slowly collected herself, stood as tall as she could and walked into the courtroom.

Before Allison could take her seat Dillon announced, "The plaintiff calls Johanna Huntington, Your Honor."

Instantly, Allison rose and objected, "Undisclosed witness, Your Honor."

"This witness is well-known to the defense, Your Honor," Dillon responded, pulling a letter from his briefcase and holding it above his head as he spoke. "Johanna Huntington is the laboratory director at Fermagro, an offshore company which Henry Holten participated in founding and for which he continues to serve as corporate secretary and general counsel. Indeed, only last February Mr. Holten himself sent a letter to Ms. Huntington about the EnviroClean situation. Do you want to see the letter, Ms. Forbes?"

"Objection overruled," Judge Cleveland stated. "You may proceed, Mr. Love."

Johanna Huntington approached the clerk and was sworn in. Wearing a tight tailored suit and high heels, she stepped into the witness box. She immediately annoyed Allison because, despite the 'corporate-sexy' look, the woman also projected a sort of European chic-professional aura that made Allison feel gargantuan and clumsy.

Johanna Huntington's initial testimony about her background and scientific credentials, delivered in her lovely accent, fully confirmed her qualifications and conveyed the impression of a poised and sincere individual. As she spoke, every member of the jury smiled. Feeling crushed, Allison looked around at Boyd Campbell and was horrified to find that he too was smiling.

"Ms. Huntington," Dillon said after inquiring about several preliminary matters, "does Fermagro produce microorganisms for use by industry?"

"Yes, we do."

"How about the species of microorganisms known as pseudomonas?"

"Not at the present time," Huntington replied

"Did you at one time?" Dillon asked.

"We did fill one large order, in 1999," she replied.

"Can you identify the name of the company and the circumstances surrounding that order?" Dillon asked.

"Certainly," she answered. "I have with me a copy of an invoice for a shipment of pseudomonas sent to a Minneapolis company, Bio-Tech Services, Inc., in 1999. July, 1999."

"Ms. Huntington," Dillon said, walking to the witness box and handing her a previously received exhibit, "I'm handing you an invoice from BTS to EnviroClean, also dated in July 1999, covering the sale of an order of pseudomonas from BTS to EnviroClean. Is there any way to know whether the organisms referred to in the BTS invoice are the same as those in the Fermagro invoice?"

"They are the same," Huntington said authoritatively. "Note that the quantities are identical. In addition, they filled the EnviroClean order on the same day the shipment was received from Fermagro. And I can tell you that BTS was no longer in the business of growing organisms at that time. The fermenting staff had left BTS a few months earlier to come to Bermuda to start Fermagro. My husband and I were involved in getting it set up. Consequently, any organisms it sold had to have come from Fermagro."

"As I understand it," Dillon continued, "Fermagro retains batch samples from all organisms it produces for its customers, and that includes the pseudomonas shipped to BTS, am I right?"

"You're correct," she replied.

"Have you had an opportunity to conduct gas chromatographic testing on the batch samples of pseudomonas that they had shipped to BTS in July, 1999?" Dillon asked.

"Yes, I have," she answered.

"Showing you what I have just marked as Exhibit 121," Dillon asked, "can you identify this as a copy of those test results?"

"Objection!" Allison shouted, rising from her seat. "May I be heard on this at the bench, Your Honor?"

The two lawyers walked to the side of Judge Cleveland's bench, and, out of hearing of the jury, Allison argued, "This document is obviously a forgery. The Bermudan authorities confiscated both the vial and the test results he obtained illicitly on Saturday night. This document can hardly be genuine, and I object to its admission."

"I think the witness can clear this up, Your Honor," Dillon said.

"I hope so," Judge Cleveland responded. "Objection overruled subject to further clarification. But I want no mention of the encounter between you and Mr. Holten over the weekend. Is that clear?"

"Yes, Your Honor," Dillon said. Allison returned to her seat at the defense counsel's table, and Dillon continued with the questioning of his witness. "Ms. Huntington," he said, "can you explain to the jury how you came into possession of this document?"

"The chromatographic testing was run on Saturday at Fermagro's laboratory in Bermuda," Huntington began. "I gave a copy of the test results to you, Mr. Love, and as you know, you were asked to turn that copy over to the constabulary. However, it's standard laboratory practice to run the test twice to insure its accuracy. I kept the other copy of the test results myself. My copy is what you have identified as Exhibit 121. It's the original graph of the analysis of the batch of pseudomonas that Fermagro shipped to BTS. I've had this document in my possession since Saturday when the test was completed."

"No objection to the exhibit," Allison said resignedly.

"Exhibit 121 is received," said Judge Cleveland.

"With reference to Exhibit 121, please explain the results of your analysis to the jury, Ms. Huntington," Dillon requested.

Huntington picked up Exhibit 121 and, holding it up for the jury to see, explained the testing procedures and the significance of the peak that indicated the presence of a contaminant.

"Do you have copies of the graphs produced by the Mayo Clinic?" Huntington asked, looking at Love. "Perhaps I might show the jury how the two graphs compare."

Dillon handed her that test result, previously received in evidence as Exhibit 66. With the court's permission, Huntington stepped from the witness stand, walked to the front of the jury box, and held each graph side by side for the jury to observe.

"Many of the peaks are different," she explained, "because the Mayo Clinic was analyzing a blood sample, whereas I examined only the organisms and their natural by-products. But what's significant is that on each graph the same peak appears at the same spot on the graph. This indicates it's the identical substance in both cases. As you can see, Dr. Gauss labeled this as 'Peak E' on exhibit 66, and I understand he testified it was the cause of Mrs. Bergstrom's illness. I can now tell you categorically that this Peak E contaminant came from Fermagro. The comparison of exhibits 66 and 121 proves that without any doubt whatsoever."

"Do you have an explanation of how this contaminant found its way into the bloodstream of Ruth Bergstrom?" Dillon asked.

"Yes sir, I do," she replied.

"Showing you what I've just marked as Exhibit 122, can you identify this for the jury?" Dillon asked.

"It's a copy of a gas chromatographic analysis of some canned tomatoes. I understand your investigator, Mr. Clapp, obtained these from the basement of the Bergstrom's home and that Ken Butler analyzed them last week."

"We offer Exhibit 122, Your Honor," Dillon said, handing the document to Allison to examine.

"No objection," Allison said, without looking at the document.

"Received," the judge said.

"What's the significance of this exhibit, Ms. Huntington?" Dillon asked.

"The same Peak E appears in this graph, indicating it also has the same contaminant we found in the Fermagro batch samples and in the Mayo Clinic samples. It's obvious. The mode of poisoning was through the tomatoes."

"But doesn't the canning process kill the organisms?" Dillon asked.

"The canning process will kill the organisms, but if they've already produced a chemical toxin as a part of their process of metabolism, that chemical will be unchanged by boiling. As she ate the tomatoes throughout the fall and winter, she continued to ingest the contaminant on each occasion, sustaining or building up its toxicity. Since the other family members did not like tomatoes, they didn't become ill."

"One more question, Ms. Huntington. Is it not true that this same batch of P-27 bacteria, this stuff that's supposed to be a godsend to humanity, this same batch, was responsible for your husband's death in November of 1999?"

Before she could reply, Allison leapt to her feet yelling, "Objection!"

Love raised his own voice and shouted "It's true, isn't it? Tell the jury the truth!"

"Objection, objection," Allison screamed while Judge Cleveland banged her gavel for silence.

"Sustained," she said, glaring at Love. "Mr. Love, this is out of line, completely out of line. Sit down and get hold of yourself." In a calm and firm voice she said to the jury, "Members of the jury, you will disregard that question, and you are not to speculate on how the witness might have answered it. The question was improper, and you are instructed to pay no attention to it or to the outbursts of counsel."

Judge Cleveland turned back to face Love, glaring at him. "Mr. Love, have you any further questions of this witness?"

"Yes, Your Honor, I have one more question. Ms. Huntington, is there any doubt in your mind that this batch of P-27 manufactured by your company, Fermagro, is responsible for Ruth Bergstrom's debilitating illness?

Allison leapt to her feet again. "Objection, this witness is not a medical doctor and is unqualified to answer the question."

Love pondered another less objectionable way to ask the question, but when he looked at Johnnie she was quietly sobbing on the witness stand. "No further questions," said Dillon, "perhaps we might have a short break for the witness?" He looked across at Allison.

"We'll take our morning recess at this time," Judge Cleveland said. "Fifteen minutes, everyone."

Allison picked up exhibits 122, 121, and 66 and left the courtroom with Boyd Campbell and his wife Kathleen. They found their way to a small conference room down the hall.

"It's obvious to me that Fermagro is responsible for Mrs. Bergstrom's illness," Boyd Campbell said as they entered the room to assess the discovered evidence. "Look at these exhibits. They all have the same peak. What more is there to say? It's definitely not our fault she got sick. Fermagro blew it, pure and simple, not us. I didn't even know Fermagro was involved. If I had, I'd have checked it out. Now you can get this case thrown out."

"I wish I could," Allison said. "Sorry to say, that's not the law. Anyone who sells a product is responsible for its safety. It makes no difference that you did absolutely nothing wrong. You sold it. You're as innocent as Ruth Bergstrom, and, in a way, you're as much a victim as she is because, if Fermagro screwed up, you'll have to pay for its mistake."

"Tell me you're kidding," Campbell said incredulously. "The law can't really be that unfair."

"Well, of course, when it's all over, you could sue Fermagro and get your money back."

"Are you sure about all this?" Campbell asked. "Henry's never mentioned anything like this."

"There's no doubt at all," Allison said. "If the P-27 was contaminated, you're liable for whatever harm it caused."

Boyd contemplated Allison's words silently for a few moments. "Well then," he said finally, "if I have to pay for Fermagro's mistake, let's get it over with. Find out how much it'll take to settle the case."

"Love's still got to prove it was Fermagro's fault," Allison said.

"Isn't that what he just did?" Campbell asked.

"You haven't heard my cross-examination yet," she said. "I've got a couple of questions that may call Huntington's testimony into question. Let's hold off for a while."

"What for? I can see plain as day Fermagro screwed up."

"Love will be totally unreasonable now," Allison said. "It's never wise to negotiate from a position of weakness. We've got to wait for the right opportunity. There are some problems in Huntington's testimony, and we've not even begun with our own witnesses yet."

"Maybe," Campbell said, "but I want you to talk with him and find out what he wants."

Allison dutifully located Dillon in the corridor.

Boyd and Kathleen were able to observe the two lawyers from a distance. Dillon had his back to them. As Allison squared off to present Boyd's desire for a resolution of the lawsuit, she looked past Dillon toward the anxious faces of her clients down the hall. They could see her speaking without animation or emotion. Her eyes were vacant and unfocused. Her long blond hair rested motionlessly on her shoulders, and her arms hung listlessly at her side. Boyd strained to hear her, without success.

At first Dillon stood straight and attentive, appearing to listen as Allison spoke. Gradually his large frame began shifting from one leg to the other, and his arms fluttered about. His shoulders stiffened, and the muscles in his neck tensed. An instant later, without waiting for Allison to finish her presentation, Dillon raised his hand, turned abruptly, and pointed his finger directly at Boyd Campbell. Turning back to Allison, he gestured wildly with both hands and left her standing alone at the end of the hall.

Boyd and Kathleen waited as Dillon's imposing figure approached them, his face contorted in anger. He stared coldly at them as he paused near them next to the entrance to the courtroom. Then he turned, pulled open the door, and disappeared inside.

"It's hopeless," Allison said, obviously frustrated by Dillon's stubbornness. "He wants five million. He's totally unreasonable because he's overconfident about the impact of Huntington's testimony. Your only hope is that Ruth Bergstrom will insist that he take a more reasoned approach. He's required to inform her about our discussion, so we'll just have to wait for her response."

Dillon returned to Ruth Bergstrom to advise her of the conversation he had just had with Allison Forbes. "We've finally got them exactly where we want them," he said. "Allison Forbes took me aside and practically begged me to settle the case. Frankly, Ruth, the jury is unbelievably sympathetic to you. I can see it clearly in their faces. I told her we were sticking with our five million demand, but, frankly, I don't want to settle this case at all. This could be one of the biggest verdicts in the history of the state."

"I don't understand," Ruth said. "This wasn't even their fault. Fermagro goofed up. Johanna Huntington admitted that herself just a few minutes ago. Why should EnviroClean have to pay?"

"They have to pay because they're the ones who put the contaminated organism in the ground."

"Just the same," Ruth responded, "why don't you just tell Ms. Forbes that we're interested in settling, and see what she proposes. I don't need five million dollars, or anything close to that. My word, where would EnviroClean get all that money anyway?"

"That's not our concern, Ruthie, but it'll probably come from their insurance company."

The hammering of the clerk's gavel interrupted their conversation. "All rise," she announced as Judge Cleveland took her seat and directed Allison to commence her cross-examination of Johanna Huntington. 'Here we go,' thought Love, 'come on Johnnie!'

Johanna Huntington resumed her seat in the witness box and waited quietly for Allison's first question. She had repaired her makeup during the break, and was once again the calm professional. She held her chin high and her shoulders back and smiled as Allison approached the witness box.

"You ran the test sample counsel has identified as exhibit 122 late in the evening on Saturday night, is that right?" Allison began. Love stifled a grin, never in the entire proceedings had Allison displayed such open aggression in her cross-examinations.

Huntington continued to smile as she quietly replied, "That's correct."

"Why was that?" Allison asked, "were you so swamped with work that you had no other time during normal business hours?"

"This was not something I was doing on my employer's account," Huntington replied. "I thought it best to do it during off hours."

"Indeed," Allison continued. "Was the middle of the night on a Saturday the only opportunity you had, or were you doing the testing at that time because you knew it was wrong and inappropriate to be doing it at all?"

"I knew the company would not approve of it, yes," Johnnie replied. "I think the reasons for that must be obvious."

"And in fact," Allison continued, "according to my sources in Bermuda, you went to great lengths to disguise your illicit activities. And you even developed a wild scheme of taxi cabs taking circuitous routes to the company with lookouts posted to guarantee your privacy, is that not correct, Ms. Huntington?"

"Yes, that's correct," Johnnie replied. "It was our intention to avoid detection in order to get the necessary evidence."

"And in your haste, Ms. Huntington," Allison asked, "did you calibrate the equipment by running known samples first to make sure it was working properly?

"I don't remember," Huntington replied.

"And is it not true that in looking at exhibit 122, we don't find any such standard samples?"

"They're not on that piece of paper, no."

"And is that not proof, Ms. Huntington, that you did not run the standard samples and cannot guarantee the accuracy of the testing?" Johnnie hesitated, so Allison pressed her. "Answer the question, Ms. Huntington. Why the hesitation? Speak up. You cannot attest to the accuracy of this equipment, nor can you attest to the accuracy of the graph marked as exhibit 122. I want you to look the jurors in the eyes and answer my question under oath."

"Objection, Your Honor," said Love, "she's badgering the witness."

"I'd like to hear the answer myself," Judge Cleveland replied. "Objection overruled."

"They would have calibrated the equipment the day before," Johnnie shrugged. "It's highly unlikely anything could have happened during the previous eighteen hours to affect its accuracy."

"Ms. Huntington," Allison asked, "is it not true that it's standard laboratory procedure to do the calibration every single day, and that you violated that standard practice in running the tests you have shown to this jury?"

"Apparently I did not run the standard samples," Huntington replied. "At least they didn't get printed on the graph paper. But the results are accurate. With all due respect, I'm afraid you're clutching at straws, miss."

Allison's neck and face flushed, which again forced Love to suppress a grin. 'Go ahead, Allie,' he thought, 'kick my butt.' With more intensity, Allison said, "What's the difference in distance between the peak that can clearly be identified as peak E and the peak on the graph paper that represents another similar substance?"

"Not much," Johnnie answered.

"We're not talking about inches, or even about centimeters, are we, Ms. Huntington?" she continued. "We're talking about fractions of millimeters, are we not?"

"A millimeter would be about right."

"So even a very small deviation in the accuracy of the equipment can be fatal, can't it?" Forbes asked. "A small, a very small, error in the machine can produce a totally erroneous result in the test, right?"

"It can," Johnnie replied.

"And if you had run the test during normal hours, under normal conditions, according to your own laboratory standards, you'd have a far more reliable result, would you not?"

"The procedure would have been better, but the result would have been the same."

"It's too bad you don't know that for sure, Ms. Huntington," Allison said.

"I am ..."

Speaking over the witness, Allison said, "You could have saved this jury from having to make an unfounded leap of faith. No further questions."

As planned, Ruth Bergstrom was Love's last witness. He rose from the counsel table, moved a few of the large exhibits which were scattered about the courtroom so he could clear a pathway for her wheelchair, and assisted her in maneuvering to a position directly in front of the witness box. She looked briefly around the courtroom until she caught the attention of her two children sitting directly behind Love's counsel table. She looked at them and smiled, then brushed her hand across her forehead. Brett looked away, but he dutifully responded by brushing his own hair off to the side of his forehead. Ruth glanced across the room at the defendant's counsel table.

Boyd Campbell sat behind Allison Forbes. He appeared pallid and drawn, his hands clasped together and resting motionless in his lap. He met the gaze of Ruth Bergstrom and nodded. She noticed the gesture and smiled at him.

Love led her through the story of her life. With great enthusiasm, she talked about her children, her church work, and her love of gardening. She described her husband's family hardware store and its recent failure along with the other small businesses in the neighborhood. With dignity, and without tears, she told the jury about her husband and the circumstances of his death. Despite frequent cues from Love, she declined to overstate the severity of her illness and resulting disability, but she did say she missed gardening, housework, and the active parenting role she used to take with her children.

Ruth knew very little about any facts or circumstances that related to the important liability issues the jury would be required to decide, and most of those facts had already been mentioned by other witnesses. But she did tell the jury all about her tomato garden next to the creek and the watering system Arne had put in place to pump water from the creek into the garden. She told how she loved canning the tomatoes, and she told the jury that the rest of her family didn't care for them and rarely, if ever, ate any.

Allison declined to cross-examine Ruth Bergstrom.

Four days and many witnesses removed from the controversial testimony of Johanna Huntington, Allison Forbes rose to assume the responsibility of her summation. The entire courtroom was silent in anticipation of her remarks. Henry Holten, now once again returned to the defense counsel table, gave his bright young partner a nod of confidence as she turned toward him before beginning her final appeal to the jury.

Allison walked directly to the jury box and placed her hands on the railing immediately in front of the jurors. She hesitated for a few seconds, looking kindly into the eyes of each juror before beginning her presentation.

"No one ever told you that being a juror would be an easy job," she began. "Quite the contrary. It's one of the most difficult jobs we require the citizens of this country to perform. It's so difficult, in fact, that we don't even trust these tough decisions to the hands of able and highly trained judges. Judges bring their own prejudices and biases with them into the courtroom, just like each witness who has appeared in this case, and just like each lawyer who is advocating his or her client's cause to the best of his or her abilities. Instead we bring in a group of citizens who are carefully screened before the start of the trial to make certain there's nothing in the facts of this case that would make it difficult for them to be fair and impartial. We then ask them all to take a solemn oath that they'll put aside whatever predispositions they might have and treat each party to this case as equals, fairly and impartially."

Allison walked slowly over to the table where Dillon and his clients were seated. She turned to face Ruth Bergstrom and her children. "Look at these wonderful people," she said softly. "Which one of you is so cold-hearted that you did not shed a tear for this woman when she took the witness stand and told you about the awful and tragic circumstances that have forever changed her life and the lives of her children? You must believe me when I tell you my own heart broke during those never-to-be-forgotten moments when she shared her anguish with all of us. What a fine and courageous woman she is, and what wonderful and vibrant young children she has with her in this room. I was so shaken by her presence that I could not bring myself to ask her even a single question."

She walked slowly across the courtroom, this time positioning herself directly behind her client, Boyd Campbell.

"But I want to tell you, clearly and unequivocally," Allison continued, "that I'm proud indeed to be representing a person like Boyd Campbell. For this man is the full embodiment of the Great American Dream, a man who rose from humble beginnings with nothing to pave his way in the world except his own energy and creativity. I have before me a person of unquestioned honesty and integrity, a university professor with an idea, a bright and innovative idea that will help make the world a safer and cleaner place for all of us. This is a man who has dedicated his life to science and the benefits that scientific discoveries can bring to the lives of everyone in this room. This is not a man who would cause harm to Ruth Bergstrom or others like her. This is a man whose mission is to improve the quality of life for all of the Ruth Bergstroms of this world."

Allison again assumed her position at the front of the jury box. "That's the reason, gentlemen and ladies, why this case is so difficult for you to decide. If only there truly were a pot of gold at the end of the rainbow, I'd join with you and gladly deliver that pot to Mrs. Bergstrom and her children. We wouldn't need this trial. We wouldn't need you to be judges of this case. But there is no pot at the end of the rainbow to give to Mrs. Bergstrom, because whatever you give to her, you must take from Boyd Campbell."

Allison glanced at Love, who was watching her with his hands clasped over the top of his head.

"You're not here today to make a choice between good and evil," she continued. "That's for juries on television to decide, where choices are obvious. There's no evil in this case, so you must choose between two goods. You have no easy decision because whatever you do will bring immeasurable harm into the life of one of the outstanding people of this community. This is why you cannot base your decision on any innate sense of fairness and justice of the sort that our mothers and fathers taught us about many years ago. You cannot look into the forlorn eyes of Ruth Bergstrom and gain any insight into what's right and wrong in this case. You cannot look at the many important contributions Boyd Campbell has made to this community and glean any useful information about how to decide this case.

"What's left for you then? What process can you follow to return a just verdict in this case? The answer lies not in the sympathy you must feel for Ruth Bergstrom. It lies in the testimony you have heard from the witness stand and the exhibits you have seen in this courtroom. Your duty is to put aside your emotions and your natural sense of sympathy because these human responses will only fail you in cases such as this. You must make your decision on the evidence alone. That's what it means to be a juror. That's what is required for you to do justice in this case.

"The simple question you must answer is whether EnviroClean has acted unreasonably in any material respect. Any sympathy you may feel for either of the parties in this case will not help you answer this question. Only the evidence will help you answer it, or rather the lack of evidence.

"And what evidence have we heard during this trial that EnviroClean or anyone associated with it has acted negligently? We've heard nothing because, whatever else you may say about this case, Boyd Campbell and his fellow employees at EnviroClean have done nothing wrong. Even if you want to accept the rather suspicious, unsubstantiated testimony of Johanna Huntington, that testimony does not prove EnviroClean acted negligently. On the contrary, it proves only that Fermagro acted negligently. No, ladies and gentlemen, the evidence is that EnviroClean was a victim like Ruth Bergstrom, a victim that has now been unfairly hauled into court to defend itself from false charges made by a well-intentioned but obviously mistaken lawyer who actually believes in pots of gold at the end of the rainbow.

"If you focus your attention on the evidence as you are duty bound to do, and only upon the evidence, the only reasonable result you can possibly reach is to conclude that Dr. Boyd Campbell was not negligent, and return a verdict in his favor. Thank you for your consideration."

Love froze for an instant, waiting for the flow of juices to ignite a passion he most certainly would need to bring home a verdict in favor of his client. He had expected Allison to make a much longer argument, undertaking a meticulous dissection of the evidence presented during the last ten days, and he wasn't yet emotionally prepared to step into the spotlight before the jurors. Worse, he thought to himself, Allison had robbed him of the emotional appeal he had planned to use to win the sympathies of the jury. Having that option preempted, he would sound schmaltzy trying to wring more melancholy from the violin. He would have to accept Allison's challenge and address the facts, the weakest part of his case.

He made eye contact with Allison Forbes and wondered whether the slightly rising edges of her lips were intended to goad and distract him by having successfully upstaged his planned presentation. He stood quietly for a moment next to his chair, considering his response to Allison's concise but effective argument.

"I'm awestruck by the responsibility I carry for the lives and welfare of the gracious and stoic family I'm honored to represent," he said softly as he stood nervously in front of the jury box. "I know that the folks over at Darby & Witherspoon have scores of cases like this, but for me this has been the case of my life. In retrospect, it's obviously been more than I could handle. Maybe I should have brought in some big-bucks firm with computers and teams of investigators, legal assistants, and lawyers to present the kind of electronic, high-tech case we've seen the defense put on for you. I ask you only to look beyond my own shortcomings to the clear facts of this case. That is all Ruth Bergstrom and her children ask of you.

"You know, folks, most of the facts in this case are really uncontested. No one is saying Ruth Bergstrom is not devastatingly disabled, or that her disability preceded the work of EnviroClean at the gas station next door to her house. No one disputes the fact that EnviroClean released into the environment some engineered microbes sent to them through a company in Bermuda that had only recently gone into business without the opportunity to adequately test the organisms. Nor does anyone seriously contest that these microbes carry the potential for producing the toxin that caused Ruth Bergstrom's debilitating injuries. No one denies the fact that what made her sick is this toxic compound which found its way into her tomatoes and from there through her digestive tract and into her bloodstream, where it has poisoned her almost beyond belief. These are all uncontested facts.

"Ms. Forbes claims the tests done at Fermagro last Saturday weren't accurate. Well, where are her own tests? Where are the tests that her own people could have done to prove us wrong? Why didn't you see any such tests in this courtroom? Either they were not done because they were afraid of the results, or they were done, and they're too embarrassed to bring them here for you to see. So don't be conned by Ms. Forbes' disingenuous cross-examination of Ms. Huntington, because if our tests were really incorrect, she would've brought different test results here for you to see.

"We, on the other hand, have offered you a plausible explanation of what happened, how it happened, and why it happened. The defense has offered you nothing but an electronic dog-and-pony show designed to distract you from the truth. It's darned easy to sit back and take potshots at someone else's theories, but unless you offer some of your own, you really are in no position to criticize those who do.

"You know what happened, I know what happened, and Allison Forbes knows what happened. And we all know it would not have happened had EnviroClean taken the necessary steps to insure that no untested, uninspected, negligently manufactured organisms were released into the backyard of Ruth Bergstrom's home. They screwed up, and it's time for them to pay the price.

"This is Ruth Bergstrom's one and only day in court. Allison Forbes and Henry Holten will have hundreds more days. I will have hundreds more days. She asks you for no mercy, no sympathy, no outpouring of emotions. She asks you only for a chance to live the rest of her life in dignity as she did before her life was made into a shambles by the mad scientists of this modern and unforgiving world.

"Ruth Bergstrom is a remarkable woman. She has survived her long ordeal with the mutated organisms from EnviroClean. She has survived the catastrophe of the untimely death of her husband just over two months ago. She has continued despite her weakened condition to be a mother for these two wonderful young children sitting next to her, to provide them a home, to provide them strength and determination to carry on as she must do, alone and sick. And she has done it all with dignity and self-respect. She's asked nothing of anyone. This inspiring woman is too proud, too determined to live her life any other way. As frail as she is, sitting over there in her wheelchair, Ruth Bergstrom is one of the strongest people I have ever known.

"This is her day, ladies and gentlemen, the day she will live with for the rest of her life."

As Dillon walked slowly back to his seat at the counsel table, he felt a powerful stillness in the room and knew that he had done his job. He slumped with relief; the case was over. He watched the lovely Kathleen Campbell take a tissue from her purse and dab away tears. Allison raised her eyebrows and nodded at him.

CHAPTER Twenty-seven

Allison and Dillon walked together through the front door of Pete's Piano Bar, each carrying a briefcase in one hand and files in the other arm. They were sweating in their dark suits after the walk from the Government Center on an unusually hot afternoon. Dillon dumped everything he carried onto the table of a corner booth, tossed his jacket into a corner as if he hated it, ripped off his tie, and used it to wipe his brow. Allison, laying her own load beside his, laughed at him as he rolled up his sleeves like a petulant boy just home from church.

They sat opposite each other and moved the files and briefcases onto the benches beside them. Dillon looked at Allison and let out a long stream of relieved breath. She smiled and said, "Pleased it's over?"

"I feel like I just got out of Leavenworth."

"Me, too," Allison admitted. "None of it turned out as expected."

The waitress arrived and asked what they wanted.

"Do you carry any porters?" Dillon asked her.

"Sweetheart," the waitress replied, "if I had a porter, he'd be carrying me."

"Everyone's a comedian," Dillon said with a straight face. "We're talking beers here, honey."

"Porter?" Allison asked. "What's that?"

"It's rich and black, the poison of choice in Bermuda, full bodied and smooth. Real smooth, I might add."

"You talking beer or women?" laughed Allison.

"Both. The combination's awesome, and you saw the results first hand in court."

"You mean Huntington? That old hen dressed up as chicken? Screw your taste, buster."

"I got Guinness, I got Sam Smith Oatmeal Stout," the waitress said.

"Two cold oatmeal stouts," said Dillon. "That okay with you, Allie?"

"Sure."

"So that's how you got Johanna Huntington to Minneapolis," Allison said after the waitress left. "You boozed her up and took advantage of her. I should have considered that for my cross-examination."

"I tried," Dillon joked, "but all I could do was induce her to come to court. Now we'll see how far that strategy gets me with you."

"Why would I want to hop into the sack with an irreverent, sweaty slob like you?"

"I been running," he said, "like you suggested."

"That's it?" she asked, grabbing a handfull of his gut, "I'm supposed to hit the sack with every fat lawyer who buys running shoes? I'm not that kind of girl."

"I've got other redeeming qualities," he said.

"Name one," Allison replied, pinching his belly even harder.

"Integrity."

Allison laughed. "Integrity. That's supposed be a turn-on for an illicit relationship with a married man?"

"Integrity's what smart girls are looking for these days," Dillon replied. "And I'll still have it when I run off the extra weight."

Allison released her grasp on his belly fat and slid back in her seat. "Smart girls want commitment. It's not your gut anyway, it's your attitude. It's always been your attitude. Me first, all the way, that's the Dillon Love I knew in law school."

"I could get a reference from Ruth Bergstrom," Dillon replied.

"How about from Laurie? What's with you and Laurie anyway? I heard you might be seeing her again."

"We were going to have dinner after the funeral, but it didn't work out. She's mad at me and I haven't had time to deal with it."

"Everyone's got the same twenty-four hours a day," Allison said. "You've just got to choose what you do with them. You've chosen to marry your law practice instead of your wife."

"Not a marriage," he said, "but a temporary fling."

"An isolated fling?" Allison asked. "Or one of a series?"

"There's only one Ruth Bergstrom," he said.

"And there's only one Laurie," Allison said quickly.

"I guess I always thought a good woman should support a man with a vision. I had the vision of getting justice for Ruth Bergstrom. Laurie couldn't handle it. Now it's over. The ball's in her court. Fuck it."

The waitress put their beers in front of them. Dillon drank off half of his while Allison, holding the glass in both hands, sipped it like it was soup. He looked at her and said, "Good?"

"Delicious," she said. "You learn something new every day."

"How long do you suppose the jury will be out?" Dillon asked.

"Well, they've got the weekend now. I'm sure we'll hear Monday sometime."

"It better be early. I don't want Ruthie on tenterhooks all day."

"See what I mean?" Allison sighed. "You're so totally dominated by this case you can't even hang loose with an old friend for a few minutes. You're in trouble, Dillon."

"Shit," Dillon said, "what is it about me that every woman I know wants to be my goddamned mother?"

Allison laughed. "I hope they return an early verdict, too," she said. "I'd just as soon end this farce as quickly as possible."

"Do I sense Goliath toppling? Are you conceding the victory to me?"

"Victory?" Allison asked, suddenly serious. "There'll be no victory here. We're all losers, Dillon. Haven't you figured that out yet?"

"Cut the bullshit, Allie," Dillon said. "The jury's got two choices, it's either you or me. One of us is taking home the gold."

"At first that's what I thought too," Allison said "good versus evil, and good always wins. The only question was which one of us represented good. But it was all only an illusion. It turns out not to be that simple."

"Jesus, Allie, what are you talking about? What's going on with you anyway?"

"Think about it for a second instead of charging off half-cocked all the time. If I win, Ruth Bergstrom will be without financial resources, her life ruined through no fault of her own. And if you win, EnviroClean will be bankrupted, and the jobs of scores of good people who had nothing at all to do with Ruth Bergstrom will be lost. What great sins have these people committed that Enviro-Clean may effectively be sentenced to death in a state without capital punishment?"

"Its sin was its carelessness in releasing toxic compounds into the environment," said Dillon.

"Bullshit," Allison said. "Its sin was its success. So many people believed in the company that it could not meet the demand for P-27 with its own inventories. Through no fault of its own, some company it had never heard of sent its supplier a few contaminated microorganisms. Now either Ruth Bergstrom or Boyd Campbell will have to pay for that mistake. Either way, an innocent party becomes a victim."

"Defeat's painful," Dillon said. "Hell, I know that. But I'm talking victory here. One of *us* is going to win, at the other's expense, of course, but win nevertheless."

"Are you so deluded that you still see the world in black and white? You're no Robin Hood, and I'm not the Sheriff of Nottingham. There's no good and evil here, there's only good, so good will lose by definition."

"If you say so. But don't tell me Boyd Campbell won't be passing the champagne if the jury sides with him."

"What celebration can there be for Boyd Campbell, knowing that his brainchild, however innocent it may have been, has produced a debilitating injury to Ruth Bergstrom? And at what price would he achieve this hollow victory? The company's financial resources are exhausted, its vigor and vitality sapped by the drawn-out battle. Many of its people have already left, and its investors are queasy from the endless bleeding of corporate assets. If EnviroClean survives at all, it'll be as a figment of the dreams of its founder."

"Well, I'll sure as hell be throwing a few down if the jury returns the verdict I'm expecting."

"Except there'll be no money to pay the verdict," Allison replied. "Our own bills are overdue."

"Bullshit," Dillon replied. "Don't tell me there's no money, because if that were true, you'd never have fought so hard. EnviroClean must have liability insurance, they'll survive."

"Isn't that what they taught us in law school?" Allison said. "Three years, all spent learning how to wage war. We learned all the rules of engagement, the rules of procedure, the rules of evidence, the rules for effective legal argument and artful cross-examination, all the strategy and tactics we'd need to win in court. But when did they teach us common sense? When did they teach us sensitivity? When did they teach us empathy and understanding? I never heard those words mentioned in three years of law school. And I've never heard them since. No, Dillon, you and I are litigators. That's the beginning and the end of it. That's all we do, that's all we know. And, if you took the macho titles away from us, there'd be nothing left. We'd be soldiers without a war."

"Jesus Christ, Allie, what the hell's wrong with you?"

"I'm serious. We walked out of law school with blinders on, and we're still wearing them. There's no one out there to open our eyes for us. The Bar Association? Our law partners? Our colleagues? Hell, these people all make their living keeping us in the dark. And when we finally figure it out on our own, we've got so much of a stake in the system we can't afford to do anything about it." Allison paused, looking down at the floor. "Today's my last day of blissful ignorance," she said, looking back up at Dillon. "Tomorrow, I'm walking out the door of Darby & Witherspoon to find a way to add some value to society instead of devoting my life to just redistributing what society already has."

"Cut the crap, Allie. You're on track to become one of the best trial lawyers in one of the best firms in the state. And, as much as I hate to say it, you've got one of the best mentors any young lawyer could ever want."

"Henry's a great mentor, all right," Allison said, "if I wanted to become a bloodthirsty gladiator, that is. He's a boy-king, entranced by the hoards that thrill at the sight of blood in the Forum. For him, engaging in battle is the primary objective, not an occasional and unavoidable evil."

"That's what it's all about, Allie," Dillon said. "We're intellectual mercenaries paid to fight the battles our clients can't fight on their own."

"I'm not so sure our clients understand it that way," Allison said. "Boyd Campbell thought we were helping him resolve a problem that was affecting his business. He only reluctantly allowed us to drag him into court. Now we've ruined him."

"What's he got to complain about?" Dillon asked. "He got the most rigorous defense any client could ever expect."

"Yeah," Allison said. "But that's not what he wanted."

"Well, what'd he expect, hiring Henry Holten, some chilled out wussy who'd hold his hand and whisper warm fuzzies in his ear? Give me a fucking break, Allie. The guy got exactly what he paid for."

"What he expected was our help in avoiding the entire mess so he could run his little business in peace and live his dreams like everyone else."

"The irony is that Campbell would've gotten away with the whole charade if Holten hadn't developed his stupid conflict of interest," Dillon said. "We'd never have known about Fermagro if Richard Blair hadn't been suspicious of Holten's dual role."

"That was inexcusable." Allison paused and shook her head. "I suppose now Boyd will hire some lawyer and sue the firm. Oh God, will it never end?"

"What a gas that'd be," Dillon said. "I'd take that lawsuit in a New York minute. Hell, I could dip into the cookie jar twice in a single case."

"Is that all this business is to you, Dillon, some Mickey Mouse cookie jar? Look at yourself. Look at Henry Holten. Look at all of us. There was only one real man in this sordid mess, and we gave him a fatal heart attack."

Allison paused and waited for Dillon to speak, but his only reply was a vacant stare.

"Didn't you feel a tremendous loss when Arne Bergstrom died?" Allison asked after a minute of awkward silence. "I only knew him from depositions, but he must have been a fine man."

"Sure, Arne was a great guy," Dillon said. "What's your point?"

"Arne was the only person who understood what was going on," Allison said, "but the system just chewed him up and spit him out."

"It wasn't the system," Dillon said. "It was Henry Holten. Holten killed the poor guy."

"We're all responsible," she said. "You included."

"Hell, I wasn't even there," he replied.

"What have you really accomplished here, Dillon?" Allison asked.

"Your practice is shot. You've lost most of your clients. You've lost your employees. You've lost your wife. What do you have left? You tell me, who are the winners here and what is their victory?"

"We'll soon find out, Allie," he said. "We'll soon find out."

"Dillon, let's go do something fun. Something exciting and unique, something worthwhile."

"What are you talking about?" he asked.

"I'm talking about just walking away from the law, doing something extraordinary, something valuable. Making something of our lives."

"You need another drink. Waitress!"

"Dillon, come on, I'm serious."

"I don't know anything but the law," Dillon said. He chugged down the last half pint of his stout and wiped his mouth on the back of his hand. "So what are you thinking about anyway?"

"I don't know," she said. "All I know now is that tonight I'm going to get drunk and make passionate love to the first sensible man to cross my path. Are you a sensible man, Dillon Love, or are you just going to carry on with this insanity for lack of energy to overcome the inertia?"

"Jesus Christ, Allie," Dillon replied. "I don't believe this stout is up to the job. Pete's got some single malt scotch that might serve my purposes better."

"Aren't we a proud lot?" Allison said. "You and I are going to spend the night trashing our brains while our clients are out doing exactly what we should have done at the beginning."

"What are you talking about?"

"Boyd and Kathleen Campbell left the courthouse today with Ruth Bergstrom and her children. They've invited her to dinner."

Dillon's eyes widened.

"Relax," Allison said, anticipating Dillon's displeasure. "It's all over. Leave them to their own devices. They can't make a worse mess of their affairs than we already have." She leaned toward Dillon across the table and in a very low voice said, "Besides, there's no pay-off. EnviroClean doesn't have product liability insurance. No matter how the jury decides, Boyd is out of business, and Ruth Bergstrom won't get a penny."

Boyd Campbell loaded Ruth Bergstrom's wheelchair into the back of his '97 Ford Bronco after Kathleen helped her into the front seat and then climbed in the back with Brett and Molly.

As Boyd pulled the Bronco away from the curb, Kathleen put her hand on Ruth's shoulder and said, "I hope you won't mind if we're informal tonight. This whole idea was a bit spontaneous so we're just going to have to throw something together. Boyd, let's stop at the store."

"Oh my," said Ruth, "it's just us. Feed my kids bread and water, it's all they deserve."

"No!" Shouted Brett.

"We want chicken," laughed Molly.

Kathleen, who sat between the children, said, "Perhaps we'll grill some chicken and make a big salad...with no tomatoes!"

"I don't like tomatoes," Brett blurted, eliciting bitter laughter from Boyd.

"I think we all know that, Brett," Ruth said, chuckling. "Actually, I don't much care for them anymore myself."

Forty-five minutes later, after a brief stop at Rainbow Foods on Lake Street, the five of them were gathered on the small, shaded terrace behind the Campbell residence while chicken pieces, bought in bulk, cooked on the gas grill.

Kathleen poured white wine for the three adults and grape juice for the children. "Only a little for me," said Ruth.

"A lot for me," said Boyd, and they all laughed.

"Here's to resolving this mess," said Ruth, raising her glass. "I'm so sorry this went so far."

"And I'm sorry we had a fool for a lawyer," said Kathleen.

"Not Allison, though," said Boyd.

"Oh, Allison Forbes can do no wrong in Boyd's eyes," Kathleen said to Ruth. "But I think she needs to take some of the responsibility, too."

"Perhaps," said Boyd. "I can certainly no longer call Holten a friend."

"Come on now," said Ruth. "Let's stay off that subject."

"I wish I could, Ruth," Boyd said. "I just keep thinking how ironic it is that we all sit here together for the first time as the jury deliberates our fates. I never wanted to be in that courtroom in the first place."

"Arne felt the same way," Ruth said, "and so do I."

"We Americans are a strange breed," Boyd continued, after taking a big swig of wine. "We're best friends with all our old enemies, the British, the Mexicans, the Germans, the Japanese, even the Russians. The remnants of opposing armies now stroll together on the beaches of Normandy and Iwo Jima, sharing stories of their bloody battles and celebrating their lives together on the anniversaries of those days of horror when they wreaked death and destruction on each other. Seeing photographs of these men arm-in-arm, together as friends, dramatically highlights the deplorable waste these awful battles caused. Now we play out this same ritual in our courtrooms every day."

"That's a bit of a stretch, Boyd," suggested Kathleen.

"Not at all," said Boyd gruffly, holding out his glass for more wine. "It's the same underlying issue, don't you see. Stupid lawyers getting their backs up and opting to fight before diplomacy has been fully exhausted."

"I thought I wrote a diplomatic letter," said Ruth.

"You did," Boyd sighed, wiping his hand across his face. "You did."

Ruth frowned, leaned across with some effort, and tapped the hand that held his wine glass. "At least now we've become friends," she said. "And maybe that makes it worthwhile."

Kathleen put her hand up to her mouth.

"That's at least something, my dear. Indeed it is," said Boyd, "but from my perspective the truce is never worth the war."

"All right, Dr. Killjoy, time to turn the chicken," said Kathleen.

Boyd Campbell, sighed, smiled, and stood up. He bent over and kissed his wife on the top of her head. "You're exactly right," he said. "It's time to turn the chicken."

Allison unwrapped herself from the comforter and stood up. She had been dreaming about Dillon—an ethereal image of lying naked in his bed wrapped in his arms, his big belly notched perfectly against the small of her back. But it hadn't worked out that way the night before; by the time something might have happened, they were both too drunk, and they went their separate ways in taxis. Now, as the bright sunlight dispersed her nocturnal fantasy, she felt ashamed.

What a dumb way to prove one's femininity. She stumbled to the shower, holding her head.

As the hot water tumbled down on her, she thought of Boyd Campbell just as he was when she first met him. She was horrified to think of him the way he was now, drawn and worried, and aged beyond his years. She also thought of Henry Holten, her erstwhile mentor, a man who apparently had no conscience whatsoever. Allison hesitated to accuse him in her mind of outright criminality, but the possibility of that being the case hovered around in her anxiety zone. Then, without even a mental transition, her mind wandered back to Dillon. Crazy as he was, at least he had integrity, along with the bullheaded obstinacy he shared with Holten. She wept as she thought all this through. What a mess. If only the shower could wash away the shame she felt at being so used by her mentor and so disappointed in her old friend.

The more she thought about it, the madder she got. She couldn't get it out of her mind, couldn't put it down, the utter stupidity of these two men. She had to talk with them, confront them, if only to put her mind at ease and get some closure for the whole sordid mess.

A few moments later she pulled on a pair of jeans and a T-shirt, drank a large glass of orange juice, and headed out the front door towards her car. She would confront Dillon first. She would surprise him; where things would go from there, she was not sure. Perhaps she would slap him, or perhaps she would fall into his arms.

It was a ten-minute drive to his apartment. She parked beside a smelly dumpster, pulled open the useless back security door, and smelled the cloying odor of roach spray as she climbed the back steps to Dillon's floor. The carpeted hallway was filled with music. How could anyone be that inconsiderate? She wondered. When she got to Dillon's door she shook her head; it was his music. She knocked, but the music swallowed the noise of her knuckles. She turned the door handle and the door opened. She stepped inside, called out, then walked down the narrow hallway to his bedroom. Through the open door she saw a slim woman's back and round buttocks rocking back and forth on top of a huge pair of hairy legs. The woman's long, dark hair swayed with her rocking. Allison stood, frozen, her stomach churning.

The woman must have seen her in the mirror of the vanity, because she turned her head and looked directly into Allison's eyes. Johanna Huntington. She smiled and gave Dillon a few vigorous thrusts so that he cried out. Then she stopped and said, "We have a visitor."

Blind with fury, Allison found herself in the parking lot beside the smelly dumpster, gasping for breath. What was wrong with her? Why did every man she ever trusted turn out to be such an asshole and let her down so completely? In law school Dillon's rebellion was exciting, fed her sense of independence. But their values were worlds apart now. Self-absorbed jerk, fucking that old piece of leather.

Then there was her ex-fiancée, perfect Eric off feeding the hungry in Africa; he thinks *she* is the self-absorbed asshole, he thinks she let *him* down. So he broke the engagement.

And of course Henry Holten, her mentor, her guide. Gullible fool that she was, she had trusted him the most, she had been taken in by the glamorous professional aura that surrounded him. His pontifications had seemed like wise guidance, good advice. Would she never learn to judge men more accurately?

A voice called, "Allie, where you going?"

It was Dillon yelling from his bedroom window. "Where the hell are you going?"

"Away from you. As far away from you as I can get!"

"Come back. You don't understand."

"You must be out of your fucking mind. What is it I'm supposed to not understand, Dillon? What? Is that bitch going to get a green card now as a reward for testifying? You asshole, you're as bad as Holten."

"You're the one who's crazy," he shouted. "Come back up and have a mimosa."

"I don't think so," Allison said, getting into her car.

"Hey!" Dillon yelled, after Allison had slid in behind the wheel, "I guess there's no chance of dinner tonight, huh?"

The main offices of Darby & Witherspoon teemed with young lawyers in blue jeans and polo shirts as Allison stepped from the elevator and slowly walked back to her office. In their informal attire her ambitious young colleagues appeared unnaturally docile as they gazed intently at their computer screens developing arguments that would be advanced in court the following week. Without the ties and tailored suits this citadel of overpowering egos looked like a coliseum of shorn Samsons or little boys playing computer games. Why had she ever thought she belonged here?

Allison walked directly to her office looking neither to right nor left or acknowledging the presence of her colleagues. Only a week before, she had been an eager participant in this weekly ritual, greeting associates by name, but today she felt depressingly out of place as she passed the offices of her colleagues for the last time. Today she had become a despondent traitor to this world that had been her home for most of the past ten years.

Henry Holten stood at her office door.

"I thought you'd take the day off," he said jovially as she approached. "But I see that hard labor just makes you stronger. You did an outstanding job yesterday, by the way, given the harsh rulings we received from Judge Cleveland. I think you've brought home another winner for the firm."

"You just don't get it, do you Henry," she replied, pushing past him into her office.

"Get what?" Holten asked, reaching for her hand, which she quickly pulled from his damp grasp.

"A winner for the firm, is that all you care about, Henry, the goddamned firm? What about our client? Do you think this will be a winner for Boyd Campbell?"

"You're certainly in a delightful mood this morning," Holten remarked dryly.

She turned away from Holten, sat down at her desk and began shuffling through some papers in a side drawer.

Holten walked over to her and put his hand on her shoulder. "You're not all bent out of shape about Fermagro, are you?"

"Why didn't you tell me about your interest in them?" she asked, brushing Holten's hand away. "Why couldn't you be honest with me?"

"I had no way of knowing this conflict would develop. Once it did, nothing could be done but attempt to serve both clients as best I could. If we disqualified ourselves, we'd have left EnviroClean without counsel in the final stages of a complex lawsuit. The situation was unavoidable."

"That's bullshit," she replied, turning wearily from her papers and glaring directly up into Holten's eyes. "You lied to me and you lied to Boyd Campbell. You even lied to the court. You knew about this from the beginning. You're the one who got Fermagro hooked up with Boyd. The moment Ruth Bergstrom's case surfaced, you knew it was the bugs from Fermagro that infected her. Boyd would never have taken any chances with his own organisms, never. He's too conscientious for that, but he trusted you implicitly. He trusted you, and you screwed him. Then you covered up the whole mess to protect your own little start-up company in Bermuda. That's why you wouldn't allow any testing of the soil in the Bergstrom's backyard. You knew Boyd would figure it out. He'd know they weren't his organisms, and he'd trace the source right back to Fermagro, right back to his own goddamned lawyer."

Allison stood up from her desk chair and moved a step closer to Holten. Her tall, graceful frame allowed her to look him directly in the eye. Holten reached for her shoulder again and opened his mouth as if to respond to Allison's accusations. But he was not quick enough. She dodged his hand and went on.

"And that's also why you put me in charge of this case," she continued. "It wasn't because you trusted my legal skills. Hell, I was a virtual rookie in the first chair. No, you knew I'd do whatever you said, I was so naïve I'd trust you just as Boyd trusted you. You thought Dillon was a bumbling moron and we'd easily win the case and the truth would never come out. Everyone would be happy, everyone except Ruth Bergstrom."

"You're way out of line, young lady," Henry said heatedly, stepping back towards the window and turning to gaze out at the Minneapolis skyline. After thinking, he said: "Boyd Campbell never did anything wrong. We were right to defend him. We had to defend him. He had no insurance, Fermagro has no insurance and no assets. Fermagro is just a struggling start-up."

He turned away from the window, pointed his finger at Allison, and continued his defense, his voice now quivering with rage. "You say I should have disclosed my role with Fermagro. Hell, if I'd told everyone up front that the bugs were Fermagro's and not Enviro-Clean's, Love would still have gone after EnviroClean. Boyd used the contaminated bugs, and it doesn't matter that he bought them from someone else and didn't make them himself. Even though he was completely innocent of any personal culpability, Boyd would ultimately have been liable because Fermagro has no money. You know that's the law. My candor would have accomplished nothing but deliver a strong indictment against my own client. So I kept all this under wraps to protect our client. It's Boyd Campbell who benefited from my secrecy. And when the jury comes back, he'll be damn grateful for all I've done for him."

"Henry," she said softly, leaning in toward him, "do you actually believe all that crap? Please tell me you don't. Give me even a tiny reason to believe you have some trace of honor and integrity, and that you weren't just covering your own ass. Or is your motto 'expediency before decency'?"

"Allison, you're the most gifted young lawyer I've ever had the pleasure of knowing," Holten said, his voice now carefully controlled. "But you're going to have to get off that damned high horse of yours if you want to understand the real world, if you want to learn to serve the interests of our clients."

Allison walked back to her desk and slid a few last folders and a half dozen CD ROMs into her briefcase, latched it shut and said "You didn't answer my question, Henry."

Without waiting for Holten to reply she strode out of her office and down the hallway toward the elevator bank.

Holten followed her quickly and caught up with her in the middle of the marble and glass reception room. Allison had paused to peer through the glass wall of the conference room at a group of casually clad young lawyers who appeared to be intently engaged in some legal debate. She remembered how exactly one week ago she had been in the same room conferring with her colleagues as she prepared for the final week of the trial of *Bergstrom v. EnviroClean*. It seemed a lifetime ago. She also remembered that at the same moment, two thousand miles away in Bermuda, Holten had also been working on the case from his own angle, thwarting Dillon's every move in his final attempt to cover up the truth about his own sins. She walked on through the doors to the reception area.

"Allie," Holten called out as he banged open the large mahogany doors separating the reception area from the internal offices. "What's wrong with you? What's really bothering you? Whatever it is, I'll fix it. I can't let you leave me."

"You changed my goddamned letter, Henry. You didn't even have the courtesy to tell me you'd done it."

"What are you talking about?" he asked.

"The letter to Ruth Bergstrom," she replied, her voice low and menacingly level. "Ruth Bergstrom did not deserve your heavy-handed approach, and when Dillon happened to see the letter, he realized something fishy was going on. No one would write a letter like that if he didn't have something to hide. And you didn't even have the courtesy to tell me. By keeping me in the dark you jeopardized the whole case."

"That's it?" Henry asked. "That's what's got your knickers in a twist? Christ, Allie, that's what senior partners do. They have to make the tough calls, and they don't have time to go running all over the office telling every young associate whenever they edit their material. But, in your case, Allison, I'm sorry. You're special, very special, and I assure you it won't happen again."

"It won't happen again," Allison repeated, her voice flat. "What won't happen again? It's not just you, Henry, although you're pathetic enough. It's the whole system. It's the whole goddamned adversarial system, the gladiator mentality that drives the legal profession to create endless battles in search of some self-defined illusive victory. The scenario plays itself out nearly every day, and it never changes, and it never will change. Who really cares about the Ruth Bergstroms apart from the legal fees some lawyer hopes to make off her miseries? Who cares about Boyd Campbell? He spends his life striving to add something of value to society. All the lawyers do is fight with one another about redistributing the wealth other people have already created. And who cares about the public? Who is looking after the unrepresented public interest? In the end, it's the public that pays the bills for the teams of lawyers and judges who perpetuate this destructive system. I want out, Henry."

"Where in the world do you get off lecturing me on your self-pitying values?" Holten said, his voice rising. "You're entirely unqualified to dismantle a legal system that generations of men far wiser than either of us have taken centuries to build."

Allison strode deliberately across the half dozen paces that separated her from her former mentor and grabbed a handful of his freshly pressed white dress shirt. "You screwed Boyd Campbell, you screwed Ruth Bergstrom, and you screwed me. I'm disappointed in you, Henry. You guys are all the same—take what you can get and never consider the consequences."

She let go of Holten's shirt, turned and walked a couple of feet towards the elevators, then suddenly turned and said loudly, so all the associates could hear, "You'd screw your own mother if it served your purpose."

As she pressed the square plastic down arrow she noticed the solemn faces in the nearby conference room all staring intently through the glass wall at her and the startled and disheveled Henry Holten, who was brushing aimlessly at the front of his rumpled shirt. Looking past Holten at the nameless young lawyers in the marble-walled conference room, she yelled loudly enough for the entire assemblage to hear, "No, it won't be Allison Forbes who dismantles the legal system. It doesn't need my help. It's sucking itself into an immense black hole, and it's on the verge of collapsing under its own weight."

Holten tried to say something, but Allison held up a hand and said, "Shut up, Henry. It's happening right before your eyes. The legal system is being destroyed by lying, unethical, small-minded lawyers like you. I'm tired of being a part of it."

Allison Forbes stepped into the waiting elevator, turned and locked eyes with Henry Holton until the doors slid closed.

Acknowledgments

It began at Blake School, Hopkins, Minnesota, where, in 7th Grade, Bill Gregory forced me into an endless regimen of diagramming sentences. Bill's interminable exercises taught me why a participle dangles and an infinitive splits. In 9th Grade John Osander invited me to undertake my first creative writing project. One of the more memorable days in my life was the afternoon I was called to Mr. Osander's classroom and accused of plagiarism. My guiltless conscience interpreted his accusation as evidence that I had some talent as a writer. My last two years at Blake included weekly writing assignments for Bill Glenn. Writing for him every week was a remarkable education. I am forever grateful to those fine teachers.

After a successful career in the legal profession I returned to my dream of writing a novel. I spent three years on the first draft, actually the first draft that I was willing to show anyone. A fellow writer, A. J. Hodges, advised me to engage Ian Graham Leask to review the work and offer commentary. That was four complete rewrites and eight years ago. Ian Graham Leask is a literary genius, and he also has a remarkable ability to use the words "love" and "crap" in the same sentence with practically no transition. Having *The Litigators* selected by Ian to be the first book published by Scarletta Press is the greatest honor I've received yet as a writer—even better than that false accusation of plagiarism. The hard work that went into the preparation of the text astounded me; this book would be nothing without the editorial attention of Ian and the two Mikes.

Special thanks to my wife, Kathy, who spent too much time alone while I wrote and rewrote this book. Thanks also to my sister, Julie Arthur Sherman, a published author herself, who has spent her entire professional life in the book business, and who helped significantly as I stumbled through the humbling process of getting *The Litigators* published. Finally I must thank my father, Judge Lindsay G. Arthur, to whom I dedicate this book, a truly gifted human being whose virtue I strive to emulate every day of my life.

LINDSAY G. ARTHUR, JR.

Eight Questions about *The Litigators*

1. When a lawsuit is filed, even the people who "win" often come away with a sense that they actually lost, feeling "I was right and had to pay all this money to prove it." Which parties in *The Litigators* feel this way? Are they justified in their feelings? Is there any way a lawyer can measure or explain the quality and necessity of his services in this situation?

2. Which lawyers seemed to understand their client's needs; which seemed only to be interested in the verdict, with almost any means to reach that verdict justifiable?

3. Today, lawyers set many fee arrangements, including contingency fees, as happens in *The Litigators*; do you feel lawyers are tempted to take on a case just for the fees and not because they feel the client's best interest is served by pursuing legal recourse in the courts? What ethical issues are raised by contingency fee arrangements? What ethical issues are raised by hourly fee agreements?

4. Civil cases between private parties still impact the general public; time is used in the courts, and decisions that have profound impact on the lives and businesses of countless people are made without their advice or consent. Do either of the lawyers involved in such cases have any responsibility to represent the greater public good in such cases? Does this happen in *The Litigators*? Should someone be responsible for striking a balance between the rights of individuals and the common right of the general public?

5. Is it too easy to file lawsuits these days? Should good faith mediation of the dispute be required before a lawsuit can be filed?

6. In *The Litigators*, both lawyers admonish their clients to have no contact with the other side. What are the pros and cons for such instructions?

7. To what extent do you think the digital age has affected the quality of justice in America? Current rules of civil procedure allow virtually unfettered and open-ended discovery. Has this altered the quality of justice? Has this inflated the cost of justice, and has it limited access to justice for those who cannot afford giant law firms?

8. As you worked through *The Litigators*, who did you think would win the case? And why do you think the author creates ambiguity about the final outcome?

About the Author

Lindsay G. Arthur, Jr., is a nationally known lawyer who has tried over 150 cases during his 35-year career. His clients have sent him throughout the United States to represent them in a wide variety of matters, particularly products liability lawsuits. He is also an entrepreneur. In 1974 he founded his current law firm, Arthur, Chapman, Kettering, Smetak, and Pikala, a highly regarded litigation firm in Minneapolis. In 1985 he founded a bio tech company that used genetic engineering to develop microorganisms the company used to degrade toxic waste.

While *The Litigators* is his first novel, he has fully lived the plot it unravels, a challenging products liability case involving genetically engineered organisms. *The Litigators* is prompted by his love for the law, whose greatest virtue is, paradoxically, its willingness to tolerate strident criticism. In that spirit Arthur speaks here, as an entrenched insider, with a bold critique of a judicial system that is increasingly tarnished by the unscrupulous and excessive practices of certain lawyers.

Arthur is also a keen sportsman and lover of the outdoors. He plays a mean game of tennis and likes to spend as much time as possible paddling through Minnesota's beautiful Boundary Waters Canoe Area, where he has guided many wilderness expeditions.

He lives in the Minneapolis area with his wife Kathy, with whom he has two sons, both physicians. His father, to whom this book is dedicated, and with whom the author proudly shares a common name, is a retired judge and an inspired writer.